S0-AAE-548

RA BOOKS

ublished by

ington Publishing Corp.
Park Avenue South
York, NY 10016

t printing: March, 1988

ted in the United States of America

INITIATION TO HORROR

Anne was the one who ventured to speak to the unseen voice. "Kathi?" she asked, forcing herself to sound pleasant and unafraid. "Is that you?"

"So you do remember me." In an odd way, the voice sounded like Kathi's. High and wispy.

"Of course we do," Anne answered. "How could we forget? What is it you want?"

"I want to be a Lorelei."

"But you *are* a Lorelei." Francine was speaking now. "We asked you to join us, remember?"

"But I was never a member. I was never initiated."

"Of course you were," Anne told her. "It was right here in this church. You must remember that."

"But it was never . . . finished."

"Kathi." It was Vali's voice now. She sounded calm and firm. "I think we should talk about this another time. We're due back at the school. We're doing our number for the Pow Wow. We have to get back before they announce us."

The voice in the dark was cold.

"You can't go back. Not until the initiation is over."

BLOOD SIST
DEBORAH SHERWOO

ZEB

are

Ken
475
Nev

Co

All
in
cor
rev

ZEBRA BOOKS
KENSINGTON PUBLISHING

Fir

Pri

NOVEMBER, 1957

A gust of cold November wind ruffled the canvas sides of the small, tentlike shelter, causing the mourners therein to shiver and hunch their shoulders against a second and possibly more forceful blast. The lavender and crimson chrysanthemums on the polished mahogany coffin remained intact, although their arrangement was not so perfect as it had been when the coffin left the church.

"And so we commit Kathi to the Lord," Reverend Teasdale intoned. His big, fleshy face was ruddy with cold, and he rubbed his bare hands together frequently, wishing he had taken his wife's advice and worn his gloves. "Our Heavenly Father awaits her and will gather her into His arms and walk beside her through all Eternity. Although the loss will be deeply felt by those of us on earth, our hearts must be made lighter knowing she has gone to her Heavenly Home, where she will know eternal peace and the greatness of the Lord's love."

He nodded to the man from the funeral home, and the casket was slowly lowered into the freshly dug grave. A low moan could be heard issuing from a small, fair-haired woman standing directly in front of the protective rope. The man next to her put an arm around her quivering shoulders. Reverend Teasdale bent down and picked up a small clump of hard black dirt.

"Ashes to ashes," he said solemnly, "and dust to dust. This is the way of nature and of God." He crumpled the dirt in his hand and sprinkled it into the grave. Then he wiped his hands with his handkerchief, a signal that the interment ceremony was at an end.

7

The man standing next to the woman who had moaned removed his arm from her shoulders in order to shake hands with the minister and thank him for his services. His wife blew her nose and dabbed at her eyes with a tissue.

"Dear," Bill Harcort said to the woman gently, "we must thank these people for joining us here."

The woman nodded and, after blowing her nose one last time, turned to the six girls standing quietly behind her. They were all dressed in neat wool coats with stocking caps or knitted scarves protecting their heads. They were all seventeen years of age—give or take a month or two—and, although their faces were tight and pinched, their grief did not mask their collective good looks. They had the appearance, each and every one of them, of young girls brought up in good, solid homes, of being accustomed to wearing good clothes, eating substantial, well-rounded meals, of being invited to the right places and being accepted by the right people.

"I'm sorry I can't place the face with the name," she said as she grasped the gloved hand of each in turn. "Kathi's letters were full of you, but unfortunately, she sent no photographs."

"I'm Liz Everly," the tall, rangy girl with thick black hair curling beneath her stocking cap and arresting smoke-colored eyes said politely. "I'm so very sorry." There was an awkward moment of silence after which she gestured to the girl on her left. "This is Valerie Porter."

"Ah, you're Vali," Helen responded, managing a small smile for the second girl. Vali, as she was indeed called, was two inches shorter than Liz, possessed of a firm, curvaceous body, shoulder-length honey-colored hair which she wore in a loose pageboy, and delicious aquamarine eyes that sometimes showed flecks of gold. She felt incapable of speech at the moment, so she simply bowed her head respectfully.

"I'm Barbara Jean Lawson." The girl next to Vali was barely over five feet tall and had hair as short and curly as Liz's and far blonder than Vali's, it being almost platinum in color. Her eyes were a vibrant blue and quite dominated her pert, round face. "I . . . I'm sorry, too."

"The cheerleader," Helen murmured as she moved on. She reached back with her left hand and gently squeezed her husband's arm.

"Anne Eastman," the fourth girl said in a deep, throaty voice. "I liked Kathi—a lot." She looked at Helen from direct, velvety brown eyes set wide apart in a strong-looking face with high, prominent cheekbones. Her complexion was slightly darker than that of the other girls, as if she had just returned from Hawaii or Florida. Her rich brown hair softly dusted her shoulders, stick-straight but thick, swinging like a bell when she moved. Indian blood, probably, Helen surmised. It was not unusual in Oklahoma.

The woman continued down the line, expressing her gratitude to auburn-haired Margie Richey and sloe-eyed Francine Briggs, accepting their faltering condolences in return. "I want you to know," she said when she had clasped the hand of each and every girl, "your acceptance of our daughter meant the world to her. Kathi's letters and phone conversations

9

revolved around the Loreleis."

The six girls nodded, several of them stealing glances at the others. Barbara Jean bit her lip; Margie Richey twisted her hands together in her soft angora gloves. Finally, Liz Everly found the words necessary for response.

"Kathi was a wonderful addition to our sorority," she said quietly. "Even though she was never . . . uh initiated . . ." she paused and cleared her throat, "we'll always think of her as one of us."

Helen nodded and choked back a new flow of tears. There was an awkward silence until an older couple, a thin, balding man and a short, plumpish woman moved toward the Harcorts. The woman took Helen's arm. "We'd better be going now, dear," she said with a firm little tug which succeeded in turning Helen away from the girls the bereaved mother would always think of as the Loreleis. "There's nothing more we can do here."

Helen turned back for a final nod in the girls' direction. She hesitated.

"Dear?" Bill Harcort said gently. "Alice is right, you know." He regarded his wife with concern.

"Oh, my," Helen murmured. Her forehead wrinkled in consternation. She studied the girls.

"Is there something else you want to say to them?" Bill asked her. "I'm sure they're anxious to get out of the cold."

Helen looked uncomfortable. "I know this isn't the time," she began awkwardly. "But there probably won't be another." She shifted her feet uneasily. "I wonder . . . would you girls mind posing for a photograph?"

10

"Now? Here?" The woman who had been referred to as Alice frowned.

"It won't take a minute." Helen took a small camera from her oversized handbag. "It would be such a nice memory. Kathi's friends."

Bill exchanged glances with Alice and nodded. He turned to the girls. "Do you mind?" he asked them. "It would mean so much to my wife."

The girls looked distressed. They looked at each other for support.

"If you'll just stay where you are..." Helen moved back a few steps and raised the camera to her eye. "I don't expect you to smile." She focused. "There." The click of the shutter was heard. Helen lowered the camera. "Thank you." She smiled faintly and allowed herself to be led to the waiting black limousine.

The girls remained where they were until the engine started up and the limo slowly headed down the black-topped cemetery road. Then they dispersed in two groups, climbing into freshly washed cars and driving off, their young bodies stiff and rigid in their seats, their dry, expressionless eyes staring straight ahead.

APRIL, 1988

Chapter One

Anne Eastman unlocked the door of her rambling West Side apartment and flicked on the light switch which illuminated the long entrance hall. Her raincoat was not wet, merely damp, but she tossed it over one of the hooks on the umbrella stand to let it dry completely before putting it in the closet. She walked with quick, purposeful steps down the hall, pausing in the living room to turn on an ornate Tiffany lamp. Then she removed an opened bottle of beaujolais from the polished mahogany liquor cabinet and poured a liberal amount into a tumbler.

The show hadn't gone well tonight. The actors had muffed lines and stumbled around the stage like a bunch of high school kids. *Damn that Ralph Blakely!* Anne thought as she sank back in the slightly tattered Queen Anne chair and took a healthy swallow of the soothing wine. *If he hadn't thrown me the wrong cue in Scene One, I wouldn't've gotten off on the wrong foot to start with.* Her timing had been off throughout the entire performance; her movements had been awkward, and she'd had to struggle for every line. It was only an

15

off-Broadway show, she told herself for perhaps the one hundredth time, but still, you never knew who might be in the audience.

And tonight wasn't the first time she had messed up on stage.

Oh, well, things would go better tomorrow night. She'd speak to Gil Hirshfeld about Ralph. A word from the director should keep him on his toes for a while at least. She reached for the pile of mail lying on the table next to her. The maid had brought it up when she came to clean. Anne grimaced as she riffled through the envelopes. Junk mail mostly. A bill from the phone company. An envelope from Bergdorf Goodman, undoubtedly a reminder that she hadn't paid her bill last month. A folded mimeographed sheet with her name typed across the outside. A sale, probably. She was about to toss it in the junk mail pile when she spotted the return address. Baxter, Oklahoma. Who did she know in Baxter that would be writing to her now? Her father had moved away ten years ago, and she'd long since lost touch with her school chums.

Curiously she pulled apart the stapled page and spread the paper out before her.

CLASS OF FIFTY-EIGHT—WHERE ARE YOU? ARE YOU OLDER, YOUNGER, RICHER, POORER, PRETTIER, UGLIER? (PLEASE CHECK TWO.) IF YOU ARE ANY OR ALL OF THESE THINGS, WE WANT YOU TO COME AND PROVE IT AT JOHN ROSS HIGH'S THIRTY YEAR CLASS RE-UNION! PLEASE FILL OUT THE FOL-

LOWING QUESTIONNAIRE AND SEND
MONEY! THE REUNION WILL BE HELD
THE WEEKEND OF JULY 29th AND 30th,
AND IT PROMISES TO BE A REAL KICK IN
THE BALLS. WE'RE HAVING A MOCK
POW WOW, SO IF YOU HAVE ANY TAL-
ENT WE'D LIKE TO KNOW ABOUT IT.
WE MIGHT PUT YOU ON STAGE!

The attached questionnaire consisted of the usual
queries pertaining to marital status, number of
children, line of work, clubs, etc.

Anne stared at it dubiously. A thirty year reunion.
Je-sus! Imagine seeing her old classmates after thirty
years. It struck her as almost obscene. Friends of one's
youth should be remembered as they *were*. Discover-
ing wrinkles and cellulite where there had once been
smoothness and slenderness seemed an invasion of
privacy somehow. And yet, *someone* must have
thought it would be a good idea.

Anne rose and walked to the round Louis XIV
mirror above the mahogany bar. No wrinkles on *her*
face. Well, not really. The small creases under her
eyes and around her mouth were more evident than
usual tonight, but that was due to the horrendous
two hours she had just spent on the stage of the
Christopher Street Playhouse. Her body was as slim,
if not slimmer, than it had been in high school, and
thanks to monthly applications of L'oreal, her hair
was as richly brown and lustrous as ever. How, she
wondered as she studied herself, did the Loreleis look
now? A faint smile flickered across her face. The
Loreleis. She hadn't thought of them in years. They

17

were that select group of girls who constituted the "in" group at John Ross High. Four of them—Vali Porter, Barbara Jean Lawson, Francine Briggs, and Anne herself—had formed a club in eighth grade; they'd allowed Margie Richey, a Baxter transplant, to become a member the following year. Liz Everly had joined after that. The Loreleis prided themselves on winning most of the honors at school. Barbara Jean was a cheerleader, Vali the Homecoming Queen, and Liz president of the senior class. They'd taken in another new member, band majorette Sunny Matthews, in tenth grade, but Sunny's family had moved from Baxter shortly thereafter, so the Loreleis numbered only six until they were seniors. That was when they decided to take in Kathi Harcort, the "new girl" in town, the girl from Wichita, Kansas. Anne's body tensed as she thought of Kathi. After her death, the Loreleis had disbanded, and Anne hadn't seen or heard from any of them since graduation.

She returned to her chair and finished her wine. *If I did go to the reunion,* she reflected smugly, *I'd make one helluva showing.* As far as she knew, none of the Loreleis had distinguished themselves; certainly none had become a part of the New York theater. But of course she couldn't go. Even if her play closed by then, July was a bad time to be away from New York. July was when casting started for the fall openings, and Anne was determined to be on Broadway next season.

Still, she decided to fill out the questionnaire. At least everyone would know she had made something of herself—if they weren't aware of it already.

She took her glass to the bar and filled it again.

Then she picked up the questionnaire and moved to her bedroom, sipping her wine thoughtfully, her head suddenly filled with long-forgotten memories.

Barbara Jean Lawson Fleagle brushed the sweat from her face with the back of a grimy hand. What a day for the milking machines to screw up! She returned her fingers to Cassie's udder. Squeeze . . . pull. Squeeze . . . pull. She thought she'd done the last of this shit five years ago.

"Okay, Cass, that's it for today." She poured the last of the milk into the sterilizing vat and tossed the pail aside. She walked heavily out of the barn, past the row of cows that stood swatting matter-of-factly at the flies that teased their ears and backsides.

"Mommy! Help! I'm stuck!" The child's voice assaulted her ears as she stepped into the bright spring sunlight. Damn! Was that Susie or Billy? *I'm too old to have six-year-old twins,* she thought as she hurried toward the direction of the frantic little cries. She'd told Woody that when she'd found out she was pregnant that last time. If she'd had her way she'd've had an abortion, but Woody didn't believe in such things. And anyway, he'd reminded her, when a couple had four kids already, another mouth to feed shouldn't make that much difference.

Only the other mouth had turned out to be two mouths, and four legs that quickly learned to scramble into two different directions, with four busy hands that consistently found the wrong things to be curious about. And now Billy—she could see him from here—was caught on the fence she'd told him to stay off of a dozen times.

"I'm gonna get you down, and then I'm gonna whip you!" she threatened as she approached her squirming, crying son. "When are you going to learn to listen to me?"

"My ball's over there." The tow-headed boy pointed with a grubby finger. His ball was indeed about eight feet inside the pasture. Barbara Jean unhooked his leg from where it was caught in the slats and lifted him over the fence.

"Run and get it, then. And don't let me catch you playing around here again."

Billy retrieved his ball and lifted his arms upward so his mother could lift him back across the fence. "I ought to just leave you out there in the pasture," Barbara Jean grumbled, "and let ol' Blackie get you."

Billy's face lit up in his cherubic smile. "Aw, Mom, you wouldn't do that." He gave her a large wet smack on her right cheek.

"Okay, you're safe for now." She released him and gave him a small swat on his rump. "Run down to the mailbox for me and see what the postman brought."

"Hey, Susie, Mom wants me to go to the mailbox!" Billy shouted gleefully at his twin who had turned her attentions to one of the field cats when Billy had gone after his ball. Susie quickly dropped the cat and dashed after him. "Me, too!" she cried, just as she always did when Billy ran away from her. Barbara Jean watched them tearing down the old dirt path on their chubby legs and sighed. Anyone who thought it would be fun to have twins didn't know what was involved.

She let herself in the back door of the white frame farmhouse, and her expression turned grim as she surveyed the large kitchen. The lunch dishes were right where the family had left them, littering the table and attracting flies. Pots still bearing food were standing on the stove; the milk that Susie had spilled on the yellow linoleum floor had not been cleaned up. "Donna Jean!" she called angrily, moving speedily toward the foot of the stairs. "Get yourself down here!" She frowned, realizing her voice couldn't be heard above the rock music blaring from her thirteen-year-old daughter's tape deck. She stomped up the steps and threw open the girl's door. Donna Jean was sprawled on her bed, eating potato chips and reading a TV fan magazine.

"Donna Jean Fleagle, just what do you think you're doing?"

The girl looked up and tossed her head so that her long, light brown hair fell away from her face. "Oh, hi, Mom. What's up?"

"What's up? I just saw the kitchen. It looks like a disaster area."

Donna Jean shrugged. "Oh, that. I'll clean it up later, okay?"

"You'll clean it up *now!*" Barbara Jean moved to the bed and snatched up the magazine. "Get your fanny down there."

"But, Mom, I was reading about Bo Hopkins. He—"

"Now!" Barbara Jean reiterated. "March." She pointed a commanding finger in the direction of the kitchen.

Donna Jean sighed. "Oh, okay." She jumped off the bed and looked at her mother accusingly. "You're uptight, you know that?"

"I'm going to be more than uptight if you kids don't start doing as you're told. I want that kitchen to *sparkle*. I'll be down to check in half an hour."

Donna Jean gave her a glowering look and flounced down the stairs. Barbara Jean went into the bathroom to wash her hands and splash water on her face. How was she going to cope with summer, when the kids were out of school for three months? Saturdays were bad enough. She stared at herself in the bathroom mirror as she dabbed her face with a towel. Forty-seven years old, and she looked over fifty at least. Her skin was brown and leathery, the result of too much sun for too many years. Her hair, once even blonder than the twins', had darkened to a mouse brown and had an inch of gray spreading out from the roots. Her body, always round, but once seductively so, was thick and ungainly; she had long since taken to wearing loose-fitting house dresses in order to hide her huge waist and hips.

Oh, well. She put down the towel and flicked off the light. There was nobody to see her out here on the farm anyway. Nobody but Woody, and he'd long since stopped really seeing her. She trudged down the stairs and barely avoided being upended by Billy, who was flying up the steps two at a time, his small head held down and forward as if to give himself more momentum.

"Ooops! Sorry, Mom. I didn't see you." He looked up at her and grinned, displaying two missing front teeth.

"How many times have I told you to watch where

22

you're going?''

Billy ignored the admonishment, as always. "I've got the mail." He held up a seed catalogue and several business-sized envelopes. Barbara Jean took them from his outstretched hand.

"Go wash your hands and face. And tell Susie to do the same."

"Susie's outside with the cats."

"Well, go tell her. Those cats are full of fleas."

Barbara Jean negotiated the rest of the stairs and went into the living room, which Woody's mother had always referred to as the "parlor." She sank down on the threadbare, old sofa and perused the mail. An auction was being held in Okmulgee. Maybe she and Woody should go. They could use a few things for the farm. There was a letter from Barbara Jean's mother, who'd moved to St. Louis after her dad had died. She put it aside. She'd read it last. She pulled open the stapled sheet of paper with the Baxter postmark and read the reunion notice. What a hoot! The old crowd getting together for a weekend of drinking and reminiscing. She wondered how many of the class of '58 would show: everyone who still lived in Baxter, probably, and maybe a few who hadn't moved too far away. Maybe she'd even go herself. The farm was only a three-hour drive to Baxter. She could go down for one night, maybe, and catch up on all the people she'd lost track of.

She put the notice and questionnaire on the lamp table next to her and picked up her mother's letter. July was still a long time off.

Valerie Porter Ellsworth Thomas slammed the

landing gear into place and smoothly glided the twin-engine Cessna onto the landing field at Fairfield County Airport. Her passengers—the five middle-aged insurance men she'd ferried to Atlantic City for a sales meeting—applauded heartily.

"Best landing I've ever had in one of these little bitty planes," the red-faced man with the receding hairline and protruding stomach announced. "Prettiest pilot, too."

"Hear, hear!" shouted the short, black-haired man in the seersucker suit. "Let's hear it for the little lady."

A loud chorus of cheers resounded through the cabin as the plane taxied toward the small terminal used exclusively by the private planes.

"Gentlemen, I thank you!" Vali looked back and bowed from the waist as she braked the plane to a stop. She removed her headphones and climbed out of her seat, her short, brown gaberdine skirt revealing a flash of her long, tawny legs. Jack Grimaldi, the terminal supervisor, ran out onto the runway to help her open the door and position the portable stairs. Vali stood aside to let her passengers deplane first, not so much out of protocol but, rather, to escape their eager eyes on her pert, well-rounded behind.

"Good flight?" Jack asked as he held out his hand to aid Vali in her descent.

"Super." She flashed him her enchanting smile. "I wish they were all like that."

The insurance men were already halfway to the terminal. Vali walked swiftly behind them, her hips swinging, her shoulder-length, honey-blond hair blowing softly in the April breeze. The short man in the seersucker suit looked back over his shoulder and slowed his pace until Vali caught up with him.

"How about letting me buy you a drink?" he suggested. His dark brown eyes looked at her eagerly.

"I'd love to. But I can't." Vali offered an apologetic smile.

"If you'd love to, let's do it. I'm staying at the Ramada. They got a real nice bar there."

"Sorry. You see, my husband would hate it." Vali smiled again and swept past him, hurrying into the terminal. She waved to Fred Wilson at the rental car counter and crossed to the pilots' lounge where she quickly filled out her day's log.

"See you tomorrow, Fred," she called as she tossed the log onto Jack's desk and walked briskly out to the parking lot. The five men were piling into a rented Ford Fairlane. "Can we give you a lift?" the man at the wheel, whom Vali had heard called "Chuck," asked her.

"No, thanks. I have my car." Vali waved as the driver put the Ford in drive and rolled out of the lot. Her own car, a bronze Mercedes 450 SL, looked conspicuous parked next to Jack's '73 Chevy and Fred's '78 Toyota. They were the only cars left in the lot.

She started the engine and skillfully maneuvered the car onto the highway and down toward Edgewater Estates. She held the steering wheel with one hand and rubbed her neck with the other. It had been a good flight, but the insurance men had been tedious. She should probably be used to men leering at her by now, she admitted, but somehow it always seemed creepy for her to be sitting in the pilot's seat knowing she was being lusted after from behind.

She made the drive in thirty-seven minutes and swung into the long, tree-lined driveway at exactly 5:53. She didn't bother pulling into the garage. She'd let Kevin do that for her later.

The house was quiet as she entered the parqueted entry. "Chase? Jen? Anybody here?" She poked her head into the living room. No one. She shrugged and turned back toward the hallway as the housekeeper, Angelina, a rotund Jamaican, hurried out from the kitchen.

"Miss Jennifer and Mr. Thomas are both upstairs, Mrs. Thomas," she said, wiping still wet hands on a paper towel. "Would you like me to call them for you?"

Vali smiled at her. "No, thank you, Angelina. I'm just going up." She retrieved the mail piled on the hall table, lightly traversed the stairway and went directly to her bedroom.

Chase, wearing a distracted look, was standing before the full-length mirror putting stays into the collar of his crisp, white dress shirt. He did not look away when Vali planted a quick kiss on his cheek; he merely addressed her with a harried air.

"It's about time you got home. Gideon and Elsa are due any minute."

"I know. I'm sorry." Vali tossed the mail and her purse on the huge four-poster bed and began unbuttoning her blouse. "Head winds outside Newark."

The stays in place, her husband carefully straightened his collar and reached for his maroon and blue striped silk necktie. "You will hurry, won't you, darling? There's only time for drinks before we're due at the club."

"I'll just take a quick shower and be ready in a jif." She shed her skirt and headed for the adjoining bathroom, fumbling with the hook on her bra. She threw her underwear into the laundry basket and quickly stepped into the shower. Chase's voice could be heard above the cascading water.

"I wish you'd come to your senses about that airline of yours, Val. It interferes with our lives more and more."

"Oh, Chase, I'm only a few minutes late." Vali heaved a sigh of frustration as she soaped her body. The airline was a constant source of disagreement between them. "Where are the kids, by the way?"

"Jennifer's around someplace. I think she said Kevin's at baseball practice."

"Oh, right." She let the water wash away the soap and turned off the faucets. She stepped out of the shower and reached for a towel. The sound of the doorbell could be heard from below.

"Damn!" Chase muttered. "Right on time."

"Look, why don't I call the club and tell them we'll be a little late? That way we can relax over cocktails."

"I don't want Gideon to get the idea we're not organized around here." His look was sour, but his answer showed he could be swayed. He paid no attention to his wife's nakedness.

"Are you kidding? Gideon's hardly the type to resent a second drink. We'll be half an hour behind schedule, that's all." Dry now, she reached for her dusting powder.

Chase frowned thoughtfully. "All right, go on and

call. I'll go down and greet them."

Vali nodded. Then, as Chase continued to frown, she smiled. "I'll be right behind you. Honestly."

Chase looked as if he didn't believe her, but he turned and hurried from the room. She heard his quick steps on the staircase.

Whew! Avoided another argument for a little while at least. She looked at her reflection in the mirror and nodded to herself in relief. Chase would never get used to her working. She supposed he was right in a way—it did cut into their time together—but she had spent almost twenty years as the devoted wife of Chase Thomas. She had the right to do something for herself.

She called the club, freshened her make up in record time, brushed out her naturally wavy hair, and slipped into an expensive, beige silk dress. She put on strappy high-heeled shoes and grabbed the sleek acrylic clutch she'd bought in Italy last fall. She was on her way out of the room when she noticed the mail still lying on the bed. She hesitated and glanced at her watch. Ah, hell. What did another minute matter? She flipped through the mail, not finding it particularly interesting. She was, however, intrigued by the folded flyer postmarked Baxter, Oklahoma, and she carried it with her as she departed. She pulled it open when she reached the staircase and grinned when she saw the opening message.

"Vali! Darling! Wonderful to see you!" Elsa Davenport, tall and elegant, with hair pulled severely back from her face and heavy makeup painted exotically on her eyelids and lips, was standing just outside the den, holding a drink. "I was just going to

28

come up and see what happened to you. You look marvelous!''

"Thank you. So do you."

"Chase said your plane was late. Honestly, darling, I don't know how you can go around in that tiny little thing. I'd be frightened to death."

"Elsa, my love, my 'tiny little plane' seats six people. And I assure you it's very safe."

Elsa made a face. "Well . . . if you say so. But I still can't understand why you would want to fly people you don't even know to God knows where."

Vali held onto her patience. "It's my business," she explained brightly. "I have a charter airline, and people pay me for my services."

"Val? Is that you?" Chase called to her from the den. "Come say hello to Gideon."

Elsa sighed. "Yes, I suppose you'd better. We never get time for girl talk, you and I."

Vali chuckled and went into the den to greet Elsa's somewhat stuffy husband. Gideon Davenport was chairman of the board of a large bank, and although he was one of Chase's closest friends, he was not one of her favorite people.

"Hello, Gideon." She offered her cheek for his kiss and dutifully apologized for being late. She asked Chase for a dry martini and seated herself in one of the leather wing-backed chairs, still holding the announcement from Baxter in her hand.

"Something important in the mail?" Chase asked, nodding toward the paper.

"What? Oh, no, I forgot I still had it." She put it on the table beside her. "It's a reunion notice from John Ross High."

"A reunion? You're kidding!" Elsa flew to the table and snatched up the paper. She peered at it nearsightedly. "You aren't thinking of actually going, are you?"

"I don't know. I haven't thought about it. The announcement just came."

"Well, I certainly wouldn't go to *my* reunion," the woman declared distastefully. "I can't imagine anything worse."

"I'm not so sure. It might be fun." Vali felt a perverse pleasure in baiting her. The Davenports were both such dreadful snobs.

"My wife still thinks fondly of her high school days," Chase offered as he placed the martini on the table next to Vali's chair. "She was a member of a sorority that called themselves the Sirens." He rolled his eyes at Gideon.

"It was called the Loreleis," Vali corrected, irritation creeping into her voice. "The members were my best friends."

"The Loreleis. How droll." Elsa let the announcement drift back down to the table. "Why on earth did you call yourselves that?"

"Oh, you know teenaged girls. We thought we were positively wicked." She looked at Chase and saw his disapproving scowl. "Actually," she amended quickly, "none of us knew much about anything, let alone the art of seduction, but we saw ourselves as perfect vamps. No one of the opposite sex was safe when we were around." She laughed. "We even had our own colors. Crimson and lavender."

Elsa made a face. "Crimson and lavender? *Together?*"

Vali nodded. "Weird, huh? We picked crimson because it seemed . . . well . . . wicked. The lavender was because of Kim Novak. After we saw her in *Picnic,* she became our favorite movie star. And, according to the fan magazines—which we devoured like popcorn—lavender was her favorite color."

"I wonder if any of them lived up to their so-called potential," Elsa mused. "How long since you've seen them?"

Vali shrugged. "Thirty years. Most of them moved away from Baxter, and I haven't been back anyway. I do exchange Christmas cards with Francine Brookfield, though. Maybe I'll give her a call and see if she knows who's going to attend."

"Just to make sure Chase doesn't go with you," Gideon said, attempting humor despite his natural lack of it. "He might get lured away from you by another Lorelei."

"If I were Chase, I'd demand to go," Elsa declared, draining her glass. "Vali might run into one of her old loves down there. And you know what those things can lead to."

Vali felt Chase's eyes on her. She looked up to see him regarding her with what seemed like a cross between anxiety and suspicion. She returned his look evenly.

"All this talk is silly," she said, turning from her husband to their guests. I don't even know if I'm going to the reunion. Why don't we all have another drink?" She gulped down the last of her martini and held out the empty glass.

Chase was still regarding her darkly as he reached out and took it from her.

Liz Everly pulled her sweater closer around her shoulders and vigorously rubbed her hands which were becoming stiff with cold. *Damned Russians!* she cursed silently, *they probably sabotaged the heater.* She glanced at the wall clock. Four-forty-five. She might as well start packing up. No more work would be done today.

"Hey, Liz, how're ya doin'?" Johnny Halprin patted her shoulder and flashed his perfect, all-American smile.

"I'm freezing, if you must know." Liz shot him an irritated look.

"We'll get the heater fixed by Monday. Lucky it's April and not February, huh?"

"Yeah. Real lucky." She jammed the papers on her desk into the bottom drawer and gathered up the stray pens and pencils that always seemed to litter her work space.

"How about my buying you a drink to warm you up? We'll go over to the Metropole."

"No, thanks. I've got to get home."

Johnny looked at her with frank curiosity. The attractive dark-haired translator had come to work at the embassy more than a year ago, and although she wasn't married, he'd never known her to go out with anyone in the American colony. Oh, she'd attended the Christmas party and some of the birthday celebrations, but that was all. If it wasn't absolutely forbidden, Johnny would swear she had a Russian lover. "What's the big deal at home?" he asked half-jokingly. "You got somebody stashed there we don't know about?"

"Yeah. His name's Sasha. He's a big gray and white tabby cat." She smiled at him for the first time, and he smiled back, struck as always by her sensuous-looking face with the smokey, enigmatic eyes, full, ripe lips, and the smooth cap of dark hair that framed the soft, creamy skin.

"There's a party tomorrow night at Eric's. Why don't you come along?"

Liz forced another smile. How she hated all these attempts to draw her into the "crowd." As if every unmarried woman was fair game for all the aggressive members of the diplomatic corps. *Watch it,* her inner voice warned her. *Don't say anything to make them wonder. Stay inconspicuous.* "Maybe I'll see you there," she said lightly. "It sounds like fun."

Johnny was about to suggest he pick her up and escort her when Brett Greenlee rounded the corner and tossed some envelopes on Liz's desk.

"Mail call," Brett announced. He handed two envelopes to Johnny. "Better late than never."

"Honestly, the mail's getting worse and worse," Liz grumbled when Brett had gone on down the hall.

"Just be glad we get the pouch," Johnny said. "Otherwise, we'd never see half the stuff that's sent us."

"Yeah, you're right about that." Liz put the envelopes in her purse without looking at them and clicked it shut. "Well, I'm off. See you tomorrow night, maybe." She grabbed her heavy, beaver-lined

33

coat from the cloak stand and slipped it on before Johnny could offer to help. *"Dasvedanya."*

He returned the Russian farewell. *"Dasvedanya. Spokoyni Nochi."*

Liz didn't look back as she hurried down the hall to the stairs leading to the ground floor. She nodded to Sam, the guard, as she opened the big embassy door and stepped out into the cold April air. It was already dark outside, and she could see her breath as she hurried briskly up Tchaikovsky Street. At the corner, she hailed a cab and asked the driver to take her to an address on Zhdanov Street. When she arrived at her destination, she paid her fare and waited until the cab had moved off out of sight. From there she walked the three blocks to the Hotel Berlin. Although not usually recommended for Western tourists, the old hotel had far more elegance than the newer, antiseptic-looking places like the National and the Rossia.

The lobby, with its graceful Victorian furnishings, was buzzing with the mixture of varied languages, although if one listened closely, he could probably pick out German as the more dominant. Carefully avoiding eye contact with either the guard at the door or the hotel personnel, Liz crossed the lobby and headed toward the bar with the assurance of someone who had been there many times before. Germans, she mused thoughtfully. Must be some kind of conference. She nodded to herself, satisfied. German was one of her better languages.

She seated herself at the end of a half-filled bar and nodded to the female Russian bartender.

"Vodka, *bitte*," she said, loudly enough for several

customers to turn and give her an appraising look. Still, she avoided looking at anyone directly. She couldn't afford to be too obvious. When the small pony of vodka was placed in front of her, she dallied for a moment, then picked it up and tossed it back in one quick movement. This done, she sat quietly, glad the bartender was busy with a group of men wearing three-piece business suits. She knew exactly how many straight shots she could handle without risking the loss of any mental faculties, but she preferred to drink as little as possible.

Finally, the Russian woman approached her again, and she asked for a refill. This time, she felt a pair of eyes on her as she repeated the act of tossing it back.

"Russkaya?" a man at her elbow asked. Without looking directly at him, she could see that he, also, was wearing a business suit. The one hand that was in her line of vision was well manicured.

"Nein. Ich bin Deutsch." She waited, almost afraid to breathe. She felt the man studying her, appraising her.

"Wohin gehst du?"

"Frankfurt."

She dared to turn and look up at him. He was about forty, on the plump side, light blue eyes and fair hair plastered back with shiny pomade. She smiled.

"Are you a tourist?" he asked, still speaking what sounded like native German.

"Ja," Liz told him. "I have been here three days. And you? Are you a tourist, also?"

The man gave a small shrug. "I am here for a

scientific conference. I've been here a week."

"It can be a little boring, don't you think?" Liz asked, keeping her tone light. "After you've seen Lenin and the Bolshoi, what else is there?"

The man laughed. "The Russians would tell you a lot more. A collective farm, a Young Pioneer camp. Gorky Park . . ." He drifted off. "May I buy you another drink? I was admiring the way you polished off the first two."

Liz smiled. "Well, all right, thank you. But I think one more's my limit."

He signaled to the bartender. "Where'd you learn to drink vodka like that? I'd have sworn you were Russian."

She tried to look pleased. "I just decided to try it. I was watching some Russians do it at my hotel last night."

The man digested this, his pale eyes still regarding her thoughtfully.

"You are traveling with a group?"

She shook her head. "No, alone. Crazy, isn't it? I was curious about the Soviet Union so I decided to come here and see it for myself."

The man slid onto the stool beside her. "And what do you think? Have you seen enough?"

This was her chance. Her answer could cause him to react in a way that would tell her whether he was really German, or a Russian trying to check her out.

"I think it's horrible. Everything's so gray—the buildings, the clothes the people wear. And nobody smiles. I don't think it's really the workers' paradise they claim it is."

He looked amused. "Careful, *Fraulein*. You don't

36

want the wrong people to hear those remarks." He gestured toward the ceiling. "Big Brother is everywhere." Her drink arrived, and he applauded as she drank it in one gulp. "Where do you live in Frankfurt?"

She named the street where she had lived when she worked as a translator at the embassy there. As they fell into an easy, casual conversation, she was aware that he was still appraising her. The slight frown on his face told her he was still uncertain about her.

"Tell me the truth," he said finally, speaking in a low, confidential voice. "You're not really German, are you? You're a Russian girl."

She suppressed a smile. She gave him a nervous look instead. "Please," she whispered after a slight hesitation, "don't tell anyone. I'm not supposed to be in here."

He smiled. "No need to worry about me, *Fraulein*. I wouldn't want to see a nice girl like you get into trouble."

She eyed him appealingly. "You really like me? You think I'm pretty?"

"Oh, yes, very pretty," he said seriously. He reached out and covered her hand with his. "Very, very pretty."

"You would like to . . . go with me?" she asked with a bright but anxious smile. "I am . . . talented."

He frowned again and studied her. "So you're a prostitute." He looked perturbed.

"Please, *mein Herr*," she said urgently. "Don't think of me as a bad woman. It's the only thing I can do to earn my way. You see, I have three children. My husband was killed in an accident at the airplane factory. I must buy their clothes, their school supplies, their medicine when they're sick."

A long moment of silence. "How much?" he asked. She could tell he wasn't completely sold.

"Twenty rubles." She watched his face as he translated the sum into marks. "It isn't too much. I will show you a good time." She paused. "Maybe you have lipstick in your room? Pantyhose?" Most western travelers brought such things to give as tips to guides. Every Russian woman would jump at an opportunity to ask for them.

He looked at her closely. "Do you have a place?"

"I . . . I was hoping . . . your room. I will speak German on the elevator and in the hall," she added hurriedly before he could protest. "No one will know I am Russian." She squeezed his hand. "I will make you happy. You will see."

The smile that spread across her face when he agreed was not for him. It was a smile of personal satisfaction.

Later, at home in her two room apartment in the American compound, she prepared her dinner. As she sat down to eat it, she remembered she hadn't opened the mail she'd received at the embassy. Quickly she retrieved it from her purse and riffled through it: a letter from her sister, a post card from one of her co-workers who was on vacation in France. She opened the dog-eared fold-over from Baxter last. A reunion notice. She read it quickly, finished her meal, poured herself another cup of coffee and read it again.

John Ross High. Good Lord. How far away it seemed now, and how long ago. Much longer than thirty years. Had she ever been a carefree high school girl?

The Loreleis. One couldn't think of high school without thinking of the Loreleis. She wondered if they'd be going back. Did she want to see them again if they did? She thought about how she'd just spent the last hour and a half. What would the Loreleis have thought of that? The question made her laugh out loud. She'd always felt a little like a fake around them. But now! She had become more of a Lorelei than the others had ever dreamed of being!

Chapter Two

Margie Richey Middleton wadded the mimeographed paper into a ball and tossed it into the trash compactor. It was the second mailing she'd had about the John Ross reunion. She hoped whoever was organizing the thing would get the hint pretty soon. No way was she going to let herself in for *that* kind of hassle. Margie saw enough of the old crowd just moving around Baxter. She had no desire to see any of the others.

"Honey? What happened to the iced tea?" Jerry Middleton came into the kitchen wearing denim cutoffs and a faded tee shirt. He was barefoot, and his lank, medium brown hair fell carelessly across his forehead. At forty-nine, he looked—and sometimes acted—like twenty-two.

Margie shoved the compactor door shut and turned toward the refrigerator. "I'm getting it right now." She busied herself putting the ice in the glasses.

Jerry took a couple of steps toward her. "You all right?" he asked, frowning.

"Sure, I'm all right. I'm fine." Then, figuring

40

further explanation was necessary, she said, "I'm just a little tired, that's all."

"Yeah. It was kind of a rough day. Here, let me help you with that." He took the lemon she was holding from her hand and placed it on the cutting board. "At least we have the evening to ourselves."

Margie smiled. "Thank Heaven for small favors." Melinda, her nineteen-year-old, was out with her current beau, and the boys, for once, had found a movie they both wanted to see.

"Let's go see what's on the tube, okay?" Jerry squeezed the lemon into the filled glasses and took one for himself.

"Sure. It'll be nice to watch uninterrupted for a change."

They had settled themselves on the couch in the den and were absorbed in *Dallas* when the telephone rang. Jerry, who was closest, grabbed for the receiver.

"Hello? . . . Yeah, this is the Middleton residence. . . . Yeah, she's here. Who's this? Mary Ellen? . . . Who? . . . Sure, just a minute." He handed the receiver to Margie, covering the mouthpiece. "She says it's a Mrs. Brookfield." He looked puzzled.

Margie felt a lurch in her stomach. She only knew one Mrs. Brookfield, and she hadn't spoken to her in at least five years.

"Hello?" She held the receiver tensely, wishing Jerry wasn't there to see her reaction. "Oh. Francine. How nice to hear your voice."

At the other end of the phone, stretched out on her white satin bedspread, Francine heard the strain in the high-pitched voice. *She isn't glad to hear from me*

41

at all, she thought, half amused. *She probably thinks I'm calling to solicit money for one of my charities.*

"It's nice to hear yours, too," Francine responded brightly. How the hell have you been, anyway?"

"Oh, fine. Real good."

An awkward silence. "I guess you've heard about the reunion."

Margie shot a sideways glance at Jerry. He seemed absorbed in something J.R. was saying. "Yes, I got a couple of notices." She wished she could change to the phone in her bedroom, but there was no way without Jerry thinking it was strange.

"Well, I'll bet you weren't notified about this. Would you believe we've been asked to do one of our old dance numbers in the Pow Wow?"

"We?" Margie repeated, confused.

"The Loreleis, dear. All us darling little golden girls have been asked to shake our forty-seven-year-old behinds for our former classmates."

"You're kidding." Margie laughed nervously.

"Nope. Dead serious. I thought it might be fun to do the 'Singin' In The Rain' number."

"'Singin' In The Rain'? I don't remember a single step." Margie was aware of Jerry's head turning in her direction, curious as to the turn the conversation had taken.

"Relax. We'll get a dance teacher to help us put it together. It'll be fun."

"Oh, Francine, I don't think so. So much time has gone by. It wouldn't be the same."

"Well, of course it won't be the same! That's what'll make it such a kick. Imagine all of us old broads up there on stage in those short plastic

42

raincoats." Francine lifted one of her long, smooth legs in the air and admired it. Thanks to endless exercise and careful diet, her body was better now than when she was seventeen.

Margie closed her eyes. Jerry had forgotten about *Dallas*, he was concentrating solely on her. "The others . . ." she said tentatively, "they won't all be here, will they?"

"It's beginning to look like most of them will. Barbara Jean's driving up from Choctaw; there was no problem about that. Annie didn't want to leave New York, but I convinced her that a week away from the bright lights wouldn't kill her career. And—get this—Vali's flying in from Connecticut in her own plane!"

"What about Liz?"

"Well, it's hard to tell about her. She's living in Moscow at the moment, working at the American Embassy. But even if it's just the five of us, we can work up a number. The out-of-towners are all coming in a week early. That should give us time to pull it together."

"Francine, I'm not sure . . ."

"Why? Have you gotten fat or something?" Francine couldn't imagine Margie Richey fat. Anyway, she'd passed Middleton Cleaners recently and had seen Margie through the window. Her hair had lost some of its rich auburn color, and she looked mature, which was to be expected; but basically Francine had been impressed with the way she'd held together.

"No. It's not that." Margie didn't even bother to make a joke about growing old. "Look, Francine, I'll have to get back to you about this, okay?''

Francine pushed her sensuous lips into a pout. There *would* have to be a holdout. ''All right,'' she agreed. ''But don't wait too long. I have to get word back to the organizers so they can get a program printed up.''

''Okay. I'll talk to you soon.'' Margie dropped the receiver into its cradle and sank back onto the couch.

''Hey! Let's have it! What was that all about?'' Jerry was looking at her eagerly.

Margie shrugged. ''It was Francine Brookfield. A friend from high school.''

''Brookfield, like in *the* Brookfields?'' Jerry was wide eyed. The Brookfields owned one of the largest oil companies in the United States. And they owned most of Baxter as well.

''She's married to Baron.'' Anyone who read the papers knew who Baron Brookfield was.

''Baron? He must be eighty years old.''

Margie nodded. ''He was about sixty when Fran married him. As I recall, it caused quite a scandal.''

Jerry whistled. ''So what'd she want? To invite you to a tea party?''

''No.'' Margie sucked in her breath. ''She's trying to get up a chorus line for our class reunion.''

''Reunion? You didn't tell me about that.''

''That's because I hadn't planned on going.'' She picked up her iced tea which was now mostly melted ice and took a swallow.

''Why not? You could see all your old crowd. The Loreleis.''

''Jerry, it's been thirty years since I've seen any of them.''

"So? That's what reunions are for. To renew old acquaintances." He cocked his head sideways. "Anyway, you've been holding out on me. What's this about a chorus line?"

Margie gave an embarrassed laugh. "Oh, I told you how the Loreleis were involved in everything. John Ross High had a big talent show every year. It was called the Pow Wow. We couldn't let that pass without lending it our stellar presence. We used to do a little dance number." She smiled at the memory. "There was a teacher in town—Miss Virginia, we called her. She must've had fantasies about working for Busby Berkely when she was young. Anyway, she always taught us some showy little piece that didn't call for much actual ability. We were usually a big hit."

Jerry's face reflected his enthusiasm. "Sounds to me like Francine's right. You *should* recreate a number. Think of it, honey. You have a chance to relive a little of your youth with the girls who were once your best friends."

Margie clenched her hands and steeled herself. "Jerry, they don't know what happened after high school."

Jerry looked blank. "What happened?" Then, remembering: "Honey, if you mean the hospital—"

"Yes, of course I mean the hospital!" Margie cut in curtly. "I'm sure they'd all just love to know I was confined to a looney bin for a year and a half."

"That was twenty-some years ago. And it was a sanitarium, not a looney bin. And, anyway, people are much more enlightened about those things now. If they were to find out, that is. Which they almost certainly won't."

"Jerry, the idea of seeing them again . . . it makes me nervous."

Jerry looked at her, concerned. "Well, you don't have to if you don't want to. But I wish you'd think about it, babe. This may be the last time the old crowd will ever get together."

Margie sighed. "I know. And I *will* think about it." She managed a smile. "Who knows? It might be fun after all."

Barbara Jean eyed her dinner plate glumly. A hamburger patty not much bigger than a silver dollar rested next to a dollop of cottage cheese. "Four weeks of this shit," she muttered, "and I've only lost eight pounds."

"Hey, Mom, how about sending the mashed potatoes up this way?" She looked over at Tommy, her fifteen-year-old son whose plate was already piled high with roast beef, green beans, macaroni salad and biscuits.

"Where do you plan to put it?" she asked as she handed over the bowl of potatoes. "On your lap?"

"Har de har," Tommy guffawed.

"This diet's making you a little crotchety, isn't it?" Woody observed, giving her an annoyed look. "Or is it the change of life that's causing you to be such a bitch these days?"

"Thanks a lot," Barbara Jean answered, glaring at him.

"What's the change of life?" Susie wanted to know. She had made a "castle" with her mashed potatoes, a ring of gravy forming the "moat."

"It's the time of life when Mom changes from a simple housewife to a gorgeous high school cheerleader," Tommy sniggered.

"Hey, you guys, stop it." Seventeen-year-old Kerry faced them all angrily. "Can't you see how hard Mom's working to lose weight? She *is* going to be gorgeous at her reunion."

Barbara Jean smiled gratefully at her understanding older daughter. But she was beginning to wonder if all this body torture was worth it. It wasn't just the diet; she did twenty minutes of excruciatingly painful exercises every morning and ten every night, providing she wasn't too tired. And what had it gotten her? Eight miserable pounds! "Maybe I'll just forget the diet," she said, pushing back her untouched plate. "Who cares if I'm fat or thin, anyway?"

"Oh, Mom, you can't forget it!" Kerry cried, alarmed. "What would the Loreleis think if you showed up overweight?"

"They wouldn't let you be in their chorus line," Woody jibed as he added more gravy to his already swimming plate.

"You think it's funny, don't you?" Barbara Jean snapped. Her face turned bright red with anger. "You think it's all a big joke. The reunion, the chorus line, all of it!"

"Hey, Mama, I didn't say that." Woody smiled at her patronizingly. "I was just needling you a little, that's all."

"Well, I'm tired of your needling. I've been stuck out here on this goddamn farm of yours for twenty-eight years. I've milked your fucking cows and fed your fucking chickens, had your kids and put up with your snoring and your smell of cow dung that even new improved Bold can't get out. I haven't had a new dress in five years; I never go outside these grounds except on Sunday, and then it's only to church. Well, I'm sick of it! I'm sick of you and this place and everything that goes with it. I'm gonna lose weight, I'm gonna go to Baxter to that reunion, and I may never come back!"

The family stared at her in awed silence as she jumped up from the table, pushed back her chair and ran from the room. Kerry jumped up to follow her, but her father put out an arm and held her back. "Let her go," he growled irritably. "Let her get over it by herself."

Barbara Jean was breathing heavily when she got upstairs and went into the hot, airless bedroom. Her thin summer dress was clinging to her perspiring body. "Damn them!" she cursed aloud. "Damn the whole sniggering bunch!" She pulled open the bottom drawer of her bureau and tore at the pile of clothing she always put away so neatly. The bottle felt cool to her touch. She pulled it out and uncapped it quickly. Her breathing became easier as the colorless liquid scorched her throat.

Fuck Woody! she thought furiously. *And piss on me for ending up this way: fat, old before my time, a dowdy farmer's wife.*

She, who could have been—was briefly, in fact—Mrs. Lawrence Holloway. Larry. Tears welled up in her eyes as his face swam before her. He was the most handsome boy she'd ever seen; ever *would* see as it turned out: warm, gray-blue eyes in a strong, chiseled face, an absolutely gorgeous straight nose, full, soft lips, and a cleft in his chin that just accommodated her little finger. Thick, silky, rich brown hair that had a roguish way of falling carelessly over his high, intelligent-looking brow.

Not a football player. That was odd because people always expected cheerleaders to date football players. Tennis and golf were Larry's games, unusual for high school kids in those days, but very much the result of family influence. The Holloways were one of Baxter's leading families, almost on a par with the Brookfields and the MacKintoches. Country club members, of course. They were patrons of the Baxter Art Museum, the Little Theater, supporters of Baxter Junior College. The family had big plans for Larry, the eldest of their three sons: first, law school, then an association with a prestigious law firm, possibly in Tulsa. Then, politics, on a local level to begin with, graduating to State Senator, and ultimately—who knew?

Who knew anything in those days? she reflected wearily. Who could possibly have predicted Larry's fate? Or her own? Life was full of surprises—and of painfully cruel tricks. Barbara Jean knew. She had had more than one of them tossed her way.

Well, she was damn well tired of being a victim. She had to grasp one of life's *bouquets*—before it was too late. She took another swallow of her own personal pain killer. Not a bouquet, exactly, but it sometimes helped make the world seem more rosy. How many calories in two fingers of vodka? Or four fingers? She sighed. Even through her pleasantly

49

fuzzy haze, she knew she'd blown her diet.

She took one more drink, capped the bottle and put it back in the drawer. Tomorrow she would go back on her diet. But tonight . . . tonight she would indulge herself a little.

That's Barbara Jean Lawson." Vali pointed to the third girl from the left in the row of seven smiling teenagers. "She was the only girl at John Ross ever to make cheerleader all three years. Very bouncy. Tons of energy. The whole school was crazy about her."

"And that's you in the middle." Jennifer grinned up at her. "The Homecoming Queen."

"Do you love that outfit?" Vali laughed, amused by the almost ankle-length straight skirt, the too-long sweater, the bobby sox and the loafers.

"Your hair looks just the same, though. Your face, too, except you're prettier now."

Vali gave a doubtful smile. "I hope other people at the reunion share your opinion." She returned her attention to the photograph. "That's Anne Eastman on the other side of me. You remember, we saw her in a movie not long ago. She played Faye Dunaway's friend."

"You had a movie star in your class!"

"She wasn't a movie star then. Annie always knew where she was going, though. We never doubted she'd make it."

Jen studied the picture and frowned. "You once told me there were six girls in your club. There are seven in this picture."

The vision flashed before her eyes so suddenly she

50

didn't even have time to will it away. A church altar, draped in black. A young girl lying motionless, her white, unclothed body illuminated by the glow of thirteen flickering candles. Six shadowy figures in the background. The sound of chanting. Jennifer felt her squirm as they sat side by side on the sofa.

"Uh, yeah," Vali said, forcing herself back to the present. "Actually, there were seven. For a while." She pointed to the girl next to Anne, a frail-looking girl with fluffy, light-colored hair and a small heart-shaped face with a smattering of freckles across her nose. "Kathi was just about ready to be initiated when this picture was taken."

"She move away?"

"No. She died."

Jen turned to face her. "No kidding. What happened?"

"I don't know. She got sick or something." Vali clapped the scrapbook shut. "That's enough show and tell for today," she said with forced lightness. "I'm sure you're sick of reliving my teenaged past."

"Wait. You didn't tell me about the last girl," Jen protested mildly. "The one standing on the other side of Kathi."

"Oh. I guess it was Liz. Liz Everly. She lives in Russia now or something."

"Russia? She lives in *Russia?* What for?"

Vali turned to her and ruffled her dark blond hair. "Jen," she said with a laugh, "I'll be darned if I know."

Curled up on her straight-lined, Danish-made

51

sofa, Liz opened the slightly yellowed yearbook and methodically turned the pages until she reached the senior class protraits. Even scattered among the pictures of all the other classmates, the Loreleis stood out. They were far and away the prettiest girls in their class; their hairstyles, most of them dated now, were the most stylish, their skin the clearest, their smiles the brightest and their teeth the most even.

"Birds of a feather," Liz murmured as her smokey eyes slid past the individual photographs. Well, not quite. She wondered what they'd think if they knew what she'd really been like. Her glance fell on the picture of Bobby Langencamp, just one row below Barbara Jean's. His light hair was cut so short it almost looked as if his head was shaved; his skin was blossoming with acne, yet he was giving the camera a confident "I'm the greatest" look. Bobby Langencamp, BMOC (Big Man On Campus): captain of the John Ross baseball team, champion swimmer and wrestler. He and Liz had made it in the school parking lot one night after a meet. It was time, he'd told her firmly, slipping his big broad hand possessively under her yellow cashmere sweater. They'd been going steady for two years. What kind of a jerk did she think he was, anyway?

Liz had told him for the thousandth time that she just wasn't that kind of girl, that she had no intention of going all the way until she got married. Bobby had hooted at that. He was planning to be a doctor; he couldn't get married for at least four more years, maybe seven. "What do you expect me to do, live like a monk?" he'd asked her sneeringly. "I'm telling you for the last time. Either we do it, or we break up."

Liz didn't want to break up. Not with Bobby, who could have just about any girl at John Ross. As a Lorelei, she was expected to have a steady boyfriend; she wouldn't fit in otherwise. And she knew most of the others had made it with their steadies—or at least they said they did. So, for the first time, she didn't pull Bobby's hand away when she felt it sliding up her leg under her brown pleated skirt. She stiffened when he reached her cotton underpants and pushed his fingers up past the elastic around her thighs.

"We have to be careful," she told him flatly. "If anything happens . . ."

"Nothing's going to happen." Bobby's breath was coming in short gasps. He removed his hand from beneath her sweater and unzipped his fly. Then he reached past her and opened the glove compartment, his other had still stroking her vagina.

The parking lot was dark. The other swimmers and spectators had long since gone home. "Let's get in the back seat," Bobby said hoarsely. He pulled away from her and opened the door on his side. Liz got a glimpse of his penis sticking out from his trousers as he got out of the car. The sight disgusted her. She opened her own door and crawled into the back seat.

"Take off your pants." Bobby was fumbling with the rubber shield. His hands were shaking. Liz removed her underpants wordlessly. She wished it was over with instead of just starting. She lay back, the arm of the seat pressing into her neck as he climbed on top of her. He was heavy, and her body was twisted in the small car. He didn't touch her again, just shoved his penis inside her. The lubrication on the rubber made it slide in more easily, but it still hurt like hell. Liz gritted her teeth. *This* was the great thing everybody whispered about?

Bobby was pumping up and down on top of her now; the top of her head was banging against the car's windowsill. In a moment he let out a loud cry and slumped over, his arms hanging out at his sides. His penis was still inside her; she could feel it shriveling up.

"Bobby? Get that thing out of me." She was referring to the rubber. She'd heard they sometimes slipped off when the penis got small again.

Bobby pulled himself up. He jerked himself and the rubber out of her and tossed the shield out the window.

"Don't leave it out there!" Liz cried, aghast. "Someone'll see it!"

"You think they're gonna know whose it is?" Bobby asked her as if she were mentally deficient. "This parking lot's full of those things."

Liz straightened up and retrieved her panties from the floorboard. "Let's go home now, okay? My folks are probably waiting up." As she got back into the front seat, she could feel a dampness between her legs. She sat pressed against the door and didn't look at him. When they got to her house, she jumped out before he could kiss her goodnight.

She and Bobby did it two more times after that, and then he stopped calling. Liz was glad. She told the other Loreleis she'd broken up with him because he was a lousy lay and invented a boy she'd met in St. Louis last summer who could screw rings around him. Her friends accepted it all, and Liz maintained her status as a Lorelei in good standing.

Cliff Berkeley leaned back and lit a cigarette, carefully holding it beneath his desk in case the camera returned to him unexpectedly. Not that there was much chance of that. All three cameras were trained on his third guest of the evening, the dark-haired singer-actress who was putting her all into a not very exciting rendition of "Maybe This Time." Actually, though, he was not totally displeased with her performance. Her voice was good, she was attractive, and she handled their pre-song conversation very well.

He hoped her performance after the show would be as accomplished. He'd met her at a party several weeks ago, and when she'd narrowed her velvety brown eyes at him, he'd made some passing comment about booking her on the show. She'd phoned him seven times since then, and her manager had phoned him five. He'd finally booked her as a last-minute replacement when Crystal Gale had been called to Hollywood to tape a country music awards show.

The song ended, and Anne bowed gracefully and resumed her seat on the sofa next to Sean Connery and Joan Rivers. "Well!" Cliff exclaimed, widening his eyes in exaggerated appreciation. "I didn't know girls from Oklahoma could sing like that."

"Careful," Anne shot back, smiling. "I can hear ten thousand TV sets being clicked off."

Cliff grimaced broadly. "Sorry, folks," he said, raising an apologetic hand. "I didn't mean it. After all, Anita Bryant's from Oklahoma—right?"

Anne gave him a you've-got-to-be-kidding look. "Right," she muttered, unamused.

"Tell me. Where are you from in Oklahoma?" Cliff had caught a disapproving look from his producer and decided he'd better make amends in the bible belt.

"Baxter," Anne replied. "It's smaller than Tulsa and bigger than Jinks. I'll be back there in a couple of weeks, as a matter of fact."

"Oh? Going out to watch the grass grow?"

"No, you wild crazy man. I happen to be going back for my high school reunion." She carefully avoided mentioning the year.

"A high school reunion in Baxter, hmmm?" Cliff mused aloud. "That oughta shake up the town."

In the semi-darkened room, the tall, solidly-built, broad-shouldered man stiffened and stared at the screen. He swung his long legs over from their stretched-out position on the sofa and reached for the TV section of the newspaper which lay in disarray on the floor. What the hell did Berkeley say her name was? He found the listing and quickly perused the scheduled shows. *New York Nightline Starring Cliff Berkeley*. That was it. *Guests: Sean Connery, Joan Rivers, Anne Eastman*. Of course! He should have recognized her. She hadn't even changed that much. Her dark hair was shorter, and she looked a little thinner; but the huge eyes were the same and the cheekbones more prominent than ever.

"I plan to stay a week," she was saying in her charming husky voice. "Some of my classmates and I

56

are going to be dancing a chorus line number."

"Sort of a poor man's Rockettes," Cliff quipped.

"Actually, we're calling ourselves the Loreleis. After a club we belonged to in school."

The man in the semi-darkened room sucked in his breath and snatched up the message pad lying on the table next to the telephone. He underlined the word *Baxter* and then made a list of the things he had to do to get ready.

Then he got up and went to the kitchen for a beer.

Chapter Three

"I've taken a room at the motel," Francine told her husband. "Everyone in our chorus line except Margie Middleton will be staying there, and I'd like to be near them. Naturally, I'll be in and out of the house, too."

Baron Brookfield looked at her. At eighty-six he stood as straight as he had at thirty; his light blue eyes were clear and sharp, his complexion remarkably smooth and unblemished. His hair was snow white, of course, but that made him look distinguished, not ancient. "Am I to meet these friends of yours, these 'Loreleis,' as you sometimes refer to them?" he asked.

"Of course, darling. I want you to meet them." Francine smiled at him, and Baron was caught, as always, by the interesting slant of her copper-colored eyes that was even more pronounced when she smiled. She seemed more beautiful than when she was twenty-one; her abundant tawny hair was glossier, her body still a perfect size ten. Even after all these years he took pleasure in looking at her, and there were times when desire for her still flared in his old man's body.

"Why not have a party for them here one night?" he suggested. "They might enjoy that."

"Yes, I'm sure they would." Francine would enjoy it, too. The only one of them she'd seen since she'd married Baron was Margie, and that was only an occasional chance encounter that stemmed from the fact that they both still lived in Baxter. She and Vali exchanged Christmas cards every year, but they'd never actually gotten together. Even though she was long since accustomed to the wealth and status that went with being Mrs. Baron Brookfield, she would thoroughly enjoy showing off her flawlessly furnished house, her impeccably trained staff of uniformed servants and her fleet of fancy foreign cars to her old schoolchums. "Yes, I'll have to do that. I'll work out something with Marie." Marie was the formidable housekeeper who kept things running with smooth perfection at Brookfield Manor.

"Fine." Baron kissed the top of her head. "I'll see you at dinner." He picked up his briefcase from atop the hall table and departed for the office, walking with his usual dignity.

Francine looked after him. She wondered what the others would think when they saw her old, white-haired husband. Probably that she'd married him for his money, which was certainly an inducement. The other reason was something they wouldn't know, must never know; even Baron was unaware of that one. Only Arthur, Baron's son, knew that secret, and he'd kept it so long Francine doubted if he even remembered anymore.

I suppose it worked out for the best after all, Francine mused as she closed the door behind her husband. She'd been happy with Baron, as happy as a woman could be with a husband thirty-nine years her senior. And, of course, there was the Brookfield wealth and social standing to compensate for anything she felt was lacking. She'd long since gotten over feeling guilty, and now that Baron's first wife, Grace, was dead, the comparisons between her and her predecessor had stopped for good.

Funny. Arthur's wife was dead, too. The woman who'd won and the woman who'd lost were both gone. And Francine remained, in robust good health and with her irrefutable trump card: the heir to the Brookfield fortune, her twenty-six-year-old son, Barry. She rarely thought about the chain of events that had led to her becoming Baron's wife, but today—maybe because the forthcoming reunion was jogging so many recollections—she was flooded with memories. Memories of herself at twenty, with two years of college behind her and indisputably one of the most beautiful women in Baxter county. She was tired of school; she wanted to get started in *life*, so she'd quite OU and had returned to her home town to begin earning her living.

To her mind there were only three places in town worth working for: The First National Bank, MacKintosh Petroleum and Brookfield Oil. All three companies had been impressed with her secretarial skills and eagerness to learn, but Brookfield Oil was the only one with an opening, so that's where she ended up. She remembered how excited she'd been the first day she'd reported for work, how plush everything had seemed on the executive floor where she'd started as a receptionist, and how incredibly handsome Arthur Brookfield had looked when he made a special point of introducing himself. He'd had the bluest eyes Francine had ever seen, and the blackest hair, so glossy it shone even without pomade. Her heart had almost stopped when he'd smiled at her; she'd been so dazzled she was almost left speechless. She'd stuttered when she told him her name and cursed herself after he walked away for being so stupid. After all, she was not a silly teenager anymore. She was a grown woman.

Obviously Arthur had seen the woman in her because he seemed to turn up in the reception room every day that week. He didn't say much to her at first, just a "Good morning," or "You're looking pretty today," and then gradually he drew her into conversation and discovered she was single, lived at home, had lots of dates but was not interested in any young man in particular.

By the end of the second week he'd taken her to lunch—to a small, out-of-the-way place on the other side of town—and bought her her first martini, delivered in a coffee mug since Oklahoma was legally a dry state. Francine had been grateful for the drink; it had relaxed her and made it possible for her to choke down at least a little of the hot turkey sandwich she'd ordered. Arthur had completely enchanted her, just looking at him gave her the shivers. A few days later he'd suggested a drink after work and had taken her to a cozy little apartment out by the junior college.

"Does this belong to a friend of yours?" she'd asked in her awestruck naivete, admiring the polished cherrywood furniture, the Herculon plaid sofa and the gilt mirror over the mantel.

"No, as a matter of fact I keep it for myself. For the

nights I can't bear to go home." He gave her a sad smile. "Loretta—that's my wife—and I don't always see eye to eye."

"Oh, I'm sorry." Francine's knees began to tremble. Arthur hadn't mentioned a wife before. "Do . . . you have children?" she managed to stammer.

"Two. Both girls, ages six and three. Poor kids. They don't exactly have the most pleasant home life most of the time."

"That's too bad." Francine took the martini Arthur had made for her and took a healthy swallow. Arthur switched on the hi fi and the apartment was filled with soft, romantic music.

"Let's not talk about that," he said, gently taking her glass from her and placing it on the coffee table. "I have a sudden desire to dance with you."

"Dance? At six o'clock in the evening?"

"Why not? It's as good a time as any." He took her in his arms and began to move to the music. Francine followed, praying she wouldn't stumble all over herself. She was so close to him she could smell his aftershave; she was drowning in the feel of his body next to hers.

She was lost as soon as he kissed her. She forgot about his wife and kids and responded to him with more passion than she'd dreamed was in her. When he'd carried her to the small, simply furnished bedroom, she hadn't even demurred for propriety's sake. A man like this, a feeling like this was what she'd waited for all her life; incredibly, she was still a virgin.

She'd moved into the apartment a week later. Her parents had been amazed; they hadn't realized her salary could support such a place, but Francine had assured them she had the situation well in hand. They never knew it was Arthur Brookfield who paid the rent. Arthur met her there three or four times a week, usually after work but occasionally on their mutual lunch hour. At first Francine had prepared elegant little meals complete with canapes and chilled wine, but Arthur never seemed to have time to enjoy them. "I wish I could stay, but I have a business dinner tonight," he'd tell her, leading her into the bedroom. Or, "Dad's expecting me to join him at the country club." Finally Francine stopped preparing the dinners and stopped chilling the wine. Arthur didn't even seem to notice.

When she first suspected she was pregnant she felt a mixture of elation and dread. What would Arthur say? Surely he'd be happy; he'd told her he loved her many times—it stood to reason he'd love their child. Francine hoped this would be the thing that prompted him to do what he'd said he wished he could do all along. Divorce Loretta and marry her. Why should he remain in a loveless marriage when the real woman of his heart was waiting with a child inside her?

She had champagne ready when he arrived that night. "What's this, a celebration?" he asked, pulling her to him and covering her face with kisses.

"A fantastic celebration," Francine told him joyfully. She expertly popped the cork and filled two tulip-shaped glasses. She handed him one and raised the other. "To Arthur Brookfield, Junior!" she announced. "Who, according to my calculation, should be arriving in just about eight months."

"What?" Arthur's face turned white. "Francy,

you're kidding, aren't you?''

"No, darling, I'm not." She laughed and kissed his nose. "Isn't it wonderful? We'll have to say he's a bit premature, but if you could get Loretta to go to Mexico right away—"

"Mexico!" Arthur exclaimed. "You can't be serious."

Francine stopped laughing and stared at him. A cold chill crept up the back of her neck. "Of course I'm serious. Arthur, I'm pregnant."

Arthur was silent for a long moment. Then: "Look, honey, I know a doctor. It's perfectly safe, nothing to worry about."

"A doctor? What kind of doctor?" Francine felt weak; she could hardly breathe.

"A perfectly capable one. He handles this sort of thing all the time. Naturally, I'll take care of the fee."

"Arthur, you're not talking about an abortion?" Abortions were illegal, carried out in secret by slimy men with dirty hands who had flunked out of medical school. Girls from the wrong side of the tracks had abortions, not girls like Francine Briggs.

He took a step toward her and took one of her hands in his. "Francy, it has to be this way. You can't have a baby now. What would people think?"

"But if we were married, if you sent Loretta to Mexico—"

"Francy, I can't do that. Not now. I know I've told you we don't get along, and everything I've said is true. But we have the girls and a certain standing in town—"

"A certain standing? What about me? What about the child I'm carrying?"

"Look, there'll be other children. Later on, when I

untangle everything, get things squared away." He looked at her evenly. "Francy, you'll have to have the abortion."

But Francine *wouldn't* have it. She wouldn't do that to her body, to her child. And from that moment she thought it as only *her* child, because when she looked at Arthur she saw—not the handsome, gallant man she'd loved—but a weak, lying bastard. "Suppose I go to Loretta myself," she posed in a flat, dead voice. "Suppose I tell her about us, about this apartment? Where will your 'certain standing' be then?"

"You wouldn't. You have too much class for that."

"Oh? Don't be so sure." She handed him his overcoat. "Get out, Arthur. And don't come back. I'll vacate the apartment at the end of the month."

"Francine, you're being too hasty—"

"Get out, Arthur." She wished she could kill him, she hated him that much.

He sighed wearily. "All right, Francy. Have it your way. But you'd do well to remember the Brookfields own this town. If you try anything cute, you'll be the loser, not I."

When she got to work the following Monday she learned that Arthur and his wife had left for an extended tour of the Orient. The reason for the trip was sort of a "second honeymoon."

Margie Middleton was becoming increasingly nervous. Chorus line rehearsals were to begin the day after tomorrow, which meant all the Loreleis would have arrived by then. Margie had agreed to take part in the talent show, but she was not comfortable with her decision; she was beginning to sleep fitfully and suffer from nausea as a result. All of which was starting to take its toll on her looks. Dark smudges had appeared under her eyes, and her face seemed drawn and sallow.

When they were in high school, the Loreleis had sworn everlasting friendship; they would never lose touch with one another, never forget the shared joys of their golden teenage years. And now, thirty years after their graduation, Margie had no desire to see any of them. She'd made a career out of putting high school out of her consciousness; now it was all about to come back and hit her over the head.

The popular one. That's what she was called then. Not that they weren't *all* popular. Popular was what being a Lorelei was all about. But it was Margie Richey who had the most "fun," the most dates and late dates, could drink the most beer, knew the most swear words, cheated on the most tests and sneaked the most cigarettes in the Girls' Room at John Ross High. Bouncy and outgoing, Margie was invited to every party, every hayride, prom and beer bust. And she never said no to anything.

What would they have said, Margie wondered as she sorted clothes for the laundry, if they knew how she had loathed it all, all the drinking and swearing and sneaking around, making out in a hundred different cars? What would they have thought if they'd known how disgusted with herself it all made her feel, how she'd come home after a date and throw up in the bathroom because she couldn't stand the boy she'd just made love to with passionate abandon?

It had all started as a natural teenage desire: to be accepted among the "in" crowd. Margie had first laid eyes on Vali, Anne and Francine in ninth grade, when the Richeys had moved to Baxter from Shreveport. Not that they had paid her any mind. She'd talked with a heavy Southern drawl, and some of the kids teased her; but her fourteen-year-old body was already filled out, and her auburn hair fell alluringly to her neat little waist. She knew the way to attract the attention of the popular girls was to attract the attention of the popular boys, and so she set out to do just that. She found it surprisingly easy once she made up her mind to do the necessary thing. In the nineteen fifties, fourteen-year-old girls didn't have sex with everyone who asked, but Margie Richey did. Her first "score" was a bungling, puffing senior named Sam Dailey who, naturally, filled in his friends about the new girl from Shreveport. After that, the phone rang constantly in the Richey house, and Margie's parents were overjoyed that their daughter had made such a rapid adjustment to the new town.

Barbara Jean Lawson was the first of the "in" crowd of girls to notice her. Barbara Jean was what Margie pretended to be: peppy, self-assured, a natural leader. Through her, Margie got to know the others, and when it became evident that they would either have to accept her or face the possibility that she would be a formidable rival, they asked her to join their newly formed club, Lorelei. From that time on, Margie could never let up. She had a reputation for being the most sophisticated girl in school, and she was terrified of losing it. She drank gallons of beer and was sick all night; she made out with boys who made her skin crawl just so no one would say she was "square." She was the first of her crowd to wear

67

lipstick, the first to shave her legs and the first to appear in a strapless formal. She stole Miss Wright's answer book for an important quiz, and she and her friends all scored one hundred. She stole stationery from the dime store and ran out of restaurants without paying the bill—all in the name of "fun." And none of it ever caught up with her until the last semester of her junior year. That's when she found out she was pregnant.

At first she couldn't believe it. All those other times, and her period had been regular as clockwork. No one had ever made it with her without using a rubber, but somewhere something had gone wrong. If she'd known for sure who the father was, she might have gotten him to marry her. But she didn't know—and, anyway, she didn't want to get married. Her heartbroken parents arranged for an abortion in a dingy little doctor's office on the south side of town, and Margie's laugh didn't ring with quite so much gaiety after that.

The experience made her seem very glamorous in the eyes of the other girls, of course. They all claimed to have slept with boys (although some of their stories were suspect), but none had ever gotten "caught." They were agog over their friend's not-so-secret abortion, and Margie pretended to love the new status it gave her. But she cried herself to sleep almost every night, and in the morning she had to push back a million unnamed terrors and force herself to go to school.

Now they were all coming back, all the people who knew what she had managed to keep buried for so long. She didn't know how she was going to bear it.

Chapter Four

Frank Bragg walked up to the registration desk at the antiquated Hotel Baxter at approximately five o'clock in the afternoon. He was wearing jeans and a sports shirt, and he carried no luggage.

"Double or single?" the thin, pinched-faced man at the desk asked, thrusting forth a registration form.

"Single," Frank answered. He surveyed the ornate lobby with its heavy, velvet-covered chairs and sofas, its carved wood doors and beams, and the spectacular crystal chandelier that hung from the domed ceiling. "Interesting old place."

"We still get the class clientel. How many nights is that?"

"I'm not sure." Frank picked up the ball point pen which was secured to the desk by a chain. He printed his name on the first line of the registration form. "Looks quiet," he observed idly.

"Summer," the clerk responded. "It's always quiet in summer."

"Well, I imagine you'll have all the business you can handle during reunion weekend." Frank took his driver's license out of his wallet to check the number.

"Reunion? There's no reunion scheduled this month."

Frank looked up and frowned. "The John Ross High School reunion isn't being held here? It's the weekend of the twenty-ninth."

The clerk shook his head. "We haven't had a reunion here in ten years or more." He cleared his throat. "Frankly, I'm just as glad. Those things get rowdy, the drinking and all . . ."

"Yes, I can see your point." Frank put a hand to his lips. "Where *are* the reunions being held these days?"

"Most things of that sort go on at the Lancelot. They've got a big banquet hall—and of course they're air conditioned."

"You mean you're not air conditioned?" Frank held on to the registration form.

"Wiring's too old. We've got fans, though, and most of the rooms get a pretty good breeze at night." He produced an enormous bronze room key. "Shall I call a bellboy?"

"No, wait. On second thought . . ." Frank paused, embarrassed. "Look, I'm very sorry. I had no idea you weren't air conditioned. You see, I have this problem—"

"A lot of people have it," the clerk answered, nodding wearily. He took the registration form from Frank's hand. "Shall I tear this up?"

Frank sighed. "I suppose you'd better." He reached into his pocket for some bills. "I am sorry . . ."

The clerk waved off the tip. "Forget it. Come back in about six months. Our heating system's terrific. Pipes hardly knock at all."

"I will," Frank assured him, gratefully repocketing the bills. "Thank you very much for your trouble."

"Just take Mission out to Fifteenth," the clerk called after him as he walked away. "The Lancelot's the building with all the turrets."

Barbara Jean checked into the Lancelot, room 513, at 2:35 P.M. on Friday, the twelfth.

"You're here for the reunion, right?" the desk clerk, a bleached blonde wearing too much makeup, asked when she'd signed the registration card.

"Sure am. How'd you know?"

"Mrs. Brookfield gave me all your names—the names of her special friends, that is. Said to give you ladies the best rooms in the place."

Three cheers for Mrs. Brookfield, Barbara Jean thought dryly when she entered her room and opened the battered piece of Samsonite she'd been given as a high school graduation present and began unfolding her clothes. She'd treated herself to two new dresses and a haircut to celebrate the fact that she'd lost twenty pounds since May, when she'd received the first reunion notice. She turned to look at herself in the full-length mirror attached to the front of the bathroom door. She was still a good twenty pounds over-weight—she was sure Mrs. Brookfield had maintained *her* high school figure—but she was no longer sloppy, and she was proud of what she'd managed to accomplish.

Barbara Jean wondered if the others had arrived. She hadn't thought to ask the desk clerk. Maybe she

71

should pick up the phone and check. She moved to the night table on the far side of the bed wondering who she should ask to speak to. Anne, the one she'd admired most in high school? No. Anne was a famous actress now, or at least *almost* famous, and Barbara Jean wouldn't know what to say straight off. Liz, who'd come all the way from Russia? No, Liz, the brain, had always made her feel slightly uncomfortable; anyway, weren't her parents still in Baxter? Most likely she'd be staying with them. Vali, then. The one she'd known the longest. It should be easy to talk to someone you'd known for thirty-eight years.

She sat down on the bed, reached for the phone and dialed "1." When the operator's nasal voice came on the other end, she hesitated, then hung up. She'd known Vali for thirty-eight years and hadn't seen or heard from her for thirty. She'd heard Vali owned some kind of airline company and flew her own plane. Would she really be thrilled to hear from a farmer's wife?

Of course she would, she scolded herself. That's what they were all here for, wasn't it? To see each other again and recapture old times. To relive the days of the Loreleis.

> *"Ain't we neat . . .*
> *Do you think we can be beat?*
> *Well, I tell you very confidentially,*
> *We're elite."*

The words of the old sorority song sprang to her lips. She and Anne and Vali had made them up to be sung to the tune of "Ain't She Sweet?"

72

> "Lor-e-leis . . .
> Loved by all the guys.
> There's nothing wrong with any one of us
> In their eyes."

Not exactly the most subtle song in the world. The lyrics were meant to be "witty and ironic," but the super-secure Loreleis thought they hit pretty close to the truth. Weren't they the golden girls, the darlings of the Class of Fifty-eight?

If I only had a drink, Barbara Jean thought to herself. She'd refrained from bringing a bottle with her; she didn't dare take a chance on losing control of herself this week. Maybe if she just went down to the bar and ordered a club soda. The atmosphere alone might help her get her courage up.

She took the elevator down to the lobby and entered the bar located directly across from the front desk. It was dark inside, and that made her feel more at ease right away. She sat at a small corner table and ordered a club soda from a young girl dressed in a sort of old English "wench" outfit. The room was empty except for two men at the bar and another man at the table across from her.

Barbara Jean felt the man at the table staring at her. She wondered if he thought she was a pickup. When the waitress brought her drink, she sneaked a peek in the man's direction. It was hard to tell in this light, but he looked attractive.

Crazily her thoughts went back to last night, when she'd been in the bedroom packing. Woody and the kids were downstairs watching television—as usual. To her surprise the door had opened and Kerry had come in. She'd offered to help, so Barbara Jean had given her the job of collecting and folding underwear. They'd talked idly about the reunion for a few minutes—about the Loreleis and what Barbara Jean knew of their present circumstances—and then Kerry had put the last pile of bras and panties in the suitcase and had turned to Barbara Jean with a solemn expression.

"Mom, you have a good time in Baxter, huh?" It was more of a command than a pleasantry.

Barbara Jean looked at her and frowned. "Sure, hon. I intend to."

Kerry's blue eyes had narrowed, and she'd taken a deep breath, as if trying to gear up for something. "I mean it, Mom. A *really* good time."

Barbara Jean had had to laugh at her daughter's earnestness. "Hey, what is this? You think I'm too old for a little fun?"

"No, not at all. I just thing you're . . . well, inhibited."

"Inhibited? What's that supposed to mean?"

Kerry had given her an intense look, then, as if suddenly embarrassed, had turned back to Barbara Jean's chest of drawers and busied herself sorting nightgowns. "Did you have any big romances in school, Mom?" she asked, not looking at her mother at all. "Anyone who might be at the reunion?"

Barbara Jean felt the familiar grab in her stomach. She'd never told her family about Larry. It was too personal, too . . . hopeless. Her hands clenched her makeup case so tightly her knuckles showed white. "I'm not eager to see any of my old boyfriends," she said, trying to keep her voice bright, "if that's what

74

you mean."

Kerry was silent for a long moment. Then she turned an eager face toward her mother. "Well, if anybody *is* there, anybody who turned out to be a hunk, you shouldn't feel guilty if you . . . well, you know."

Barbara Jean stared at her. Was her daughter telling her to have an affair?

"I mean," Kerry went on carefully, "you and Daddy have been married a long time. You've been stuck here on the farm . . . and you look so great now that you've lost all that weight."

Daddy. Barbara Jean nodded, understanding now. Clearly Kerry was aware of the fact that her parents no longer had the hottest sex life in the world. Woody treated Barbara Jean more like a live-in relative than a wife. Barbara Jean had long assumed that he— who, if anything, had gotten more handsome with the years—pleasured himself with women when he went out of town for auctions or on selling trips. The assumption must have transmitted itself to Kerry; that's why she was trying to tell her mother about the what's good for the goose bit.

Barbara Jean's eyes misted. It had been a long time since anyone had suggested *she* grab a bit of fun. She'd gone to Kerry's side and given her a warm hug. "I'm glad you're my daughter," she whispered. Suddenly she didn't feel quite so much like a stranger in her own house.

Frank had come into the bar because he felt conspicuous sitting in the lobby watching people

arrive. He was pretty sure most of the Loreleis would
check in this evening, this being the Friday previous
to the commencement of the reunion. Anne Eastman
had told Cliff Berkeley she'd be in town a week, and
he suspected the week would be spent rehearsing the
dance routine she'd talked about. When Barbara Jean
walked in alone, he wasn't sure she was one of them;
that's why he had looked at her so hard through the
dimness. Short, fair, overweight. The overweight
part was to be expected, he supposed—didn't it
happen to most housewives approaching middle
age? Fair. Hmmm. Could be Vali, although Frank
pictured Vali more patrician. Couldn't be Francine
Brookfield, nee Briggs. Not stylish enough. Barbara
Jean Lawson? Possibly. Wouldn't hurt to check it
out.

He rose from his table and strode over to hers. She
saw him coming and watched cautiously.

"Hi. Can I buy you a drink?" He smiled, showing
even white teeth.

He looked nice. Normal. Not like a pervert or
anything. "I'm just having club soda." If he *did*
think she was a pickup, that should put him off.

"Then I'll buy you a club soda. Unless you'd prefer
something else."

Barbara Jean hesitated. She knew she should either
leave or tell him to get lost, but he *was* attractive; and
so far he hadn't done anything except ask to buy her a
drink. And what if one of the other Loreleis
happened to come into the bar at this moment?
Wouldn't it be more interesting to be found sitting
with a handsome man than nursing a club soda
alone? "Okay. White wine. Thanks." One glass of

white wine wouldn't hurt; anyway, she needed it.

He signaled to the waitress. "Mind if I sit down?"

"Go ahead." She gave him a guarded smile. Better not let him think she was too eager.

"I hope you don't think I'm being too familiar. I just hate drinking alone, and you seem like a sharing person."

"Are you from out of town?"

"A little north of here. How about yourself?"

"I'm from a little town called Choctaw." She shook her head. "That is, I'm *from* Baxter, but I live in Choctaw now."

He put out his hand. "Glad to know you. My name's Frank Bragg."

She reached out for the handshake. His palm was warm; she could feel the strength in his arm. "Barbara Jean Fleagle."

He smiled again and moved his chair closer to hers.

The anchor man of Baxter "Eyewitness News" was at Indian Hill landing field when the twin-engine Cessna smoothly glided onto the air strip. "You get that, Jim?" he asked his cameraman as the plane taxied to a stop several yards from where they stood.

"No problem." The camera continued to whir. Jim carefully focused on the plane's door, which was being lifted aside by one of the landing field's mechanics. The camera caught a flash of shapely leg, a sleek mane of golden hair and a picture perfect smile on a lovely and still young-looking face.

"And she's landed!" the anchor man announced to

his viewing audience. "Valerie Thomas has arrived for her high school reunion."

The mechanic held Vali's hand as she lept lightly to the ground, smiling and waving at the cluster of people standing just beyond the runway. The anchor man approached her. "Welcome to Baxter, Mrs. Thomas," he greeted heartily.

Vali was all white teeth and flashing dimples. "Why, thank you, thank you very much! Gee, it's great to be here." She laughed and fanned herself with her hand. "I'd forgotten about the heat, though."

"How was the flight? Have any trouble?"

"Oh, no, it was perfect all the way. No trouble at all."

"Well, tell us, Mrs. Thomas. How does it feel to be back in the old home town?"

Vali gave a charming shrug. "To tell you the truth, I don't know. I only just got here. I like the welcome, though."

"Looking forward to the reunion?"

"Oh, yes, very much." She waved an energetic fist. "Rah, Rah, Class of Fifty-eight!"

"I think I can say with certainty you're the only John Ross graduate who ever returned in her own plane. Think your friends will be jealous?"

"Heavens no. Why should they be? I'm just the same as I always was." She smoothed her silky hair with her palm.

The anchorman looked into the camera. "Well, you heard it, Class of Fifty-eighters. Valerie Porter Thomas is the same as always. That's it from Indian Hill landing field."

The camera ground to a halt. Jim hefted it from his shoulder and turned back toward the sound truck. The anchor man turned to Vali. He put an arm around her shoulders.

"Hi, there."

She looked at him with heartstoppingly familiar aquamarine eyes. "Since when does the anchor man do remotes?" She was smiling, but he felt the sting in the question.

He faced her squarely. "I wanted to do this one. It's good to see you, Val."

She met his gaze. "Good to see you, too, Donald." Her voice was soft. Whispery.

He stared at her, then looked away. He suddenly wished he hadn't taken the assignment after all.

Chapter Five

Anne hurried to the information desk at the Tulsa airport. Her slingback pumps clicked purposefully on the terra-cotta floor.

"I'm expecting someone to meet me," she said loudly to the young, crisply uniformed man behind the counter. "Perhaps someone's been asking for me?"

"No one's asked for anyone since I've been here," the young man told her politely. "Would you like me to page the party?"

"No. I don't know his name. He's from the newspaper."

"Oh? *World* or *Tribune?*"

"I don't know. Maybe both." When the young man looked confused she went on quickly. "Just say Miss Eastman is waiting at the information desk."

"Miss Eastman?"

She glared at him. "Miss *Anne* Eastman."

She waited irritably as the young man's voice resounded through the large, modern lobby. "Will the party meeting Miss Anne Eastman please come to the information desk? The party meeting Miss

Anne Eastman . . ."

Damn that Mark! Anne thought with murderous rage. He'd promised to have a reporter here! Maybe even a photographer. Why couldn't people do what they said they'd do? Lord knew she paid him enough every month. When she heard the announcement for the third time, she knew it was hopeless. And here it was Saturday—fat chance of catching Mark at home *or* the office.

"I'm sorry, Miss Eastman, your party doesn't seem to be around." The young man looked at her apologetically, and Anne was struck by how much he resembled the young Robert Wagner. She smiled. No sense in blaming *him.*

"Thanks, anyway. Could you direct me to a pay phone?"

The young man pointed. "Over there. Across from the gift shop."

"Thanks." Anne made for the phone. Damned if she was going to play this scene without an audience. She asked the operator for the number of the *Tulsa World,* dialed, and asked for the entertainment editor.

"I'm sorry. Mr. Jones isn't in the office on weekends."

"Give me the feature editor, then." That was better, anyway. Entertainment news was always relegated to the back pages.

"There's no one there, either, ma'am. Can you call back on Monday?"

"No, I cannot call back on Monday. I won't be here on Monday." Anne took a deep breath. "Do you mean to tell me nobody's in the office now? What if a

81

fire destroys City Hall? What if the mayor gets shot? What if a swarm of killer bees arrives at Third and Main? What do you do? Say 'sorry about that, you have to wait till Monday so we can send out a reporter'?"

There was a moment of silence at the other end. Then: "I can give you Mr. Bishop."

Mr. Bishop. Who the hell was he, the religious editor? "Fine," she sighed. "Give me Mr. Bishop." She waited while the operator rang through.

"Bishop here." The voice was strong. Aggressive. Anne put on her best English accent.

"Hello, Mr. Bishop, this is Miss Caldwell in New York."

"Miss who?"

"Caldwell. Of Caldwell, Black and Donahue. The public relations firm."

"Yeah? What can I do for you?"

"It's *I* who can do something for *you* Mr. Bishop. Miss Eastman has arrived in Tulsa, and your man was not there to meet her at the airport."

"Miss Eastman? What Miss Eastman is that?"

"Miss *Anne* Eastman. The well-known actress. She's on her way to Baxter to attend her high school reunion."

"Oh, well. We don't usually meet people on their way to Baxter. Try the *Baxter Chronicle*."

"But, Mr. Bishop, it was all arranged. Your reporter was to do a feature story on her. This could be your last chance."

She could feel his discomfort over the phone wires. "Look, Miss Caldwell, I'm just a stringer. I don't know anything about an interview with Miss

Eastman. I can't even check it out for you. The assignment editor's gone home."

"Then I suggest you get out to the airport yourself. I'll contact Miss Eastman and ask her to wait. She's very gracious about these things, actually."

"Look, I don't know anything about—"

"I'll call her this minute," she interrupted. "How soon can you be there?"

"Lady . . ." He stopped. "Oh, hell. Tell her twenty minutes."

"Fine. I'll ask her to wait in the coffee shop."

Anne put down the phone and smiled thinly. She'd proven once again what she'd learned long ago. If you don't blow your own horn, no one else is sure as hell gonna blow it for you! She freshened her makeup in the ladies' room and went to the coffee shop to wait. It was only five-thirty. Her connecting flight didn't leave until seven. Sipping a diet soda, she thought about what she was going to tell this hot shot stringer. All about her career, naturally. How she'd just closed in a marvelous play—she'd leave out the off-Broadway part, they didn't know off-Broadway from the Bronx down here, anyway—and about her recent appearance on the Cliff Berkeley show. And she'd certainly tell him about the movie that was in the offing, though she'd be careful not to say anything that could be checked.

But if Bishop was like most reporters, he'd probably want to bring in the "local girl" aspect, even though Baxter was a hundred miles from Tulsa. Since she was on her way to a reunion, she should be prepared to discuss her high school years. But exactly *what* should she tell him—that was the question.

Should she tell him that she was the girl the others felt sorry for? Not because she wasn't pretty or popular—God, no! She was a Lorelei, after all. But as far as she knew, she was the only girl in her class who didn't have a mother.

"That's Anne Eastman, her mother's *dead*," she'd hear her classmates whisper to people who weren't aware of her circumstances. She learned early on that having a dead mother gave her a certain status—and she only had to allude to the situation to patch up a quarrel, snag a dinner invitation to a friend's house or persuade a teacher not to report a cut class to the principal. No one wanted to further injure a poor motherless child.

The truth to tell, Anne's mother had died when Anne was so young the motherless child could neither remember nor grieve for her. As a matter of fact—though she never admitted it to *anyone*—she was glad her mother was dead; she had a feeling she'd have hated her had she been alive.

The tragic story of Jessica Coffee Eastman was one Anne had heard so many times she could recite it perfectly and never skip a single detail. Jessica's beauty was legendary, her mixture of Cherokee and Scottish blood gave her skin the color of hazelnut, eyes as black as a starless sky and a mane of ebony hair that shone like satin and fell so far down her back she could sit on it. She was a petite thing, light as a feather. Men stood in line for hours on end to dance with her the time she sneaked into the Christmas Ball at the country club. She was *always* in wonderful spirits; her cherry lips didn't know what a frown was. And she was good, inside and out. She had a perfect church attendance record and thought nothing of walking a mile and a half just to take a sick old lady a bowl of her homemade navy bean and bacon soup.

Naturally, she had her pick of men to marry. Why, every bachelor for *miles* was head over heels in love with her. She'd decided on Philip Eastman, a Baxter transplant from Little Rock. Philip was older than the fellows Jessica usually dated, already established at the First National Bank where he was taking part in a junior executive training program. (One day he would become president of First National, but Jessica didn't live to see that.)

Jessica's wedding was absolutely *perfect,* she walked down the aisle of the First Baptist Church in a dress from Duncan's department store, and there were so many flowers people suspected some of them had actually been *bought.* The marriage was perfect, too, although a few people thought Philip was disappointed when the first child Jessica presented him with was a girl. But Jessica was a wonderful mother and homemaker; her house positively *reeked* of Lysol and homemade bread. Even when she started to feel poorly, her skin lost its satiny glow and her famous high cheekbones were prominent to the point of alarm, she baked pies for the church sale, babysat the neighborhood kids and drove around town in her brand new Pontiac delivering Christmas baskets to the poor. When she went off to the T.B. sanitorium, she wrote her husband and child every single day.

Jessica went to the sanitorium when Anne was three, and although she didn't die until two years later, Anne never saw her after that. But she heard about her—oh, Lord, how she heard about her. Friends and relatives sang her mama's praises day and night; Anne sometimes wondered if Mama was more perfect than the little baby Jesus. She received one reprieve, however, when, after her mother died, she was sent to live with her father's parents in Little Rock. The Eastmans had only met Jessica once and were not so aware of her perfections, therefore they were not wont to glorify her day and night. But when she was ten, Philip decided he wanted his daughter back, and Anne was shipped back to Baxter unaware that her destination was her mother's shadow.

At first Anne loved being the lady of the house. She already knew how to fry chicken and make biscuits, and what she didn't know, she improvised. She loved to fix dinner and have it waiting when Daddy came home from the bank of an evening. She loved to have the house all sparkling, too, and she hardly ever burned one of his dress shirts or broke one of the knickknacks she so carefully dusted. But her daddy never seemed to appreciate her efforts. No matter how crispy her chicken, her mother's was always crispier; Anne's flaky biscuits didn't melt in the mouth the way Jessica's had. And if she *did* break something, her daddy was usually furious, calling her clumsy and sometimes even stupid. To please him, she tried harder, not just at home but at school, too. But "A" report cards didn't impress him. Sometimes she'd see him looking at her over the top of his ever-present cocktail glass, shaking his head as if he didn't know her.

She wondered if there was something wrong with her appearance. She studied herself in the mirror, but found nothing wrong with her rapidly developing body and even, perfectly placed features. One day when she was thirteen, she compared her mirror image to a photograph of her mother. She brushed her hair straight back the way Jessica's was, made her eyes slant upward with a few strokes of a Westmore pencil, and darkened her cheeks so that the bones showed more. That night she put on one of her mother's silk nighties (all Jessica's clothes were still in the house) and crept into her daddy's bed while he was asleep. He had, as always, a faint aroma of liquor about him; she knew he'd had several bourbons alone in the den after dinner. She didn't mind the smell, or even his snoring. Those things were what made him Daddy.

When he sensed her presence, he put an arm around her and pulled her to him without even opening his eyes. Then, to her joy, he smothered her face with kisses and ran his hands along her body which made her tingle deliciously. He murmured "Jessica" once or twice, but she was so enraptured she hardly heard the word.

What he did next was not what she expected, but it was so loving, so *intimate*, that she welcomed it, pain and all. She was lying pinned beneath him, reveling in the musky warmth of his body, basking in the knowledge that things would be different from now on, when she heard his gasp of horror and felt him leap from the bed as though it were on fire.

"Oh, my God! My God!" He was pacing the room, head in hands, shoulders heaving, his voice quivering with anguish. "Forgive me. Oh, Lord—forgive me."

Anne rose from the bed, went to him and put her arms around his waist. "There's nothing to forgive, Daddy. It was wonderful."

He pushed her away so hard she almost fell, and then he ran into the bathroom where he stayed until Anne finally went back to her own room and cried herself to sleep. After that, he stopped talking about her mother's perfections; in fact, he barely talked to her at all. If Anne was the girl without a mother, she was the girl with a ghost for a father. He drank more bourbon than ever. He never so much as hugged her again, and he always kept his bedroom door locked at night.

Anne compensated for her loveless home life by finding things to do that kept her from home as much as possible. School plays required evening rehearsals, and acting offered a release from her misery. In playing a part she could lose herself, pretend to be anyone other than the person she most detested: herself. She carried her self-hate through high school and on to Northwestern where she received excellent theatrical training. After that, she went to New York, driven by the desire to make something of herself, make people sit up and take notice. And if one of those people happened to be her father—now retired and living in La Jolla, California—well, better late than never.

She finished her diet soda and asked for her check. No, she decided, her true life story wasn't fit for Mr. Bishop's ears. She'd have to invent something to tell him.

*　　*　　*

Liz was pretty sure she'd win the prize for having traveled farthest. She flew Aeroflot from Moscow to New York and TWA to Tulsa, where she was met by her parents. Had she taken the earlier flight, she would have been on the same plane as Anne. Veda and Jack Everly plied her with questions about life in Moscow during the drive to Baxter, then filled her in on local gossip before she could answer most of them. Her mother fixed fried chicken and corn on the cob for her first meal at home, and she slept on the sofa bed in the condo her parents had bought after her sister had married and Liz had gone off to see the world.

The following morning she phoned Francine and learned the first official meeting of the Loreleis was set for seven-thirty that night at Margie Middleton's house. Then she borrowed her mother's car and drove around town, amazed at how much Baxter had grown. John Ross High looked exactly as she remembered it, except that it was abandoned now, soon to be torn down to make way for the construction of an office and shopping complex that would cover several blocks. She sighed. That was progress, she supposed. Anyway, high schools had sprung up in other, more convenient areas since the Loreleis had graduated.

At noon she decided to go to Riley's Drive-In for the one thing she'd missed most since leaving: a good old-fashioned hamburger. Although Riley's was still open, it looked as if it, too, was ready for the wrecking ball. The red and white aluminum canopies were sadly in need of paint, and the car hops' uniforms— once crisp and flattering—were faded and ill-fitting.

Liz ordered a "hamburger in a basket," which meant french fries were included, and a cherry coke. She smiled as she waited for it, recalling how she and her friends used to pull into the place so tightly packed in a car there was barely room to move their arms. They'd order hamburgers, onion rings, malts and Riley's specialty, black bottom pie, calling out to other kids jammed in other cars as they waited, singing school fight songs, listening to Elvis on the car radio. Occasionally someone would get out of a car in order to talk to someone across the way. This would usually result in a stern rebuke from Jake, the cop who patroled Riley's day and night.

Today the drive-in was less than half filled, and most of the customers seemed to be young housewives with small children. Liz supposed the high school kids had found another hangout. It was after the car hop had brought her order that her eyes suddenly fell on the ancient, dark blue Mercury parked in the opposite aisle and directly in her line of vision. It had been blocked from view before by a car that had just pulled out. The sight of it caused Liz's stomach to lurch involuntarily. The car was clearly out of place among the Celicas and Rabbits; one fender was dented, and what was obviously the original paint job was faded and scratched. But it jogged something she couldn't quite grasp, which made her feel suddenly uneasy.

This is dumb, she told herself, fighting the inexplicable nausea that suddenly swept over her. It's just a car. But somewhere in her subconscious was the feeling that it was *more* than just a car, and the feeling was so disturbing she deliberately tried to push down any memories that might be fighting their way to the surface.

It was the sight of the car's occupant that made definite identification impossible to deny. When Liz had first spotted the car, the occupant, a lone female, had been turned away from the window; all Liz had been able to see was a fluffy mass of red-gold hair. But she suddenly turned around and faced Liz fully, looking at her with what seemed like complete recognition. She appeared to be about seventeen, and her red-gold hair was parted on one side and loosely framed her delicate heart-shaped face. Her eyes were clear and probing, and even from this distance, Liz knew they were green. Liz was also aware of a small smattering of freckles across the small, straight nose, though to anyone else they would not have been discernible from another car.

Liz began to perspire, while her body was wracked by a sudden shaking. A vision swam into her head, a vision of a girl with fluffy red-gold hair and a freckled, heart-shaped face lying lifeless on a black draped altar. Her body was surrounded by tall black candles whose reflected flames bobbed like dancers on her cold, frozen features. She heard sounds in her head—horrible sounds, sounds of sobbing. Then, as quickly as the vision had appeared, it went away, and she was once again confronted by the relentless stare of the girl in the opposite car. She knew with chilling certainty that the girl of her vision and the girl in the car were one and the same.

Kathi Harcort.

Liz closed her eyes tight and forced herself to try and think logically. Of course it wasn't Kathi. Kathi

91

Harcort had been dead for thirty years. The girl in the car had only resembled her, and the fact that Liz had encountered her here at Riley's set her imagination working for a moment. But those eyes . . . those piercing green eyes that seemed to say "I know you . . ." And that red-gold hair that no one at John Ross had ever seen before . . .

Stop it! she commanded her whirling inner thoughts. *Lots of people have green eyes and red-gold hair. You're making a big thing out of nothing.* All she had to do, she told herself, was look again. Just open her eyes and look at the girl squarely, and she would see how foolish she was being.

Liz opened her eyes and looked toward the opposite aisle. The dark blue Mercury wasn't there. As she jerked her head around in an almost frantic attempt to locate it, she spotted it pulling out of the driveway onto South Peoria. All she could see of the driver was the back of her fluffy, red-gold head.

Chapter Six

"My, God, look at you! You look fucking fantastic!" Vali threw her arms around Francine and hugged her enthusiastically. "You haven't changed a bit. Except to get prettier."

Francine laughed. "Valerie Porter, you always were the best liar in school. *You're* the one who hasn't changed. Good Lord, it seems like yesterday!"

"And just look at this one!" Vali reached out and took Margie's hand. "What would you give to be this thin?"

"I burn a lot of calories," Margie retorted with a bold wink. She was quaking inside, but so far she'd managed to dredge up the old bravado. "I'm still the hottest girl in town."

"Better not let your husband hear you say that!" Francine roared. "He'll lock you up for reunion weekend."

"I know. That's why I sent him off with the kids this evening."

The doorbell rang and Margie went to answer. There were whoops of delight as Barbara Jean's voice was heard sounding the old school cheer the Loreleis had revamped and made their own.

"Gimme an L! Gimme an O! Gimme an R! . . ."

Barbara Jean flew into the room and embraced the three women all at the same time. "I don't believe it! You guys have found the fountain of youth. Fran! Margie! Oh, shit—this is too much!"

"Hey, why don't I get us some wine?" Margie suggested. "This calls for a drink!"

Vali laughed. "Same old Margie. Always sneaking the booze."

"Except now I don't have to sneak it. I just have the liquor store deliver it by the truckload." That, too, was part of the Margie Middleton Act." Margie hadn't touched alcohol since her release from the hospital twenty-five years ago.

Anne and Liz arrived together, having run into each other in the Lancelot lobby. Anne was wearing a figure-hugging, black jump suit and full makeup. Liz was in the jeans she had put on early this morning. After her experience at the drive-in she had been inclined to change her plans and spend her whole stay at her parents' condo; but Francine had insisted it would be more fun if everyone stayed at the motel, and she hadn't wanted to disappoint anyone. Still, she found it impossible to match the others' exuberant moods.

"Oh, God, isn't this great?" Barbara Jean was shouting, hopping from one to the other. "Annie, I saw all your movies. And Liz—what the hell are you doing in *Russia?*"

"Hey, one question at a time!" Francine yelled. "We'll never get caught up that way."

"Maybe we should all take turns," Margie suggested. "Everybody stand up and give a little speech about herself."

"No! No speeches!" Vali declared. "Let's just take it easy, okay? After all, we've got a whole week."

"It's gonna take me a week to learn one dance step," Barbara Jean giggled. She took a healthy swallow of wine. "I'm a farmer's wife now."

"Oh, don't worry about the dance number," Francine told her. "We'll manage somehow."

"Hey, Francine, is it true you're Miss Gottrocks now?" Anne teased. "I hear you're married to Brookfield Oil."

"It's nothing, darling," Francine tossed back, holding up the seven-carat diamond that sparkled on the third finger of her left hand. "We always knew I was destined for bigger things."

"Does your husband have any brothers?" Anne asked after clapping her hand to her eyes as if the ring had blinded her. "Maybe you could introduce them to Liz and me."

"Yeah, how come you two have escaped wedded bliss?" Barbara Jean asked, whirling on them. "You're not homo, are you?" She broke into peals of laughter.

"I want to hear about Vali," Liz said, smiling good-naturedly. "I understand you have your own plane."

"Not just my own plane—my own airline," Vali confirmed with a note of pride. "It's pretty small potatoes at the moment, though. Just a little charter operation."

"Anyone for pizza?" Margie entered from the kitchen carrying a bubbling hot tray.

"Oh, jeez, pizza!" Barbara Jean whooped. "Re-member the time I dropped a whole one in Bobby

Langencamp's car? We were picking up pepperoni for weeks!"

"Bobby Langencamp—whatever happened to him?" Vali asked. "Liz, you used to date him, right?"

"That was thirty years ago," Liz said.

"You know, I think he's a policeman now," Francine broke in. "I caught a glimpse of him in a patrol car not long ago."

"I wonder how many of our old flames'll be at the reunion," Anne mused.

"Well, if all of Margie's come we'll have a full house," Barbara Jean chortled. Then she turned to Margie. "Sorry about that," she said, giving her a gentle squeeze.

"Hey, Liz, what are Russian men like?" Francine asked gaily. "I'll bet they're wild in bed."

"Please," Liz said with a small grimace. "I could get into real trouble for fraternizing with Russians."

"But that only makes it more exciting!" Margie exclaimed. "Imagine the intrigue!"

"You can have the intrigue," Liz told her seriously. "Believe me, no man would be worth what they'd put you through."

Francine studied the tall, dark-haired friend of her youth. "You know, Liz," she said thoughtfully, "you've changed more than anyone here. Not in looks—you look terrific. But you seem so . . . I don't know . . . subdued. Is that what living in Russia's done to you?"

"Partly," Liz admitted. Her eyes darkened. "But there's another reason. Something happened this afternoon." She swallowed hard, not really wanting to go on but impelled all the same.

"You ran into Bobby Langencamp!" Barbara Jean

hooted. "And you're going to marry him and take him back to Russia."

"No. Nothing like that." Liz's expression was so solemn the others felt it and all the joking stopped.

"What was it, then?" Vali asked, concerned. "It wasn't anything bad, was it?"

Liz took a deep breath. She hadn't intended to tell them; they'd laugh at her, think Russia had made her nuts among other things. But there was no containing it. "You're not going to believe this.... I thought I saw Kathi this afternoon."

"Kathi?" Several gasps could be heard. Margie's face became a frozen mask of fear.

"You don't mean Kathi Harcort?" Vali pressed. Her voice was thin and unusually high-pitched. "I mean, that can't be . . ."

"I know. But if it wasn't her, it was someone who looked exactly like her. She was even driving a '55 Mercury. Dark blue. The same color as Kathi's."

"You're crazy," Francine snapped testily. "Is this supposed to be some kind of a joke, or what?"

"I wish it was a joke," Liz said quietly. "And maybe I am crazy, but whoever it was, she looked at me like she knew me. Her hair was exactly the same as Kathi's, and she had those enormous green eyes . . ." She broke off and ran her hand across her forehead. It was wet with perspiration. "I'm sorry. I didn't mean to spoil the party."

"Liz, for God's sake," Anne said angrily, "we made a pact thirty years ago. We were never going to mention Kathi again."

"I know. But seeing . . . whoever. . . . It spooked me." Liz cleared her throat. "Look, forget it. It must've been my imagination."

"If you ask me, you've been in Russia too long," Barbara Jean announced. "You'll probably see Stalin next. Hey, Margie, how about some more vino? Margie?"

She took a step toward their hostess as the others turned in Margie's direction. The "most popular girl in school" was staring straight ahead, mindless of her guests, her eyes wide with unspeakable terror.

"You see what you've done?" Barbara Jean muttered, annoyed. She placed a gentle hand on Margie's shoulder. "Margie? Margie? Snap out of it."

She gave her a slight shake, and Margie turned her eyes in her direction. "Barbara Jean . . ." she gasped. "Liz said Kathi—"

"Liz is crazy. She's trying to scare us. Hey, what's the big deal? Kathi's been dead for thirty years."

"Yes. Yes, of course." Margie fought for control and managed to succeed well enough to make an excuse to leave the room. "I have to get some more food from the kitchen," she said. "I'll just run out and get it."

Alone in the kitchen she hugged herself as she bent over double. "Oh, dear God," she moaned. "I'm not strong enough for this. Please, please don't let it all come back."

The new girl from Wichita had been more or less forced on them by Miss Winters, Dean of Girls at John Ross. Margie was the one who had figured out how to make the situation bearable—and entertaining. Kathi Harcort was as different from the rest of them as potatoes were from grits. They were high-spirited and irreverent; she was subdued and disgustingly moral. They laughed at her for that—behind her back, of course—but because of a stupid mistake they'd made, they were stuck with her.

Margie had decided the best way to deal with Kathi was to invite her to become a Lorelei. The others had practically vomited. They had had enough of Kathi as it was.

"But we'll have some fun with her," Margie told them, her eyes shining mischievously at what she had in mind. "I've got a new idea for a POL."

POL was short for Proof Of Loyalty, something each of the girls had had to endure in order to be a Lorelei in good standing. It was their own special form of hazing, and the POL tests were different for each girl.

Vali, the undisputed beauty and the one with the largest, most expensive wardrobe, had been ordered to get a dress from the Good Will and wear it to school every day for two consecutive weeks. Liz, the "brain" of the bunch, had to fail a test. Francine, the vain one, had to go without makeup for a month.

"What is it?" Anne asked, only vaguely interested. Margie knew her own POL still rankled. She, the dedicated actress, had had to screw up a performance.

"An initiation!" Margie announced excitedly. "A whole ceremony, like they have at college sororities."

"You mean make her eat cold spaghetti and tell her it's worms?" Barbara Jean asked. Her POL had been to lead cheers minus her bra at three football games.

"Right!" Margie replied. "Lots of stuff like that. I've got some ideas that are really gross." She smiled happily.

"Suppose she won't go along with it?" This from Vali.

99

"Then she won't get to be a Lorelei." Margie took a more direct approach. "Don't you see? This could be a way to get her off our backs."

Francine began to nod. "I think she's right," she said thoughtfully. "If she won't go along with it, at least we'll be able to say we gave her the chance. And if she does go along—" She shrugged. "We'll be disbanding at the end of the school year anyway. We can stand her for that long."

The others weighed the situation and finally agreed.

Margie set about creating the initiation. She spent days poring through books checked out of the Baxter Public Library, trying to glean things that would be most repulsive to the irritating interloper.

But when IT happened, that awful thing they'd sworn never to talk about, Margie—irrationally, perhaps—couldn't help blaming herself. IT was on her conscience all the time. IT happened on Halloween of their senior year, and somehow she got through to graduation and even endured a year at the University of Tulsa. The following summer she was driving through town in her very first car when she suddenly started to cry, and couldn't stop crying. It got so bad she couldn't see the road, and when the police found the car smashed into a tree, they found her still crying.

Word was put out that she had to go to the hospital because of the accident, but in truth the hospital she went to was not for broken bones or whiplashes or concussions. It was for people who had lost touch with reality, and Margie was there for a year and a half. When she got out, she went back to Baxter where she met Jerry Middleton whose family had recently arrived and had opened a dry cleaning establishment. Jerry was good looking and kind and gentle. Best of all, he didn't know anything about Margie's past. When, after six months of proper dating (during which time he did no more than fondle her breasts), he asked her to marry him, she accepted. In order to be fair, she told him about the hospital, but she never mentioned the abortion or the thing that still haunted her twenty-four hours a day.

Back in the living room, Barbara Jean continued to rail at Liz. "You scared the shit out of her! What's with you, anyway?"

Liz bit her lip. "I'm sorry. I shouldn't have said anything."

"No kidding! Listen, Liz, if this is the way you plan to get your kicks while you're here—"

"Hey, cool it," Vali broke in softly. "Liz was just making a joke, that's all." She smiled at Liz understandingly. "I guess she didn't realize some of us are still sensitive about what happened."

"Yeah, let's not make a big deal out of it," Francine agreed. She turned to Liz. "Obviously, the pact still holds," she said a little apologetically. "No Kathi quips, okay?"

Liz sucked in her breath and nodded. "Right. No Kathi quips." She smiled wryly. "I guess I just lost my head."

The room was wrapped in an uncomfortable silence. "Hey, we're together ten minutes and it's just like old times," Anne said, trying to lighten things up. "We're already yelling at each other."

Francine laughed. "Only this time it's not over

guys." She picked up her wine glass. "Speaking of which, guess what I heard about Tiger Jackson!"

"Tiger?" Barbara Jean screeched with laughter. "I haven't thought of him since graduation!"

Liz barely heard the news about Tiger. She was too busy berating herself. *Terrific, Everly,* she thought angrily. *You knew better than to tell them, and you told them anyway! Now they not only think you're nuts, they think you're a troublemaker.* She was lost in her own thoughts when she felt a soft hand press gently on her arm.

"Hey, you're not upset because Barbara Jean flew off the handle, are you?" She looked up. Vali was regarding her with sympathetic concern.

Liz sighed. "I really put my foot in it, didn't I?" Vali's hand slid down her arm and grasped Liz's. A shudder went through Liz. She curled her fingers around Vali's.

"It's really okay," Vali said softly. "Don't worry about it."

Liz looked at her and smiled. "Thanks, Vali. You always were the most sensitive one of this bunch."

Vali squeezed her hand and pulled away. "Look, Margie's made a salad. Let's go get some." She smiled and led the way. Liz felt a sudden urge to cry.

Barbara Jean excused herself early, pleading exhaustion from all the excitement. "We farmers are used to going to bed with the chickens," she quipped. "I'll see you all tomorrow." She hugged each in turn, giving a slightly cooler farewell to Liz. She glanced at her watch as she pulled her car out of Margie's driveway. Eleven-ten. Frank was waiting for her at the Lancelot bar.

He was still there at 11:33. She arrived flushed and out of breath. She hated to seem eager, but she was terrified he'd given up and left.

"Hi." She caught her breath and slipped into the chair beside him.

"How was the big meeting?"

"Fun." She smiled at him nervously.

"Everyone looked just the same, right?"

She laughed. "That's what we all told each other."

He took her hand under the table. His touch was warm and reassuring. "Tell me about it."

She shrugged. "There's nothing to tell. We talked about old times. Very boring unless you happened to have been there."

"How about some wine?"

"I thought you'd never ask." She mentally calculated the number of drinks she'd had so far tonight. One here earlier with Frank, three—or was it four?—at Margie's. Oh, what the hell. She was feeling good; she was feeling *great!*

"So." Frank was smiling at her affectionately. "You were all there. All you Loreleis."

She was impressed. She'd told him a little about the club earlier. "You even remembered our silly name."

"I think it's a great name. Just the kind of name high school golden girls would choose for themselves." He paused. "You said there were six of you. Not many members for a sorority."

"Well, we were kind of cliquish." Cliquish? she thought to herself. Bloody little snobs is what we were. But what was high school without its resident snobs?

"You never thought of taking in anyone else?"

Barbara Jean looked at him. "Actually, we did once. But she . . ." She cleared her throat. "It didn't work out."

"She wasn't a golden girl, huh?"

The waitress, a redhead this time, brought the wine, and Barbara Jean took a healthy swallow. "Something like that." She was thinking of what Liz had said tonight, about seeing Kathi at Riley's. Damn that Liz Everly, how could she bring up such a thing? She took another swallow of the wine. She felt nervous all of a sudden, nervous and apprehensive. Frank must have sensed it because he put an arm around her shoulders.

"All right?" he asked.

She tensed. "I just hope one of the others doesn't walk in. We're all staying here, you know. All except Margie."

"Would you feel better if we continued this in my room?" She shot him a skeptical look. "We can talk better there. And I have a bottle of scotch."

She hesitated. How could she go to his room? That was *asking* for trouble. But he was right; it would be more comfortable. It was one thing to be seen with a man who wasn't your husband at five o'clock in the afternoon—and quite another to be seen with him at eleven-thirty at night. And scotch . . . oh, how she would love a drink of real liquor! "I . . . I can only stay a little while. Just one drink."

He inclined his head. "Whatever you say." He signaled the waitress for the check.

Chapter Seven

Even on Sunday it was unusual for Margie to sleep so late. She peered fuzzily at the clock on the table next to her side of the bed and reached out an arm for Jerry. His side of the bed was empty.

"Jerry? Honey?" She called out in confusion.

He appeared in the adjoining bathroom doorway, a toothbrush dangling from his foamy mouth. "Yeah, hon. I'm here." He disappeared to rinse out his mouth. "You all right?"

Margie sat up and rubbed her eyes. "Sure. Why wouldn't I be?"

"I don't know. I thought maybe you were sick or something. "You're usually up before this."

"I guess last night kinda wore me out." She yawned. "I slept like a rock." The truth was she'd taken a sleeping pill. Last night of all nights she'd needed a drugged sleep. Otherwise, she'd surely have had THE DREAM. "You have breakfast?"

"Just coffee and juice, I thought I'd wait for you."

"What about the kids?"

"You kidding? They're still dead to the world." He watched her as she got out of bed and put on her robe.

"So how'd it go? Was it fun seeing the old gang?"

She picked up her brush and ran it through her hair. "Ummm."

"Well, how'd they look? What'd they have to say?"

She shrugged. "Barbara Jean's overweight. Anne wears too much makeup. Francine is gorgeous."

"Mrs. Brookfield *should* be gorgeous. All it takes is money, right?"

She smiled wanly. "I guess."

"Honey? It really was all right, wasn't it? Nothing came up, did it?"

She tensed. "No one knows about the looney bin, if that's what you mean."

"Hey, come on." He put an arm around her. "I guess I shouldn't've mentioned it. How about coming out to the kitchen with me?"

"Let me get dressed first, okay?"

"Okay. I'll be in the family room. I took the newspaper in there earlier so I wouldn't disturb you."

She nodded and he ambled off. When he was gone, she put a fist to her mouth to stifle the scream building in her head. It had been horrible seeing them again. From the moment Francine—the first to arrive—had come through the front door it had been a nightmare. All the talk about boys and drinking and petting in parked cars! The way they'd dredged up all the things it had taken her years to forget. And then, when Liz said she'd seen Kathi. . . . It was horrible, too horrible to think about. With the help of a valium, she'd managed to get through the evening—but how could she get through the rest of the week? It could only get worse. And sleeping pills or no, she knew she'd have THE DREAM.

THE DREAM still came occasionally, even though the doctors at Lakeview had said it would eventually disappear entirely. It took place in Our Lady of Guadelupe Church where the Black Sabbath was being held. The girls, all seven of them, were there. Six wore long black robes and carried black candles. But it was Margie, not Kathi, who was stretched out on the altar, naked, her body covered with crazy symbols drawn in crimson lipstick. She heard the chanting . . . chanting . . . so loud she thought her head would burst. She saw the girls' faces as they bent over her: evil, distorted, terrifying. Then IT happened. Exactly what IT was, Margie could never remember. She always woke up just then, perspiring, shaking, afraid to make a noise for fear of waking Jerry. It was always so real and so frightening, not like a dream at all, but more like a premonition.

She shuddered and reached for the vial of valium. She would keep going as long as she could, but she couldn't guarantee how long that would be.

She swallowed the pill, put on shorts and a T-shirt, and went to find Jerry.

Anne sat propped up against the pillows and sipped the coffee she'd ordered from Room Service. She flipped over the last page of the *Chronicle*'s television supplement and smiled. So Vali's ex, Donald Ellsworth, was anchor man of the local Eyewitness News. She closed her eyes and tried to remember what he looked like. He was in the Class of

Fifty-six, but she vaguely remembered seeing him with Vali at parties and football games. Not terribly tall, but broad-shouldered and rugged-looking. He was handsome enough—would a Lorelei date, let alone marry, a man who wasn't handsome? She wondered how he'd ended up back in Baxter. She'd once heard something about him and Vali living in Los Angeles. She gave a rueful grimace. Probably couldn't make it anywhere but here. Oh, well. At least he ought to be good for a little local exposure.

She picked up the phone and asked the switchboard to connect her with television station KBTV. She waited until she heard the answering operator.

"KBTV. May I help you?"

"I'm trying to reach Donald Ellsworth. Can you connect me, please?"

"I'm sorry. Mr. Ellsworth isn't here on Sunday."

Predictable. Damn these little towns! You'd think the world stopped on weekends.

"Would you care to leave a message?"

She sighed. No use trying to get his home number; people here considered respect of privacy next to cleanliness and Godliness. "No, thanks. I'll try him again tomorrow."

She put down the phone. God! Would she be able to endure seven more days of this place? She looked at her watch. Nine-thirty. What the hell was she doing up so early? Then she remembered. Central Daylight Time. She toyed with the idea of going back to sleep, but she was already wide awake. Should she call Francine or Barbara Jean? No, she'd be seeing enough of them in the coming week. Maybe she should go downstairs and have breakfast.

She switched on the radio. A loud angry voice filled the room. "And the devil came to me, and he sat on my shoulder, and he said, 'Son, I've got a proposition for you'!" Anne turned the tuning knob. Church music. Of course. What did she expect on a Sunday morning in Baxter?

Sunday morning! That was it! She'd get dressed and go to church. Forget that she hadn't been to church in thirty years, think what a nice touch it would add to Donald Ellsworth's interview with her.

"What have you done since you've been in Baxter, Miss Eastman?"

"Well, the first thing I did was go to church. I have such happy memories of the First Baptist Church."

Humming to herself, she dressed in a neat summer suit and placed the hat she'd almost left in New York on her head. She surveyed herself in the full length mirror. Perfect. Very pious. All she needed was a pair of white gloves. She called downstairs and ordered a taxi. She'd wanted to hire a limo and driver for the duration of her stay, but it seemed there were no limousines in Baxter. Except, of course, the one belonging to Baron Brookfield.

The First Baptist Church looked just the same. It was pitifully small compared to churches in New York, but its carefully polished, etched glass windows glistened proudly in the morning sunshine. The service was just beginning as Anne walked down the center aisle and slipped into a rear pew. She saw a few heads turn in her direction, obviously aware of a stranger in their midst. Anne looked toward the pulpit. Her eyes widened; she couldn't believe what she was seeing. Old Reverend Teasdale was announcing the first song! *Why,* Anne thought, *he must be a hundred and ten.* But he looked exactly the way he had when she'd come to church as a bored teenager.

It's just my imagination. Of course he's changed, she told herself as she found the page in her hymnal for "Master, The Tempest Is Raging." He looked the same because he'd seemed old *then.* She sang the song in her lusty alto, proud of the way her voice rose above the congregation. It felt good to be singing the old Baptist hymn. Maybe she'd start going to church in New York once in a while.

The hymn ended, and she replaced the book on the little rack attached to the back of the pew in front of her. She settled back on the hard bench and waited for the sermon to begin. There were announcements first: The Juniors For Christ were having a picnic next Saturday; Mrs. Alan Beasley had had a baby girl; donations were being accepted for the Trowbridge family whose house had burned down last week. Anne listened idly, her eyes on the pulpit. Then suddenly Reverend Teasdale drifted off, and Anne was aware of the sound of moans and cries. The air became thick; she felt as if she was suffocating. She blinked her eyes. Reverend Teasdale was no longer at the pulpit. A young girl was stretched out in front of the baptistry, her body stiff and cold. She was surrounded by black candles, her skin flamed with crimson markings. Huddled near her, in a shadowy haze, were six black-robed figures. The moans and cries grew louder. Anne put her hands to her ears and gasped for breath. She was choking; she felt as if the walls were closing in on her. She looked frantically

110

toward the windows. The glass no longer sparkled; there was only darkness beyond, as if some great cloud had come and covered the sun.

Desperately she forced herself to rise from her seat and stumble out into the aisle. Her legs were rubber, and she could hardly stand on them. Somehow, she made her way outside and fell onto the scorched grass. The next thing she remembered was being surrounded by a sea of concerned-looking faces. A glass of water was thrust at her, and she drank eagerly. The moans were gone; a gentle breeze ruffled her hair. The sun shone on her body. She could breathe!

"Honey, are you all right?" Worried voices. Anxious whisperings.

"Yes . . . thank you. I guess I'm just not used to this heat."

Heads nodded. "It's bad here in the summertime. You could fry an egg on this here sidewalk."

Another voice. "You're the actress, aren't you? Anne Eastman?"

She smiled. "Yes, that's right." She hoped the incident would at least make the paper. *Actress overcome by heat while attending church service.* Not the best kind of publicity, but something anyway. She struggled shakily to her feet, thanking all the nice concerned people. Then she thought her heart would stop. Standing on the edge of the small circle of church goers, regarding her with curious green eyes, was Kathi Harcort.

Frank waited for Room Service while Barbara Jean

111

took a shower. He smiled as the sound of water beating the bathtub drifted out to him. Things had gone well, so far, very well indeed. He'd arrived in Baxter without a definite plan; all he knew for sure was that he had to somehow find the Loreleis and keep track of their comings and goings. He'd never thought of himself as a spy, but he figured that was what his program for the rest of the week amounted to.

What incredible luck meeting Barbara Jean in the bar that first night. He hadn't thought of actually getting involved with any of them, but that meeting turned out to be the perfect solution. She was unhappy and worried about the reunion; he could tell that right away. Not surprising, either, since she was clearly overweight, and although her haircut was fairly stylish and her cotton sundress practically timeless, she didn't have the look of a woman who'd taken care of herself for the last thirty years. Married to a farmer, she'd told him. Mother of six. A dull, humdrum life. Perhaps that was why it had been so easy to gain her confidence and develop their relationship so quickly.

Mother of six or no, the woman was sex-starved—that was for damn sure! He hadn't even intended to take her to bed last night; all he'd wanted was to make a tiny place for himself in her life this coming week. But one thing had led to another, and when he'd suggested drinks in his room, well, that did it.

Quite a little boozer, too, was Barbara Jean. She'd been pleasantly smashed by the time they'd hit the hay; could be an advantage in that, too, maybe. He didn't want to ask too many questions right off the

112

bat, though; she might get suspicious even after a few drinks. Then he'd *never* find out what he wanted to know.

He answered the waiter's knock and told him to put the cart next to the bed. It would be nice to have breakfast in bed with a woman. Frank had almost forgotten when he'd done it last. The waiter left and Barbara Jean came out of the bathroom wearing his white terrycloth robe. With her face all scrubbed and shiny and her hair curling slightly from the steam in the shower, she looked fresh and innocent as a kid.

"Ummm, that looks good." She went to the cart and took a strawberry from the bowl. With her free hand, she lifted the stainless steel cover from one of the plates. "Eggs Benedict! Yum!"

He smiled at her. "Nothing but the best for the queen of John Ross High."

"Vali was the queen. I was a cheerleader."

"That's even better, right? You got to wear those short pleated skirts."

"And nearly froze to death half the time." She propped some pillows against the headboard and crawled into bed, taking her plate with her. Frank followed her example.

"What about the other Loreleis? How did they distinguish themselves?"

She stirred sweetener into her coffee. "Well, Anne was the star of all the school plays. Naturally. Liz was president of the senior class. Margie was voted most popular. And Francine was voted most likely to succeed. Boy, were we right about her!"

Frank chewed his food slowly, thoughtfully. "What about the other girl you mentioned?"

113

"There was no other girl. No other Lorelei."

"But you mentioned somebody else that first night we met. Somebody you were thinking of taking in."

"Oh, right." Barbara Jean gave a dry smile. "She distinguished herself by—" She broke off and shrugged. "Nothing."

"What were you going to say?"

"It was cruel. Sick."

"So be sick. What was it?" He offered an encouraging smile.

"I was going to say she distinguished herself by dying." She grimaced. "There. Wasn't that gross?"

"How'd she die?"

"I don't know. She just did."

"Was she sick?"

"No, I don't think so. Although we heard she had a bad heart."

"She had a heart attack, then?"

Barbara Jean concentrated on her food. She did not look up. "Something like that, I guess."

"I didn't think young girls had heart attacks."

She became defensive. "Look, I told you, I don't know what happened to her. She was found dead outside Our Lady of Guadelupe Church." She reached across him to put her plate on the cart and swung her legs over the side of the bed.

"What's wrong? Where are you going?"

"I just realized what time it is. I've got to get ready to go to rehearsal."

"On Sunday?"

"We have to start today. We don't exactly have a lot of time."

"You're not upset about something, are you?" He

114

looked worried.

She was very busy now, getting into her clothes. "No. Why should I be?"

"I thought talking about your friend who died might have upset you."

"It was a long time ago. I hadn't even thought about her till you asked if we'd considered taking in anyone else. Look, Frank, I hope you won't think I'm being rude, but I'd better go to my own room and finish putting myself together."

He got out of bed and kissed her on the forehead. "Whatever you say. I know I can't monopolize all your time. See you later?"

She looked up at him and smiled. "How about the bar? Say, five o'clock?"

"Five o'clock."

"What'll you do while I'm gone?"

"Miss you."

Her eyes took on a soft look. "You're sweet." She moved to him and put her arms around him. "You could become a habit, you know?"

He pressed her to him. "Only for the week. We made a pact, remember?"

"Yeah, darn it." She pulled away, grinning wryly. "After that, Cinderella turns into a plough horse. See you at five."

The door closed softly behind her.

Liz checked her watch. Twelve-thirty. Plenty of time. She was driving east, toward the Ramada. She'd considered going downtown, but from what she'd heard, the Baxter didn't have much action anymore, mostly old people who didn't know where else to go. She parked the car in the Ramada lot and walked through the lobby. A few men with paper name tags stuck to their lapels stood talking together. Good, she thought. There's a convention going on.

She found the bar and stood just inside the door as her eyes adjusted to the dim light. It wasn't exactly humming, but she could see that one of the tables was occupied by three men and a woman. A lone man sat at the bar. He was wearing a suit but had discarded his jacket and tie. She slipped onto the stool next to him and asked the bartender for a vodka and soda. It seemed strange to be able to get a drink after all the years of Oklahoma's being a dry state. When it arrived, she played with the stirrer and looked at the man out of the corner of her eye.

He didn't appear to be interested in her. He was quietly drinking a highball, sipping it slowly but purposefully. Killing time, Liz decided. Didn't have any place to go.

She swiveled toward him on the barstool. "Here for the convention?" she asked.

He turned and looked at her. He wasn't bad looking: late forties, she guessed, not fat, but on the heavy side, a pleasant face, brown eyes, gold band on the third finger of his left hand.

He nodded. "Pharmaceutical. How about yourself?"

She shook her head. "I'm just visiting. My folks live here."

He shrugged. "Not a bad place. Little more action than Hugo."

"Hugo? You're from Hugo?"

"You know it? Little jerkwater town. Two pharmacies. I got one. My brother's got the other one."

Liz smiled. "Sounds like you've got a cartel."

He frowned at her. "You a teacher?"

"No. An interpreter. I live in Moscow."

"Come on. You're pullin' my leg."

"It's true. I'll show you my visa if you like."

He finished his drink. "Well, I'll be damned. Moscow." He signaled to the bartender for a repeat. "That's why you drink vodka, right?" He laughed.

"Right. You kind of develop a taste for it there. Keeps you warm." She sipped her drink. She didn't really want it. "So." She gave him her full attention. "How long are you here for?"

"The convention ends tomorrow."

"Then it's back to Hugo."

He gave her an ironic grin. "Back to Hugo." He raised his fresh drink and clinked his glass against hers.

"Finished with your meetings for the rest of the day?"

"Free as a bird till nine in the morning."

He was making it difficult. Not making any suggestions.

"Well, I'd buy you lunch," she began lightly, taking the bull by the horns, "but I'm only free for the next hour."

He was unimpressed. "That's how it goes."

"Of course, a lot can be done in an hour."

He squinted at her. "Yeah? Like what?"

Thank God, she thought. He's finally beginning to get the idea.

She gave him an all-knowing smile. "Whatever

you like." She looked around furtively to make sure no one was listening. The table of four was involved in its own conversation. The bartender was washing glasses.

He leaned over, his mouth close to her ear. "You a hooker?" he asked in a low voice.

"Let's just say I'm someone who likes to show a man like yourself a good time."

He studied her. "What was all that crap about Moscow?"

He looked worried. Maybe he thought she was some kind of secret agent. She decided to put him more at ease. "A joke," she said airily. "You don't think I'd really live in Russia, do you?"

He relaxed visibly. "Nah. I figured you were shittin' me." He studied her again. "How much?"

She twirled her drink stirrer. "A hundred's the going rate."

"You got to be kidding." He turned back to his highball.

"But you look like a nice man, and I'm partial to pharmacists from Hugo."

"Bullshit." He kept his eyes averted.

"For you I could make it seventy-five."

A long silence. She watched him steadily. "Make it fifty," he said finally.

He didn't see the smile that played across her face. "Well, since you're from Hugo . . ."

She was teasing him. He looked very nervous.

"Listen, I don't fool with hookers. I want a woman, I go get one. I don't have to pay."

She smiled charmingly. "Suit yourself." She opened her purse and took out her wallet. Her drink tab was lying on the bar next to her glass.

"Hey, wait a minute. I'll take care of that."

"I don't want you to feel obligated."

"Hell, it'll be fun. Different. What's fifty bucks?"

"Might be the best fifty you ever spent."

He fished his room key from his pocket and handed it to her. "Why don't you go on up? I'll pay for the drinks and be right behind you."

"Aren't you afraid I'll take something?"

"Honey, if you can find anything work takin', help yourself."

She closed her hand around the key and stood up. "I'll go on, then. I'll be waiting for you."

He was fumbling in his wallet as she made her way out of the bar.

Chapter Eight

Barbara Jean was the first to arrive at Miss Virginia's School of Dance. Although the first "Singin' In The Rain" rehearsal wasn't scheduled until three o'clock, the front door was open when she got there at two-forty, and she walked inside calling for whoever had preceded her.

"Yoo hoo, anybody here? Get on your tap shoes, all you Miss Twinkle Toes, the Lorelei chorus line is about to live again!"

Her words echoed hollowly through the empty anteroom and filtered into the deserted studio in back. As she looked around, a little shiver ran down her back. Miss Virginia's! How much time had she spent here in her life? From the age of five she'd been shepherded here weekly by her mother in the hope that lessons in ballet, tap and acrobatic dancing would usurp some of her boundless energy and help her acquire the poise she would need when she became a young lady. It had all become something of a bore by the time she reached her teens; but she supposed she had Miss Virginia to thank for the fact that she'd won the state cheerleading competition, and later, in high school, when the Loreleis decided to put together a chorus line for the annual talent show, she was made dance captain.

You'd never know it now, she thought ruefully as she wandered into the studio and caught her reflection in the long, mirrored wall. She dreaded having to put on the leotard and tights the women were going to wear under their plastic raincoat costumes. Maybe she could talk them into getting slickers instead of those stupid see-through things.

Although, she mused, a flush of warmth suddenly enveloping her, Frank Bragg hadn't seemed to mind her generous body. Generous body. There was definitely a double entendre there. Her body had been generous, all right. God, she hadn't screwed like that since the early days with Woody. She walked closer to the mirror and inspected her bloodshot eyes, wondering if anyone would notice. Jesus, she hadn't expected the night to end up the way it did. One drink in Frank's room, that's all she'd had in mind. But one drink had led to two, and she'd been so comfortable curled up on his king-sized bed with her shoes off, she seemed to lose track of time and drinks and everything.

Frank was so easy to talk to; she hadn't talked to a man like that in years. And he looked . . . well, she hated to say it because it sounded corny, but he looked a little like Larry. He had the same soft brown hair with sun-bleached highlights, and his eyes had that same gentle look she'd so loved in Larry's. When he'd leaned over the bed and kissed her, well, let's face it, she'd thought of Larry, maybe even pretended he *was* Larry. What was wrong with that? Women were allowed fantasies, weren't they? His arms felt so good around her, she felt as if she could get lost in them. She knew she was committed when he laid down on the bed beside her. There'd been a brief flash of guilt; she'd never cheated on Woody before. "Nice girls" didn't do that, no matter what their life was like at home. But she'd firmly pushed the guilt out of her mind. This was *her* week, wasn't it? She was in Baxter for the sole purpose of having a good time. And what Woody didn't know wouldn't hurt him.

Funny, she'd thought she'd seen Frank standing across the street when she'd pulled her car up in front of the studio a few minutes ago. He'd only been there for a split second, standing in the doorway of Kramer's Drug and Pharmaceutical store, looking in this direction. But when she'd turned to get a better look, he'd ducked inside, and she'd decided her eyes were deceiving her—it wouldn't have been him anyway. Their relationship was strictly a fling; he had no reason to keep tabs on her. Anyhow, she'd be seeing him later; she'd promised to have dinner with him after rehearsal. She supposed her mind had conjured him up because she *wanted* him to be there, wanted to have a man care enough about her to follow her and wait in the shadows, as though he were wildly jealous and suspected she was meeting someone else.

"Hey! How is it out there in Dreamland?"

She looked up and saw Francine standing in the doorway leading to the studio. Barbara Jean hadn't seen her come in.

"Oh, hi. I guess I was kind of reliving the past. Being here at Miss Virginia's and all."

"Spooky, isn't it? Everything looks just the same. That even looks like the same old dilapidated piano."

"I think it is," Barbara Jean agreed.

Francine took a step toward her. "Wait till you see Miss Virginia's daughter. She's the one who runs the studio now."

"I didn't know Miss Virginia had a daughter." In high school, the Loreleis had speculated on whether the unattractive Miss Virginia had ever actually "done it" with a man. The consensus was she hadn't; obviously they had the lady all wrong.

Francine laughed. "Apparently she was away at boarding school all the time we were coming here. Anyway, she's the spitting image of Miss Virginia herself. You'll die when you see her."

"Oh, good. All we need is another spook." Vali came in smiling, her golden hair shining silkily, her perfect teeth showing white against her tanned face. "This town's already starting to give me the creeps."

Francine frowned. "You're not letting Liz's crazy story get to you?"

"Well, it *was* creepy." Vali looked from Francine to Barbara Jean. "And Liz was never one to make sick jokes."

"Then she's either changed, or her mind was playing tricks on her at Riley's," Francine said positively. She turned at the sound of voices in the anteroom. "Speak of the devil," she whispered conspiratorially.

Liz and Anne arrived at the same time. Liz looked well-rested and alert, but Anne looked wan, despite her liberal use of makeup. Barbara Jean wondered if she, too, had had a busy night.

"Well, are you all here?"

They turned in unison toward the doorway where a tall, thin woman was now standing. Her gray-streaked, brown hair was pulled severely back from her face and fastened in a secure knot at the nape of her scrawny neck. Her face was almost skeletal, so prominent were the cheekbones and the indentation of the sunken, light blue eyes. She was wearing black polyester slacks and a blue cotton blouse tied at the waist. Francine smiled at the expressions of shock on her friends' faces.

"What'd I tell you?" she asked delightedly. "Isn't she Miss Virginia all over again?"

The women all stared. "You're her daughter, right?" Vali asked a little uncertainly. The resemblance was not merely great, it was uncanny.

"Let's just say I'm carrying on the Miss Virginia tradition," the woman replied. She looked at each of them in turn. "Where's Margie?" she asked finally.

"She should be here," Vali answered. "We told her three o'clock."

"Oh, you know Margie," Francine said. "She wouldn't be on time to her own funeral."

Barbara Jean wondered if she was the only one who felt a sudden grabbing in her stomach. How did this stranger know it was *Margie* who was missing?

By the time Margie arrived, Miss Virginia—as she insisted on being called—had handed out five pairs of plastic see-through rain boots with taps attached to the soles. She told them she would hand out the raincoats later.

"I don't believe it; these are my old boots!" Vali

124

exclaimed as they slipped securely over her size six-and-a-half-narrow foot.

"Did your mother keep all this stuff?" Liz asked as she, too, found a perfect fit.

The teacher shrugged. "You never know when something will come in handy."

Margie's face, when she saw Miss Virginia, was a study in fright. She had come in panting, apologizing profusely for being late, explaining that she'd misplaced her car keys and spent half an hour looking for them. Then her eyes lit on the teacher and she turned white. She gave such a strangled gasp that Barbara Jean hurried over to her to explain who this "Miss Virginia" really was.

"It's her daughter; she looks just like her," Barbara Jean whispered, patting Margie's arm reassuringly. "It's amazing. It scared us all half to death."

When Margie regained her composure, she was handed the last pair of boots, and the women were instructed to line up according to the order in which they'd made their appearance in the original dance.

"Let's see, Barbara Jean was first," Francine remembered aloud. "And then Liz . . ."

"No, Anne was in front of me," Liz corrected. "I was between her and Vali."

"Just stand where I place you," the teacher suggested crisply. "Barbara Jean first, then Francine, Vali, Margie, Liz and Anne."

"But Anne was in *front* of me," Liz protested stubbornly.

"No. That was the 'Mississippi Mud' number. The year before," Miss Virginia corrected.

"Oh." Liz and Anne exchanged stares.

"Now, you enter stage right. Flap-ball-change. Flap-ball-change . . ."

They straggled out of the studio two hours later, breathless and laughing about this brave attempt to recreate a scene from their youth.

"Talk about two left feet!" Francine exclaimed. "Have I gotten klutzier with the years, or what?"

"You were always a klutz," Barbara Jean chided her. "Wait till the society editor hears about this!"

"How about Miss Virginia the Second?" Vali asked. "Is she too weird for words?"

"I think she's a little crazy," Francine declared, becoming more serious. "The day I came to ask her to help us recreate our dance, she took me down to the cellar below the studio. The place is filled with old costumes, and there are trunks full of photographs of the original Miss Virginia's students."

"That's how she was able to recognize us, then," Anne said thoughtfully.

Francine nodded. "She also has all the notes her mother wrote about each number. She must have looked them over before we got here. That's how she knew who followed who."

"Whew! That's a relief!" Barbara Jean said with a laugh. "I was beginning to think she was a witch."

"Hey, how about a burger and fries?" Vali suggested, changing the subject. "Or, better yet, onion rings."

"Onion rings at Riley's!" Francine specified. The two of them turned to the others.

"Pass." Liz shook her head firmly.

"I want to get back to the Lancelot," Barbara Jean said. "I've got a couple of things I want to do." Maybe soon she'd tell them about Frank. But not yet. Not yet.

Anne also begged off.

"Margie?" Vali asked, disappointed in the others' excuses. "Is your husband expecting you at home?"

Margie hesitated. Despite the shock of seeing Miss Virginia's daughter, the rehearsal had lightened her spirits. And she had promised herself she would try to fit in this week, try to push back those dreadful fears and be a Lorelei one more time. "Hell, no!" she said adamantly. "I'm with you two!"

They decided to go in Francine's car and leave Margie's and Vali's where they were. They would pick them up later. After they had all exchanged goodbyes, Anne took Liz aside.

"Are you in a hurry to get back?"

"Not really. I just don't want to go to Riley's, that's all."

"Then, how about coming with me for a cup of coffee?"

"Where?"

Anne shrugged. "Anywhere. The coffee shop at the Baxter Hotel."

"Okay." They got into Liz's father's car since Anne was traveling by taxi. They headed in the direction of Main Street.

The Baxter Hotel was one of the oldest buildings in town. It had been an eyesore in the fifties, but now it was so ridiculous it looked almost "camp."

"I *love* this place," Liz said as she slid into her side of a dingy booth.

"You're kidding. Why?"

"Because it doesn't remind me of anything. I never came in here when I was in school."

"It does feel funny confronting the past, doesn't it?" Anne paused to ask the waitress to bring two coffees. "I guess we'll get used to it before the week's over." They were silent for a moment. The waitress placed ceramic mugs in front of them and filled them with coffee. "Liz," Anne began when she'd moved away, "about what you said last night at Margie's. About seeing Kathi . . ."

Liz's head shot up defiantly. "Look, I've already apologized for that! If you asked me to have coffee with you so you could give me a lecture about what to say and what not to say—"

"No." Anne broke in quickly. "That's not what this is about." She swallowed hard; her fingers fiddled with the scallops on the paper place mat. "I . . . I saw her, too."

Liz frowned. She wondered whether Anne was putting her on. "When?" She looked at her dubiously.

"This morning. I went to church."

"Not—"

"No. First Baptist. It wouldn't have occurred to me to go to Our Lady of Guadelupe."

"Kathi was at First Baptist?"

"Yes. No. She was outside. At least that's where I saw her. Liz, I fainted this morning." In a voice barely audible, she told her about the vision she'd had while Reverend Teasdale was speaking, how she'd run outside and passed out on the grass. "When I came to, there were some people around me. They gave me some water."

"Kathi was one of the people?"

"She was standing off to the side, watching."

"She didn't say anything?"

Anne shook her head. "She just stared at me. Liz, she looked just the same! She was wearing that old white dress with the lace collar, the one she had on the night we fixed her up with Butch Ferguson."

Silence. Then: "Anne, it couldn't have been Kathi."

"I know that! Don't you think I know? But she had Kathi's face, her eyes, her hair—and that dress!" She slumped dejectedly in her seat. "Why am I trying to convince you? You saw her, too."

"I *thought* I saw her. It could've been my imagination."

"We both had the same vision?"

Liz sighed. "I don't know, Annie. Maybe what I said last night brought Kathi so vividly to your mind, your subconscious conjured her up."

"Do you really think so?"

Liz's eyes bored into her face. "No."

"Then . . . what?"

"Someone's playing some kind of sick joke on us. Trying to scare us."

"But no one knew—"

"Six of us knew."

"But we made a pact."

Liz's voice was strong. "Pacts get broken, Anne. People tell their parents, their husbands, their friends . . ."

Anne nodded. It was true. Someone knew. Someone who was using it against them now. "Shall we tell the others?"

"Let's wait and see if anything else happens. Maybe if we don't panic, whoever it is will get bored and give it up."

"Ummm." Anne sipped her coffee thoughtfully. A joke. Yes, it had to be. It was a joke that would mean nothing if they all kept their heads. She looked at Liz with a faraway smile. "Remember the day we met her?"

Liz nodded. "It was right after the great department store heist."

"I don't know which was more stupid. Ripping off Duncan's or allowing Kathi into our circle."

The prank was meant to be more mischievous than malicious. There was to be a scavenger hunt. Each of the Loreleis was assigned an item which must be acquired and shown to the others as proof of possession. The catch was, the items were to be stolen from Duncan's, the leading department store in Baxter.

"The plan," Francine announced at their first official meeting at the beginning of their senior year, "is to go into Duncan's, fan out, and grab what we're looking for. We then meet at Vali's car, which will be parked nearby, show the items to each other and then return them to the store."

"That's stealing," Liz protested, shaking her head defiantly. "If we got caught, we'd end up with a police record."

"We won't get caught," Barbara Jean said with certainty. "The things we'll take will be very small and inexpensive. We'll just slip them into our purses and walk out with them. People do it every day."

"Those people are professionals," Anne argued. "I think Liz is right. It's taking too much of a chance."

"Since when are the Loreleis afraid to take chances?" Margie asked with her usual flippancy. "That's what we're all about."

"And it's not *really* stealing," Francine emphasized. "We're going to take the stuff right back."

Only Vali hadn't commented. She sat thoughtfully on a wooden folding chair in Anne's basement club room and deliberated. Her aquamarine eyes looked troubled. "What's the point of all this, anyway?" she asked finally.

"What's the point of anything we do?" Margie was, as always, ready with the answer. "It's a kick. Sort of a test to see how much we can get away with."

"It's just something crazy to start off the school year," Barbara Jean added. "After all, this is our last year together. We have to do lots of stuff so we'll remember it later and laugh about it."

"At least we *hope* we'll laugh," Anne murmured.

"Look, everybody." Francine addressed them impatiently. "You're turning this into too big a deal. It's just a little joke. It's harmless fun, and it's not going to take more than half an hour."

"And we *are* returning the merchandise," Vali reiterated for confirmation.

"Absolutely. That's the whole point. Now, how about taking a vote?"

The vote was five to one in favor, with only Liz holding out. "Majority rules," Margie told her firmly. "You have to join in, like it or not."

Liz nodded wearily. "Okay. What do we take?"

Francine and Barbara Jean had already made a list of small, insignificant items and written them separately on six small slips of paper. The papers were then folded over and tossed into the center of the game table. They were shuffled around until everyone was convinced not even the instigators knew what was written on what slip, and then, one by one, they each drew one and opened it to reveal their prospective bounty.

"You're kidding!" Vali laughed when she saw what was written on her paper. "Revlon's 'Kissing Pink' lipstick!"

"I've got to get a bra!" Anne hooted. "Size forty-two C!"

Barbara Jean was directed to take a bottle of Coty nail polish, Liz's assignment was a cheap plastic bangle bracelet, Margie drew a ball point pen, and Francine got stuck with a paperback novel.

The sizes and insignificance of the articles made even the more nervous of the group feel better, and by the time they piled into Vali's red convertible, they were confident they could do the deed with very little effort and practically no risk.

"You have to park a little way from the store," Barbara Jean told Vali as they cruised past Duncan's. "We don't want anyone to see us come out and show the stuff to the others."

"And we've all got to keep a straight face right up until the end," Francine warned. "Someone could get suspicious if we start laughing on the street."

"Okay, here we go," Margie said as Vali eased the car into a space a block and a half from the store.

"Everybody meet back here in fifteen minutes."

The girls checked their watches and climbed out of the car. Margie and Barbara Jean hurried ahead, while the others walked somewhat more leisurely. When they crossed Fourth Street, Liz broke out of the foursome and headed for the store on her own.

Saturday was always busy in downtown Baxter, and Duncan's was bustling with people. "This has to be a snap," Vali muttered under her breath to Francine. "There are so many people here no one will pay any attention to us."

Francine nodded. "The book department's on Two. I'll see you at the car." She and Vali exchanged a conspiratorial grin and parted.

The Revlon counter was to the rear of the store. Vali was dismayed to see that it wasn't exactly crowded with customers. The clerk, a youngish woman with heavy makeup and dyed black hair, was showing an automatic eyebrow pencil to a middle-aged woman who was studying it carefully.

"It's the latest thing on the market," the salesgirl was saying. "But if you don't like it, you can always get a regular pencil."

"I just don't know," the customer mused. "I've never used anything like this before."

"Excuse me." Vali decided to speak up while the saleslady was occupied. "Would you mind showing me some lipstick?"

"I have a customer, miss," the woman replied sharply. She turned back to her customer.

"I know, but if I could just look while you're waiting on this lady, I'll have decided by the time you're free." Vali smiled at her sweetly.

The saleslady gave her a sour look. "Look, you have to wait your turn, okay?" Her voice reflected her irritation. She obviously thought Vali was a smart-aleck high school kid.

The customer unexpectedly came to Vali's aid. "Why don't you show her the lipstick?" she said. "Then you can write up this pencil."

The clerk shrugged. "What color?" she asked Vali.

"Something in the pink family. Isn't there a color called Kissing Pink?"

The clerk nodded. "There's a whole series of pinks." She produced a tray of samples and put them on the counter in front of Vali. Then she returned to the middle-aged woman and proceeded to write up the sale.

Vali carefully studied the lipsticks. Kissing Pink was among the samples; but the case was glued to the display card, and she couldn't figure out how to pry it off inconspicuously. The clerk was finished with the woman who'd bought the automatic eyebrow pencil, but another customer was approaching the counter.

"Excuse me," Vali said hastily. "Would you mind showing me some of your regular stock? These samples are kind of gooey."

The woman gave her a resigned look. "All right, but you have to be careful. If you sample anything, you have to buy it."

Vali smiled. "Sure. I understand that." When the clerk had placed several boxed lipsticks in front of her, she gestured toward the customer who had just arrived. "Why don't you go ahead and wait on her? I'm not in a hurry." She was relieved when the saleslady followed her suggestion.

She took her time. Her heart racing, she opened several of the boxes and made a show of uncapping the tubes and peering at the lipstick. When she got to Kissing Pink, she opened it up, looked at it, palmed it, and pantomimed putting it back into the box. Then she closed the flap carefully and put it back on the counter. She glanced at the saleslady. She was busily trying to sell a box of face powder.

"I've changed my mind," Vali said apologetically. "Thanks, anyway." To her relief, the clerk did no more than nod. Vali walked away, leaving the five lipstick boxes she had asked to see lying on the counter.

Liz had her arm lined with bangle bracelets. "I can't decide which color," she said to the gray-haired woman who worked behind the counter. She turned to a customer who was searching through a basket filled with earrings attached to small squares of cardboard. "Which do you like?"

The woman looked at the bracelets and then into her face. "Yellow'd be good with your coloring," she offered.

"Mmmm. You may be right. I like yellow." A woman with a baby pushed up to the counter. "Do you have any turquoise earrings?" she asked the saleslady. "Not too big, but nice, you know?"

"We keep our turquoise on the other side," the woman said. "If you want to come around, I'll show it to you."

"Turquoise. That sounds pretty." Liz smiled in the direction of the woman looking through the basket and began slipping the bangles off her arm. "I think I'll go look, too." As she slipped the last, ice-blue bracelet over her hand, she slid it into her purse and walked quickly in the direction of the woman with the baby. When she got to the other side of the counter, she headed straight for the door.

The lingerie department was on the third floor. A sale on robes was in progress, and perhaps a dozen ladies and one or two men milled about the area. The girl behind the bar counter was showing a thin, birdlike woman a sampling of padded bras. Anne approached the counter confidently and smiled at the girl. "May I see what you have in forty-two C, please?" she asked.

The clerk looked at her. "Are you sure that's the size you want? You look—"

"Oh, it's not for me. It's for my aunt who's . . . well, you know."

The clerk smiled and nodded. Then, seeing the thin woman was still studying the padded bras, she opened a drawer labeled "42" and lifted the contents onto the counter. "These are all different cup sizes," she told Anne. "You'll have to go through them to find the C's. I have to help this lady first."

"Oh, that's okay," Anne assured her. "I don't mind helping myself."

"Just remember bras are not returnable," the clerk reminded her. "If it doesn't fit, your aunt won't be able to bring it back."

"I know. It'll be all right." Anne smiled again and turned to the pile of bras. The one on top was a forty-two C. With studied casualness, she draped it over her right arm, riffled through the rest, and addressed the clerk again. "I think this is the one I want," she told her. "But I want to look at some slips, too. May I just hold onto this for a minute?"

"Certainly," the girl responded pleasantly. "I'm Cindy, when you're ready."

"Thanks, Cindy." Anne drifted away from bras and made her way to slips. She made a point of fingering several designs which were hanging from a standing t-bar, and then drifted toward the robes and the denser area of customers. She glanced back toward bras. The birdlike woman had been joined at the counter by a plump lady in blue jeans. The clerk seemed totally absorbed. Anne slipped the bra from across her arm into the pocket of her full cotton skirt.

Margie was first to arrive back at the car. Lifting the ballpoint pen had been easy; there must have been ten of them on the counter, and the salesman had slipped away. Since Stationery was near Books, she had wandered over to see how Francine was doing and had chuckled to see her friend carefully studying a paperback murder mystery. She was also happy to see that Francine was carrying an oversized purse that day.

Barbara Jean arrived shortly after Margie, and she was followed by Vali, Liz and Francine in fairly short order. Anne was last to arrive, her full skirt swishing, a smile of satisfaction on her face.

Margie was ready to pop. "Well? Anyone have any problems?"

"Easy as falling off a log," Francine declared. "I could have taken ten books."

"Those salespeople are idiots," Barbara Jean gloated. "They don't see *anything*."

"Okay, here's my bracelet." Liz stuck out an arm on which dangled the ice-blue bangle. "Let's see what the rest of you have."

Barbara Jean produced her nail polish, Margie her pen, and Vali her Kissing Pink lipstick.

"You know, when you return this, I may go back and buy it," Francine said, studying the lipstick. "It's a neat color." She pulled the paperback out of her bag. "Anyone want to read *God's Little Acre?*"

"Oh, Franny, you didn't!" Margie snatched the book from her and began turning the pages. "We can't take this back. We have to read it first."

"We're taking everything back," Liz said firmly. *"Everything."*

"I'll take those if you don't mind."

The girls hadn't seen the man in the neat gray suit approach the car. He was standing on the curb, his hand outstretched. He was looking at them sternly.

"Uh, we'd better go, Val," Anne said, making motions for Vali to start up the engine. "We have to get home."

"Not just yet, you don't," the man said. He reached into the inside pocket of his jacket and brought out a badge. "Detective Wayne Hamilton of the Baxter Police Department. You girls are in big trouble."

They exchanged panic-stricken glances. "Uh, it's not what you think, Mr. Hamilton," Barbara Jean began politely. "We didn't do anything wrong."

The detective took the book and the pen from Margie's hands. "Didn't these come from Duncan's?"

"Yes, but . . ." Margie started to sputter.

"Do you have the sales receipts?" His eyes were regarding her coldly.

"No, but . . ." No one knew what to say. Finally,

Anne, the actress, decided to explain.

"It was supposed to be a joke. A game, really. We decided to take these things to prove we could do it, and then take them right back to the store. We were about to go back when you stepped up."

The detective frowned. "Some game. Shoplifting's what I call it."

"But we were really going right back with them," Vali said urgently. "The store wouldn't have been out anything."

"We'll see what the people in the store have to say about that." He opened the door on the passenger side. "Everybody out."

The Loreleis were visibly shaken as they climbed out of the car. "All right, let's go," Hamilton snapped. He made up the rear as they silently made their way back to Duncan's. He shepherded them through the store to the back elevator, on which they ascended to the sixth floor. There they were met by a grim-looking, florid-faced man with an older, distinguished-looking, white-haired gentleman.

Hamilton introduced the florid man first. "Girls, this is Rolf Nielsen, head of store security. And this is Mr. Edward Duncan."

The Loreleis stared at the older man. Mr. Duncan himself!

"They took the items to a car," the detective explained to the men. "They claim it was a game. That they planned to return them to the store immediately."

Nielsen reflected on this. "Let's see what you have," he said quietly. With shaking hands, Vali handed over the lipstick, Liz proffered the bracelet, and Barbara Jean produced the nail polish. Detective Hamilton turned over the book and pen he had taken from Margie. "Anything else?" Nielsen asked. Red faced, Anne took the bra from her pocket. At the sight of it being drawn slowly out, its outsized cups dangling in the air, Margie burst out laughing.

"So you think it's funny." Nielsen turned on her. Margie turned immediately sober.

"No, sir. I'm sorry."

"Suppose we have the girls come into my office one at a time," Edward Duncan suggested. "I'd like to hear their stories from each of them individually."

Rolf Nielsen nodded. He turned to Liz. "We'll start with you. The rest of you can sit down."

One by one, the Loreleis told their story to the three men. From the way they looked and spoke, it was obvious they were not a malicious gang, only a group of silly high school girls engaged in what they considered a harmless prank. Edward Duncan recognized several of their family names. The Porters, Lawsons and Everlys had been preferred charge customers for years.

"I don't think there's any reason to press charges," Duncan said when the last girl had left his office. "Under the circumstances, I think a warning will do."

"I'll call their parents," Nielsen said. Privately he resented these well-dressed, well-spoken girls getting away with theft simply because they were from respectable families. "They might want to know what their daughters have been up to."

"I'd call the school principal, too," Detective Hamilton suggested. "Wouldn't hurt to keep an eye on them for a while."

The girls were released, humiliated and humbled. By the time they returned to their respective homes, most of their parents knew what had happened, and they were dealt with accordingly. Margie, Liz, Francine and Barbara Jean were grounded for several weeks. Vali was denied the use of her car. Anne got off with a brief reprimand from her father.

The most serious consequence occurred on the following Monday, when they returned to school. Each girl was summoned from her classroom and told to report to the office of Miss Erskine Winters, Dean of Girls. Miss Winters was a tall, stately woman with steel-gray hair and a no-nonsense demeanor. She greeted the girls by name and asked them to find a place within the semi-circle of chairs she had arranged in front of her desk.

"It's come to my attention that you six girls have had a brush with the law," she began, looking at each of them in turn. "I wonder if you realize how serious that is?"

"Yes, ma'am," Barbara Jean said politely. "We're sorry. It won't happen again."

"It was really just a joke, anyway," Francine added. "We didn't mean any harm."

The Dean of Girls nodded. "I have been apprised of your explanation." She paused and cleared her throat. "I know you girls aren't bad girls. In fact, all of you excel here at John Ross in one way or another." The Loreleis relaxed slightly. They sat looking at her attentively, their hands resting quietly in their laps. "But you should be aware that pranks such as yours can get out of hand. You all seem to be fairly high-spirited, and if not kept in check, this can lead to trouble."

"We've learned our lesson, believe me," Margie avowed fervently. "We'd never do anything like this again."

Miss Winters seemed to discount the answer. She moved on to a new tack. "I know you girls have formed a club," she said matter-of-factly. "The 'Loreleis,' isn't it?" The lines around her mouth were drawn down, registering her disapproval.

"It's just a silly name we have for ourselves," Vali offered with a small grin. "Most of us have been friends since eighth grade."

Miss Winters was not impressed. "The thing is, these social clubs, or 'cliques,' as some people call them, can be very bad for girls your age. They encourage an attitude of superiority. Of snobbishness."

"Oh, but we're not snobs," Anne assured her. "We're just good friends who like to do things together."

"Hmmm." Miss Winters looked thoughtful. "Until now," she began again, "I haven't tried to interfere with your little club because, exclusive though it is, I thought it was fairly harmless. However . . ." She paused as if to emphasize her next thought. "I'm afraid it's leading you onto the wrong path."

Barbara Jean dared to sneak a glance at Margie, who did a very good imitation of the prim Dean. She looked as if she was about to burst into a fit of giggles. Barbara Jean looked away quickly, lest the mirth should be contagious.

"I think," Miss Winters continued, "it would be wise for you to disband the Loreleis."

Six gasps were heard, practically in unison.

142

"But we're not hurting anyone," Liz cried in dismay. The other girls echoed her protest.

Miss Winters held up her hand for silence. "I'm afraid you may be hurting yourselves," she declared. "You should be using your free time positively, not thinking up ways to test your bravery."

"But we don't—"

Margie was interrupted by Anne. The insightful actress sensed arguing would only make things worse. "What do you mean by 'positively'?" she asked. "Maybe we could do something as a group."

The Dean awarded Anne with a small, dry smile. "Yes, as a group, I think you could be quite effective. You're all bright and energetic. If you turned the Loreleis into a service club, you might have something worthwhile."

The girls stared at her. "What's a service club?" Francine ventured to ask.

"A club that does good works. You could spend an hour or two a week working as candy stripers at a hospital. Or you could go out to the county home and read to the elderly." She had a sudden thought and reached for the phone on her desk. She buzzed her secretary. "Maxine, find out what class Kathi Harcort has this period and send her in here, please," she said into the mouthpiece. When she replaced the receiver, she turned to the girls with new enthusiasm. "There's a new girl beginning her senior year here," she told them. "She hasn't lived in Baxter long, but she's already distinguishing herself by setting a wonderful example. I believe she's involved in any number of service projects."

"Kathi Harcort," Liz mused aloud. "I think she's

in my Algebra class.

"She's a relatively quiet girl," Miss Winters said. "She may not have attracted your attention as yet. She could, however, be of help to you should you decide to direct yourselves toward service." She looked at them expectantly. "Does the idea interest you at all?"

The girls were mute, none of them knowing what to say. "Would that mean we could keep on being the Loreleis?" Vali finally asked. "We wouldn't have to disband?"

"I don't think the name is exactly fitting," Miss Winters answered with a slightly distasteful wrinkle of her nose. "But, yes, that would be the idea."

Vali turned to the others. "Then I think we should do it. Miss Winters is right. It would give us something *positive* to do. Broaden our horizons." She smiled as if she had a great secret.

"I agree," Francine said, following her lead. "I think it's a good idea."

The phone on Miss Winters' desk buzzed. The Dean picked up the receiver. "Yes, Maxine?" she said. Then, after a pause: "Send her in."

Presently, the office door opened and a girl entered. As if cued by a director, the Loreleis turned around to stare at her. She was of medium height and had a rather frail look about her. At first glance it was hard to tell whether she was plain- or interesting-looking. She had a small, heart-shaped face capped with a cloud of fluffy, red-gold hair. Her nose was a bit sharp, but her eyes were a mesmerizing, brilliant green. Her white complexion was dotted with pin-point-sized freckles.

"Girls," Miss Winters announced grandly, "this is Kathi Harcort."

Kathi nodded shyly in the general direction of the semi-circle. Liz, who recognized her, reminded her of their common Algebra class. The others followed suit and introduced themselves.

"These girls," the Dean explained, "are interested in getting into service work. I thought you might be able to help them decide on a plan of action."

"It takes a lot of time," Kathi said doubtfully. "Once you sign up, you have to be dependable."

"We'd be dependable," Anne declared, annoyed at the inference that the Loreleis could not be counted upon. "Just tell us where we can do the most good."

Kathi looked slightly abashed by Anne's assertive attitude. "I'm going to the Crippled Children's Home after school today," she replied. "They always need help there. Maybe you'd like to come with me."

"That sounds like a fine idea," Miss Winters said brightly. "How do you feel about it, Barbara Jean?" She turned her probing eyes on the head cheerleader.

"I . . . I have to go to the dentist after school today," Barbara Jean answered. Then, uncomfortable under the Dean's gaze, she added, "I could go tomorrow, though."

"I can go today," Francine announced. She nudged Margie, who quickly spoke up.

"Me, too. Sounds great." She looked as if she was about to gag.

"I can go today," Vali said. "Why don't we meet outside the main entrance at three o'clock?"

Anne had play rehearsal and Liz had a piano lesson, but it was agreed that the three that couldn't make it that day would accompany Kathi to the county home the following day.

The Crippled Children's Home was a large mansion on Baxter's north side. It was formerly owned and occupied by one of the town's leading families, but when the south side became the more desirable section, the family donated it to the March of Dimes which turned it into a convalescent home. Because the home consisted of three stories, the children who were not confined to bed needed help moving from floor to floor. The three volunteers Kathi introduced to the home's director were warmly received and set to work pushing wheelchairs, delivering orange juice and reading aloud; the capacities in which they were needed were numerous.

"This is the pits," Margie muttered to Vali when they passed each other on the huge, circular staircase. I'm going to be crippled myself from going up and down these stairs."

"Just keep smiling," Vali trilled as she urged a small child on crutches toward the third floor.

Francine ran into Kathi in the solarium. The Loreleis' mentor was patiently spooning jello into the mouth of a child in an iron lung. "Do you really do this every day?" Francine asked in disbelief. She herself was becoming profoundly depressed by the handicapped children.

"Not *every* day," Kathi told her, smiling. "I divide my free time between here, the county home and St. John's Hospital."

"But why?" Francine asked. "I mean, it's admirable, but—these are the years when you're supposed to be having *fun*."

"There are other things besides fun," Kathi said softly. She turned back to the child in the iron lung. "Okay, Jamie, this is the last bite."

At the end of their two hours of service, Francine, Vali and Margie agreed that Kathi was completely beyond their comprehension.

"Miss Goody Two Shoes," Margie called her disdainfully. "She makes me want to throw up."

"She *is* doing something worthwhile," Vali said, frowning. "To tell you the truth, she makes me feel a little guilty."

"Look, we'll all be doing charity work when we're older," Francine declared. "I don't know why we should be expected to do it while we're still in high school."

"It's either this or disband the Loreleis," Vali reminded her. "I don't see that we have much choice."

The other two agreed soberly. They lapsed into momentary silence. Then Francine came up with a new thought.

"Maybe our folks'll lift our restrictions," she said, her spirits rising. "They won't have the heart to ground us if we say we're coming to the Crippled Children's Home."

"I think my father will give me my car back, too," Vali said, her face brightening. She laughed. "Maybe this thing will have its advantages."

"As long as it doesn't go on too long," interjected Margie. "I wouldn't want to end up like Kathi. We might actually start *liking* this crap."

They hooted at that, linked arms, and set off down the street.

Chapter Nine

Vali could tell Chase was listening to her account of her activities in Baxter with half an ear. "Wonderful, darling!" he declared with no real enthusiasm when she told him how much she was enjoying being with her old high school girl friends again.

"The dance routine is a scream," she said with a droll chuckle. "You'd think my feet would remember something about tapping, but it's like I never had a lesson in my life."

"I'm sure you'll be fine. Look, darling, I hate to interrupt; but I'm working on a proposal, and I'm afraid I'm rather preoccupied."

Vali gave in to the inevitable feeling of deflation. Things would never change where her husband was concerned. "Yes, of course," she told him evenly. "You'd better get back to it before you lose your concentration. Give my love to the kids, okay?"

"Absolutely. 'Bye, darling. Miss you."

"I miss you, too. See you soon."

She hung up the phone with a sigh. She supposed she couldn't blame him for not being more interested. After all, Chase had no real link to her high school days. By the time they married she'd been away from Baxter over six years, was divorced from Donald and had two children. Hardly the "Lorelei" her friends here remembered.

She reached for the message she'd picked up when she'd returned to the Lancelot from Riley's. *Donald Ellsworth. 555-3520. Please call.* She looked at her watch. Six-thirty.

Should she call? She supposed he wanted to talk about the kids. She probably should have brought them with her, but somehow having a full grown son and daughter at a high school reunion seemed almost obscene. Anyway, the Class of Fifty-eight was her special time, and she wanted the freedom to relive it without the distractions of the present. She'd suggested to Kevin and Jennifer that they visit their father for a couple of weeks in August.

She decided to get back to Donald. He had a right to hear about his own children—both of whom were terrible correspondents. She reached for the phone, then withdrew her hand, leaned back in the chair and became thoughtful. It had been funny seeing Donald at the landing strip yesterday. She hadn't seen him since she'd married Chase, although she'd talked to him by phone from time to time when it was necessary to discuss something concerning the kids. Oddly enough, he'd looked pretty much the way she'd remembered him: big, firm, and very handsome. His eyes were still that incredible blue, the kind of eyes that attracted you instantly. Kevin had those eyes, although they weren't *quite* so intense. She smiled at the thought of her charming, devil-may-care son. God help the girl who fell in love with Kevin.

Donald answered the phone on the second ring.

"Hi. It's me."

His voice took on a warmth Chase's never had when he spoke to her. "How're you doin'? Big day today?"

Vali laughed. "Real big. We had the first rehearsal for our dance number. Boy, are we in trouble!"

Donald laughed in return. "I can't wait to see it."

"What do you mean, 'see it'? I don't want you anywhere near that Pow Wow." Vali tried to sound stern, but she knew the amused note in her voice was giving her away.

"Man, do you have a lot to learn. Didn't anyone tell you I'm taking a camera crew over there Saturday night?"

"You wouldn't dare."

"Wouldn't I?"

"You'd lose all your ratings. Everyone would switch to KOTV."

They laughed together.

"Hey." Donald's voice was low. Intimate. "How about having dinner with me tonight?"

Vali felt a tinge of disappointment. "Would you believe I just came back from Riley's? I had a bite with Margie and Francine."

"Define 'bite.'" Vali could imagine the teasing expression on his face.

She chuckled. "Hamburgers with everything, french fried onion rings, cherry cokes and black bottom pie."

"You've got to be kidding."

"Believe me, the next time I step on a scale, I'll wish I were."

A pause. Then: "Could we have a drink? Say, an

hour from now?"

Vali hesitated. Something about this bothered her, but she didn't know what. *Come on,* she chided herself inwardly, *he's the father of your children. It's perfectly natural that you should get together. You can show him the pictures of Jen's birthday party.*

"Sure," she said with slightly forced brightness. "I'd like that."

"Good. Pick you up at . . . say, eight?"

"Fine. I'll see you then."

She replaced the receiver thoughtfully and a tiny bit disturbed. Why? She'd known she'd be seeing him this week, hadn't she? She could hardly come to Baxter and avoid him completely. Inexplicably, she felt butterflies begin to stir in her stomach. Why was she so nervous? Was it because she'd seen him at Indian Hill? Seen how terrific he looked? Was she afraid he wouldn't think she looked as good?

She rose from the chair. A nice long bath was what she needed. A bath always calmed her down. She went into the bathroom and put the stopper in the tub. She found some bubble bath among the grooming products the hotel provided and poured it under the gushing faucet.

Stepping out of her clothes, she pinned her hair atop her head to keep it out of the water and studied her face in the mirror above the sink. Faint lines were etched around her eyes, but all in all, her skin was still exceptionally smooth. Her hair was touched up these days, but the manufactured honey color was an almost perfect match with her own natural color. She stepped back and ran her hands down her naked body. She'd been lucky there, too. She was still a perfect size eight.

She turned off the water and stepped into the tub. The bubbles soothed her. It was almost, she thought whimsically, like getting ready for a date with Donald when she was sixteen. She smiled at that long ago memory. Being sixteen had been so exciting. And so poignant.

She sank back against the end of the tub and sighed. Exciting and poignant. Her whole life seemed to have been that way. Or at least her life after the "Big Split."

The "Big Split" had happened when Vali was thirteen. It hadn't been particularly traumatic, no big blow up or anything like that. Her mother had simply sat down with her and her sixteen-year-old sister, Tori, one day and told them she wouldn't be living with them anymore.

"It's not that I don't want you, darlings," she'd said, smiling her beautiful smile and smelling of the wonderful perfume she always wore. "It's that I'm not going to be living in Baxter anymore. I'm going to New York, and I don't think you'd be happy there. At least, not until you're older. You'll be better off to stay here with your father until you're out of high school."

Vali and Tori hadn't even asked her *why* she and their father had decided to divorce. They knew grown-ups did strange things sometimes. And since neither Mummy nor Daddy seemed particularly upset by the turn of events, they decided to accept things in the same good grace. After Mummy moved out, their big, comfortable old home on Bent Oak Drive seemed a little emptier; but their housekeeper, Mamie, was still there to see that they got to school on time, and Daddy was always available to help with homework or to lend an advance on their already liberal allowances.

Frequently, large packages would arrive from Mummy in New York, and Vali and Tori would open them to find fine cashmere skirts and sweaters, silk underwear and glittering costume jewelry. In fact, as time went by, Mummy's departure seemed almost like a bonus. No other girl of their acquaintance was so well-dressed or was allowed such freedom from parental authority.

Then one day Mummy phoned with an announcement. The girls were about to gain a stepfather. "You will positively adore him!" she had assured them, gushing. "His name is Fisher Farrow, and he's the most handsome thing you ever saw!"

He was also, they soon found out, extremely rich; much richer, apparently, than their physician father. They met "Fish," as they learned to call him without sniggering, the following summer when they went to New York to pay their mother a visit. He was indeed handsome, although the girls found him a bit stiff. Tori, however, found New York very much to her liking, and at the end of the summer she elected to stay on and attend Miss Finch's Finishing School instead of graduating with her class at John Ross High.

So Vali had returned to Baxter alone. That was the year she entered high school, and she found herself caught up in such a whirl of activities, she had no time to miss her sister. In high school, classes were harder, boys were more important, and there were many more things to gossip about with best friends. And, of course, for Vali high school meant Lorelei. The club she'd formed in junior high with Anne, Francine and Barbara Jean went into high gear.

As Vali luxuriated in her bath, the memories of those days seemed as frothy and sparkling as the bubbles surrounding her body. Although the club was comprised of the most popular girls in school, she was clearly the envy of its members. Even at fourteen, she was a classic beauty, and the fact that she was a doctor's daughter, lived in a grand old house, wore expensive clothes and spent her summer and Christmas vacations in New York and Palm Beach gave her a glamor none of the others could hope to possess.

She met Chase the summer she was fifteen. Her sister Tori was being launched as a debutante, and Vali went to New York to attend some of the festivities surrounding this exciting event. While she was too young to attend the cotillion, she was very much present at the "tea dance" Tori gave for her friends at the Farrow's Park Avenue home. Although petite, platinum-blond Tori was in her glory as a deb, taller, quieter Vali with her silky curtain of dark gold hair and her natural elegance caught the attention of handsome, twenty-year-old Chase Thomas, one of the young men in Tori's new set of friends. Chase brought her a glass of punch, danced with her three times, and invited her to a matinee of "Damn Yankees," which was playing on Broadway. Although Vali enjoyed the dances and the attention,

154

her time in New York had been carefully planned by her mother, and there was not a moment that wasn't already filled. "Thanks anyway," she said with a shy smile. "Maybe I'll see you again sometime."

By the time she did see him again, at Tori's wedding, Vali was going with Donald Ellsworth. The wedding was a society affair, held in Palm Beach, and both Vali and Chase were in the wedding party. Tori's new husband was Gregory Cooper, a recent graduate of Harvard and an executive-in-training at a top Wall Street brokerage firm. Chase had also graduated from Harvard and was learning the ropes of investment banking.

"Chase's family is extremely prominent in both New York and Washington, D.C.," Vali's mother had told her when, a few days after the wedding, Chase had phoned and asked Vali for a date. "And so handsome, too! A girl could certainly do a lot worse for herself."

"But I've got a boyfriend," Vali had protested. She'd known Donald since her sophomore year of high school, but since he was two grades ahead of her, they'd merely been nodding acquaintances then. But in the summer of her junior year, they'd met at a swimming party, and Donald had noticed that Vali was no longer just a kid. They'd started to date, and it was beginning to get serious—although, of course, they hadn't actually gone "all the way."

"It won't hurt you to go out with Chase while you're here," her mother had insisted, smiling that lovely, but firm smile. "Anyway, you're too young to go steady. You're going to be meeting lots of nice young men."

Vali had dutifully agreed to see Chase and had enjoyed their riding and boating dates; but her heart belonged to Donald Ellsworth, and when she returned to finish her senior year, she didn't give Chase Thomas another thought.

First love. Nothing like it on earth, Vali thought as she stepped from the tub and wrapped herself in a thick, white terrycloth bathrobe. By the end of her senior year she was deeply in love with Donald and wanted desperately to enter the University of Oklahoma in the fall so they could finally have a full-time romance. But two years before, Vali had promised her mother she would go to Wellesley, and since she had been accepted, there was no way out of it. "Just give it a year, darling," her mother had urged, patting Vali affectionately. "Then if you want to go to OU, we'll discuss it." Nor would her father help her in this cause. He had recently married again and was considering leaving Baxter to join the practice of his bride's doctor-father in Atlanta. Dr. Porter thought that, under the circumstances, Wellesley was a good place for Vali.

She had endured that first year—had actually enjoyed much of it—but the following fall she entered OU. She and Donald became inseparable, and when, on the evening of his graduation, he asked her to marry him, she accepted wholeheartedly.

Naturally, her mother tried to talk her out of it, and her father urged her to at least finish college; but she was adamant. The wedding took place in the senior Ellsworth's living room, with only Donald's parents and Francine Briggs present.

Donald had majored in Journalism and had been

expected to win a spot on one of the larger Oklahoma newspapers, but as they discussed their future, he surprised her by saying he wanted to go to Los Angeles to attend a school for television announcers.

"Broadcast journalism is the way to go," he declared, looking very young and very intense. "Why should I confine myself to a paper when I could be covering the news live, on the air? Besides, television pays more."

Donald's parents considered their financial responsibility toward him and his education at an end with his graduation from college, but Donald cheerfully said he wouldn't mind working nights to pay his way through broadcasting school. Vali, who could type and file and was a whiz at handling people, said she would look for a job as a receptionist as soon as they got to L.A.

At the beginning, it was pretty much the way they had planned. Vali got her receptionist job almost immediately, and Donald tended bar nights at a Santa Monica watering hole to pay for his tuition at the Lee Gordon School of Radio and Television Broadcasting in Hollywood. They found a small apartment in Santa Monica, which Vali kept spotlessly clean, where she prepared the rare meals their conflicting schedules allowed them to enjoy together. It was hectic and frustrating. They talked and made love on the run; but they knew it was all only temporary, and they endured the inconveniences with good grace.

Then Vali got pregnant with Jennifer. She worked as long as she could, but once she had the baby there was no question of going back. In the 1960's, day care centers were not the norm; young mothers stayed home to raise their families. They got by on the meager amount of money they'd been able to save, and Donald found a job at another club which was busier than the first and netted a bit more in tips. But poverty and a crying baby put a strain on their relationship, and Vali wondered why being young and married wasn't the way it was in the movies.

She appealed to her parents for help, and her father agreed to pay the tuition for Donald's second year of broadcasting school while her mother sent liberal checks for household expenses and baby care. Vali hated having to depend on them, but as soon as Donald graduated and got a job, they could pay it all back.

Donald did graduate and get a job, but the job was with a small radio station in Costa Mesa, not with a big T.V. station in L.A. Still, it was a start, and Vali loyally kept her radio tuned to 830 on the dial as she tended Jennifer, cleaned the Costa Mesa apartment and prepared for the arrival of baby number two.

"It's a start, and I'm lucky to have a job at all, Donald told her when she complained that he seemed to be more of a disc jokey than a newscaster. "I was one of only five guys in our graduating class who got anything at all. The business is overloaded with talent."

Stretching pennies had Vali at her wit's end. Although her mother still sent checks in the form of "presents," her father's aid had stopped, and she was too proud to ask for anything else. She had married Donald against their wishes; she could hardly ask them to bail her out now. The new baby was a boy,

Kevin, and as soon as he was born Vali went on birth control pills. The two children seemed to sap all her strength. She never had time to read or see a movie, and when she looked in the mirror, she hardly recognized herself. Her figure, once considered svelte, was too skinny to be attractive now. Her once shining hair seemed dull and lifeless, and worry showed in her face twenty-four hours a day. She found herself nagging at Donald, and she was too tired to make love more often than not. Still, she and Donald plodded on, telling themselves and each other that a really good job was sure to turn up any day. "Can't give up at this point," Donald told her with characteristic optimism. "Otherwise, what's it all been for?"

The day Vali found out about the other woman, she simply packed up the kids and left. The girl was one of the secretaries at Donald's radio station, and Vali happened to spot them in the station's parking lot the day she stopped by to bring Donald his forgotten lunch pail. They were kissing passionately, oblivious to the fact that they were outside in a public place. When Vali saw them, she hit the brakes, causing a tire squeal that instantly broke them apart. Donald came running toward her, and for a moment she actually considered stepping on the gas and running him over. Instead, she listened to his apology and floundering explanation and silently handed him his lunch pail. By the time he got home that night, she and the kids were on the plane to New York.

*　　　*　　　*

Margie's improved spirits lasted throughout the evening. Going to Riley's had been fun; she and Francine and Vali had giggled over the myriad memories that kept cropping up, new ones triggered by each in turn. Margie almost *felt* like a teenager again, only this teenaged Margie was snug and secure. The old Margie who'd had to constantly prove herself was dead and buried.

When she got home, she fixed spaghetti and meatballs for Jerry and the kids and watched "The Sunday Night Movie" snuggled against her husband's familiar, protective body. At eleven-fifteen she went into Brian's room to turn off the radio. Brian, age fifteen, was fast asleep, his face in repose looking as innocent as a five-year-old's. He'd been listening to the "Big Burke Show," one of those call-in D.J. shows where listeners could dedicate songs to each other. Margie doubted if Brian ever called in—so far, he wasn't that much into girls—but it was possible that he was occasionally the recipient of a dedication. Gangly and awkward as he was, the boy had a definite appeal.

"And here's a request for an oldie but goodie," Big Burke's hearty voice thundered through the speaker. Margie's hand reached for the knob. "Seems Like Old Times" for Vali, Anne, Francine, Liz, Margie and Barbara Jean . . . from Kathi!"

Margie doubled over and vomited at the foot of her son's bed.

Francine stripped down to the pink leotard and flesh-colored tights she'd worn under her skirt and blouse. The others had all worn slacks to rehearsal, but somehow she felt a leotard was a more professional touch. Not that there was anything professional about the "Singin' In The Rain" number. From the start of today's rehearsal, it had been obvious that none of the Loreleis could be noted for their dancing ability. Anne, of course, had a sense of rhythm which was natural since she was a professional singer, and Francine herself had acquired a certain grace through years of body exercise; but they had all agreed it was a good thing their dance routine was simple. Otherwise, they'd end up looking like idiots up there on the stage.

She moved into the bathroom and ran a comb through her long, silky hair. Thank God for this age of natural-looking hair dyes, she thought as she stared at her face in the mirror. She couldn't believe Barbara Jean had actually come to town with streaks of *gray* showing in her mouse-brown hair! The others had managed to maintain themselves pretty damn well. In fact, Francine was a little taken aback to realize she wasn't the only one who could be called beautiful at the age of forty-seven.

She was glad, though, that they all looked so well; it was a credit to the Loreleis of old. There was no doubt in her mind that they would outshine all the other women at the reunion. She was putting her skirt on a hanger when the knock sounded at the door. Probably one of the other Loreleis; they couldn't seem to get enough of gossiping together. She dropped the skirt on the bed and hurried to the door.

At first she thought there must be something

wrong with Baron. Why else would Arthur Brook-field be standing there staring at her that way? But it wasn't her husband, Arthur assured her as he walked past her into the room. Baron had never been sick a day in his life. What made her think that was going to change now?

"Then what are you doing here?"

Arthur looked at her evenly. "I wanted to talk to you. I've been waiting for the chance for a long time."

A small, bitter smile crossed Francine's face. "You've had over twenty years to talk to me."

"You know what I mean. Really talk. Away from your husband and all those big-eared servants." He seated himself in the room's one upholstered chair. Francine remained standing.

"I don't have any secrets from Baron."

"You sure as hell have one."

Her heart almost stopped. What was he trying to pull?

"You haven't forgotten about Barry, have you?"

She met his eyes and kept her voice perfectly controlled. "Is that what you want to talk about? My son?"

"*Our* son." He was leaning back in the chair, looking at her. She suddenly felt naked. She snatched up her skirt and wrapped it around herself, tying it at the waist.

"After all these years you want to talk about Barry." It wasn't a question; it was a statement of disgust.

"After all these years we're *going* to talk about him. I've wanted to do it for a long time now."

162

"Arthur, he's no concern of yours."

"He's my son."

"Only in terms of genes. He's Baron's son in every other way."

He shrugged and leaned forward. "You're looking very well, Francine."

"Thank you."

"Having fun at this reunion of yours?"

"The reunion hasn't started yet. This is just the preamble."

"I imagine all your friends are impressed with what you've managed to accomplish."

She tossed back her hair. "I don't know. Maybe. Arthur—"

"*I'm* certainly impressed. I have been for over twenty years."

She faced him squarely. "Okay, Arthur, what is it you came here to say? Let's stop pussyfooting around."

He leaned back again and nodded slowly. "I want to tell Barry the truth."

"No!" It was a cry of real pain.

"He's entitled to know who his father is."

"He loves Baron."

"I wouldn't expect that to change."

"Then, *why*, Arthur? Why tell him now, when he's a grown man?"

"Because he *is* an adult. I want to make him my heir."

"You can do that without bringing up the past."

"I want him to know the truth."

She sank heavily onto the edge of the bed. "What about Baron?"

"What about him?"

"Don't you have any consideration for him at all? Think what this would do to him. He's eighty-six years old!"

"And apparently getting stronger all the time. Francy, I wanted to wait. I didn't dream the old man would last this long. He's going to outlive us all if we're not careful."

She glared at him. "How can you say such a thing?"

His expression changed to a smirk. "I suppose you're going to tell me you love him."

She jumped up and raged at him. "Yes! I do love him! Maybe I didn't when I married him, but he's a wonderful man, Arthur! The finest man I've ever known."

He rose, smiling, and reached out to curl a strand of her hair around his finger. "Still the same beautiful hair. Remember when I—"

She whirled away from him. "Fuck off!"

"Francine, listen to me."

The phone rang. She rushed to answer it. Incredibly, it was her son. He wanted her to stop by the house the following afternoon. He was bringing someone over he wanted her to meet. A girl.

Arthur stood close enough to Francine to overhear. "That's another reason I want him to know," he said when she'd hung up. "He's a grown man. He'll be having children of his own one day soon. My grandkids."

She glared at him. "You should have thought of that all those years ago when you recommended an abortion."

Her sarcasm didn't faze him. He answered calmly,

with the assurance of one who believes he's always right. "There were reasons for that. If you hadn't been so stubborn, if you'd just waited, there might have been a future for us."

"If I hadn't been so stubborn, Barry wouldn't be here, and you wouldn't be worrying about grand-kids."

Arthur smiled thinly. "Touché, my love. But, nevertheless, he exists, and I want to take my rightful place in his life."

Francine fought panic. He *couldn't* tell him. Imagine what it would do to Baron, to her marriage, her position. All those years down the drain. He stepped up behind her and put his hands on her shoulders, gently massaging them.

"I used to do this when you were tense. Remem-ber?"

"Yes," she replied. His lips touched her neck. What the hell did he think he was doing?

"I've never forgotten you, Francy. I've never forgotten *us*."

She wrenched herself free and walked to the door. "Goodbye, Arthur."

He stood looking at her. Then he gave her a careless shrug. "Have it your way, Francy. For now."

"Arthur—"

He held up a hand. "We'll talk about it later."

"I'll thank you not to come to my room again."

"What's the matter? Don't you trust yourself?" He opened the door. "Goodbye, Francy."

He walked down the corridor without looking back.

*　　　*　　　*

165

The phone in her room rang at ten minutes to eight. Vali, wearing a full-skirted, Adele Simpson silk dress, moved to answer, long crystal earrings dangling from her hand.

"Hello?"

"Hi. It's me."

She checked her watch. "Donald. You're early. I'll be down in just a—"

He cut her off. "What are you wearing?"

"What?"

"What do you have on? A dress? Pants? Shorts . . . ?"

She looked down at her delicately printed skirt. "A dress. You didn't say where we'd be going. I thought it would be suitable for—"

"Take it off."

She frowned. That didn't sound like Donald. "I beg your pardon?" Her voice held a cautious note.

"Take it off. Put on shorts. Or jeans. We're going to the county fair."

"The fair? You're kidding." She blinked in surprise. Then she smiled.

"I just got a call from the station. The reporter who was supposed to cover it had a boating accident this afternoon. They couldn't find anyone to fill in, so I volunteered. Do you mind?"

Vali's hand was already reaching for the zipper at the back of her neck. "No, not at all. I haven't been to a fair in years."

"The camera work won't take long. After that, we'll do the midway. I may even win a stuffed animal for you."

Vali felt a pang of nostalgia. Once she had strolled the midway with Donald and come home with more stuffed animals than she could hold in both arms.

"Are you in the lobby now?" she asked, anxious to be off.

"Sure am."

"Just wait right there. I'll be down in a jif."

She hung up and pulled off her dress. She hadn't thought to pack jeans, but she had a pair of jungle-patterned cotton pants and a blouse to match. She tossed her crystal earrings back into her velvet-lined travel case and reached for dangly shell ones.

When Donald spotted her getting off the elevator, he whistled. "Man, these Baxter women get more beautiful every day." He planted a light kiss on her temple, against her soft hair. "Hi, there."

"Hi." Vali stood still, liking his nearness.

He put his arm around her waist and gave her an affectionate squeeze. "Shall we go?"

They rode to the fairgrounds in Donald's new Le Baron convertible. "The camera crew will meet us there," he explained, looking at Vali out of the corner of his eye. She looked completely at ease in his car, not minding the way the wind whipped at her hair as they picked up speed.

"The reporter who was in the boating accident. Was he badly hurt?"

"*She*," he corrected. "Apparently she was more shaken than anything. And not exactly in the mood to cover a fair."

"I'm glad."

He smiled. "I'll give her your good wishes."

She looked surprised. "I didn't mean that. Oh, I *am* glad she's okay, but what I meant was—I'm glad you're taking her place."

"You dig fairs, huh?"

"Doesn't everyone?"

They laughed.

The van carrying the camera crew and sound equipment was waiting at the fairgrounds entrance. Donald made brief introductions and then went into a huddle with the director for the fair segment. When all the shots were explained to him, he motioned to Vali, and the entire group traipsed around the grounds, cameras photographing livestock and thrill rides, Donald interviewing midway barkers and winners of bake-offs and knitting competitions. Watching from the sidelines, Vali marveled at his graceful self-assurance in front of a camera and his effortless way of putting his subjects at ease.

This is what those years in California were about, she reflected, as if a great light had suddenly dawned. This was what he had struggled for, what their marriage had come apart for. He had known what he wanted, and he hadn't let anything stop him from getting it.

Now that she saw the end result, she felt nothing but admiration.

The taping lasted less than an hour. When the crew left, apparently satisfied with what they'd managed to get, Donald took Vali's hand and led her toward the bustling, brightly-lit midway. "Hungry?" he asked as they passed a vendor offering hot dogs on sticks.

"No, but I could use a cold drink."

Donald bought two cokes in paper cups. They sipped companionably as they strolled and observed.

"You seem quiet," Donald said after a bit. "Tired? Or isn't the fair living up to your expectations?"

"Neither," Vali assured him. "I was just thinking."

"Anything you'd care to share? Or is it none of my business?"

"I think you could say it's definitely your business." She smiled at him. "I was thinking about you." There was a moment's pause as he waited for her to go on. "I was wondering—why this?"

"This? You mean the fair? I told you—"

"No, I don't mean the fair. I mean Baxter. Donald, I watched you on the late news last night, and I saw how you handled yourself out there this evening. You're *good*."

He made a motion as if to tip his hat. "Thank you, ma'am."

"I mean it. You're a complete professional. Why aren't you in Oklahoma City? St. Louis? New York?"

He finished his coke and tossed the paper cup into a nearby trash bin. "I was in Chicago for a while."

"I know that. Jen and Kevin visited you there. I didn't want to ask what happened, but . . ."

"I didn't get fired. I chose to come back."

"But *why?* Surely the money—"

"The money was better, yes. And I'm not going to go all cliché on you and tell you money isn't everything, but personal satisfaction *is* everything. Or a hell of a lot, anyway."

"You weren't satisfied in Chicago?"

"I was one of fifty hotshot newscasters there. The jockeying for position in a place like that is incredible. The bullshit you have to go through . . . the playing up to people . . . the cocktail parties . . . the flattery . . ."

"In other words, you weren't your own man."

He snorted. "Hell, I didn't know *whose* man I was for a while. I didn't even recognize myself. Here, I can have some validity. Call it ego if you want, but, believe me, there's a lot to be said for being a big fish in a small pond." He smiled. "Anyway, I like Baxter. I'm a hometown boy. It's nice living here."

She nodded thoughtfully. "Did anyone ever tell you you're a very unusual man, Mr. Ellsworth?"

He shrugged, as if embarrassed, and ignored the question. "Speaking of unusual . . ." He gestured toward a huge sign in front of a tent proclaiming the dubious fact that a half-man/half-woman resided within. He looked at Vali. "Shall we?"

Vali rolled her eyes. "I don't know. Think we can handle it?"

"I'll catch you if you faint."

Laughing, they paid the admission and hurried inside, forcing their eyes to adjust from the bright electric lights on the midway to the rather dim atmosphere in the tent. They followed other curiosity seekers along a roped walkway until they were directly in front of the main attraction, a man (or was it a woman?) with a full beard and bare, hairy chest wearing a black satin mini skirt, fishnet stockings and high heels.

"That's it?" Vali whispered, suppressing a laugh.

Donald frowned. "I've seen better than that in San Francisco."

The barker, who had momentarily stepped inside, overheard.

"You want proof the other half's a broad?" he asked brusquely. "It'll cost you fifty bucks."

Donald and Vali exchanged looks. Donald shook

his head. "No, thanks," he said, tugging on Vali's hand. "We've seen enough."

They came out of the tent giggling like school children.

"What next?" Donald asked.

"I don't know." She looked around. "A ride?"

"The Loop-the-Loop? The whip? The roller coaster?"

She squinted at him. "How about the Ferris wheel?"

He grinned. "You've got it."

Leaning back against the seat of their capsule, they gave in to the giddy feeling accompanying the wild swings of the wheel. When the ride came to a stop with their capsule at the top, they clasped hands and gazed up at the stars.

"Having fun?" Donald murmured, venturing a look at her.

"Ummm." She closed her eyes for a moment, then opened them to give him a wry look. "This may be as close to Heaven as I'm going to get."

"I doubt it," Donald said softly, turning his body toward hers. "You're al—" His words were interrupted by the motion of the wheel. The ride was back in action, and they held onto each other in silence until it stopped and they were ushered from their cocoon of privacy.

Later, Donald won her a green stuffed snake and a cheap vase.

The ride back to the Lancelot was completed in almost total silence. Vali was deep in troubled thought, and Donald seemed just as preoccupied. When he swung into the parking lot, he stopped just before reaching the lobby entrance.

"Tired?" he asked quietly.

She smiled faintly. "A little."

"Can I buy you a nightcap?"

She shook her head. "No, Donald, thank you." She hesitated, then leaned over and kissed his cheek. "And thank you for tonight. It was wonderful."

"Vali—"

She stopped him before he could go on. "I hope you don't mind if I don't keep the snake and the vase. I couldn't. It wouldn't be right. You understand."

He wrinkled his brow. "You won't even take them to your room?"

"No. What's the point? I couldn't pack them and take them home. Chase . . ." She drifted off, uncertain how best to continue.

He nodded slowly. "I see." He looked at her. She was turned slightly away from him, looking down, as if afraid to meet his eyes. "Will I see you again while you're here?"

"No. I don't think so." She smoothed an unseen crease in her jungle print pants.

"Vali. Look at me."

She stiffened her back and raised her head. Her eyes were guarded.

"Is something wrong? Have I done something—or said something?"

"No. Of course not. It's just that—"

"It's just that we had too much fun tonight." His voice was hard. "That's it, isn't it?"

"No. I . . . don't know what you mean."

He caught her wrist and held it. "You do know what I mean. We were close tonight. We felt things. Things for each other."

She tried to pull away, but he would not release her wrist. "Please, Donald, let's just drop it, okay?"

"But it's not okay. Admit it, Vali. It was like it used to be with us. Easy. Warm. Fun." He lowered his voice. "It doesn't have to end. We could go to my place—"

"*No!* Are you crazy? I can't do that. You know I can't."

He let go of her wrist, put his hands on her shoulders and turned her to face him. "But you want to. Admit it."

She met his eyes with her own. She studied the desire there. And the love. She drew in a breath.

"Yes. I want to." There. It was said.

"Then why—"

"Because I can't, Donald! I'm someone else's wife now. I made a commitment, and I'm not going to let a fling at a high school reunion betray it."

He seemed to recoil. He removed his hands from her shoulders. "A fling," he repeated softly.

"I'm sorry, Donald."

Wordlessly, he put the car in gear and eased up to the entrance. He shut off the motor, got out and hurried to open her door. When she got out, they stood face to face, looking at each other.

"You're sure you know what you're doing?"

Her heart was pounding.

"Yes. I'm sure."

He nodded and stepped aside. "Goodnight, then, Val. Thanks for coming out with me tonight."

She forced a smile. "Take care of yourself."

She hurried toward the lobby before he could see the tears springing to her eyes.

173

Chapter Ten

Jerry wanted to call a doctor, but Margie wouldn't hear of it.

"I'm all right. It's just this reunion thing. It's giving me a nervous stomach."

"But you were fine all evening. Why a nervous stomach all of a sudden?"

"It was just an anxiety attack. You know how I used to have them."

Jerry's eyes were full of concern. "You're sure you don't want me to call Dr. Feinstein?"

"No, really, I'm fine now. I'm through with all this 'poor, delicate Margie' bit."

He smiled at her. "I hope so, honey." He turned off the lamp next to her side of the bed and kissed her on the cheek. "You try and get some sleep so you'll be fresh for tomorrow's rehearsal."

Her voice came out of the dark, after Jerry had turned off his own lamp and crawled into bed beside her. "I'm not going to tomorrow's rehearsal."

"I thought you said you were all right."

"I am all right. I'm dropping out of the dance."

"You're kidding."

174

"No." She could feel his eyes on her, even without being able to see him.

"But they're counting on you. It won't be the same old number without you."

"They'll manage. It'll be five instead of six, that's all."

He rolled over on his side, facing her in the dark. "Honey, I think you're making a mistake. If you back out you'll regret it. How often do you get the chance to relive old times?"

"My old times don't need reliving. I prefer today."

"Margie, listen to me—"

"I mean it, Jerry. If I go through with this, I'll have another nervous breakdown and end up back at Lakeview. *Then* where would we be?"

"You're over dramatizing. You have me to lean on now. I'll help you through the rest of the week."

Silence.

"Honey?"

"Yes?"

"Will you sleep on it, at least?"

She sighed. "Yes. I'll sleep on it."

That night she dreamed about Kathi. She saw her clearly, heard the exact sound of her voice. Somehow, the dream soothed her, made her feel that perhaps Kathi wasn't dead after all. When she woke up the next morning, she told Jerry to stop worrying. She'd see the reunion—and the dance number—through.

Rehearsal went badly. Almost everyone seemed under some kind of strain. No one could remember the steps. They lost count. They couldn't keep their line straight. Miss Virginia's daughter lost patience and told them they'd better shape up or they'd make fools of themselves at the Pow Wow. They were all glad when it was over.

Someone suggested lunch, but Francine wanted to get to the house. Barry often brought friends home—occasionally even girls—but he had never asked her specifically to meet any of them. This girl must be important to him.

She peeled off her sweaty tights and took a shower. She piled her hair atop her head, washerwoman style. It was coolest that way. She had slipped into a pale yellow sundress when the door to her bedroom opened and Baron walked in.

"Darling! Why aren't you at the office?"

He moved to her and kissed her cheek. "Barry told me you were coming home to meet his friend. I wanted to be here. I've missed you."

She smiled and kissed his mouth. "It's only been two days."

"It seems like much longer."

"I've missed you, too."

"How's the dance number going?"

"Okay, I guess."

He took her hand and led her downstairs. They had a glass of sherry while they waited. Barry and the girl he introduced as Christina Freeman were right on time. Barry was all smiles. He cracked jokes a mile a minute, and he asked his mother about the dance number. He sat holding the girl's hand.

The girl said practically nothing. She sat looking at Francine with huge green eyes. She was wearing pedal pushers and sandals, outdated but right for her somehow. When they left, she extended a hand to Francine. It was soft and cool. Francine's hand was drenched with sweat.

The girl Barry had brought home was Kathi Harcort.

Liz, her legs curled beneath her as she lounged on the blue velour sofa, smiled expectantly as her mother deposited the scrapbooks on the coffee table in front of them.

"I don't want to bore you with these, honey, but you've been gone so long."

"I know, Mom." Liz mentally resigned herself to a long afternoon. "And I want you to help me catch up. I want to see each and every photograph."

"Well, of course, a lot of them are of Diana's family," Veda Everly replied. "Although we have every picture you sent us, too, honey."

"Those can't be very interesting. Me standing in front of the Coliseum, the Eiffel Tower, Lenin's Tomb." She reached for the first album and began leafing through the pages, making sure to go slowly enough to convince her mother of her interest. Diana. Always Diana. With her Elizabeth Taylor face and Raquel Welch body.

"That's your sister's new house in Tulsa," Veda explained, pointing to a photograph of a rambling ranch-style home which, to Liz, displayed no character whatsoever. *Like my sister,* she thought, then berated herself inwardly for having such an uncharitable reaction. "And that's Skipper on his twelfth birthday. And there's Mary Anne going to her first prom."

"She looks like Di," Liz observed, studying the photo of the dark-haired teenager decked out in pink tulle.

"Yes, she does, doesn't she?" Veda beamed. "She's following in Diane's footsteps, too. She was Prom Princess in her junior year. I wouldn't be surprised if she's named Queen next year."

Same ol' Mom, Liz reflected irritably. Prom Queen, that's what matters. Forget being smart, forget being president of your class, forget winning scholarships and making a career for yourself. Win beauty contests! Find a man, settle down and have kids, and spend your life baking cakes and going to bridge parties! Those are the things that matter!

Those were the things that had always mattered to Mrs. Everly. To Liz's father, too, probably, although he rarely took much interest in either of his daughters. "Diana's my pretty one, and Liz is my smart one." How many times had Liz heard her mother say those words? And the emphasis was always on the *pretty*, the part about Liz always came as a polite afterthought. At an early age, Liz had steeled herself against the phrase, trying hard to rationalize it, not wanting to admit that—to her mother and people like her—"pretty" was by far the most preferable.

"Smart" was good, too, wasn't it? The teachers at school seemed to think so, and Liz's reputation as a "brain" had followed her all the way through high school. She had put her intelligence to practical use, too. When, around tenth grade, her mother had encouraged her to be more outgoing so she would be "popular" (another of Veda Everly's favorite words), she had traded on her brains to gain entree to a golden circle of girls, Valerie Porter being, at the time, the most golden of all. The day Liz had come home and told her mother she'd been asked to join Vali's club, Lorelei, Veda had almost fainted from joy. And, Liz had noted, she hadn't been able to conceal her surprise. Her withdrawn, studious daughter hobnobbing with the glamorous Vali Porter and her friends?

Liz never told her mother she'd gained admittance to Lorelei by risking her own dishonor at Horace Mann Junior High and, later, at John Ross. She not only did the other girls' homework for them, she'd arranged an elaborate system of passing along answers to quizzes and tests. The fact that they all received good grades made Liz much in demand by the Loreleis, and they returned the favor by offering her their friendship together with the aura of glamour that surrounded them all and made them the envy of every other girl at John Ross.

Liz knew the Loreleis' acceptance of her had been beneficial to her as well. Having been sprinkled with their gold dust, she developed self-confidence, became more outgoing, and ended up being popular enough in her own right to be elected president of the senior class. But, still, the old wounds, the certain knowledge that being "pretty" and having boys flock around was what really mattered, had left their mark and provided her with an aberration she still carried. After her first intimate experience with Bobby Langencamp, Liz had no desire to enter into another affair. Later, maybe, when she was mature enough to handle it, and when the "right" boy came along. But, her insecure inner voice asked her, how would she be able to prove herself desirable if she turned the boys away?

In the end, she had found the solution. Dateless one Saturday night and unable to face her mother's looks of sympathy mixed with exasperation, she drove to Spirit Lake and pulled into the parking lot behind "Slick's," a raunchy barbecue place frequented by reprobate locals and a few wild college kids. She had gone in, found a small corner table, and ordered a beer and a plate of ribs. Before the food even arrived, she was joined by a college man from OU, who'd slipped away from campus to "tie one on" and catch the action on the wrong side of the tracks. His name was Danny Simmons, he was from Okmulgee, and in his words, he was "horny as hell."

"Hey, Lizzie," he suggested after talking to her for no more than five minutes. "How about you and me gettin' it on?"

She had recoiled inwardly. She knew only too well what "gettin' it on" meant. Hot hands fumbling with her bra and panties, wet, slobbery kisses smearing her lipstock—and that *thing* being pushed inside her, pumping, thrusting, till its owner finally collapsed on her chest with a series of animal groans.

"Who do you think you're talking to?" she had replied indignantly, glaring at him from beneath her mascara-covered lashes. "You've got a lot of nerve, buster!"

"Yeah! Then what're you doin' out here all by yourself on a Saturday night?" Danny challenged, draining the last of the beer in his glass. "You're lookin' for action, same as I am. Admit it!"

Liz blinked. She supposed he was right. When she'd driven out here she wasn't sure *what* she was looking for. Revenge? A way to get back at her mother for intimating that there was something wrong with a girl who didn't have a date on a Saturday night? Looking for action probably summed it up as well as anything. Still, the idea of going off with this stranger and "doing it." . . . How could she?

"Listen," she told him with an embarrassed smile, "you may be right. I mean, maybe I was looking for action when I came out here. But . . ." She looked down at the plate of ribs which had just been placed in front of her. "I've changed my mind." She pushed the plate aside and tossed her napkin on the table. "I'm going home."

"Wait!" Danny cried as she stood up. "Let's talk about this thing. I think you're a real nice girl. I like you, Lizzie, I really do. It wouldn't be anything you'd have to be ashamed of. We'd have a good time. And, hell-fire, nobody'd have to know."

Liz picked up her check and opened her purse. "Sorry. You're talking to the wrong girl." She walked to the cashier's desk and paid for her uneaten meal. Danny followed her out to the parking lot.

"Hey, Lizzie. I got some money on me." He pulled a roll of bills from his pocket and proceeded to count them. "I got twenty . . . twenty-eight dollars." He waved it at her. "I'll give it to you. Will you do it for twenty-eight dollars, Lizzie?"

She froze. He was offering her money, like some kind of whore! Of all the nerve!

And yet . . . a secret smile played over her face. What would her mother think of that? A boy—a college man, yet—not only wanted her, he was willing to *pay* for her charms. What better proof of one's desirability than that? She turned and looked at Danny again. He wasn't bad looking. In fact, he was kind of handsome in a gawky sort of way. He was drunk, of course. But she'd been out with guys who got drunk before. In a way, that was good. He'd probably pass out after he did it, and she'd be free to go on home.

She hesitated. Should she? Did she dare? The idea of doing it for money intrigued her. None of the other Loreleis had done it for money, that was for sure. It would be an experience, a kick. And it wasn't as if it were something she hadn't done before.

"You got anything," she asked, "for protection?"

"Sure thing, hon," Danny grinned idiotically. He pulled a condom out of his pocket and held it up. "I never travel without my friend here."

Liz felt her stomch turn. She remembered the cool rubbery feel of Bobby's condom in her vagina. "Where'll we go?" she asked warily.

"I got a room at the motel down at the end of the road. It's clean, too. There's not a damn thing for you to worry about, Lizzie, honey."

So she had gone. She'd never told the Loreleis or anyone else about her experience. It was almost as if she divorced herself from it, as if it was another Liz, separate from herself, who went with a man for money. But one night, several months later, she'd found herself leaving a party at the country club with the father of one of her friends. He gave her a one-hundred dollar bill for her services, and for her promise she'd never tell anyone what they'd done.

Almost before she realized it was happening, it became an addiction to her, a game she played, a test of her physical worth. Since high school, she'd played the game all over the world: in Frankfurt, where she'd had her first job with the foreign service, in Italy where she'd vacationed several times, on a cruise ship touring the Greek Isles. She even played the game in Russia, where the reward was more than money. By now the game had become a test of her own ingenuity as well as desirability. Each time she pulled it off without getting caught, the more powerful she felt. And she could laugh at them all. While they were huffing and puffing and relieving themselves in her body, she could tell herself what idiots they were The last laugh was had by Veda Everly's "smart" daughter.

"Darren's making forty thousand dollars a year and due for a promotion any day now," Veda was saying as she took the album from Liz's hands. "Your sister's sitting on top of the world."

"That's terrific." Liz faked a smile. "I wish I could see them while I'm here. Any chance of their driving down?"

"Well, they're so busy all the time. And with you staying at the Lancelot . . . even your father and I have to make an appointment."

Liz avoided the reproachful look in her mother's eyes. "I'm sorry, Mom. I told you how it would be. Francine made the plans . . ."

"I know, honey. I know." Veda patted her hand understandingly. "And it's nice for you to be with your friends again. Such nice girls. I must say Francine did well for herself, didn't she?"

Liz nodded resignedly. "Yes, Mama. She certainly did."

Seeing the annoyance flash across her daughter's face, Veda picked up another album and shoved it at her. "Look here. I'll bet you didn't know I saved these."

The whole album contained memorabilia of the Loreleis. The silver pin in the shape of a siren sitting on a rock which they'd had made and wore every day on their sweaters and blouses. Programs from the Pow Wows in which they'd danced. Endless photographs: Vali, poised atop her palomino horse; Francine in a one-piece bathing suit lounging beside the pool at the Eastman house, Anne dressed for her role as Mary, Queen of Scots; Barbara Jean in her cheerleader's uniform. . . . Liz smiled as she viewed them. How stupid they all were in those days.

She turned the page. A picture of three Loreleis mugging for the camera. Anne, Margie, and . . . who was the third one? The picture was slightly blurry. Liz squinted at it and snapped the book shut. The third girl was Kathi Harcort.

She placed the album on the coffee table and unfolded herself from the sofa. "Mom, I'm sorry, but I'd better be getting back to the hotel. Some of the others are waiting for me. Francine—".

"Yes, yes, of course." Her mother was impressed with Francine and her rich husband. If she was waiting, Liz had better go.

"I'll pop back over tomorrow or the next day. And you're coming to the Pow Wow Saturday night, right?"

"We'll be there."

Liz kissed her mother's cheek. "Thanks. This has been fun. If you talk to Diana, tell her hello for me."

"I'll do that." Veda followed her out to the condo's guest parking lot. "'Bye, honey. Drive carefully."

Liz waved from inside her parents' car. She wasn't sure where she was going, but she was definitely going to drive carefully.

When the call finally came, it was not from Donald Ellsworth. Joe-Dean Farber, co-host of the daily talk show *Good Morning, Baxter*, made the call himself.

"This has been Anne Eastman day," he said jovially, when Anne expressed surprise at finding herself on the phone with someone she hadn't even known existed. "Saw the article in the Tulsa *World* this morning. Then, when I got into my office, the press release from New York was sitting on my desk."

Anne breathed a sigh of relief. Mark Donahue was doing his job after all. "I'm flattered you called, Mr. Farber," she said pleasantly. "I know how busy you must be, hosting a daily show."

"I try to get my priorities straight. I understand you're something special."

Anne preened. "Why, thank you." She unconsciously smoothed down her hair.

"I understand we have a mutual friend."

"Why, yes, I suppose we do. I've known Donald Ellsworth since high school."

"I'm not speaking of Ellsworth, Annie."

She started and frowned at the casual use of the nickname she despised. "No?" she asked coolly. "Who, then?"

"Cliff Berkeley. We started out in radio together in Minneapolis. We still keep in close touch. We're like brothers."

A tiny alarm sounded in the back of Anne's head. Cliff Berkeley was a first-class creep. She'd had to sleep with him to get on his show.

When she answered, she forced herself to sound impressed. "How wonderful. I did Cliff's show before I left New York."

"I know. I caught it. That's why I decided to call Cliff when I found out you were in Baxter. To see if he thought you'd be good for my show."

"And?" Anne felt tense. She decided humor might be the best way to handle this one. "Did he recommend the bit where I set my hair on fire?"

Joe-Dean chuckled. "He gave you an A-1 rating all the way."

Anne relaxed. Three cheers for Cliff.

"So, how about it? Think you could find time to appear on *Good Morning, Baxter?*"

She tried not to appear eager. "I *think* I could manage that. Of course, it'll have to be this week. I'm going back to New York on Sunday."

"I was thinking of tomorrow."

Anne was pleased. Now that he knew she was here, he couldn't wait to have her as a guest. "Hmmm," she mused, as if consulting a busy calendar. "I suppose I could squeeze it in."

"Terrific. I'll be over within the hour."

She frowned. "Over? Over where?"

"Your hotel. The Lancelot. That's where you're staying, isn't it?"

"Yes, but . . . I have plans for this evening."

"This won't take long." Joe-Dean sounded firm. "We'll just go over your spot on the show."

Silence. Anne thought hard. Was there something she didn't know here? "Oh, but surely we can wing it, Joe-Dean," she said airily. "I'm a very good conversationalist."

Joe-Dean seemed perturbed. "Cliff told me you understood these things," he said, a frigidity creeping into his voice.

Anne closed her eyes and gripped the receiver, hard. So Cliff had sold her out. Told this Joe-Dean clown what Anne Eastman would do for a gig. But Cliff's show had been network. Surely some local yokel wouldn't think . . .

"Do you understand?" Joe-Dean asked pointedly.

Anne hesitated. Jesus. A local morning talk show. Who would see her? A bunch of housewives with smelly diapers in their hands? The nerve of this Farber creep. She didn't even know what he looked like.

She took a breath and gave in to the sinking feeling in the pit of her stomach. "Sure, Joe-Dean," she answered in a flat, dull voice. "I'll expect you within the hour."

Chapter Eleven

Margie picked up a copy of *Pyschology Today*, flipped through it, and returned it to the magazine table. Restlessly she fished in her purse for her compact and lipstick, found them, and applied the lipstick with a slightly unsteady hand.

"Mrs. Middleton?" The nurse was smiling at her through the sliding glass window. "Doctor's ready to see you now."

Margie nodded and went into Dr. Feinstein's office, smoothing her cotton print skirt as she walked. The cold, bare walls echoed her footsteps on the spotless linoleum floor. How long had it been since she'd been to Dr. Feinstein's office? Two years? Three? She hadn't come on a regular basis for at least ten, just occasionally when something was troubling her and she needed to talk.

The doctor was standing at his door, waiting for her. As she nodded her greeting, she noted that he looked the same as always, a little older, maybe, but very authoritative, all-knowing, regarding her with inscrutable eyes.

He offered her the chair facing his desk. "It's good

to see you, Margie. You're looking very well."

"Thank you. It's nice to see you, too." She hated making inane conversation with him, but after two years she supposed there had to be some kind of opening dialogue.

"Your family okay? Husband? Kids?"

"Yes. Everyone's fine." She forced a smile.

Dr. Feinstein tilted his chair backward and observed her. "You seem a little nervous. Aren't you comfortable with me after all this time?"

"Yes, of course." She answered quickly. "It's just that . . . I didn't expect to be seeing you. It was Jerry's idea"

"As far as you're concerned, this visit is un-necessary?"

She looked away. "I'm a little tense, that's all."

He nodded thoughtfully. "What's been happening? Are you under some kind of stress?"

"Margie took a deep breath. "My high school graduating class is having a reunion. Thirtieth year."

"Ahhh." He obviously thought he was getting the picture. "High school reunions always dredge up a lot of memories. Many of them traumatic. High school can be a very difficult time." He paused. "Women—and men, too—sometimes worry about how they'll look to their friends after all those years. Whether they've aged more than the others, whether they've gotten fat or haven't made a success of business or marriage."

"It's not that." Maggie was sitting very straight in her chair. Her hands were clenched in her lap. "Doctor, you know what happened to me after

189

high school."

Another long pause as he regarded her. "Your friends don't know? Are you afraid they'll find out?"

"No. Not exactly. I mean, I don't know how they could find out. No one knows except Jerry, and I'm not afraid he'll tell them."

"Then . . . what?"

She steeled herself. Might as well tell him. He wasn't going to let up until she did.

"It's that dream I used to have. It's come back. It's gotten to where I'm afraid to go to sleep at night."

He smiled sympathetically. "Margie, it was only a dream."

"But it always seems so real. The black altar and the candles and the chanting—" She broke off. Tears were beginning to form in her eyes.

"Margie, we've discussed this dream so many times." He reached for a folder on his desk and rifled through some papers. He found the one he wanted and studied it. "The last time we discussed it was nineteen seventy-eight. I thought we had put it to rest."

"I know. I did, too. But it's back. And I don't know what to do."

He cleared his throat. "If memory serves, you began having that dream after that friend of yours died. Your high school classmate. Isn't that right?"

She nodded. A lump was beginning to form in her throat.

"Tell me about the girl again. What were the circumstances of her death?"

"She was new in town. We took her into a club we'd formed. Lorelei."

He pursed his lips . "I remember now. Go on."

"Well . . . she died. In our senior year. Suddenly, on Halloween."

"And you never found out why?"

"They said she had a weak heart—rheumatic fever as a child or something—but it bothered me. I never had a friend who died. And the way they found her. Outside the church. Just . . . lying there."

His face was expressionless. "Did you have any reason to suspect foul play?"

Margie felt the nausea rising in her stomach. "No. There were no marks. She hadn't been murdered, or raped or anything."

His eyes penetrated hers. She wanted to look away, but his gaze held her fast. "And the dream started coming afterward."

She nodded.

"Margie, I've asked you this before. Many times. What is the link between the dream and your friend's death?"

"That's just it. I don't know." Her heart was beating—too loud and too fast. "I can't think of any link."

"And yet you said you were having that dream—in a waking state—the day you plowed your car into a tree. It caused your condition. Or—" he paused. "Was it your friend's death that caused the break-down?"

"I don't know!" The tears were surfacing now. Margie's shoulders began to shake. "I don't know! I've never known what caused it. I thought I'd gotten well."

"You did get well. You *are* well. You don't feel on

the verge of another ... *problem,* do you?"

"I don't ..." She took a breath. "No. Of course not."

"It's just the dream that's disturbing you. It's robbing you of your sleep."

She nodded dully. "I took a pill a couple of nights ago. It was from an old prescription. It helped, but ..."

The doctor reached for his prescription pad. "Throw what you have away. I can give you something newer. It's very mild—no after effects—and it should give you a dreamless sleep."

"Thank you."

"If it doesn't work—or if you still feel anxious—will you call me?"

"Yes. Certainly."

Dr. Feinstein stood up. "I don't think you should worry about your reunion too much. I'm sure all your former classmates have certain fears. Yours are not unique."

She smiled wanly. "I'm sure they're not. Thank you, Doctor." She rose and offered her hand. His closed around it.

"Goodbye, Margie. Call me if you need me."

"I will."

As she hurried out of his office and out to the parking lot, her brain was whirling. Why on earth had she allowed Jerry to make that stupid appointment? She'd nearly given it away! All the time she was talking, she could see Kathi lying there, the candles flickering around her, her naked body covered with those idiotic scribblings. For the first time since it happened, she had almost screamed out the truth.

She slid into the car and closed the door. Margie sat still for a moment, her hands rigid on the steering wheel. *I've got a get control,* she admonished herself. *I can't start slipping now.* All those years . . . all the time in the hospital, and in outpatient therapy, she'd never even hinted that Kathi's death and THE DREAM might be related. Or that Kathi . . . she shuddered. Today, Dr. Feinstein had come close to unearthing the entire secret!

Get a grip on yourself, she commanded firmly. *The reunion's only a few days away. All you have to do is get through that, and you're home free.* She could do it. She knew she could.

Her face set in determination, she started the car and headed for the pharmacy to fill the prescription that would put an end to THE DREAM.

They were in Vali's room at the Lancelot. Vali was sitting cross-legged on the bed; Barbara Jean was stretched out on her stomach beside her. Liz sat in the upholstered chair, Anne in the straight-backed chair next to the table. Margie was on the floor, her back supported by the edge of the bed. Francine was perched on one end of the lowboy.

"It can't be Kathi." Vali made the statement clearly, as if there was nothing else to talk about. "Kathi's dead."

"It had to have been a girl who *looked* like Kathi." Barbara Jean bit into the apple she'd taken from the basket of fruit the management had put in each of their rooms.

"She was wearing Kathi's clothes." This from Anne. Francine and Liz nodded firmly.

"I saw her up close," Francine added. "She was as near to me as Margie is. Christ, I carried on a conversation with her!"

"Maybe we should call the men with the butterfly nets." Vali pounded against the mattress with her fist. "Are you all nuts? Kathi's *dead*. God, who knows better than we do?"

"It's somebody playing a joke on us," Barbara Jean declared. "They've found someone who looks like Kathi, and they're playing a cruel, sick joke."

Anne turned to her. "Have you told anyone, anyone at all about that night?"

Barbara Jean blanched. "No! Never!"

Anne looked at Vali. "Vali? How about you?"

"Are you kidding? We made a pact."

"We were kids then. People change their minds."

"You think I wanted to admit what happened?"

Anne shook her head and turned to Francine. "Fran?"

"God, no. I've tried to forget about it for thirty years."

"You didn't mention anything to your husband? Or your son?"

"I swear."

Anne took a deep breath. "Liz and I talked this over yesterday. We've both kept quiet." She addressed Margie, who was looking at her blankly. "Margie? Did you tell?"

"Tell? About K-Kathi?"

"Yes, about Kathi." Anne exchanged a look with Liz. What had been wrong with Margie the last

194

couple of days? She looked and acted like she was freaked out on drugs. "Did you tell your husband?"

"No. No!" Margie's eyes opened wide. Behind the dull gaze there was fear.

Anne spread her hands on her lap. "That's it, then. If nobody told, nobody else knows."

"Maybe someone else has known all along." Vali's theory.

"We made sure no one was around." Liz was adamant in her answer. "If you remember, *I* was the one who insisted on taking all the precautions."

"You were the one who put us in danger," Barbara Jean snapped. "We should have left her in the church and gotten out fast."

"With those horrible marks all over her?"

"Lipstick. Big deal."

"They'd've known it was some sort of initiation. They'd've come to us sooner or later."

"We shouldn't have put the lipstick on her," Vali said grimly. "It was weird. Uncalled for."

"A Black Sabbath isn't supposed to be weird?" Anne countered hotly. "Whose idea was that, anyway?"

"Well, it wasn't mine," Vali shot back. "I'd never even heard of a Black Sabbath."

"You went along with it, though, didn't you?" Francine said accusingly. "Everyone went along with it."

There was silence. Then Barbara Jean muttered, "We shouldn't have made her drink the blood."

"It wasn't blood. It was catsup mixed with bitters." This from Liz.

"She thought it was blood. She almost threw up."

"She ate a worm." Margie's voice sounded as if she were sixteen again. And incredulous.

"She ate cold spaghetti," Vali corrected.

"No. She ate a real worm. Mixed in with the spaghetti." Margie knew. She had put the worm on the plate.

"People don't die from eating one little worm. Or drinking catsup," Francine said irritably. "Kathi died because we scared her to death."

"She had a weak heart," Anne reminded them. "Her parents said so."

"Then why didn't we admit what we did?" Barbara Jean demanded. "Why were we so fucking scared?"

"Because we were afraid they'd think we killed her anyway. We were afraid for our own precious hides." Vali faced Barbara Jean squarely.

"The autopsy report would have proved we didn't kill her."

"We didn't know that, stupid!" Liz snapped. "We were seventeen years old, for Christ's sake! All we could think of was getting away from there."

"The mark," Margie murmured, putting a hand up to her mouth. "The mark didn't wash off."

An old familiar horror gripped the room. That tiny red mark on Kathi's left shoulder. They'd thought it was the lipstick, but no amount of rubbing could erase it.

"What the hell was that mark, anyway?" Barbara Jean asked after a moment. "It looked like the imprint of an animal foot. A goat or something."

Margie cleared her throat. They all turned to look at her. "It was a cloven hoof. The devil's mark."

*　　　*　　　*

Later, they appologized to each other for their heated reactions to the conversation.

"We can't let this ruin the reunion for us," Francine said placatingly. "I don't know who this imposter is, but we can't let her cause problems between the six of us." She passed around the bottle of white wine she'd had sent up from Room Service.

Vali poured some of the wine in her glass and smiled thoughtfully. "Funny, it's almost like she's getting back at us," she mused. "For all the stuff we did to her."

"If she hadn't been so persistent, we'd've left her alone," Barbara Jean said. "We agreed to let her get us involved in charity work. We never said we'd *marry* her."

To their disgust, Kathi had begun joining them for lunch in the school cafeteria. The first time she brought her tray over to where Margie and Francine were sitting, she asked permission to share their table.

"Uh, Anne and Vali are supposed to be here any minute," Margie said quickly, flashing an apologetic smile. "We promised to save their places."

"You must be mistaken," Kathi said sweetly. "I just saw Vali on her way to P.E. She has late lunch period today."

And she sat.

Margie and Francine decided it was in their best interest not to appear rude. They tried to keep the conversation going.

"How come you moved here from Wichita?" Margie asked, not really bothering to look at her.

Kathi's answer was not what she expected.

"My parents had to go to Africa for a year because of my father's work. I came here to live with my aunt and uncle."

"Africa," Francine repeated, intrigued in spite of herself. "Couldn't you have gone with them?"

Kathi sighed. "I wanted to, but they didn't want to take me out of the American school system. Particularly in my senior year."

"What kind of work does your father do?" Margie pried open her milk carton and inserted a straw.

Kathi straightened her shoulders. "He's a writer. A good one."

"He is?" Francine tried not to sound impressed. "What's he write?"

"Lots of things. Books, mostly. Did you ever read *Full Harvest*? Or see the movie?"

Francine thought hard and shook her head. "I guess not," she admitted. She attacked her pot roast feeling slightly stupid.

Margie frowned. "Who was in it? The movie, I mean."

"Oh . . . Cary Grant. Elizabeth Taylor. Doris Day . . ."

Francine was agog. "You're kidding! I thought I'd seen all of Elizabeth Taylor's movies."

"Well, this one was a while back." Kathi bit serenely into her barbequed beef sandwich.

"Did you meet any of those movie stars?" Margie asked. Her secret dream was to meet Elvis Presley.

"Only Cary Grant. We went out to Hollywood while they were filming. He was neat. I got his autograph."

Margie began to think Kathi might be an asset to the Loreleis after all. "What does your uncle do?" she inquired. "He a writer, too?"

"Oh, no. He's a car salesman, and my aunt's a social worker. She helped start the Frances Willard School for Troubled Girls."

Margie lost interest.

"Did you have a boyfriend in Wichita?" Francine asked idly.

Kathi looked taken aback. "Oh, no. I wouldn't want a steady boyfriend." She shook her head with certainty.

Margie widened her eyes. "Why not?"

"Well, it could be . . . dangerous. You know. You get to kissing in the car, and then . . . well, you know."

"Kathi, that's not the sin of the world," Margie said indignantly. "Making out is normal. It's what makes the world go round."

"Oh, I know. But it's for married people."

Francine looked interested. She'd always felt torn between wanting to wait and keeping pace with her more liberated peers. "You mean you intend to wait until you're married?"

Kathi smiled shyly. "I think a girl has to save herself. I don't even like to think about sex." She leaned on the table with her elbows and addressed them earnestly. "You do agree, don't you?"

Margie glanced at Francine and almost choked on her sandwich. "Oh, right," she said airily. "Absolutely."

*   *   *

It was Margie who came up with the idea of getting Kathi laid. "It'll do her good," she said with an exaggerated wink at the rest of the Loreleis. "Clear her complexion up."

Vali giggled. "There's nothing wrong with Kathi's complexion."

"Except maybe her freckles," Francine said with deliberate sarcasm. Secretly, she thought Kathi's smattering of freckles was cute.

"Well, maybe it'll clear her freckles up," Margie urged them on energetically. "Come on. It'll be fun. We'll fix her up with one of our BMOC's and let him take it from there."

"Yeah? Like who?" Barbara Jean was becoming interested.

"I don't know. Larry Everett. Jack Shagan."

"I've got it!" Francine was suddenly full of animation. "Butch Furguson!"

"Butch Furguson?" Anne looked doubtful. "He's a junior at BJC."

"The last I heard, he was going steady with Sandy Cullen." Vali had a certain loyalty toward any girl who was going steady.

"Oh, who cares about that," Margie scoffed. "I think Butch is a terrific idea." She laughed. "If Kathi doesn't want to go through with it, I'll take her place."

Because he was two years ahead of them, Butch Furguson had not had much contact with the Loreleis. When they were lowly sophomores and he a lofty senior, they had admired him from afar, but no one had been lucky enough to actually go on a date with him. After he graduated from high school and went on to Baxter Junior College, they saw him occasionally, mostly at football games at which he was the star player. Butch was tall and brawny, blond, blue-eyed and ever so macho. He also had a reputation for being on the wild side, and they had heard he'd had more than one small brush with the law.

"How do we get him to go along with it?" Liz asked. She wondered privately whether making it with Butch the first time would be any more pleasant than it had been with Bobby Langencamp.

"Butch Furguson will go along with anything for a joke," Margie said positively. "We'll tell him we've made a bet he can't lay Kathi, and he'll jump at the bait. If he doesn't," she added, "we'll pay him."

"Pay him?" Barbara Jean squealed. "Are you serious?"

"Sure I am. We'll take up a collection and give it to him." She laughed. "It'll be worth it."

"Who's going to ask him?" Liz looked at Margie suspiciously.

"I will," Francine said suddenly. "My brother's in one of his classes at BJC. I'll have him get Butch's number, and I'll call him."

Vali was silent. She seemed to be wrestling with something inside herself. "Why are we doing this?" she asked at last.

"Because Kathi's such a prig." Anne was almost hostile. "Because she's so pure and perfect, and she screwed up our fun by attaching herself to us."

"She saved our asses," Liz reminded her, her dark eyes bemused. "If it wasn't for Kathi, the Loreleis would've disbanded by now."

201

"That trouble at Duncan's was weeks ago," Barbara Jean argued. "We don't need Kathi for our image anymore."

"Apparently Miss Winters thinks we do." Francine made a face. "We're probably going to be stuck with her for the whole year."

Margie nodded. "That's why we might as well get some laughs out of it." She howled. "Can you imagine what she'll think when Butch pulls his thing out? It must be huge."

"Maybe she'll like it," Barbara Jean suggested. "Maybe she and Butch'll go off and get married."

"Good. Then she'll be out of our hair." Anne walked over to the refrigerator that had been installed in the clubroom and took out a bottle of Coke.

"Okay, it's settled then." Francine began making plans. "We'll arrange a date with Butch and then one of us will have a party. It should be someplace where we won't have parents interfering." She looked expectantly at Anne.

"My father's never around." Anne shrugged. "We can have it here."

Butch Furguson agreed to go along with the joke, particularly after they offered him twenty dollars. "I always wanted to get paid for doin' it," he said with a grin. "Just don't let Sandy get wind of it, okay?"

Everyone promised to keep the secret within the Lorelei circle.

Kathi was thrilled to be invited to a party at Anne's house. She asked Vali to help her shop for a dress. "You have such good taste," she told her, gushing. "I want you to help me find something really great."

Kathi wasn't told a date was being arranged for

her. She arrived at the party alone, looking winsome and virginal in a princess style dress made of white voile with a lace collar and long, poofy sleeves. Seeing her, Francine gave Vali the "high" sign, registering her approval of Vali's shopping advice.

When Butch was introduced, he put on all of his considerable charm. "Where have you been all my life?" he asked, looking at her the way a dog looks at his master's T-bone steak. "You and I have to get acquainted."

Kathi looked up at him with her shining green eyes and sighed.

"It's going to be easy," Liz whispered to Anne as they watched from across the Eastman living room. "She's flipped for him already."

As the evening progressed, Butch didn't leave Kathi's side. He gave her liberal helpings of punch from the heavily spiked bowl in the dining room and held her close as they danced to soft music supplied by the record player. "You're so pretty," he whispered in her ear, brushing back her soft cloud of hair with his big, warm hand. "I think I'm in love with you."

Kathi smiled her sweet smile and cuddled against his chest. Anne lowered the lights, and the Loreleis and their own dates danced or necked on the sofa or searched for places to be alone.

A current of electricity ran through the room as Butch was observed leading Kathi toward the stairs, an arm around her frail shoulders, the dangling hand lightly brushing against her small breasts.

"I can't stand it!" Francine exclaimed when they were out of sight. She jumped up from the sofa so suddenly her date, Chuck Metcalf, was startled. "It's actually working!"

"Where's Margie?" Vali asked, suppressing an excited giggle. "She's going to die."

But Margie was in the downstairs bedroom with Terry Anderson, busily assuring her continued popularity.

It was almost eleven when Butch came roaring down the stairs. "Goddammit, Francine!" he yelled. His face was red with anger. "I'll get you for this!"

Everyone jumped up.

"What's wrong?" Francine asked, suddenly frightened. "What happened?"

"That little girl you talked me into getting it on with. What do you think I am, anyway?"

"A sexy guy," Anne offered. She took a step toward him. "A guy no girl can resist."

"Well, you were wrong about one girl," he growled. He took some bills out of his wallet and threw them on the floor. "And you can keep your goddamn money!"

As he stomped toward the door, Francine caught up with him. "Wait a minute. You can't just leave like that. What happened?"

Butch turned and glowered at her. "I'll tell you what happened. I get her up there, and everything's all lovey-dovey, right?" Francine nodded. "So I kind of ease her back on the bed and start fooling around a little. Know what I mean?"

Vali and Barbara Jean exchanged glances.

"Then I pull my pants down and tell her to get undressed. And you know what she does?"

Francine took a breath. Her eyes were big as

saucers. "What?"

"She tells me she likes me and she'd fuck me if it wasn't for one thing."

Anne ventured to ask the question. "What was that?"

Butch looked as if he was about to have apoplexy. "She said she's going to become a nun!" He turned and stormed out, slamming the door behind him.

The Loreleis stood stock still for a moment, letting the words soak in. Then, when they dared to look at each other, they collapsed on the floor in hysterical giggles.

The next day, Anne found three glasses of unconsumed punch behind the potted ficus tree.

Margie was intrigued. She'd never known anyone who was a Catholic—let alone anyone who wanted to become a nun. When she was younger, Catholicism had frightened her a bit. The nuns in their awesome black habits had a forbidding look. She pitied the kids who had to be taught by them; she imagined them to be unsmiling and even a little cruel.

The Catholic population of Baxter consisted mostly of Mexicans, immigrants who had come over the border at Juarez to help out on the farms and oil fields in Texas and Oklahoma. Our Lady of Guadelupe, which was kitty-corner from John Ross High, was the first Catholic church to be built in Baxter. Later, as the town grew and a more affluent Catholic community sprang up, other, more elaborate houses of worship were built. But "Our Lady," with its purple-hued, stained-glass windows, its shining gold cross that reached heavenward and its young, good-looking Mexican-American priest, continued to be the solace of the poor, and passing it, Margie often wondered what mysterious things went on inside.

The next time she saw Kathi at the Crippled Children's Home, she asked her whether she attended Our Lady of Guadelupe. Kathi looked embarrassed.

"Well, actually, I haven't found a church here yet. In Wichita, I attended St. Mary." Her heart-shaped face seemed to glow. "It was so beautiful. The candles and the music . . . The altar was hung in dark red, and the whole place smelled of incense."

"Is it true you want to be a nun?" Margie asked bluntly. "Butch Furguson said—"

"Oh, Butch . . ." Kathi seemed very uncomfortable. "About that night at your party. . . ." She drifted off, unable to go on.

"Yeah, I'm sorry. I guess it was my fault. I thought you'd like him. I didn't realize . . ."

Kathi offered a weak smile. "I didn't tell you about my plans because . . . well, it's a very private thing. And you and the other Loreleis have so many boyfriends . . ."

"But," Margie probed, "don't you want to get married and have kids?"

"Being a nun *is* getting married. Nuns are the brides of Christ. Nothing could be more rewarding than that."

Margie thought about Kathi and her religion for a long time. She didn't want to do anything really sinful, naturally, but somehow she sensed that

Catholicism could be used against the irritating newcomer. Margie was Baptist herself. All the Loreleis were, except for Vali, whose family was Presbyterian, and Liz, who had recently declared herself an Agnostic. Although she had a vague belief in something called God and had attended Sunday School regularly since the age of four and a half, Margie was not very pious. She did not believe she would be struck dead if she uttered the Lord's name in vain, or if she occasionally delved into other religions in the name of research.

That's how, with a clear conscience, she was able to study witchcraft.

Ever since she'd seen Anne perform in a Little Theater production of *The Crucible*, Margie had been somewhat fascinated by the idea of putting hexes on people and flirting just a wee bit with the devil. The trouble was, she could never get anyone to take a crack at it with her. Now she saw a way.

"Remember the idea for the initiation I told you about?" she asked at the Lorelei meeting following Kathi's encounter with Butch Furguson.

"Yeah? What about it?" Francine was filing her nails as she listened.

"We're having a Black Mass."

"What?" Five heads popped up.

"Are you out of your mind?"

"How could we have a Black Mass?"

Barbara Jean and Francine giggled. Anne and Liz stared. Vali looked vaguely uncomfortable.

"Easy. I've got a book about it. All we need are candles, preferably black, a bunch of black robes, and an altar."

"Oh, very good," Anne scoffed. "Where are we going to get any of those things?"

"We can get candles anywhere. If they're not black, we can paint them or something. And they must have black robes at the church."

"What church?" Five voices asked the question almost in unison.

Margie shrugged. "Our Lady of Guadalupe. That's the altar we'll use."

"Are you crazy?" Anne demanded. "We can't walk into Our Lady of Guadalupe and use their altar for a Black Mass. They'd kick us out. Probably report us to the police."

"Not if they don't know." She paused. She knew she had them. "We'll do it at midnight. Or later, if necessary."

Silence swept over the room as everyone became thoughtful.

"How will we get in?" Barbara Jean asked.

Margie made a face at her. "Everyone knows Catholic churches are open all night in case someone wants to pray, or light a candle or something."

"But if they do . . ." Liz looked doubtful.

"Look, we'll do it on Halloween. That's the perfect time for a Black Mass, and no one will be in the church because it's a big night for the Mexicans. They call it the Night of the Dead. They stay home and make shrines with pictures of dead relatives." She grimaced. "They even put food in front of them in case any of them want to eat. Any of the *dead* people."

Again, the thoughtful silence. Then, with certainty:

"Kathi would never go along with it." Vali had issued the ultimate challenge.

Margie's answer was breezy and indisputable. "Then she won't get to be a Lorelei." She spoke more earnestly. "Look, it'll be like what we did with our proof of loyalty tests. Only, instead of going without a bra or wearing a dress from the Good Will, she'll undergo a Black Mass."

"But," Vali persisted, "isn't that against her religion?"

Margie smiled broadly. "You've got it."

Although none of the girls thought Kathi would really go along with such a thing, they agreed with Margie when she said they had to plan a Black Mass just in case. Armed with Margie's copy of *Witchcraft, Magic, and Sorcery*, which she had obtained from the public library, they set about creating the Black Mass of Black Masses.

There were peals of laughter as they read about the witches of the fourteenth century. "They actually thought they were making love to the devil!" Barbara Jean squealed, her eyes glued to a fairly explicit account of the goings on. "Only he used a phony cock, made of iron or horn!"

"Sometimes they did it with animals," Margie, who had read the book from beginning to end, volunteered.

"Barf!" declared Francine. "Forget about that!"

They carefully collected thirteen candles which were large enough in circumference to allow them to be placed around the required nine-foot circle without danger of tottering and falling over. They found a crucifix at a religious store in the Mexican section of town and hid it in Anne's basement until the big night. As a lark, they all attended mass at Our Lady of Guadelupe one Sunday and happily noted that the choir members wore long black robes. After the service, Margie, looking innocent, followed one singer to the back of the church and discovered the room where the robes were kept. Using *Witchcraft, Magic, and Sorcery* as their "bible," they painstakingly copied down things they would have to say in the course of the ceremony and traced pentagrams and hexagrams in order to become familiar with their designs.

Then came the moment of truth. *Would* Kathi go along? Because their victim seemed to have slightly more regard for Vali and Anne than for the others, those two were delegated to put the carrot in front of her too-sharp nose. They proceeded by inviting her for an after-school snack at Riley's, a less than perfect choice due to the fact that there was always a great deal of distraction at Riley's. Two Loreleis and a girl nobody knew seated in Vali's convertible attracted all kinds of attention, but between raucous greetings and polishing off their hamburgers-in-baskets, they managed to put forth the proposal.

"You know Lorelei is a club," Anne began, feeling slightly squeamish but determined not to let the others down. "We meet every Thursday after school."

"Oh, I know!" Kathi breathed, her eyes alight with the wonder of actually being seen with these two golden people. "Everybody at John Ross knows about the Loreleis."

"We were thinking we'd like to add another member," Vali went on, taking over for Anne. "Since it's our last year of school and everything."

Kathi looked at them wide-eyed, almost afraid to breathe.

"We wondered if you'd consider joining."

"Join the Loreleis? *Me?*"

Anne's stomach lurched. She was almost pathetic in her excitement.

"Since we've gotten to know you, we've . . . uh, really gotten to like you," Vali said, smiling her silvery smile. "You're so . . . uh . . . *good* and everything."

"But I can't begin to compare to the rest of you. I'm not pretty enough to be Homecoming Queen, or talented enough to be in a play. And I could never be a cheerleader, or—"

"Hey, don't worry about it," Anne interrupted. "We want you for yourself. Okay?"

Kathi gulped. "Okay. I guess." Her green eyes sparkled. "What do I do to join?"

"Well, you'll have to go through an initiation," Vali said coolly. "Naturally."

"Oh, naturally." Kathi nodded furiously. "Ummm . . . when?"

"We thought the last day of this month," Anne told her. "October thirty-first."

Kathi laughed. "That's Halloween."

"Uh, huh. It'll be fun." Vali wished they could pay their bill and leave. What they were doing seemed wrong to her somehow.

"So I should show up somewhere on Halloween? Like for party?"

Anne nodded. "Come to my house. You remember where it is." She paused. "The thing is, Halloween's on a Monday. Do your parents care if you stay out late on a week night?''

''I thought I told you. I live with my aunt and uncle.''

''Oh, right. Do they care?''

Kathi shrugged. ''I'll manage it.''

''Good.'' Anne smiled at her. ''Come to my house about ten o'clock, then. We'll take it from there.''

Kathi looked as if she would die of happiness.

On Halloween, they were all gathered in Anne's basement. Barbara Jean, Vali, Liz and Francine had told their parents Anne was having a slumber party in honor of the spooky night, and they had been allowed to attend after promising they would not stay up too late and would be at school on time Tuesday morning. Margie's parents had not been so accommodating, forcing Margie to crawl out her bedroom window after the house was quiet.

Barbara Jean had made cookies, and Anne had stirred up some punch in order to give the event a party atmosphere. They awaited Kathi's arrival anxiously.

''I don't know if we should go through with it,'' Liz said, biting her lip dubiously. ''What if we get caught?''

''Trust me,'' Margie urged confidently. ''I tell you no one will be there. Anyway, we can always lock the door to keep anyone from coming in.''

''I think it's a dirty trick,'' Anne said, finally giving voice to her private feelings about the matter. ''Kathi has no idea what she's getting into.''

''If she doesn't like it, she can lump it,'' Francine snapped. ''That's the whole point, anyway.''

"What if she goes through with it?" Vali asked. "Then we'll be stuck with her permanently."

"If she goes through with it, she deserves to be a member," Liz declared. "I, for one, will welcome her."

They quieted down as the doorbell pealed. Anne hurried upstairs to answer and came back leading Kathi by the hand. The frail-looking girl was wearing a frilly blue dress, appropriate for a party. Obviously, she hadn't held the Butch Furguson incident against them. She was game to put herself in their hands once again.

"Hi!" Margie called the greeting. "It's good to see you, Kath."

Kathi smiled and looked around. "Hi, everybody."

"Come in and have some cookies." Francine stepped forward holding the tray. "There's punch there, too."

Kathi looked confused. "Where's everyone else?" she asked.

"Everyone else? Like who?" Barbara Jean was dipping up the punch.

"I don't know. You all always seem to have boys around."

"Not tonight." Margie moved toward her and smiled. "Tonight's your initiation. Only Loreleis are allowed."

"Oh, yeah." Kathi swallowed. She was visibly nervous. "What . . . what do I have to do?"

"First, sit down and get comfortable." Vali patted the cushion next to her on the sofa.

Margie had spiked the punch ever so slightly. Just enough to get everyone relaxed. This time, Kathi accepted a glass and drank it down. When she had consumed a second, Francine announced it was time to get the initiation started.

"First, we blindfold you," she said, taking a silk scarf from her purse and dangling it in front of Kathi. "Okay?"

Kathi shrugged. "Sure. Go ahead." She grinned as Francine tied the scarf securely around her head, covering her eyes.

"Now," Barbara Jean said, "you have to drink some blood." She exchanged glances with the others. They all looked as if they were about to break into fits of giggles.

The "blood" was actually catsup doctored up with bitters. Kathi was given a small portion in a glass and told to drink it up. She downed it in one swallow, making a face at the end. The others watched, impressed.

"Now," Margie said, her excitement increasing, "you have to eat a worm." She brought forth the plate of cold spaghetti they had prepared. But before she gave it to Kathi, she looked boldly around and, when she was sure she had the others' attention, dropped a real, dead worm onto the plate.

"Ooooh!" Francine gasped. "How disgusting!"

Margie smiled and offered the plate. "Go ahead, Kathi. Pick one."

They watched, mesmerized, as Kathi's hand unfalteringly found the worm, snatched it up and gulped it down.

"I think I'm going to vomit," Liz whispered to Barbara Jean.

But Kathi was smiling triumphantly, unaware of

214

the distressed looks being exchanged. Margie was standing stock still, seemingly speechless. She hadn't expected Kathi to choose the real worm.

The stunned silence was eventually broken by Francine, who announced it was time to take Kathi on "a little excursion." The blindfold still intact, they guided her up the stairs and out to the driveway where Anne's father's Cadillac awaited. Anne's father was out of town on business.

Kathi was relaxed and in high spirits as they arrived at Our Lady of Guadelupe. Just as Margie had predicted, the church was empty of parishioners. A few candles burned, welcoming the potential worshipper, but their footsteps echoed hollowly on the bare wooden floor as they entered the foyer.

Kathi wrinkled her nose and sniffed. "Where are we? What's that smell?"

Barbara Jean was first with the answer. "We're in a church. Our Lady of Guadelupe."

Kathi stiffened. They waited for her to protest, but she said nothing, simply digested the fact. Determinedly they led her through the main part of the church, up to the altar. As she stood there uncertainly, Anne and Francine scrambled to set thirteen black candles in a nine-foot circle. Margie hurried back to the robe room and returned proudly bearing six black robes.

"I had a skeleton key with me," she announced, "but it wasn't even locked." She passed the robes around to the Loreleis.

"What's going on?" Kathi asked, her voice sounding faint and bewildered. "What's happening?"

Francine moved toward her. "We're preparing

your initiation. A Black Mass."

"A what?" Kathi looked frightened, even with her eyes covered by the blindfold.

"It's all right. We won't hurt you," Liz soothed. "Just take it easy."

"What . . . what am I supposed to do?"

"You have to get undressed," Margie told her matter-of-factly. She herself was wearing one of the long black robes.

"Undressed? You mean . . . everything?"

"It's how Black Masses are done," Barbara Jean explained. "It won't take if you're dressed."

"We're all girls here," Anne added, to give Kathi confidence. "There are no boys."

Kathi looked dubious. "You swear?"

"Swear to God." Margie held up her hand as if taking an oath. "Hope to die." She was clearly on the verge of laughter.

"You can refuse," Liz said bluntly. "You don't have to go through with it."

"But then I won't be a Lorelei." Kathi sounded wistful.

"No. Not if you're not initiated." Francine's voice was firm.

Kathi hesitated. She seemed to be weighing the pros and cons. Six pairs of eyes regarded her expectantly.

"Okay," she said finally. She fumbled with the buttons on her dress. "As long as there are no boys."

The Loreleis watched breathlessly as she stepped out of the blue dress and then methodically removed her slip, bra and panties. They looked away, embarrassed, as she stood naked in the center of the circle, the flames of the thirteen candles casting dancing shadows on her slender white body.

"Uh . . . what next?" Barbara Jean asked Margie. Everyone seemed too surprised to move.

Margie thought. "The symbols. We have to write them on her body." She found her purse, pulled out a lipstick, and gingerly stepped between the candles. "Kathi, there's sort of a table right next to you." She took the blindfolded girl's hand and led her to the altar table they had draped with black satin. The crucifix they'd bought was turned upside down behind it. "Can you climb up and lie down?"

Wordlessly, Kathi stretched out on the table. Margie, soon joined by Francine and Barbara Jean, began to draw hexagrams and pentagrams, together with certain other symbols they'd seen in their book, on her bare flesh. Their hands were shaking, but by the time they stepped back, Kathi looked rather like a tattooed lady they'd once seen at the county fair.

"I can't believe she's going through with it," Anne whispered to Vali.

"She wants to be a Lorelei," Vali replied, awed that entree to their circle could possibly be worth such degradation. The girls were beginning to perspire. The church was hot, particularly within range of the candle output.

"What are you going to do now?" Kathi asked tremulously. Her body seemed wracked with shudders. Still, she went gamely on.

"We have to conjure up the devil," Margie declared. "We're going to chant." She motioned to the others to gather round, and they all stepped into the circle.

"Eko, Eko, Azarak," they chanted, recalling the words they had memorized from *Witchcraft, Magic, and Sorcery.*

"Eko, Eko, Zamelak."

"What . . . what is that?" Kathi called out. "What are you doing?"

"Shhh! Be quiet!" Francine admonished her. "You're not supposed to talk."

"But this is spooky." Her voice was barely audible. "Please hurry and finish."

"Sau Thor Malcus Ve Geverah," the girls continued. They held hands and tried to avoid looking at Kathi, but they were all aware that she was shaking uncontrollably.

"I think we should stop," Liz said suddenly. "We've done enough."

"But we're not finished." Margie was annoyed. She looked at Liz impatiently.

"This is more than any of us went through," Liz replied, moving away from the others and toward Kathi. "She's had her initiation. She's a Lorelei now."

She stepped up to the altar and reached for Kathi's blindfold. The girl's head felt like a dead weight; it fell back against the table as Liz untied the knot.

"Hey! I think she's fainted." Liz's fingers pulled at the silk scarf.

"Quick! Get some water!" Vali directed the order to Margie and quickly joined Liz at the altar. Together, they pulled the scarf away.

Kathi's eyes were wide open. She was staring—at nothing.

"My God!" Vali gasped and stepped back.

"What is it? What's happened?" The others gathered round. Margie came flying in with a paper cup filled with water.

Liz took the scarf and dipped it in the water. Then she dabbed at Kathi's face. But the eyes still stared; the body seemed leaden, immobile.

"My God! She's dead!"

Barbara Jean stifled a scream. Francine began to cry. Margie froze in horror.

"She can't be." Anne took Kathi's hands and began to massage them. "She's ice cold," she said tonelessly.

"She's dead," Liz said again. "I'm sure of it."

"We'd better call a doctor." Vali started for the door.

"No. Wait." Liz stopped her. "If we call a doctor, we'll have to explain. Tell him what happened."

"But she—" Vali swallowed the word, nearly choking on it.

"She's beyond help. There's nothing we can do."

"What about artificial resuscitation?" asked Barbara Jean. "I took a life guard test once, and—"

"It won't do any good. Her heart's stopped. There's no pulse." Liz stepped aside. "See for yourself."

Barbara Jean remained where she was.

"Liz is right," Francine declared. "If we tell, they'll say we murdered her."

"But we can't just leave her here. Like this." Anne gestured to the candles and the writing on Kathi's skin.

"Barbara Jean. Anne"—Liz was snapping orders —"blow out the candles and get them out of here.

Francine. Vali. Help me get this lipstick off her. Margie, you take the robes back where you found them.''

They sprang into action. Removing the lipstick was the hardest. The harder they scrubbed, the more it seemed to streak and run. At last, they succeeded in removing most of it, all except for a tiny horseshoe-shaped spot on her left shoulder.

''This won't come off,'' Francine said, rubbing at the spot desperately.

''We've got to get out of here,'' Vali announced. ''It's almost two o'clock!''

''All right, leave it,'' Liz told them. ''We did the best we could. Let's get her into her clothes.''

With great effort and much despair, they dressed her and carried her outside, through the church's back door.

''What'll we do with her?'' Vali whispered. She shivered. The night had turned cold.

''Just put her down.'' Liz pointed to a grassy spot near a flower bed. ''They'll find her in the morning.''

''Are you sure?'' Francine looked doubtful.

''What else is there to do? Unless we turn ourselves in.''

''No!'' The others, who had followed them outside, joined in the frantic chorus. Kathi was gingerly laid on the grass, after which the Loreleis turned away, most of them finally giving vent to the tears of panic that had been rising for the past hour.

They saw the car as soon as they pulled up in front of the Eastman house. Kathi had driven her dark blue

Mercury over earlier and left it there. They had gone to the church in Anne's father's car.

"We can't leave it here," Liz said, forcing herself to think clearly. "They'll know she was here."

"But what can we do about it? We can't take it to her aunt's house. There'll be all kinds of questions." Margie's eyes were huge with fear.

Francine's voice was controlled and definite. "We'll have to take it back to the church."

"No! We can't go back. What if someone's there? What if they've found her?" Barbara Jean was beginning to tremble violently.

"No one will be there. Not at this hour." Liz checked her watch. It was 2:45. "Francine's right. We have to take the car to the church."

No one wanted to drive Kathi's car. In the end, they drew straws. Vali and Margie drove the Mercury to the church. Barbara Jean, Liz, Francine and Anne followed and brought them back.

Later, huddled together in Anne's basement, they took the oath.

"We, the Loreleis of John Ross High School, solemnly swear that we will never reveal what happened to Kathi Harcort, that we will guard the secret unto death."

Their eyes darted from one to the other. The carefree days were gone.

Miss Winters broke the news to them herself. Dabbing at red-rimmed eyes with a tissue, she explained how Kathi Harcort had been found outside Our Lady of Guadelupe Church by a janitor coming to work on Tuesday morning, the first day of November.

"She had obviously gone there to pray," Miss Winters said softly, shaking her head at the unfairness of it all.

"What did she die of?" Liz asked. The others looked at her, amazed that she could ask such a question in such an innocent-sounding way.

"We don't know for sure." Miss Winters sniffed and straightened her shoulders. "Apparently her heart simply stopped."

The Loreleis twisted their hands on their laps. None dared to catch the other's eye.

"It's a terrible loss. Dreadful. And I know how you girls must feel."

"Yes," Vali replied in a choked voice. "It's hard for us to believe she's really gone."

"I'll tell you this." Miss Winters forced a faint smile. "The six of you made Kathi's last days very happy. Only last week she came to me and told me what a difference you'd made in her life." She sighed. "Poor child. She wanted so much to be accepted here at John Ross."

"Well, she was certainly accepted by us," Anne volunteered. "We liked her very much."

"Yes, I'm very proud of myself for introducing her to you girls. It's obvious the friendship was beneficial to all. You . . . ah . . . Loreleis," she paused as if the name caused a bad taste in her mouth, "have set a fine example for the whole school with your charitable and civic work. I do hope you won't let this tragedy affect that."

"Ummmm . . ." Francine was trying to form a thought. "The thing is, the Loreleis won't be the same without Kathi. With her gone, there doesn't

seem to be much point in our continuing as a club."
She bit her lip and glanced quickly at the others.

"That's true," Barbara Jean put in, nodding her blond head vigorously. "I think I'm speaking for everyone when we say we don't have the heart to go on."

"Well, of course that's up to you." Miss Winters looked at her warmly. "But I want you to know that if you decide to continue as a club, you will have my support."

"Thank you." Barbara Jean looked apologetic. "May we be excused now?"

"Yes, certainly." Miss Winters rose. "Thank you for being so brave. I'm sorry to have been the bearer of such terrible news."

That night in Anne's basement, the Loreleis tossed their silver pins on the game table.

"What shall we do with them?" Anne asked, fingering her lady on the rock for the last time.

"What difference does it make?" Liz asked sharply. "I never want to be reminded of the Loreleis again."

Margie looked at the small pile of pins wistfully. She wondered if it would ever be possible to forget.

Chapter Twelve

Jerry was worried. Margie had been acting strange since the commencement of reunion week, and now Francine had called and said she hadn't shown up for rehearsal. He tried to think what might have happened to her. Since her upset stomach two days ago, she had seemed in good physical shape. Mentally, though, he wasn't so sure. She seemed a bit on edge a good deal of the time; she was having trouble sleeping, and at times Jerry thought her voice seemed unnaturally high and trembly.

He knew she'd been worried that the Loreleis would find out about those two years in the mental hospital. Although she'd been released over twenty years ago and had lived a perfectly normal life since, she was still bothered by the fact that she had had a nervous breakdown.

Jerry hadn't known her at the time of the breakdown. He'd met her after she returned home and hadn't even suspected she'd had a problem until he asked her to marry him. Then she'd told him everything, explaining it was only fair that he knew and assuring him she would understand if he decided he didn't want to marry her after all. But Jerry never once considered backing out. He'd fallen in love with the Margie he knew; as far as he was concerned, the past was over and done with. He hadn't even questioned her about what had caused the breakdown. He had received the impression it had had something to do with the girl who died, and he supposed the death of a friend could cause a young girl to go off her rocker for a while. But the fact was, she'd been cured, and in the many years they'd been married she'd carried out her duties as wife and mother with easy assurance and loving dedication.

But where was she now? She'd never been particularly enthusiastic about being in the Loreleis' dance number, but once she'd agreed, she'd seemed determined to do her best. It didn't figure that she'd just decided to chuck the whole thing and not bother to tell anyone.

Jerry pursed his lips, a facial expression he often fell into when he was thinking hard. It was too early to be worried, he reflected. Francine had only just phoned. And yet . . .

He picked up the phone and called his mother-in-law. Margie often stopped by her folks' house to say hello when she was driving around town doing chores.

Ellen Richey's greeting was warm. She considered Jerry the perfect husband for her somewhat fragile daughter.

"Jerry, do you know I was just thinking about you? I just took a homemade lemon meringue pie out of the oven, and I said to myself, 'I wish Jerry was here to have a piece of this.' Do you have time to come over and pick it up?"

"No, Mom, I'm sorry. Not today." He cleared his throat. "Actually, I was looking for Margie. Is she there with you, by any chance?"

"Margie? At this hour? I haven't seen her all week." She paused and her voice took on a worried note. "Nothing's wrong, is it, Jerry?"

"No, Mom, nothing. I just wanted to talk to her for a minute."

"Well, I don't know for sure, but you might try that Miss Virginia's dance studio. She's been spending a lot of time there with her friends this week."

Jerry stifled a sigh. "Yeah, Mom, good idea. I'll try that."

He hung up frowning and dialed the house again. Brian answered.

"Oh, hi, Dad. You looking for Mom, too?"

"Why, son? Did someone else call?"

"Just that Mrs. Brookfield, Mom's friend. I told her I just got home from swimming, and I didn't know where she was."

"Yeah? You have a good practice?"

"I beat Bobby Wilson by fifteen seconds!"

"Hey! Great. We'll talk about it when I get home. If your mother comes in, have her give me a ring, okay?"

"Sure, Dad. 'Bye."

He couldn't think where else to call. The hospitals? Could she have been in an accident? But if she had, wouldn't the hospital call him? His name and number at the store were on the I.D. card in her purse.

He finally decided to call Dr. Feinstein, although Margie had been furious when he'd set up the appointment with him for her yesterday. She was adamant about keeping her occasional need to talk to a psychiatrist separate from her family. The doctor took his call right away and sounded a little disturbed when he heard his patient had missed rehearsal.

"She seemed a little nervous when she came to see me yesterday, but I didn't think anything was seriously wrong," he said thoughtfully.

"I didn't think so, either," Jerry told him. "She was just losing a little sleep."

"I gave her a prescription for that. I also told her, her anxieties about her reunion were perfectly normal. She seemed to accept that."

"She didn't say anything to indicate she was thinking of . . . doing something? Going away, or—" He broke off.

A pause. "No," the doctor answered slowly. "Nothing."

Jerry nodded, the phone still in his hand. "Well, thank you, Doctor. I was just checking."

"Mr. Middleton." Dr. Feinstein stopped him before he could hang up.

"Yes?"

"When you find her, have her give me a call, will you? I'd like to know how she is."

"Yes, Doctor. Will do." He replaced the receiver in its cradle.

He had the urge to get in the car and drive around and look for her, but he knew it would be useless. Baxter was a big town now, almost a city. She could be anywhere. He decided the best thing to do was get back to work. She would surely turn up. Work would keep him from worrying until she did.

The call from the Baxter Police Department came at 4:37.

"Jerry Middleton? Sergeant Harry Andrews here. We have your wife at the South Main Station. Think you could come down and pick her up?"

"She's at the police station? What happened?"

"Oh, nothing much. She's not under arrest, if that's what you're worried about. We picked her up because she seemed a little . . . disturbed."

"Disturbed? How do you mean?"

"One of our men picked her up over on South Lewis. She was wandering around like she was in a daze. Said she was looking for the Crippled Children's Home."

Jerry frowned. "You're kidding."

"One of the officers here remembers the place. It was torn down twenty years ago."

Je-sus. Jerry didn't know what to think. "I guess she was just confused. If you'll keep her there, I'll come right down."

"There's just one more thing," Andrews told him.

"What's that?"

"We found your name in your wife's purse. Her name, too. Marjorie Middleton, isn't it?"

"Yes, that's right. Why?"

"She have dark red hair and sort of greenish eyes?"

Jerry felt a prickle of apprehension. "Yes. But I don't—"

"Your wife may be more confused than you think," Andrews said. "She told us her name was Kathi Harcort."

*   *   *

Anne was wearing less makeup than she usually wore on camera, and she was dressed in a casual slack outfit that was cut to show off her still-good figure but not tight enough to look cheap.

"And how does it feel to be back in the old home town?" Joe-Dean Farber asked. They were sitting in comfortable chairs facing each other in the studio's "living room" set.

"Terrific. Even more fun than I expected." Anne smiled, displaying her perfect white teeth.

"I suppose your old high school classmates are pretty impressed to have you in their midst. Movie star and all that."

Anne gave a modest shrug. "I don't know why they should be impressed. I don't consider myself a movie star. I'm just an actress trying to make a living."

They briefly discussed the films and plays in which she had appeared, Joe-Dean asking the usual, unimaginative questions, and Anne making her "featured" roles sound as important as possible.

"Anything we can look forward to seeing you in, in the near future?" Joe-Dean asked. He had a whimsical, Pinnochio-type face, with a large, irregular-shaped nose, dark eyes set too close together, and a funny, lopsided smile.

"Well," Anne hedged. "There are several things brewing. I'm superstitious about talking about things before they happen, though." She grinned. "Let's just say I'm very hopeful."

"Any advice for Baxter's young people who might be aspiring to follow in your illustrious footsteps? I'm sure they'd be grateful for it."

Anne cocked her head as if to give it a moment's thought. "Work hard. Study. Persevere. Don't ever give up."

"Hmmm." Joe-Dean nodded at her appreciatively. "Sounds good to me." He turned to face the camera full on. "Well, that's it, then, kids. You have advice from an expert. Thank you, Anne Eastman, for taking time out to chat with us this morning. We wish you the best of luck with your career. And have a wonderful time at your reunion."

"Thank you, Joe-Dean. I enjoyed it." She smiled again, and the camera returned to the host. During the commercial break, Anne was motioned off the set, profusely thanked by the show director, and sent on her way. The car and driver that had been sent to fetch her from the Lancelot was waiting to take her back.

Sitting in the back seat, the driver either too intimidated or too uninterested to attempt conversation, she felt deflated. The interview had been hurried and poorly conducted. She had felt at a disadvantage the entire time she was on camera.

For that she had let Joe-Dean fuck her?

When the car deposited her at the hotel, she went straight up to her room and stretched out on her bed without even removing the spread. Arms folded behind her head, she stared at the ceiling. Why had she even bothered with any of it? Why the frantic calling of the newspaper reporter in Tulsa; why the fierce determination to get one lousy television spot here in Baxter? Was she so insecure she couldn't attend her high school reunion without trying to make it a media event?

Damn right she was. She closed her eyes as if to block the discovery. But it was there. Why? Why this need to call attention to herself, to her accomplishments? Deep down, she knew if she'd been a *real* celebrity, she'd have preferred to sneak into town and *avoid* publicity, and she hated herself for not using that approach. But something inside her cried out to be noticed; somehow it was always her number one priority.

Maybe, she decided, it had something to do with what had happened with her father. Maybe it had to do with things that had happened after that, after she'd left home and struck out to set the world cn fire? Northwestern? Those seemed like pretty conventional years. She'd enjoyed campus life and had had the opportunity to study with one of the best drama teachers in the country. She'd snagged some good roles there, too, roles she knew she'd done well in.

New York? Maybe *that* was where it had started. From John Ross to Northwestern to New York. Between those three points, there had been worlds to conquer. Making her mark in high school and college had been fairly easy. But New York. That had been different.

Manhattan, when she got there, was overflowing with aspiring actresses. They poured out of the subway exit at Forty-fifth and Broadway clutching their black zippered portfolios which held their precious photos, resumés and, if they were lucky, press clippings. They made the rounds of casting offices, trudging the streets in high heels and their best dresses or suits. When Anne thought of today's actors, running around in jeans and t-shirts, she was amazed.

She had—like thousands of young women before her—moved into the Barbizon, a carefully supervised hotel for women pursuing a career in the big, bad city. How naive she was then. And how moral! The first time a producer made a pass at her, she had told him off and marched indignantly from his office. There would be no casting couch route for her, not Anne Eastman, who was an *actress,* not an aspiring starlet!

Fortunately, she was a good actress, and she got her first job through strictly legitimate channels. It was a recurring role on a television soap opera, and it paid very good money. At the time, however, soaps didn't enjoy the public acclaim they later achieved, and many "theater people" considered appearing in one something of a comedown. Anne felt that way, too, but she couldn't pass up the money. So she emoted her way through her character's trials and tribulations and used her days off to look for a "real" job.

Ironically, it was the soap opera that got her, her first movie. Antonio De Benedetto, the "new wave" director of the sixties, was looking for a young, unknown American actress to play the lead in an art film he was making in Italy. He happened to spot Anne when he came home early one day and found his wife watching *Love of Life.* Her smoldering good looks and intense way of acting arrested him, and he called the studio and made an appointment with her. When he saw her in person, he was as impressed as he had been when he saw her on television; even more so when she did not take kindly to the advance he routinely made toward attractive women. He gave her the role, and Anne went to Italy.

The picture was low-budget and did not have popular appeal, but it was highly acclaimed in the world of the art film and went on to win a series of awards at the Cannes Film Festival. While Anne's notices were all good, she did not find herself besieged with other offers once the film was released. Still, she had done something prestigious, and she had no desire to go back to doing soap opera. Instead of returning to New York, she went to London and applied for acceptance at the Royal Academy of Dramatic Arts. Once again, her phenomenal luck held. One of the judges observing her audition scene was directing a play in London's West End and decided on the spot that she was perfect for one of the parts. This time it wasn't the lead, only a small role, but Anne eagerly accepted. The Royal Academy could wait a while longer.

It was in the play that she met Geoffrey. His role was considerably larger than hers, and he was considered one of the rising young stars of British theater. His perfect, chiseled features, tall, elegant carriage and wonderful, resonant voice would soon qualify him as a genuine matinee idol. Until London, Anne had had practically no romance in her life. Her early experience with her father had left her emotionally scarred; sex was something with which she was extremely uncomfortable. There had been men she'd found attractive, and she enjoyed dating and male companionship; but as soon as a relationship threatened to become physical, she found herself withdrawing and eventually discouraging the man in question so that he stopped seeking her out.

With Geoffrey, it was different. From the moment they met, they seemed to form an instant bond. Anne adored Geoff's clipped British accent and wry, droll sense of humor. They took to having late suppers together after performances and could sit for hours in bistros or coffee shops discussing their respective careers, dreams and ambitions. They began spending their Sundays together, Geoffrey showing Anne all the famous London sights. Hand in hand, they listened to the speakers in Hyde Park, watched the changing of the guard at Buckingham Palace, and took pictures of each other at the spot in the Tower of London where Anne Boleyn lost her head.

Between the time they spent at the theater and their leisure activities, they seemed to be together more than they were apart. To Anne, it seemed as if a miracle had happened. This wonderful, talented, incredibly handsome man had chosen *her* for his constant companion. Once or twice she got up the nerve to ask him about the other women in his life, but he had merely smiled and said, "There was never anyone like you, Annie, luv." She had had to be content with that.

It was obvious to her that he really cared for her and wasn't simply using her. During the months of what Anne could only think of as their courtship, Geoff was never less than a gentleman. Soft, warm goodnight kisses at the door of her flat were all he demanded, although he would occasionally look at her in a wry way and murmur, "Better watch it, Annie, luv. A girl could get in trouble causing a man to feel this way." As Anne fell more and more in love with him, her inhibitions about sex vanished, and his gentlemanly goodbyes left her frustrated and filled with desire. One Sunday evening, after a romantic excursion to Hampton Court, she enticed him into her flat and all but threw herself at him. His response was to cradle her in his arms and murmur that he could never compromise her or involve her in anything she might regret later.

"But, I *won't* regret it," she had assured him, snuggling against his strong, trim chest. "If you're afraid I'll insist on marriage—"

She broke off, and he cupped her face in his hand and looked at her intently. "But that's just what you *should* insist on, Annie, luv," he told her gently. "You're not like any actress I've ever known. You're not the type to have an affair with every leading man."

"Geoffrey, you're not 'every leading man.' You're you, and I adore you." She faced him, embarrassed. "If you want the truth, I'm in love with you."

"Oh, Annie!" He had laughed joyously and cradled her in his arms. "Annie, Annie, do you mean it? Is it possible that we feel the same way about each other?"

"The same way? Geoff! Oh, Geoff, are you saying you love me, too?"

Again, the wonderful, melodious laugh. "Yes, my darling, that's exactly what I'm saying. And, if you'll have me, I think we should get married right away."

They celebrated by opening a bottle of champagne Anne had received on opening night and fell asleep on the sofa in each other's arms. When they awoke, both still dressed, Geoffrey realized he was late for an appointment and went tearing out, promising they would discuss wedding plans after that night's performance.

When Anne confided their plans to Winne Roberts, the actress with whom she shared a dressing room, Winne looked at her in surprise. Instead of congratulating her, she said bluntly, "Oh, Annie, are you sure? Marriage to a man like Geoffrey?"

Anne knew Geoff's good looks would always make him prey for beautiful women, but it didn't matter. He had proven himself loyal and honorable, and she had no intention of being a jealous wife. "Yes!" she told Winne happily. "I'm very sure. Geoff's all I want in this world."

They were married in a small chapel near Covent Garden and celebrated afterward at a small, private dinner at Rule's, their favorite restaurant and a hangout for the theater crowd. Anne was deliriously happy. Goeff held her hand tight all through the afternoon and evening, and when they went back to her flat—they were in the process of looking for a bigger one—they drank a private toast to their future.

The marriage was consummated that night, and if Anne's newly inflamed desires were not entirely sated, at least she was not left with the sense of longing she had experienced up until now. Geoff made love to her in a slow, languid way, his long, lean body moving rhythmically to the final climax. It was not rockets and fireworks, but it was loving and warm; and since Anne's only other experience with sex had been so shameful, it seemed good and clean and right.

Soon after the wedding, Geoff decided to leave the play and accept an offer from Stratford-On-Avon. "It's the right move, Annie," he said as they discussed the decision over one of Anne's good, American breakfasts. "I've been seen in the West End. Now I have to polish my Shakespearean technique. I want a spot with the Old Vic one of these days."

Anne frowned thoughtfully. She was reluctant to say, "But what about *me?*" Geoff's reasoning in his own case was probably correct, but Stratford-On-Avon had not come knocking at *her* door. How could she make a case for togetherness without seeming selfish?

Geoff seemed to read her thoughts. "You stay here and finish out the run. They'll have to close in two or three months' time; business is wearing thin. Then you can join me at Stratford, and we'll see if we can't get something for you there. All right, luv?"

Anne sighed. What choice did she have? Even though her role in the play was small, it had proven a wonderful opportunity for her. Not many American actresses were seen in the West End these days. And Stratford-On-Avon was not really so far away. She could run down to see Geoff every Sunday. She knew he was right about the play's future, too. The theater was only about half full most nights.

"All right, darling," she agreed. "I'll miss you, but I know we have to make these sacrifices."

"Good girl." He leaned across the table and kissed her. "Annie, there's no limit to how far we can go in this business. You'll see."

Geoffrey's attitude toward their respective careers gave Anne another reason to love him. Unlike many actors she'd met, he was not so conceited as to insist on being the "star" of the family. He obviously felt there was room for both of them in the theatrical world, and he had as much faith in her talent as he had in his own. The discussion ended on a positive note, and Anne vowed to work harder than ever on her English accent so she wouldn't stick out like a sore thumb at Stratford.

Handling Geoff's absence was not really so hard. Anne kept busy with the play and decorating the new flat they'd managed to find, and she enjoyed her Sunday excursions to visit her husband. The actors at Stratford-On-Avon instantly accepted her into their circle, and she always returned to London with a warm feeling of camaraderie, something she hadn't experienced since the disbanding of the Loreleis six years before.

Geoff proved right about her play. Only three weeks after his departure, the closing notice was pasted up backstage. Anne was sorry to see it come to an end, but she looked forward to being a full-time wife again. They had decided to sublet the flat since they expected to be in Stratford at least six months, so Anne told Geoff she would see to it and join him as soon as all the details were taken care of. She succeeded in wrapping things up a little ahead of schedule and headed for Stratford one Wednesday afternoon with three heavy suitcases and a light, excited heart. Geoff wouldn't be expecting her as early as this, and the thought made her smile. She could imagine his delighted reaction to an unexpectedly early reunion.

She took a taxi from the train to the theatrical boarding house where Geoff was staying. The concierge knew her by now and greeted her enthusiastically as the cabbie helped her in with her suitcases.

"Ah, Mrs. Redding," he said, giving her a friendly, gap-toothed smile. "It looks like y'er 'ere to stay."

Anne smiled back. "Yes. Finally." She paid the driver. "Is my husband in?"

"To tell you the truth, I don't know. Just got on duty, I did." He checked the key slot and found Geoff's missing. "Looks like he's there, all right. Shall I give 'im a quick ring and tell 'im y'er on y'er way up?"

"Oh, no, please don't do that. I'd like to surprise him. I'll just leave my things down here, and you can send them up later. All right?"

"Right you are, missus. And welcome again to ye."

Anne took the rickety lift to the third floor and ran lightly down the hall to room three-o-five. Barely able to contain her excitement, she threw open the door and burst inside.

Geoff was lying facedown in bed, totally naked, his beautiful body moving in languid rhythm over the body beneath him. Soft moans were coming from both participants in what was obviously a pleasurable activity; neither heard the swoosh of the opening door or the gasp from Anne as she stood staring at them in horror.

No. Oh, God, Geoff, no! Her panicked thoughts were actually a silent prayer. She couldn't believe this was happening. Another woman—and their marriage not six months old! She wondered wildly if she could have gotten the wrong room, opened the wrong door.

But it was Geoff, and when her mind accepted the fact, she couldn't contain her fury. "Bastard!" she shouted, flying at him, hitting him with her fists.

Two screams answered her cry. Geoff rolled over to avoid her blows, and his companion, also lying

239

facedown, became fully visible. Through a blur of tears Anne saw a shining cap of blond hair, a delicate, tapered back, a small round ass, and well-developed legs covered with dark blond fuzz.

"Je-zuz, Geoff!" a nasal, effeminate voice complained as the person in question raised up and looked at Anne. "Who the hell is that?"

Oh, dear God, please. No. Please. Not a man. Anything but that. Anne felt faint. She had to reach out and put a hand on the bureau to steady herself. Geoff had leaped from the bed and was wrapping a towel around his waist. "Annie . . . luv . . . Annie, let me explain." He reached out to touch her, but she shrank away. The young man on the bed was sitting up now. He seemed barely out of his teens, a beautiful boy with big blue eyes and soft, pink and white skin.

"Tommy, get out of here, for God's sake," Geoff hissed at him. "Get your clothes and get out."

"Well, I like that!" the boy retorted indignantly. "I was here *first*, after all!"

If it hadn't been so tragic, Anne would have laughed. A farce, straight out of the theater. Wife catches husband with his beautiful young lover. Only the lover turns out to be another man!

"Anne? Are you all right? Sit down, love, and let me get you something to drink."

Anne sat. She accepted the brandy he splashed into a tumbler and drank it straight down. It gave her strength. When she was controlled enough to speak, she turned to him. "How long has this been going on?" Her voice was cold. To her ears, it sounded as if a person other than herself was speaking.

He swallowed. "Will you believe me if I say I love you?"

"How long?" She glared at him.

A moment's hesitation. Then: "All my life, Annie. I'm homosexual."

She felt the rage rising in her again. "No kidding?" she retorted sarcastically. "Who would have guessed?"

He dropped to the floor on his knees next to her chair and studied the mud-colored carpet. "I'm sorry."

"But how could you—?" She broke off. It was useless, discussing it impossible. She rose and put her glass on the bureau.

"Where are you going?"

"Right now, to another hotel. The flat's been sublet." She offered a cold, ironic smile. "I'll figure out the rest tomorrow."

"You have to give me a chance to explain. Please, Annie."

"Would explaining change anything? Turn you into a . . . real man?"

He winced under the verbal blow. "No," he said sadly. "I suppose it wouldn't. But it might help you to understand."

"I don't want to understand! I want my husband back. I want *us* back. The way we were before." She unexpectedly burst into tears. "Oh, God, Geoff!"

He rushed to put his arms around her, and she sobbed into his bare chest.

"I'm sorry, Annie. I didn't think. Oh, Lord, what have I done to you?"

When she was in control again, she turned her face

to his. "Why, Geoff? Why did you take up with me in the first place? Why, in God's name, did you *marry* me?"

His eyes were gentle, earnest. "Because I thought—still think—you were wonderful. We became such good friends, Annie. We had so much in common, so many hopes and dreams. I couldn't imagine sharing my life with anyone but you."

"But you're gay. You admit it. What about your . . . friends?"

He sighed. "They have nothing to do with you. Or with us. To tell you the truth, I thought you knew."

"Are you out of your mind? Would I have married you, *knowing?*" She remembered Winne's reaction when she'd told her they were engaged. She'd misinterpreted her meaning. She wondered if the whole cast had known.

"Women have been known to accept it. Some of our greatest actors, some of your greatest American film heroes have been homosexual."

She shook her head. She felt numb. "Geoff, I can't talk about it anymore. I'm in shock, and all I want is to be left alone."

He nodded understandingly. "Suppose I arrange for a room at the King's Arms. I'll help you get your things over."

She spent one night at the King's Arms. The next day she was on her way back to New York, her marriage—and her life—in shambles.

In retrospect, she supposed her need for attention stemmed from that night in Stratford-On-Avon, although at first she was conscious only of a need to keep the pain away. She plunged back into her areer, accepting any decent role, small or large, that was offered. She'd done well over the years. She just hadn't done well enough. Featured roles in films, leads in TV series that failed, second leads off (and occasionally on) Broadway paid the bills, but never established her as a bona fide star. She studied singing and put together a respectable nightclub act, but it was considered "pleasant," never "great."

On her thirtieth birthday, the first doubts about ever really making it set in. When she reached thirty-five, she was on the verge of panic. She began engaging in indiscriminate and meaningless affairs, attempting to prove to herself over and over that men still considered her attractive. By the time she was forty, she was using sex to secure jobs, sometimes even to secure interviews. Was it any wonder, she asked herself, that she wanted to bring to her high school reunion something to show for all those years of hard work, all the humiliating moments of her self-imposed degradation? She may not have made it to the top in New York or Hollywood, but here in Baxter, for seven short days, she could be a star.

Couldn't she?

She rose from the bed. The self-disgust she'd felt every day for as long she could remember, clung to her like a second skin. She wished she'd never come back to Baxter, never put herself in the position of having to prove herself once again. But she *had* come, and it was too late to back out. She brushed her hair back from her face with a weary hand and reached for the telephone. What the hell. She would call her friends and see who was free for dinner.

243

Chapter Thirteen

Vali switched off the *Baxter Eye Witness News*. The special interest piece about the county fair had come off well. Donald's interviews and commentary had brought out the full flavor of the fair: the simple, homespun aspects in his coverage of the baking and knitting, the color and excitement when he moved on to the bustling midway.

As on the night of the taping, she was struck by his professionalism, the ease with which he did his job. His parents had been disappointed when he'd chosen to go into journalism instead of business. She wondered what they thought of him now.

She sank down on her bed and wrestled with the impulse she'd had since the newscast had begun. She'd told him when he'd brought her back on Sunday that she wouldn't be seeing him again. She'd made the decision knowing it was in his best interest as well as her own. Now it was Thursday, and the fact was, she was sorry. She had thought about him all week, couldn't get her mind off the way his hazel eyes had looked at her, the old easy smile she remembered so well, the general feeling of well-being she'd had when his big, warm body was close to hers.

All the more reason not to see him, her cautionary inner voice told her. *There's such a thing as liking something too much. Especially when that something is the wrong person.*

But he's my ex-husband, she argued back. The father of my two children. What's wrong with seeing him while I'm here in town?

She knew what was wrong with it. The children were virtually grown now; she didn't need to spend time with him because of them. And there was Chase. Chase was her husband now.

She hadn't dared call her mother, but she knew Tori would be understanding. She received an instant invitation to come to the Coopers' Manhattan townhouse for as long as necessary. Tori even called the airline and arranged the tickets for her. Once in New York, it had simply been a matter of moving the kids into the nursery with Tori's four-year-old and sinking into the luxury of living in a beautiful home with servants to do her bidding. Soon her figure was trim and firm again, her hair glossy, and her face as pretty as ever. And if her heart felt as weary as she herself had felt in California, she was the only one who knew.

Donald begged her to come back. He took the blame for everything, cited his own stupidity for causing the problem, but Vali knew he had been driven to another woman's arms because of her selfishness and self-pity.

"I love you, Vali," Donald had told her. "If you'll

245

come back, I'll give up this whole idea. We'll go to Oklahoma; I'll get a newspaper job the way we planned. Things aren't so expensive there. We can make it; I know we can."

Vali thought of Donald's beautiful hazel eyes and the way his arms felt when he put them around her at night, before they went to sleep. She thought of his warmth and ambition and of the plans they had made and the dreams they had dreamed.

"I'm going back," she told Tori one night, as the sisters sat in the living room enjoying a glass of Harvey's Bristol Creme.

"You've got to be kidding!" Tori erupted. "Vali, the man was *unfaithful* to you! He screwed another woman! You can't go back to him after that!"

"But it was my fault as much as his. I wasn't a good wife. I didn't make time for him. I was too busy with the kids . . ."

Tori called in another force: their mother. "Darling, the man's a failure," Mrs. Farrow said, shaking her head sympathetically. "He'll never amount to anything. You can't spend the rest of your life being a slave to a man like that. You aren't prepared for it. You've never known anything but privilege."

Vali told Donald she needed time. She had some thinking to do. Donald, wounded, yelled at her and hung up the phone. He didn't try to contact her again, in fact he wrote a crisp note in which he said divorce was probably the best solution.

Chase was there to help her pick up the pieces. Chase, who cheered her up by taking her to Twenty One for lunch and Le Pavillion for dinner. Chase, who escorted her to the theater and kept her out dancing at El Morocco till two o'clock in the morning. Chase, who brought her flowers and played with her kids and told her she was beautiful. Chase, who finally asked her to marry him and who put a nine-carat diamond on her finger almost before she knew what was happening. By the time she learned about the deceit—her mother's phone call to Donald informing him Vali was involved with someone else—and the attempted "financial settlement," which Donald refused to accept, she was Mrs. Chase Thomas.

Chase has been good to me, Vali thought as she snapped the clasp on her pearls and smoothed her simple little St. Laurent dress. He's been good *for* me. Once she had agreed to marry him, she had moved forward on a tide of approval and urging from her family. The wedding had been a chic, Park Avenue affair, and the handsome groom and beautiful bride had moved to Connecticut, from which the groom commuted to his office on Wall Street. Vali had thrown herself into the life of the young society matron, getting involved in various charities, lunching daily at the country club, making sure her kids attended the right schools and had the right friends, until she got so bored she had taken up flying and gone into business.

Still, it was an exciting, fulfilling life, and she had not allowed herself to look back on those frustrating, exhausting days from which she had escaped. That is, not until now.

She rose from the bed, walked into the bathroom and looked at herself in the mirror.

"Valerie Thomas," she said aloud, "tonight's the

last night before the reunion begins. You aren't going to get another chance. Whatever you do, you'd better do it and get it over with."

Nodding to herself firmly, she whirled around and marched purposefully to the telephone.

Donald answered on the third ring. Vali took a deep breath and plunged in.

"Hi. It's me. Miss Baxter County Fair."

His voice sounded surprised, but cautious.

"Hi."

"I saw the newscast. It was great."

"Thanks." He waited for her to continue.

Vali hesitated. The hand holding the receiver was trembling slightly. "What are you up to tonight?"

"Nothing special." Again, the excruciating silence.

"Have you had dinner?"

"No. Not yet."

"Good." Vali's voice was stronger now. Brighter. "Just stay right there."

"I don't understand."

"You will. Can you hold off for an hour or so? Before you eat, I mean?"

"Sure, but—"

"Then just stay where you are. And don't ask any more questions."

She hung up the phone with a feeling of triumph. There. She had taken the first step.

She arrived at his expensive and ultra modern condominium forty-five minutes later, her arms weighed down with grocery bags. Donald grinned when he saw her.

"Well, don't just stand there. Help me with these."

She thrust one of the bags into his hands and directed him to lead her to the kitchen.

"Am I to take this to mean we're dining in?" he teased as he helped her remove her purchases and lay them out on the counter.

"How about that? You guessed!" She smiled at him as she stuck the salad vegetables under the water faucet. "Have you got something to put these in?"

"You mean like a salad bowl?"

She shook her head in mock impatience. "Yes. Like a salad bowl."

Half an hour later, they sat down to what Donald called "the best dinner of my life." The salad was crisp and tangy, the New York steaks were just the right color of pink and the broccoli was oozing a lemony Hollandaise. She'd even provided the wine, a good California cabernet.

"All right," Donald said, leaning back against his chair and observing her. "What's this all about?"

They'd finished the meal, but the second bottle of wine was barely touched.

Vali eyed him levelly. "I've decided," she said coolly, "I want to make love to you."

She saw the surprise in Donald's eyes, the flicker of cautious joy.

"Are you serious, lady?"

"I've never been more serious." She smiled at him. "Pretty wanton of me, isn't it?"

He whistled. "I've always dreamed of encountering a wanton woman." He stared at her. "Well? Do we just do it, or do we wait for our dinner to digest?"

She laughed and rose from her chair. "I suggest we have at least one more glass of wine," she told him, gathering up the plates and napkins. "And if you've got some nice music for that fancy-looking stereo over there, it might add to the mood."

"You're on." Donald jumped up and rummaged through his cassette collection. He settled on Rachmaninov. He dimmed the lights as Vali rinsed off the dishes. When she returned to the living room, he was seated on the sofa, the wine bottle and two glasses on the coffee table in front of him. He patted the cushion next to him.

"Come here, baby."

She kicked off her shoes and snuggled in next to him. He kissed her hair.

"You smell good. Even your hair smells good."

She smiled and turned so she could kiss the corner of his mouth. "I washed it earlier."

He pulled her closer and they were silent, letting the music wash over them.

"More wine?" He reached out and retrieved both glasses. He handed her one.

"Thanks."

"You have good taste. In wines, I mean."

She cocked her head to one side and looked at him. "I hope I have good taste in more things than that."

He studied her, sipping his wine. "I'm afraid I may be dreaming this."

"Why?"

"Well, Vali, the other night, after the fair, I asked you to come home with me, but I didn't expect you to say yes. And now, this . . ."

She kissed him full on the lips. "Shhh. Don't question it."

She started to pull away, but he put his free hand

against the back of her head and pressed her forward again. He kissed her deeply, their lips becoming more and more greedy as they tasted the sweetness remembered from long ago.

One hand trailed its way around her body, seeking her breasts. He found one and cupped it through the thin silk of her dress. She shuddered and made low moans in the back of her throat.

He was kissing her face, her neck, peppering her with a hundred baby kisses. His free hand found the zipper at the back of her dress and gently tugged at it, causing the V-neck to fall away from the shoulders, exposing her flesh above her lacy white bra. Hungrily he pushed the cup down, not bothering to unhook the restraining strap. His mouth devoured her naked breast, his tongue teasing the erect, quivering nipple.

She began to laugh. He rose up, staring at her.

"What's so funny?"

"We are. Are we going to do it here, or do you have a bed?"

He groaned. "We have to move?"

Her eyes were shining. "I think it would be slightly more comfortable."

He nodded soberly. "Come with me." He led her to a darkened bedroom and pulled her to the bed without turning on the light.

"How come you're still in that dress?"

"I haven't had time to get it off."

"Well, do it, dammit. Fast."

"Yes, sir." She bobbed her head smartly. She tapped on his trousers with a long, rounded fingernail. "How about you getting out of these?"

Naked, skin burning against skin, they kissed and fondled and explored, awakening memories long forgotten, finding new, hidden places, the touching of which caused the other to gasp and groan.

His penis was huge, much bigger than she remembered it. Her mouth couldn't get enough of it; she ran her tongue across the head which was so full it threatened to burst at any moment.

His hands were at her thighs, teasing the soft inner flesh. He parted her and felt her wetness with his fingers. Suddenly, he pushed her back on the bed and entered her. He pushed himself in sharply; she gasped in surprise, and then her thighs began to move, pulling him in deeper, begging him to fill her completely.

He thrust hard; he could hear a tiny grunt with each movement. They were in perfect rhythm, pumping, thrusting, both gasping for breath.

"Don't stop!" Vali begged. "Don't stop. Don't—" She gave a strangled cry. "Don-ald . . ." Her body writhed and trembled. He released his own explosion within seconds.

When they were quiet, bodies limp with relief, he realized she was crying. He could feel her tears trickling down his chest.

"Vali? Vali, honey, what's wrong?" He kissed her face, stroking her hair tenderly.

"Nothing. It's nothing."

"I didn't hurt you, did I? I didn't mean to."

"No. You were wonderful. *It* was wonderful." She swallowed back a fresh flow of tears and smiled at him. How could she tell him she was crying for the past that never was?

When they were more controlled, he went into the living room and returned with the wine. They finished it in bed, holding hands, neither saying much of anything.

It was Donald who broke the silence. He had to know.

"Can you stay the night?"

She gave him a longing look. "No."

He nodded. A pause. Then said, "Will I see you again?"

She squeezed his hand. "How about tomorrow night?"

"The reunion will have started. Isn't there a dinner dance?"

"Uh huh. I need a date." She eyed him flirtatiously.

He was thoughtful. "Won't people wonder if they see us together?"

She shrugged. "Do you care?"

"No, ma'am. But you might."

She leaned over and kissed his ear. "Donald Ellsworth, I don't care what people think. Tomorrow night I'm going to be Vali Porter again. Vali Porter could do no wrong."

"Then may I say something to you, Vali Porter?"

"Please do."

He looked deep into her eyes. "I love you."

She caught her breath and looked away. "Please, Donald, don't—"

He straightened up. "I'm sorry. I guess I don't know the rules of the game." His mouth hardened.

Her voice was soft. "There are no rules. Let's just take it as it comes, okay?"

253

He sighed. "Okay. You're the boss." He reached out to devour her again.

Francine returned her husband's smile across the polished Chippendale dinner table. He was obviously so glad to have her there she felt a twinge of guilt for having moved to the Lancelot for the week. Despite his upright carriage and his insistence that he was in the best of health, Baron was an old man, and as his wife, Francine knew she should be more solicitous of him. Still, he continued to go to the office every day, and when he was home there were plenty of servants to look after him.

The truth was, the only reason she was here tonight was because of Arthur. When Baron had called her and said Arthur was joining Barry and himself for dinner, an alarm sounded. In the more than twenty years she had been married to Baron, the number of times Arthur had joined them for dinner could be counted on one hand. She doubted this was the night Arthur actually planned to tell Baron about Barry; more likely, he had arranged the dinner merely to frighten her. If he had, she told herself grimly, he had succeeded.

"Tell us about the reunion, darling," Baron suggested as he prepared to tackle the sizzling T-bone steak the maid had set in front of him. "Are you and your friends having fun?"

"Oh, we're having fun," Francine replied. "But of course the reunion doesn't start officially until tomorrow."

"How about your dance, Mom?" Barry asked. He

grinned at her, and for a moment her heart seemed to do a flip flop. He looked so much like Arthur when he smiled. "You handling those high kicks okay?"

Francine laughed. "There are no high kicks in our routine, thank God. Just a bunch of slap-ball-changes and shuffle-off-to-Buffaloes. Your mother may not exactly be Miss Twinkletoes, but I don't think I'll embarrass you at the performance."

"You know," Arthur began idly, sipping at his wine as he addressed her, "I think I'd like to catch that performance. Barry? Would you mind if your uncle tagged along with you Saturday night?"

Barry shrugged. "Heck, no. Dad's coming, too, aren't you, Dad?"

Baron smiled and winked at Francine. "Wouldn't miss it for the world."

"Oh, really, you guys," Francine said, embarrassed. "I don't know why any of you want to come. Class reunions are known to be incredibly boring for non-class members. Why do you think Vali's husband didn't come with her? Or Barbara Jean's?"

"Perhaps their legs aren't as good as yours," Baron offered dryly.

Francine decided to change the subject. She didn't really care whether they came or not. "Let's talk about you, Bear," she said, turning to her son. "How's it going in the corporate world?" Barry was beginning to distinguish himself at Brookfield Oil after learning the ropes from the ground up.

"Oh, terrible," the young man deadpanned. "They keep me chained to a desk for eight solid hours, and if I get hungry they toss me a day-old tuna sandwich."

"Ungrateful brat," Arthur said affectionately. "You're lucky to have a job at all, the unemployment rate being what it is."

"Yeah, I guess you're right," Barry agreed. "If I didn't have a job, I'd have to spend all my time chasing girls."

Baron suppressed a smile. "Speaking of girls," he said, eyeing Barry with an inquisitive gaze, "what happened to that little number you brought here the other day? The one with the freckles?"

Francine froze, her fork suspended in mid-air. The girl's face flashed in front of her. Fluffy, red-gold hair. Emerald green eyes. Smooth white complexion dotted with pert little freckles. *Kathi's* face.

"Christina?" Barry was saying. "She's around. In fact, now that you mention her, maybe I'll invite her to Mom's performance, too."

"No!" Francine gasped. Then, seeing the bewildered expressions on their faces as they turned to her, she forced herself to smile. "Listen, if you three guys want to come, okay. But let's not bring any strangers into it, huh? It's embarrassing enough as it is."

"I'll make her promise not to laugh," Barry assured her with the same dryness with which Baron and Arthur often spoke. "I'll threaten her with a horrible death if she so much as smiles. Okay?"

Arthur's eyes were on Francine. He did not know the girl being discussed, but it seemed to him Francine was overreacting to what was being said. Was it that she didn't like the girl? Or was she starting to get protective now that Barry was beginning to try his own wings?

"Who is this girl?" he asked, feigning nonchalance as he looked from Francine to Barry.

"Just a girl," Barry replied. "Nobody special."

"Special enough for you to bring home to meet your mother," Baron put in. He smiled at Francine and was puzzled to see she seemed to have lost all interest in her dinner. Her steak had barely been touched, and the vegetables seemed to simply have been moved from one side of her plate to the other.

"I brought her here because she asked me to," Barry explained. Unlike his mother, he was devouring his meal, speaking between hearty mouthfuls. He looked at Francine. "She wanted to meet you."

"Why?" Francine began to feel cold. *Stop it!* she commanded herself. *Don't let them see that any of this is bothering you.* "Why would someone you just met want to meet me?"

"Beats me," Barry said, stabbing his last piece of steak with his fork. "Maybe she just wants to be able to say she met the glamorous society queen of Baxter." He chuckled.

Arthur was becoming more and more perplexed. Francine looked as if she were about to jump out of her skin. Did she know something about the girl that Barry didn't? Was she afraid this Christina had some ulterior motive, like casing the house for theft, or wanting to use her in some way?

"Where'd you meet her, anyway?" he asked Barry. "Is she a Baxter girl?"

"No, she's just here for a couple of weeks. She's visiting an aunt or something. I think she lives in Illinois."

Well, that should make Francy feel better, Arthur

257

thought, shooting a glance at her from the corner of his eye. But, surprisingly, the news that the girl was only visiting seemed to have an even more disturbing effect on her. Her face was deathly white, and her hand holding her wine glass trembled so violently, he feared she was going to spill the wine.

"If you'll excuse me, I've got some phone calls to make," Francine said, suddenly rising. "I'm sorry."

"But you've hardly touched your meal," Baron said. He, too, was concerned by her unusual behavior.

"I know. I'm just not hungry. I had a big lunch today." She offered a tremulous smile. "You all go on and finish. I'm sure Olivia baked a terrific pie or something for dessert."

"Don't you at least want coffee?" Baron asked.

"Maybe later. I'll see." She turned to Arthur. "Nice seeing you, Arthur. You must come to dinner more often."

"Thank you. Maybe I'll do that." His eyes caught hers and held them. Francine had to get away. She felt as if her legs were about to buckle beneath her. She turned abruptly and headed for the staircase, praying she wouldn't stumble.

Alone in the bathroom that adjoined her luxurious bedroom, she bent over her hand-painted ceramic sink and splashed cold water on her face. When the dizziness that had threatened to overpower her subsided, she stood up straight and stared at herself in the mirror. What the hell was going on, anyway? She was a grown woman of reasonable intelligence. She did not believe in ghosts of people appearing from beyond the grave. But ever since the Loreleis had arrived in Baxter, a dead girl from their past had been making what seemed to be physical appearances. When Liz had first reported seeing her at Riley's, Francine had thought she was trying to scare them. And when Anne had seen her in church, well, Anne was an actress, and actresses were given to theatrics.

But when the girl had come into Francine's own home, sat in one of her pale blue chairs, partaken of a cup of tea, and shaken Francine's hand . . . what had she thought then? That she was losing her mind?

A hoax, Francine decided as she dabbed at her face with a towel and freshened herself with her favorite spray cologne. Someone was *impersonating* Kathi; it was a joke to frighten the Loreleis. But who? Someone who knew the truth about what happened thirty years ago? Or simply someone with a sick sense of humor?

Sick. The word tumbled around in her head. Margie Middleton had once been sick. Although she hadn't told the others, Francine had heard Margie had been committed to a mental hospital for a while after high school. She had suspected at the time that Margie's problems had had to do with Kathi. Suppose Margie was still disturbed and was re-creating Kathi somehow. She went back to her bedroom and sat down on her bed. She closed her eyes, trying to picture Margie. Auburn hair, fair skin, *green eyes*. She sucked in her breath. No, not emerald green, not as brilliant as Kathi's, but green. Same size as Kathi, the two had once exchanged clothes in high school.

Could Margie be impersonating Kathi?

A wig could easily account for the red-gold hair, freckles could be handled with makeup. Add pedal-pushers from the fifties . . . *But I had tea with her,* Francine argued. *I talked to her, shook her hand. I'd have known if the girl was Margie.*

But the shock of first seeing her, she countered, carefully creating the details of that meeting, *could have jarred me so much, I wasn't aware of the possibilities.*

She recalled being nervous, forcing herself to behave naturally. She remembered enduring the afternoon as if she were in a dream; it had seemed unreal, like a movie where everything is seen through a distorted lens. Margie could have been made up to look like Kathi, and Francine's mind could have done the rest. But why? What would Margie gain from it?

Again, the memory of the hospital. She had lost touch with reality once. Perhaps she had never regained it.

A knock sounded on her door. She straightened her shoulders and reached up to fluff her hair. "Yes?" she called out. "Who is it?"

The door opened. Arthur poked his head inside. "It's me. I came up to see if you were all right."

Francine stiffened. Arthur! In her own bedroom! She jumped up. "I'm fine, thank you." She tried to avoid his eyes. "Where are the others?"

"Barry had a hot date and Dad's watching a news special on television. I told him I was coming up to say goodbye."

He was standing still, inches from her, not touching her. Yet she felt his magnetism so strongly he might have been holding her in his arms. She braced herself and looked into his eyes.

"That's very nice of you, Arthur. Goodbye." She held herself in rigid control. Her voice was ice cold.

Arthur took another step inside and closed the door. Francine took two steps back.

"What are you doing? Get out of my room."

"I want to talk to you, Francy. We didn't finish the conversation we started the other day."

"I was under the impression we *did* finish it. You are not to tell Baron about Barry."

"I didn't intend to tell Dad. I intend to tell my son."

"Can't you see it's the same thing?" Francine cried out, the old panic beginning to take over. "Barry won't be able to handle a thing like that!"

Arthur eyed her coolly. "And what if Dad does find out? What do you think will happen?"

"He's an old man! Anything could happen. He could have a heart attack and die, for God's sake."

Arthur smiled and moved closer to her. His right hand went out and gently touched her face. "Is that what you're afraid of, Francy? That he'll die? Or . . ." He looked at her. "That he *won't* die?"

Francine slapped at his hand. "What the hell is that supposed to mean?" Her eyes blazed at him. Her knees threatened to buckle again.

"If he finds out you duped him, he could become very angry, even after all these years. Angry enough to kick you out. Disinherit you." His mouth curled up in an evil smile. "That would be the final irony, wouldn't it, Francy? If he disinherited you after you put up with him all this time?"

"I didn't 'put up with him,'" she answered tartly. "I love Baron. My life with him has been wonderful."

Again the evil smile. "But think how much more wonderful your widowhood will be, Francy. Dad can't live forever. If he dies while you're still beautiful and desirable . . ." He let the words drift off.

"Arthur . . ." Francine took a deep breath. "Will you please leave? Baron could come up and find you here. He could be outside that door this minute, listening to everything we've been saying."

"Oh, I doubt that. Dad's too much of a gentleman to eavesdrop. But you're right. This is not the time nor the place." He reached out and put his hand on her arm, holding it tight. "We'll discuss it Saturday night," he said flatly. "After your performance at the Pow Wow."

"I can't do that. Baron and Barry—"

"You can send them home," he interrupted, sensing her protest. "Tell him since it's your last night with your friends, you want to go and celebrate. We'll go to my house. The servants will be off. No one will know."

"Arthur . . ."

He bent down and kissed her forehead. His nearness made her head spin. She hated him. God, how she hated him. And yet, even now her body seemed to be responding to him, yearning toward him.

"Shhh." He put a finger to his lips and smiled at her. "It's what you want, Francy, you know that. It's what we both want."

"No!" She pulled away and ran to her writing

desk. She snatched up a paperweight and hurled it at him, missing him by inches.

The smile on his face froze. His eyes narrowed and glared at her. "Very well, Francy," he said coldly. "Have it your way. But your 'command performance' still stands. Maybe"—his voice was thick with sarcasm—"you can think of it as a way to change my mind about telling the truth to my son."

He bent down and picked up the paperweight. "I'd be careful about throwing these things around. You might actually hit something with one of them." He placed the paperweight on the bureau behind him and walked quickly from the room.

Chapter Fourteen

Barbara Jean climbed the steep cement steps leading up into the stands. Less than halfway to the top she stopped, panting heavily. She turned around and faced the playing field. It was smaller than she remembered. Baxter Stadium was definitely smaller. She stepped into the bleachers and took the first seat in Row R. Funny. She'd never watched a game from the bleachers. She'd always been out on the field, leading the cheering section.

"Gimme a B! Gimme an A!" The exuberant shouts of the six boys and six girls in white sweaters with red lettering and white trousers or short pleated skirts rang in her ears. She had been elected cheerleader in her sophomore year and had kept her place throughout high school, becoming Captain of the squad when she was a senior. No one had been able to jump higher or do as many acrobatics. Once, a movie company had come to Baxter to film locations and had shot additional footage of Barbara Jean's cheerleading performance. The footage never made it to the final print, but Barbara Jean had been a celebrity for a while because she had been singled out.

Idly she snapped open her purse and removed the neat, silver-plated flask she had placed in it before leaving the Lancelot this morning. She unscrewed the cap and put it to her lips. The vodka felt like fire as it roared down her throat. Her whole body flushed with the heat, and the present-day despair that had been creeping into memories of the past backed off a bit.

Larry Holloway had loved watching her cheerleading performances. He loved the way she looked in her uniform, the way the white sweater displayed her generous breasts, the way the short skirt showed off her sturdy, bare legs. She smiled to herself and took another drink as she recalled the times she'd had to perform without a bra as proof of loyalty to the Loreleis. The game was the secondary event on those three occasions. Barbara Jean Lawson's boobs were much more fun to watch.

Larry hadn't liked the idea of her displaying herself so blatantly, but he hadn't been outraged enough to make her choose between him and the Loreleis. He was understanding of just about everything she did. That was what made him so special. She sighed, remembering those last, final weeks of love, the spring of their senior year.

They were so besotted with each other, they couldn't find enough time to spend together. Barbara Jean became an expert liar in order to get out of the house after dinner and meet him on the corner for an explosion of furtive, passionate kisses and fervent words of love.

His parents didn't approve of her—they wouldn't have approved of any serious romance at that stage— so Barbara Jean wore his senior ring on a chain around her neck, carefully tucked inside her blouses and sweaters. "Next to my heart," she would tell him tenderly. Theirs was the most talked-about romance at school. They couldn't pass each other in the hall without touching hands, they scheduled their lunch hours so they could eat together every day, then they would fly to the parking lot as soon as the final bell rang and smother each other with kisses in Larry's baby blue Thunderbird.

They made love in the car at drive-in movies, in deserted lovers' lanes and out under the stars on the grassy banks of Spirit Lake. They felt no guilt; it was right, it was good, the perfect expression of their perfect, glorious love.

But the pressures on them mounted increasingly. Larry's parents, alarmed by their son's slipping grades and lack of interest in home life, called Barbara Jean's parents and suggested more rigid control of their "uninhibited daughter." The Lawsons were hugely embarrassed and began making Barbara Jean account for every spare minute of her time. In desperation, Larry and Barbara Jean decided on affirmative action. They couldn't—wouldn't—be separated by their cold, unfeeling parents.

The cheerleader clinic in Stillwater provided the excuse Barbara Jean needed to spend four days of Easter Week away from home. Larry told his parents he was going camping with some guys from school. The young lovers simply got in Larry's car and drove all night to Las Vegas, where they were married in a gaudy wedding chapel that seemed to Barbara Jean like the most beautiful place on earth. They spent their wedding night at the tawdry Diamond Bar

Motel, and their lovemaking was all the sweeter because they truly belonged to one another.

They knew they'd been found out as soon as they returned to Baxter. Mrs. Lawson had tried to call Barbara Jean at the cheerleader clinic to tell her her grandmother had died, and was duly informed that no Barbara Jean Lawson was registered there. Mrs. Lawson imediately phoned the Holloways who soon discovered that Larry's friends from school hadn't gone camping at all.

The newlyweds were defiant at first, insisting they were old enought to know their own minds and that they were bound together legally and could not be separated, no matter what. The annulment proceedings began the following day. Larry was packed off to Europe with a tutor; he would receive his high school diploma by mail and enter Harvard in the fall. Barbara Jean thought she would die. For two weeks she prayed she was pregnant, thinking that would make a difference. But she was heartbreakingly regular. Somehow she got through the spring and summer, and she enrolled at OSU in September. Larry wrote often at first, then his letters dwindled down to a few lines once a month. In the end Barbara Jean married the first boy who asked her, sturdy, freckled Woody Fleagle, and settled down on two hundred acres he'd inherited from his deceased parents.

She wouldn't even see Larry at the reunion. She'd followed his career avidly, from his emergence as a junior partner in a Colorado law firm, to his involvement in civil rights, to his election to the House of Representatives. She'd read about his marriage to a Miss Alicia Conover, the plane crash that left him crippled for life and, finally, just three years ago, his death from a gunshot wound inflicted by his own hand.

Still deep in thought, she put the flask to her lips and realized with surprise that it was empty. Obviously she'd been taking sips she hadn't even realized. Oh, well, she consoled herself, time she got back to the hotel anyway. Maybe Frank would call and take her to dinner.

She rose from her seat, steadying herself against the back of the bleacher. Sitting down, she'd felt fine. Standing up, she felt decidedly dizzy. Carefully she picked her way down the steps, holding on to the railings for support. When she reached the end, she looked around, confused. Where was the ramp leading to the parking lot? She couldn't remember. She couldn't even remember how she'd come in.

Oh, the hell with it! Without another moment's concern, she hiked up her dress and slipped over the wall separating the bleachers from the playing field. It was only a short drop, but she fell on all fours when she landed. Giddily she picked herself up and made her way along the wall to Section E.

Section E was where the Red Feathers sat. They were the girls' cheering squad. The Scalpers, the boys' squad, sat across the aisle from them, in Section F.

"Gimme a B!"

Barbara Jean planted her feet the required distance apart and bent her knees. She raised her arms above her head, closing her hands around an imaginary sign bearing the letter B.

268

"Gimme an A! Gimme an X!" The other cheer-leaders had held the other letters, but Barbara Jean took everyone's part. "Gimme a T! Gimme an E! Gimme an R! B-A-X-T-E-R. Yaaay . . . Baxter!"

Barbara Jean began the short running steps as the "yaaay" began. During a game, she would run in front of the entire line of male and female cheer-leaders, gathering speed as she neared Tommy Simmons at the end. She would do her somersault first, Tommy's cue to kneel down on the field. Then she would leap to her feet, spring onto her hands, and flip over onto Tommy's shoulders. Tommy would then jump up, and Barbara Jean would rise to a standing position while the crowd yelled its ap-proval.

She was going too fast for the somersault. The hell with it. She didn't want to grovel in the dirt anyway. She would go right into the handspring. She threw her arms outward and hurled herself into space. *Yaaay . . . Baxter!*

She heard the crack before she felt the pain. Her arm collapsed under her, and she hit the ground with the full force of her overweight body.

"Oh, my God . . ." she whispered as she shifted her position, trying to free her arm from its imprison-ment beneath her. "Je-sus!"

She knew it was broken. Gingerly, she eased it up, gaping at the hand which hung limply from her wrist. She felt nauseous. She was hot. So hot. She struggled to her feet, took a step, fell to her knees and vomited. The vomit splattered on her dress. She couldn't stop retching, even after her stomach was emptied. She started to cry.

"Barbara Jean! Honey—it's all right."

She stiffened. Suddenly she felt terribly cold. Freezing, she looked up. No . . . no . . . not *him*. Frank Bragg was running toward her, looking alarmed. She couldn't face him. She couldn't. She turned her body away. The pain in her right wrist was nothing compared to the pain of her humiliation.

She felt his hands on her shoulders. Gently, he pulled her to her feet.

"Are you all right? Are you hurt? God, you gave me a scare."

Barbara Jean closed her eyes for a moment. There was no escaping him. "I think I've broken my wrist," she said foolishly. She held it up for him to see.

"Oh, Christ! Come on. We'll take you to Emergency." He put an arm around her shoulders. "Can you walk?"

The question struck her as funny. "Only on my feet," she replied, starting to giggle. Then she remembered the vomit. "Oh, Frank, I'm such a mess." She began to cry again.

"Here, try this."

He handed her a white handkerchief. She held it in her left hand and wiped her face. Then she dabbed at the spots on her skirt.

University Hospital was only a few blocks from the stadium. Emergency accepted her immediately. Frank stayed by her side as Dr. Benjamin Unger set her wrist and encased her arm in a plaster cast. Afterwards, he took her back to the Lancelot, helped her out of her soiled clothes, ran a bath and sat on the closed toilet seat, talking to her as she soaked, her

270

right arm dangling over the side, out of the water.

"I don't know what to say," she told him, still unable to look him fully in the eyes. "I'm so embarrassed."

"It's all right." His voice held no disgust or disapproval. "I'm just glad I was there."

Barbara Jean looked at him then. "What were you doing there, anyway? How did you know where I was?"

"I came to the dance studio. I wanted to buy you a drink after rehearsal. I got there just a minute too late. You were driving away as I pulled up."

"You followed me?"

He nodded. "I thought if you were coming back to the hotel, I'd buy you a drink here. Then, when you turned in the opposite direction, I decided to follow anyway. I don't know why."

"You were in the stadium the whole time?"

"As soon as I saw you go in, I realized you were probably going to relive some old memories. I thought I'd wait."

She became thoughtful. "I didn't see you."

"I was all the way at the top. That's why it took me so long to reach you when you fell."

She nodded, then grinned sheepishly. "You must've loved my act."

He smiled. "We all wish we could relive the past at times." He looked at her. "I'll bet you were a hell of a cheerleader."

She blushed. "I was a lot lighter on my feet then."

He rose and walked toward her. "Need some help washing your back?"

She nodded and smiled at him.

271

"Frank?"

"Yes, honey?"

She felt a flood of warmth for him. "Thanks."

He bent down and kissed her nose.

Francine's long, tapered fingers closed around the cold, smooth metal of the twenty-two caliber pistol. She had removed it from the bottom drawer of her bedside night stand, where it had lain undisturbed for at least a year. She'd purchased it for self-protection when a pathological sex murderer had been terrorizing Baxter. For a while, it had been as much a part of her personal paraphernalia as her lipstick and comb. She had even taken instruction in the use and maintenance of it at the local police academy. After the criminal had been caught, there didn't seem to be a reason to continue carrying it in her purse.

She spun the empty cylinder. Although it turned easily, she supposed she should take it apart and oil and clean it. If she had to use it, it had to be in perfect condition.

If she had to use it. How would she feel if Arthur Brookfield were dead? And she, the instrument of his death? Relieved? Triumphant?

Desolate?

Francine had had her dry martini that night at The Derrick, the private club off the lobby of the Brookfield Building. All Brookfield Oil employees were members; this enabled them to buy liquor by the drink. Francine had never been in a bar by herself before. She saw several men look curiously at her as she made her way through the darkened room to a small table in the back. She didn't return their glances. She couldn't have cared less what people thought.

She showed her Brookfield employee card, but the waiter asked to see her driver's license as well. When it was produced, he shook his head and told Francine he couldn't serve her; she was not yet twenty-one. She was arguing with him, insisting that *all* Brookfield employees were allowed the services of The Derrick, when a tall, distinguished-looking gentleman walked up to her table.

"What seems to be the problem here?" he asked the waiter.

"I'm sorry, sir. The young lady isn't old enough to be served."

The man looked at Francine. "Do you have a membership here?" he asked.

She nodded. "I'm a receptionist upstairs. I was told I could come here any time."

"A receptionist, you say? What did you order?"

"A dry martini." Francine could feel the eyes of the other patrons on her. She knew she should forget it and leave, but some stubborn streak was making her hold her ground.

The distinguished older man pulled out his wallet and handed the waiter some bills. "Bring us two dry martinis, Luther," he said with authority. "You've made a mistake about the lady's age."

"Yes, sir!" The waiter hurried back to the bar, stuffing the bills in the pocket of his red coat. The man pulled out the chair next to Francine's.

"Do you mind if I join you? I'm afraid it's the only way you're going to get your drink."

"No, not at all." Francine gave him an ironic little smile. "I shouldn't have pressed the point. It's not that important."

"Of course it's important if you wanted the drink." The waiter returned and put the glasses in front of them. "Thank you, Luther," the distinguished man said.

"Thank *you*, Mr. Brookfield."

Francine looked up, startled, as the waiter moved off. There was only one other Mr. Brookfield—Arthur's father, Baron. He had his own private entrance and his own private elevator to the seventh floor, which was why she'd never seen him before. "Mr. Brookfield," she stammered, aghast. "I'm sorry. I had no idea . . ."

He smiled, and she noticed how much warmer his blue eyes seemed than Arthur's. "It's all right. I don't often get to help damsels in distress."

Their two martinis were followed by two more, and two more after that. Then Baron took her for dinner at a small restaurant not far from The Derrick. By the time he escorted her to her car, he knew she was not quite twenty-one, was a native of Baxter, was unmarried and unattached. She knew that he was already a little bit in love with her.

Two nights later, they dined in his private dining room on the seventh floor of the Brookfield Building on food catered by the Baxter Country Club. He told her he was married but that his wife, Grace, had not been a "real" wife in many years. He didn't blame her. She'd simply fallen out of love with him. When he kissed her the first time, Francine told him she *was* in love with him.

Baron's reaction to her announcement—barely three weeks later—that she thought she was pregnant was very different from Arthur's. He and Francine had been together almost every night since they'd met; he had no doubt that the baby was his. Furthermore, he loved Francine and wanted their child. "There's no fool like an old fool," he told himself wryly as he set the wheels in motion that would make this incredibly lovely young girl his wife. Grace was packed off to Juarez with a divorce petition in her purse and seven million dollars in her bank account. Francine and Baron were married—to the astonishment of the Baxter social set—before Arthur and Loretta returned from the Orient.

From then on Arthur and Francine were polite to each other when they crossed paths, but they kept a distance between them as much as possible. Baron attributed it to Arthur's shock at the sudden change in his parents' marital status and in having a twenty-year-old girl for a stepmother.

Now, twenty-seven years later, Francine was undeniably the First Lady of Baxter. Grace had died ten years ago in Beverly Hills, where she'd gone after the divorce. Loretta was buried six months ago, following a stroke that had left her helpless for years. Since her death, Baron had issued frequent dinner invitations to Arthur, hoping to ease his loneliness, but Arthur never accepted. Baron was saddened, not understanding how his son could still refuse to accept such a lovely woman as Francine as his father's wife.

What would Francine be willing to do to keep her position and fine, distinguished reputation? Kill Arthur? And if she did, what then? Prison? The electric chair? A fine way of protecting her position *that* would be.

But if she wasn't caught . . . if no one knew . . . No one knew what happened to Kathi, did they? The Loreleis hadn't gone to prison.

She carefully wrapped the pistol in a blue silk handkerchief and returned it to the bottom drawer. She would clean it later, just before she needed it.

Maybe she wouldn't actually have to use it.

Maybe she would use it anyway.

Maybe she would.

Margie stretched out on the chaise lounge, shaded by the Middleton's huge weeping willow. She was thinking. It seemed to her there had been a lot to think about this week. Since the Loreleis had come back, so many memories had returned. Like the old POL's somebody had mentioned the other day. The Proof of Loyalty tests they'd all gone through before officially becoming members. Margie's POL had been to sleep with David Olsen, the class nerd. She'd often wondered why they'd chosen that particular test for her. The other girls had been assigned things that would make them uncomfortable. Anne, for instance, had protested long and hard her assignment of blowing her lines in the sophomore play.

"It's unfair to ask me to do something like that!" she'd shouted defiantly. "It won't affect just me. The audience and the rest of the cast will suffer for it."

She had blown her line anyway.

Liz had strongly resisted failing an algebra test. She took pride in her straight A grades and had her sights set on a college scholarship. She'd wanted to remain a Lorelei, however. She dutifully failed the test and so shocked the teacher she was permitted to take it over—whereupon, her duty to the club members over, she scored a neat one hundred.

But Margie's whole reputation was built on making out. What made them think sleeping with David Olsen would make *her* uncomfortable?

Or did they *know?*

David was almost seven feet tall, wore thick eyeglasses and had terrible teeth and breath. Margie breezily sidled up to him one day during lunch hour, made a date and—to his astonishment—practically raped him. She'd spent the rest of the night soaking in a hot tub trying to wash away the guilt and disgust that covered her body like mud.

Kathi's initiation seemed easy compared to Margie's POL. God. How many times had she wished she were Kathi?

Barbara Jean told everyone she'd broken her arm in a fall off a horse.

"I can't believe I did anything so stupid," she

declared impatiently. "Me, a farmer's wife!"

"Who were you riding with?" Anne wanted to know.

"It certainly wasn't one of us," Vali teased lightly.

Barbara Jean hesitated. Should she tell them about Frank? She knew her secret would be safe with them. They'd never tell Woody, or anyone else for that matter. But one reason why her affair had been so delicious was the fact that it had been so private. She wasn't sure she wanted to share Frank with them.

"I think she's having an affair," Francine said with certainty.

"Come on. Fess up." Liz was smiling encouragingly.

She supposed it didn't matter if she told. Reunion week was almost over, and she wouldn't be seeing Frank after Sunday. Anyway, the revelation might make her seem more glamorous in their eyes; she wouldn't be the dowdy one nobody wanted.

"He's a man I met the day I got here," she confessed awkwardly. "His name's Frank Bragg. He lives north of here."

"Well, I do declare!" hooted Francine. "Little B.J.'s really been pulling a fast one!" She leaned toward the former cheerleader. "Tell us everything. Is he tall, dark and handsome? Enormously rich? What?"

"Forget the tall, dark and handsome," Anne said, winking exaggeratedly. "Tell us about his cock. How big is it, and what all does he do with it?"

"Really, Anne!" Barbara Jean had turned bright red. "That's too disgusting! I'm sorry I even told you about him."

"I agree with B.J.," Vali said. "She's obviously having a great time with the guy, and we're turning it into a dirty joke. I say more power to her."

"I'm with you," Liz announced. "And I think we should change the subject."

They wouldn't hear of her leaving the dance number. Ways of disguising her awkward-looking cast were batted around as enthusiastically as the comments about her lover had been.

"We'll wrap it in yellow satin," Vali suggested. "To match our leotards. She can carry her umbrella in her left hand."

"But I can't dance," Barbara Jean protested. "I'm off balance with this heavy thing on my arm. What if I fall down?"

Everyone thought hard.

"I've got it!" Liz said at last. "We'll have someone put an old bench onstage. Barbara Jean can be sitting in the park while the rest of us dance. She can tap her toes in time to the music."

Everyone agreed it was a good idea. Except Barbara Jean.

"That'll look stupid," she insisted. "I can't just sit there while the rest of you dance."

"Yes, you can," Anne declared. "We'll talk to Miss Virginia's daughter about it tomorrow at the final rehearsal. She'll work out some extra business for you to do."

The others agreed positively. Barbara Jean was still in the dance.

Chapter Fifteen

The sign, painted in huge red letters on a white background, read "Welcome, Class of '58!" It had been carefully placed over the Lancelot's entryway early that morning. Now, at ten o'clock, the lobby was overflowing with high-spirited men and women; the air was filled with joyous greetings and shrieking laughter.

Earlier, the Loreleis had tried to decide how they should best approach the registration proceedings.

"Should we go down one by one, or descend on them *en masse?*" Francine asked as they discussed the problem over breakfast in the hotel coffee shop.

"I think we should make solo entrances," Anne said positively. "That way no one will steal anyone else's thunder."

"But if we all go down together," argued Liz, "we'll make an impression. Everyone will see that the Loreleis are still a formidable team."

"Anyway, I'm not sure I have the nerve to go down alone," Vali said with a little self-conscious chuckle. "Frankly, the idea of seeing everyone again scares me to death."

"I don't know why," Barbara Jean told her, squinting at her appraisingly from across the table. "You've hardly even changed."

Vali blew her a kiss. "That's sweet, B.J., but we've *all* changed."

"I agree with Liz and Vali," Francine declared. "We were known as a clique in high school. I think we should keep it that way."

"Margie?" Liz asked. "How do you feel about it?"

Margie had been unusually quiet this morning. While the others had wolfed down their omelets and pancakes, she had merely pushed the food around on her plate.

"I'm like Vali," she told them, smiling weakly. "I'd rather go with everyone else."

"Well, that makes five of us," said Francine. "Anne? Do you still want to go alone?"

Anne shrugged. "I've always been taught that the majority rules. We'll make our entrance a mob scene." She laughed to show she had no hard feelings.

They decided to meet in Francine's room at ten. As per the directions in the last reunion bulletin, they were all attired in casual wear. Anne wore a sporty white jumpsuit with pushup sleeves and a shirtwaist top. Liz wore white cotton pants with a turquoise blouse which she had knotted at the waistline. Vali and Barbara Jean were in sundresses, B.J.'s arm held in a sling fashioned from a lavender scarf belonging to Francine. Francine herself was wearing daringly short shorts which showed off her gorgeous tawny legs. Only Margie was not present. She had gone back home after breakfast, saying she had some

281

laundry in the washing machine which needed to be transferred to the dryer. She phoned at five to ten to say she was running late.

"I think we should go on down without her," said Anne, whose nervous energy was making her anxious to get the show on the road. "We can look for her, and when she gets here, we can give her a big Lorelei greeting."

"We might as well go on," Liz agreed. "We're all revved up, and there's no telling when she'll get here."

Vali took a final look at herself in the mirror above the bureau. "I say let's get it over with," she declared, fluffing her freshly washed hair. "Let's go."

They trooped to the elevator, giggling like teenagers. "Oooh, I wish Donald was with me," Vali lamented as they arrived at the lobby floor. "I mean Chase," she corrected quickly when four heads turned to give her curious looks. "Moral support, you know."

The registration desk was manned by four of their former classmates, only two of which any of them remembered.

"Debby Beasley!" Anne greeted the tall, rather colorless woman who was handing out name badges. "I can't believe it!" She gave the others a conspiratorial wink before running behind the desk to give her an enthusiastic hug.

Debby returned the hug awkwardly. She was clearly surprised. In high school, the Loreleis barely deigned to say hello to her, let alone show any pleasure at seeing her. She smiled, basking in the glow of Anne's graciousness. And Anne a movie star, too!

A portly man with thinning hair wearing a Cardin sports shirt tapped Vali on the shoulder.

"Hi! Remember me?" he asked, grinning at her. "I tried to get a date with you all through high school and never succeeded once."

Vali looked at him. "Bo Barlow!" She laughed. "Hey, it's great to see you!"

"I've put on a little weight and lost a little hair," he offered wryly. "But I've made a little money along the way, so it hasn't been all bad."

Debby handed them their badges, which were plastic-covered name tags bearing their senior class photographs.

"Eeek!" Francine shrieked as she studied her likeness. "I always *hated* this picture!"

"Hey, Barbara Jean, look at you!" Liz exclaimed as the former cheerleader pinned the likeness of the blond, Miss America-wholesome seventeen-year-old to the top of her sundress.

"Embarrassing, isn't it?" Barbara Jean grimaced. "I sometimes wonder if that girl was really me."

"Carole!" "Diane!" "Fred!" They found themselves surrounded by people whose faces they vaguely recalled, but whose names would mostly have been mysteries if it hadn't been for the badges. Still, the most commonly heard phrase throughout the morning was "You haven't changed at all!"

Almost everyone had a camera. Everyone posed with everyone else; those who had brought their spouses dutifully introduced them and then left them to fend for themselves in this special-interest crowd.

"Where are you living? Corpus Christi? No shit? I

live in Houston!"

"How many kids? Eight? How on earth have you managed to *survive?"*

"You're *what?* A media products analyst? What the hell is *that?"*

The din was reaching ear-splitting proportions. "Hey, everybody," Debby Beasley shouted. "The hospitality suite's open. Room two-twelve. Why don't you go on up? There's a full bar and hors d'oeuvre table."

"All *right!* Bloody Marys!" People swept toward the elevator as if on a tide.

"I still don't see Margie," Liz said, looking worried.

"Guess she got hung up," Barbara Jean declared.

"Do you think we should call her house?" This from Vali. "Maybe there's some problem."

"She'll be here," Francine insisted. "She probably got stuck doing something at home. I told her she should have moved over here."

"I hate to go to the suite without her," Vali said.

"Oh, come on," Anne argued. "She's not a child. When she gets here, Debby'll tell her we went up, and she'll join us."

"She's right," Liz agreed. "Come on. Let's go get a Bloody Mary."

"Hey, you Loreleis! Move it!" The cry came from someone in the crowd trying to get to the elevator. "You're blocking traffic."

Taking their cue from each other, the Loreleis laughed and joined the group heading upstairs.

It was after three when Margie pulled into the Lancelot's parking lot. She had spent the hours at home sitting in her den, curtains drawn, trying to get up the nerve to come and register. The phone had rung several times, but she hadn't answered it. Jerry and the kids expected her to be out all day; she knew it was the Loreleis. What could she say to them? That she felt she was losing her grip on reality because THE DREAM had come back? That since the beginning of rehearsals for their dance number, she had been filling herself so full of drugs she hardly knew what day it was?

That she was terrified of attending the reunion because she knew a dead girl would be there?

She had tried to think things through rationally, taking deep, even breaths the way they had shown her at the hospital all those years ago. First, THE DREAM. Why did it frighten her so much? She wasn't the only one who knew what had happened the night of the initiation. Five others knew it and, apparently, were not affected by it in the least. "We, the Loreleis of John Ross High School, solemnly swear that we will never reveal what happened to Kathi Harcort, that we will guard the secret unto death." They had sworn the oath on a bible at Anne's house that same night. And, in fact, no one had ever questioned them about their activities that Halloween. The discovery of Kathi's body had not even prompted an investigation.

The drugs. Why was she doing this to herself after all these years of being "clean"? Until last week, she hadn't even needed valium to steady her nerves. But THE DREAM had robbed her of her sleep, necessitating the taking of the sedative prescribed by Dr. Feinstein. Then, when she woke up, she found she

needed something to keep the horror from followin
her through the rest of the day. She couldn't face th
best friends of her high school years or the rehearsal
in the old familiar dance studio without bein
bolstered by pills. So far, she had managed to ge
through, but now that the first day of the reunion wa
here, she needed twice as many to even think abou
going to the Lancelot.

The dead girl's showing up? That, Margie knew
was impossible. And yet . . . Liz had seen her a
Riley's. Driving the same car she'd driven in fifty
seven. Anne had seen her at church—the Firs
Baptist, no less! And what about Francine? She'
served her iced tea, for God's sake!

All the Loreleis had claimed to believe someon
was playing a trick on them, though so far no on
had been able to figure out who. But how could tha
be anyway? The girl they had seen *looked* lik
Kathi—the way Kathi had looked at seventeen. Wh
would go to all that trouble to find a Kathi doubl
just to scare six grown women?

A dreadful foreboding overtook Margie. Some
thing was going to happen at the reunion. Some
thing evil. She wouldn't go. She would simply si
here in this room and wait it out.

But that was crazy. Impossible. Jerry would b
home later, so would the kids. They'd been urgin
her to go all along, couldn't understand he
reluctance from the beginning. The reunion woul
be going on through Sunday. No way could she sit i
out in this room.

She had to go. Had to prove she could do it. If sh
didn't, Jerry might send her back to Dr. Feinstein

And if she went back to see him, she might not stop short of telling him, the way she had managed to do last week. If she told him about Kathi, about what they'd done . . .

She remembered the hospital. She shuddered as she recalled being plunged into a bathtub filled with ice water. She could almost feel her body jerking as the electric shocks that came later invaded it.

"No!" In her distress, she cried aloud. "I'm over all that now. The baths, the shock treatments . . . they cured me. I'm fine. I'm mentally fit."

She had to show them. Had to go to the reunion to prove her sanity was still intact. She rose in the darkened room and pulled the curtains to let in the sun. She blinked. Her friends would help her get through it. She would go.

Debby Beasley was no longer at the registration desk. The morning crew had been replaced by another two former classmates. Cheryl Todd and Jack Higgins were sorting out the registration forms. The table which had been filled with name badges bore only a few which had not been picked up.

"Margie! Hi!" Cheryl smiled at her when she walked in. "You're one of the last ones."

"Sorry. I had a lot to do today." Margie looked around nervously. The lobby was quiet, almost empty. "Where is everyone?"

Cheryl shrugged. "The hospitality suite, probably. Or maybe resting up for the dinner dance." She rose and walked to the table bearing the badges. "Your badge is here somewhere."

Margie joined her at the table. Together, they picked through the remaining badges. Margie recognized a few of the faces from the past.

"Margie Richey—here we go. Hey, great picture."

Cheryl was handing her the badge, but Margie was paying no attention. She was standing so still she could have been turned to stone; her face was deathly pale, and she was staring fixedly at the face smiling up at her from one of the other badges on the table.

"Oh, my God—Kathi Harcort!" Cheryl gasped, snatching up the badge as Margie fought the blackness that threatened to surround her.

"How . . . how did that get here?" Margie asked, gasping for breath.

"That stupid woman who's organizing this thing. She's supposed to be a professional, but she's goofed more than once. We *told* her which ones were dead. Hey, Margie?" She turned in surprise. Margie was no longer standing by the badges.

She was in the ladies' room pinning Kathi's picture on her pink polyester blouse.

The theme of the dinner dance was "Western Night." The suggested dress was jeans, prairie skirts, cowboy shirts and ten-gallon hats. Anne's jeans came from Henri Bendel in New York. They were skin tight, with two rows of rhinestones traveling down the outside of each leg. She wore a bright red, satin shirt with a huge black eagle embroidered on the back. Her white cowboy hat wasn't ten gallons, but it gave her a youthful look as it set pertly atop her dark, heavy hair.

Liz's jeans were ordinary Levis, but she enhanced them considerably by tucking them into sleek, high-heeled boots made of the finest Italian leather. She wore a blue checked shirt and a leather belt with a hammered silver buckle.

Francine was in white satin. Her outfit had been whipped up by her personal dressmaker and consisted of form-hugging, jean-style pants and a fringed, western-style blouse. Her boots were also white, cut short and fringed along the top. The outfit was offset by a spectacular turquoise and silver squashblossom necklace with matching bracelet, earrings and belt. She wore her white hat slung low at the back of her neck, held there by its chin strap.

The three women stood together at one side of the room, sipping white wine and observing the parade of former classmates who were still engaged in animated conversation.

"You'd think they'd've gotten it all out this afternoon in the hospitality suite," Liz commented. "How can they possibly have so much to talk about?"

"Are you kidding?" Francine replied. "Look at us. We've been here all week, and we still haven't covered everything that's happened over the past thirty years."

"Personally, I'm more interested in what's been going on over the past week," Anne said, her eyes narrowing as she stared at the entrance. "Of all the people to have an affair . . ."

Francine and Liz followed her glance. Barbara Jean, wearing a bright yellow "squaw dress," her arm encased in the yellow sling she'd fashioned for the dance number, was entering with a tall, good-looking man. "It's unbelievable."

"I think it's terrific," Liz declared. "She was

obviously in need of something she wasn't getting at home."

"But *Barbara Jean*," Anne reiterated, shaking her head in amazement. "Of the six of us, she's aged the most. So overweight—and all that gray hair!"

"Jealous?" Francine asked with a catlike smile. Basically, she agreed about Barbara Jean, but she was feeling bitchy enough to act the devil's advocate.

"Don't be ridiculous. What's to be jealous about?"

"Just thought you might be envying her her man," Francine purred. "Look, there's Margie and Jerry."

Margie was wearing a full, ruffled prairie skirt with a matching blouse. She had her hair tied back with a bandana and was wearing ballerina-style slippers on her feet. From across the room, she looked young and carefree, almost like the high school girl she had once seemed to be. Her hand tight in that of her husband, she looked around, saw the three women and pulled Jerry toward them.

"Hi. I want you to meet my husband. Jerry, this is Francine, Liz, Anne."

Jerry smiled at each one in turn. "Well, *finally*. I've been hearing about you all week. I was beginning to think Marge was going to keep you hidden."

"If you'd been home the night we met at your house, you'd've seen us then," Anne replied flippantly.

"Oh, ho—not a chance of that. She sent me off to a movie with the kids that night."

Anne turned to Margie. "We looked for you all day today. Where were you?"

Margie looked blank. "I don't know. I mean . . . I didn't get back." She looked out over the room which was filled with large round tables covered with bright red cloths. "Where are we sitting?"

"It's open seating," Liz answered, "but maybe we should grab something early. How many will we be?"

"Well, there are six of us." Francine made the calculation. "And Barbara Jean's friend. And Jerry."

"That's eight," Anne said. "It looks like the tables hold ten, so there's no problem." She walked toward one of the center tables. "Let's put our purses here and hold it."

Barbara Jean and her date made their way through the crowd and joined them. "Is there room for us?" Barbara Jean asked. "By the way, this is Frank." She smiled triumphantly as Francine, Anne, Liz, Margie and Jerry each said their names and shook Frank's hand.

"Well, we weren't going to let you sit with us," Francine said drolly. "But since you're with such a handsome man, we decided to let you stay."

Frank smiled and held onto Barbara Jean's hand. The two looked very comfortable together.

"Has anyone talked to Vali since this afternoon?" Anne asked. "She's been acting very mysterious all day."

"She said she has a surprise for us tonight," Liz said. "Maybe she's going to buzz the hotel in her plane and land on the roof."

"Uh, uh." Francine was looking toward the door. "It's better than that. Will wonders never cease?"

They all craned their necks to look. Vali, wearing a coffee-colored buckskin mini with a matching vest over a beige silk blouse, was entering on the arm of

Donald Ellsworth. They were walking very close together and laughing at some private joke. As the others watched, Vali looked up at Donald and smiled into his eyes.

"My God!" Barbara Jean gasped. "She looks hooked!"

"Look at Donald," Liz said, gaping. "If that's not love, I don't know what is."

Almost as if she heard them discussing her, Vali looked up, spotted them and waved. She said something to Donald, and they hurried over.

"Is this the Lorelei table?" Vali asked. Her eyes were shining. She never let loose of Donald's hand.

"The Loreleis plus three," Margie said. Those who didn't know each other introduced themselves and they began to pull out chairs and seat themselves. Their conversation was interrupted many times by other people stopping to say hello; but by the time Rick Wyatt, the evening's MC, mounted the podium to offer greetings, they were at ease in each other's company, and even the shock waves surrounding Vali's entrance had subsided.

The dinner consisted of green salad, barbequed chicken, chili, corn on the cob, rolls, and ice cream sundaes. Between courses, various prizes were handed out. Liz won a blue ribbon for having traveled the farthest for the reunion, but Barbara Jean was beaten out of the "Has the Most Children" category by Beulah Wilson, who laid claim to nine. Vali won for "Most Unusual Job," and Anne took the prize for "Most Famous."

"How about that!" Barbara Jean exclaimed proudly. "The Loreleis have done it again."

"Well, not quite," Francine reminded her. "You and Margie and I didn't win a thing."

"Three out of six ain't bad," Jerry quipped. He leaned over and kissed Margie's cheek. "My girl gets the prize in my book, anyway."

After the awards, there was dancing to a live combo. Jerry and Frank gallantly escorted each of the Loreleis to the floor in turn. Only Donald refused to relinquish his hold on Vali. When the two of them took to the dance floor, he held her close and buried his lips in her hair. Vali closed her eyes and smiled a secret smile.

"What does this *mean?*" Barbara Jean demanded of Vali when the two of them went off to the ladies' room. "Even *I* am not being *that* blatant about my affair."

Vali shrugged. "We're acting the way we feel like acting." She carefully applied her lipstick with a tiny sable brush.

"But suppose your husband finds out? Everyone's talking. Some creep might write him, just for spite."

Vali dropped the lipstick back in her purse. "I doubt that. But if somebody does . . . well—" she tossed her golden head—"I'd have to handle it."

Barbara Jean looked at her carefully. "Is it . . . serious?"

Vali turned and faced her fully. "Is your affair with Frank serious?"

Barbara Jean was taken aback. "I . . ." She stammered, stopped and said lamely, "I don't know." She took a breath. "I mean, it can't be, can it? There's Woody, and the kids." She gave a wry smile. "And I'm not exactly Bo Derek."

"Then it's just a fling." Vali was looking at her, hard.

"No. It's more than that. I care for Frank. This week has been wonderful." She looked at Vali helplessly.

Vali nodded slowly. "Now," she said quietly, "you know where I'm coming from."

Francine insisted they all go to Riley's after the dance. "It may be the last time we'll ever be there together," she said fervently. She looked at Jerry, Frank, and finally at Donald. "We'll *all* go. We'll share the men between the six of us."

Before they left the ballroom, Rick Wyatt made an announcement about the following day's activities. "A continental breakfast will be served in the hospitality suite starting at eight A.M. Complete with Bloody Marys, of course." This news was received with appropriate enthusiasm. "There'll be a picnic in Mohawk Park beginning at noon. Hot dogs, hamburgers and all the beer you can drink. And you can bring your kids." This last proclamation was greeted with a chorus of boos.

"Finally"—he rolled his eyes comically—"there's the event you've all been waiting for. The Pow Wow!" He bobbed his head in response to the wild applause. "Even though John Ross has a date with the wrecking ball, we have received permission to stage the talent show in the old auditorium. A buffet supper will be offered afterward in the cafeteria, and it won't be you-know-what on a shingle!" A hearty laugh greeted this reference to the old name for the school's infamous chipped beef luncheon entree. "As for tonight, the dancing will continue for as long as you're able to stand up." He gave an exaggerated bow and stepped down from the podium. The class of fifty-eight gave him a rousing cheer.

Vali and Donald stayed at Riley's only long enough to be polite.

"You two might as well leave," Francine muttered to Vali as the cherry cokes were passed around. "It's obvious you're dying to get it on." She turned to Liz, with whom she was sharing the back seat of Donald's car. "Why don't we go and join Margie and Jerry? They'll drop us off at the hotel."

Vali and Donald didn't have to be persuaded. They left the drive-in, blowing the car horn and shouting their farewells. Alone in Donald's apartment, they laughed over the fact that they had been too horny to see the evening through.

"Just like high school," Donald said, leering at her playfully.

"High school," Vali said meaningfully, "was never like this."

They made love as they had the night before, but this time Vali was less uninhibited, more clingy than passionate.

"Something wrong, sweetheart?" Donald asked, smoothing back her hair as he lay facing her in bed. "You seem awfully quiet tonight."

She gave a small smile. "I'm sorry. I guess I'm just . . . thoughtful."

He regarded her carefully. "What are you thinking about?" A faint look of alarm flared in his hazel eyes.

She shook her head. "Nothing." She sighed.

"Everything."

"Worried about Chase?"

"I never thought I would cheat on him. Even when things go wrong . . . I never considered cheating."

He lowered his head and kissed the hollow in her neck. "Funny," he murmured softly. "It doesn't feel like cheating to me."

"Oh, Donald . . ." She took his face between her hands and stared at him.

"Yes, honey?"

"I—" She stopped, unable to communicate her feelings. She pulled his face toward hers. "Just love me," she said hopelessly.

Frank and Barbara Jean toasted each other with wine. They were in Frank's room at the Lancelot.

"I guess this is it," Barbara Jean said softly, forcing a stiff smile. "Our last night."

"There's still tomorrow night. After the Pow Wow."

"Maybe." She sipped her wine and placed the glass on the table next to the bed. She looked at him earnestly. "Earlier this evening, Vali asked me if it was serious between us."

"Oh? How did you answer?"

"I said it was—and it wasn't." She pushed back a lock of hair that had fallen onto her forehead.

He watched her. In the week since he'd met her, he'd become quite fond of her. The fact that she was no raving beauty didn't concern him one way or the other. The other women in Frank's life might have been younger or prettier, but none of them had

otten under his skin the way Barbara Jean had.
Maybe it was her vulnerability that made her so
appealing. When she'd gone onto the football field
and attempted to do that acrobatic stunt—God! His
heart had broken for her. Of course, his interest could
em from something else. That fact that she had
once been—No. Better not think about that. He was
ealing in today, and he somehow had to handle this
obviously confused and unhappy woman.

"Would you like it to be serious?" he asked quietly.

"No. I mean, yes. I mean . . . how could it be?"

He took her hand. "There's a chance it could be, I
suppose."

"And a chance it could not be."

He nodded. "We've only known each other a week.
t would take time to tell about the future." He
smiled at her. "I want you to know I think you're very
special. This week hasn't just been a fling as far as
'm concerned."

She squeezed his hand gratefully. "Thank you for
hat."

"But as far as the future goes . . . it would be a risk.
That is, if you were to break up your home or do
anything rash."

"I know." She closed her eyes as if to gain some
urther insight. "I hardly even know anything about
ou." She looked at him. "Are you married?"

"No." He saw the relief in her eyes. "I've come
lose a couple of times. But . . . no."

"I don't even know what business you're in." She
smiled, feeling foolish.

"Mail order. I have my own company."

She nodded. "Well, that's a start." She paused,

then sighed deeply. "I don't know what to do. What want. In some ways, my home life's the pits; but love my kids, and I've been married to Woody a long time. . . ."

"In that case, the best thing to do is nothing Barbara Jean, I don't want you to do anything that will cause you trouble or pain. I'm not worth it."

She picked up her glass and balanced the stem on her plaster cast. "I guess that's something I'll have to decide for myself."

Margie was humming to herself as she got ready for bed.

"Have a good time tonight, honey?" Jerry asked He was relieved to see that she seemed like her pre reunion self.

"Great." She slipped out of her prairie skirt and put it on a hanger.

"I enjoyed meeting your friends. They're very nice."

She smiled. "I knew you'd like them. Everyone likes the Loreleis."

She removed her blouse and underwear and went to her chest of drawers. She rummaged around until she drew out a faded pink nightgown. Slipping it over her head, she crawled into bed and reached up to turn off the lamp.

"Honey?" Jerry was perplexed.

"Yes?"

"What's the deal?"

"What?"

He laughed self-consciously. "Well, I don't want

make a big thing out of it, but you usually don't wear a nightgown to bed. I haven't seen that pink thing in years."

She turned her head to give him a surprised look. "Don't you like it?"

"That's not the point. What's caused the sudden switch?"

She turned off the lamp and slipped under the covers. Her voice, when she answered, sounded trembly and poignant in the darkness.

"Nuns don't sleep naked."

If there was one thing around Baxter that hadn't changed at all, it was Slick's. But then, Liz reflected as she parked the car behind the dilapidated, wood frame building, there was very little chance it could look any worse than it had looked in the fifties. It still seemed to be an action spot, however. Liz could hear the rock music blaring as she made her way through the unlit parking area toward the restaurant.

Just what had prompted her to drive out here at one o'clock in the morning, she couldn't say. All she knew was, after the dinner dance at the Lancelot and the hour she'd spent at Riley's, she felt the need to get away from the Class of Fifty-eight, to go someplace where she was unknown, where she could nurse a beer and observe the crowd and not have to keep up any kind of pretense.

Making a score was the last thing she had in mind as she settled into a corner table and placed her order with the black waitress whose hair was held in tight braids all over her head. When the young man

299

approached her, she allowed him to sit down becaus[e] she thought his conversation might be amusing, no[t] because he happened to be good-looking. Over si[x] feet tall, he wore his lank brown hair on the long sid[e] and looked at her with direct brown eyes that hinte[d] at some secret joke only he knew. His face was deepl[y] tanned, and at first she took him for a cowboy.

"Excuse me, ma'am. Would you think I wa[s] terrible if I invited myself to sit here?" he asked[,] smiling down at her in an apologetic yet friendl[y] way. "I don't want to bother you; but this place i[s] gittin' pretty crowded, and there aren't many seat[s] left."

"Oh, I'm sorry!" Liz felt genuinely embarrassed[.] "I shouldn't be taking up this whole table all b[y] myself. Please. Have a seat."

He smiled again and eased his long, lean body int[o] the chair opposite hers. He was holding a beer he'[d] brought with him from the bar.

"Lotta action, huh?" he commented as he looke[d] out over the room where people who were mostly i[n] their twenties drank and smoked and engaged i[n] boisterous conversation.

Liz nodded.

"You come here often?" The man turned to he[r] and looked into her eyes.

"I haven't been here in years. It does seem to be a[ ] hot spot, though." She smiled, disconcerted by the[ ] directness of his look.

His eyes held hers for a long moment. Then he[ ] shifted in his chair and took a swig of beer. "Guess [I] should introduce myself," he said in his slow, comfortable drawl. "Name's Brett Donnolly. From[ ] Beaumont, Texas."

He stretched a long arm across the table and offered her his hand. She gave him hers, noting as they shook, the firmness of his grip.

"Liz Everly. Are you just visiting, or what?"

He leaned back in his chair and shook his head. "I'm a wildcatter. Got a job on an oil rig not far from here."

"One of the Brookfield wells, by any chance?"

"Nah. An independent outfit. We're about to pack it in, anyway. Haven't hit anything but water."

"Then you'll be going home to Beaumont." Liz was keeping the conversation going mostly for politeness' sake. She was beginning to feel sleepy and starting to wish she hadn't driven all the way out here.

Brett answered her question with a shrug. "I don't know yet what I'm gonna do. I like it around here. Except for the fact that it gets kinda lonely."

"You haven't made any friends?" Liz had wondered from the beginning what such a good-looking man was doing here alone.

"Men, sure. Great guys working in the oil fields. But there hasn't been much in the way of female companionship, if you know what I mean."

Liz nodded and looked away from the intense brown eyes. She wondered if she should pay for her beer and leave.

"I hope you don't think I'm being crude," Brett said, moving his chair closer to hers, "but you're the kind of little lady I'd like to get to know better." He reached for her hand, but she pulled it away.

"That's not possible, Brett," she said in a firm but friendly way. "I'm from out of town, too. I'm leaving day after tomorrow."

He grinned and gave her a "Well, what the hell?" look. "There's still tonight." He looked at her hopefully. There was something charming about his frankness.

It would be so easy, Liz told herself, still carefully avoiding body contact. *He's good for a hundred, at least. Maybe two.* But money had never been what her proclivity was all about. It had always been a game, a test of her sexuality over an unsuspecting male. Except for the boy she'd met out here at Slick's all those years ago, she'd never been solicited.

"I've got to be getting back to my hotel," she said briskly. She put up a hand to signal the waitress.

"So we'll go back together." He snatched up the bill the waitress brought and dug into his jeans pocket for some cash.

"No, really. I'm not interested." Liz stood up.

Brett rose and stood close to her, raising a cupped hand to her face at eye level. He was holding a fifty-dollar bill. "This is all yours," he murmured, putting his other arm around her shoulders.

Liz hesitated. Then she began moving toward the door. "Good night, Brett. Nice talking to you."

He followed her outside. "Come on, little lady, I know what you were doin' in there alone. Fifty not enough? I'll double it. Hell, I'll triple it!"

One hundred and fifty dollars. A pretty good offer for a woman forty-seven years old. Besides, the irony of having it offered to her here at Slick's was appealing. A joke, really. Why the hell not?

She slid the fifty out of his hand. "A third now, the rest later. Only, we don't go to my hotel. There's a little tourist court down the road—"

The bright light was blinding in the dark parking

lot. She instinctively threw up an arm to shield her face.

"You won't be going to the tourist court tonight," the voice from behind the light said. "There's a nice little cell waiting for you—*ma'am.*"

She lowered her arm and looked at Brett. He was perfectly calm. "You bastard!" she hissed. "You set me up."

"You ought to know better than to turn a trick out here," he said with a careless shrug. "We raid Slick's on a regular basis."

"I'm not what you think!" She looked at her hands and realized, to her horror, she was still holding the fifty-dollar bill. She thrust it at him. "Take this, and leave me the hell alone!"

Brett took the money and was pocketing it as a uniformed policeman moved into the light. A pair of handcuffs dangled from his right hand.

"It's my duty to inform you you're under arrest for the crime of soliciting for the purpose of prosti—" He broke off and stared at her. She stared back. The policeman was Bobby Langencamp.

Brett Donnolly noticed the break and moved up to Bobby, concerned. "You okay, Bob? You look like you've got a problem."

Bobby jumped as if the other man's voice had startled him. He turned to him. "I'm okay, Brett. I'll handle this. You can go home."

Brett looked from him to Liz. "Are you sure? I'll be glad to go back to the station with you."

Bobby shook his head decisively. "I'll handle it."

Brett frowned, gave him a puzzled look, and finally shrugged. "Whatever you say. See you tomorrow."

Bobby didn't even turn to watch him leave. His

eyes were locked with Liz's. They remained that way for a long moment.

"Well?" Liz's voice reeked of acidity. "Are you going to handcuff me?" Her shock at what had occurred was offset by the realization that the policeman who had come to arrest her was an old beau. She was sure she was safe now.

"Depends."

"On what?"

"Whether you intend to go quietly."

A small gasp escaped Liz. "You're not really planning to take me to the police station?"

Bobby's eyes narrowed. "Prostitution's illegal in this county. Even for the Class of Fifty-eight."

"You've got it all wrong," Liz said coldly. "Your friend was soliciting *me*."

"Don't give me that. It's obvious what you were doing in there. You were just smart enough to let him mention it first."

"Entrapment is illegal, too."

"You took the money he offered you."

They glared at each other. The handcuffs were clinking in Bobby's hand. Liz decided to back off.

"All right, Bobby, I did something stupid," she said placatingly. "I tried to get rid of him, but when he followed me outside and offered me the money, well, I thought it would be a kick."

"Like living in Russia?" Bobby sneered. He made the word *Russia* sound like something slimy and obscene.

"I work for the American Embassy," Liz retorted, her head held high. She hesitated, then tried a brighter note. "Hey, how come you weren't at the dinner dance tonight?"

"I drew night duty. Besides, I don't dig that reunion shit."

"Why not? It's a hoot." She grinned. "Guess who's dancing in the Pow Wow?"

"I heard. The Loreleis are back in town."

"Why don't you come tomorrow night? It'll be fun."

He frowned, eyeing her steadily. "What'll you do for me if I do?"

She swallowed. Another trap? "What do you mean?" she replied nervously.

"I always dug you, Liz. We had some good times in high school."

Liz forced a smile. "The greatest."

"I still think about it sometimes, you know? You were the only virgin I ever popped."

Liz's stomach turned in disgust. "Well," she said uncertainly, "that's really something."

His eyes were hard. "It's my duty to take you in, you know." He held up the cuffs.

"Bobby, please . . . can't we just forget it? I admit I did something stupid. But nothing happened, and—"

"What room are you in at the Lancelot?"

"What?" She was beginning to shake all over.

"What's your room number?"

"Uh . . . three seventeen. Why?"

"You got anything to drink up there?"

"Like what?"

"Beer. Bourbon. Something for a nightcap."

She looked at him. "I thought you had to work."

"I'm talking about tomorrow night. After the Pow Wow."

Liz felt nauseous. He was trying to make a deal. An

exchange for letting her go tonight. She thought of that night with him in his car all those years ago. He had made her sick; she'd almost vomited. He was making her sick now. She thought of his stiff penis in its rubber encasement. She thought of his hand creeping in under the elastic band of her panties.

She thought of her job, the headlines if she was arrested. And on *prostitution* charges. Suppose someone did some digging, started asking questions? The whole world could cave in on her.

What was Bobby Langencamp's penis compared to that?

"I could pick up a bottle," she said dully.

"So you get the idea. Good."

She smiled coldly.

"How about picking up some cotton panties, too? Maybe with little red hearts on them or something."

"Oh, Bobby, really." She looked at him with disdain.

He grinned. "So I'm kinky—so what? It'll be fun. Like old times."

She sighed. "Yeah. It sure will."

"Which is your car?" Liz pointed it out. "I'd tail you back, but I've got to get back to my rounds."

Her relief knew no bounds. "It's okay. I'll be all right."

"I'll tell Brett you pulled a gun or something and got away."

"Thanks a lot."

"It'll be okay. He won't go looking for you, unless I tell him to." His eyes bored into hers. "I'll see you tomorrow night. After the Pow Wow."

Liz nodded. Might as well face it. She was trapped.

Chapter Sixteen

Picnics were not their style. They decided to forgo that particular reunion activity in favor of lunching at the Brookfields'.

"I've always wanted to see this house," Barbara Jean said eagerly. "We used to drive past it every Sunday on the way to church. It always seemed like a palace or something to me."

"I know what you mean," Liz agreed. "I used to think, 'that's too big to be a house where people live. It has to be a hotel, or maybe a museum.' Come to think of it," she added dryly, "it *could* be a museum."

"But to our Francine, it's just 'home, sweet home,'" Vali said with a wry little laugh. "Modest by royal standards, maybe, but good enough for the ol' U.S.A."

"Oh, come now," Francine replied, embarrassed. "I invited you all over for lunch, not to make jokes about my house."

The Loreleis were seated on the spacious verandah which overlooked the huge free-form swimming pool with its natural rock waterfall and accompanying jacuzzi. A large yellow and white striped umbrella shaded the white wrought iron table from the sun, and a Mexican maid had just served tall frosted glasses of iced tea. They had just completed a tour of the house which, as Anne had whispered to Barbara Jean, was "worth at least twenty-five cents." In her role as hostess, Francine had shown them through twenty-two of the twenty-seven rooms, the others being servants' quarters. She had pointed out objets d'art from both Ming and Romanov dynasties and introduced her white-haired husband who had bowed in courtly fashion and bid them a genuine welcome.

The fact that they were now being just a wee bit snide was definitely rankling. She knew that Vali had also married well, but the others were definitely middle class and ought to have been truly impressed. Perhaps they didn't know enough about fine things to *be* impressed, she decided, as she gave the signal to Maria to serve lunch. Or, what was even likelier, they were just plain jealous.

"I think it's wonderful," Margie said, seeing the frown on Francine's face. "A beautiful house for a beautiful lady. Francine deserves it."

"I'll drink to that!" Liz declared, lifting her glass of iced tea. "To our hostess."

The others followed her lead and drank the toast. Francine's good humor was further restored when Maria appeared with the cold curried chicken salad scooped into papaya halves and served on delicate Lennox China.

"Where on earth did you get this fresh papaya?" Vali asked, gaping at the dish. "I haven't seen them

308

that big since I was in Hawaii.''

''We have them flown in from Honolulu,'' Francine said. ''Baron always has papaya for breakfast.''

As the Loreleis devoured their lunch, they continued the exchange of high school anecdotes and ''Do you remembers?'' that made up the major part of every conversation they had when they were all together.

''Do you remember that boob, Denny Kirkpatrick?'' Barbara Jean asked, her big blue eyes questioning each of the others. ''He asked me to dance last night, and I nearly threw up.''

''Danny Kirkpatrick!'' Francine exclaimed. ''Would you believe he's the first boy I kissed?''

''You're kidding!'' Liz made a face. ''Why would anybody kiss Denny Kirkpatrick?''

''Well, I wouldn't have done it except that I was scared half to death,'' Francine explained with a chuckle. ''He took me out to the graveyard and threatened to leave me there if I didn't comply.''

''The graveyard!'' Vali clapped her hand in glee. ''I'd forgotten all about that. It was Donald's and my favorite trysting place.''

''I used to go out there with Eddie Dale,'' Margie recalled with a smile. ''We used to make out on the grave of Maude Chissom.''

''Who?'' Liz looked at her in disbelief.

''Maude Chissom. Let's see. . . . She was born April . . . tenth . . . eighteen eighty-five, and she died September seventeenth, nineteen . . . twenty . . . seven.'' She gave a quick, satisfied nod. She had remembered correctly.

"But who was she?" Anne asked. "A relative of yours?"

Margie shrugged. "I have no idea. We just happened to pick her tombstone for a meeting place. Eddie and I used to make up all kinds of stories about her and her life. It was sort of a running gag."

"You know . . ." Vali said slowly, her forehead wrinkled thoughtfully. "Kathi Harcort's buried in that cemetery."

"You're telling *us,*" Francine responded. "I can remember her funeral as if it were yesterday. It was the worst thing I'd ever been through."

"It was facing her parents that was hardest for me," Barbara Jean said soberly. "They were so sad. And they seemed so grateful we turned out that day."

"Hey, let's not talk about Kathi, okay?" Margie said. She was feeling the coldness creep through her body. "Haven't we talked about her enough already?"

"I was thinking maybe we should go visit her grave," Vali said, as the others turned to her in surprise. "You know. Pay our respects."

"Oh, Vali, that is definitely not one of your better ideas," Francine declared. "The thought of it gives me the creeps."

"I don't know," Liz mused. "Vali may be right. We *should* pay our respects to Kathi."

"Not me," Margie said, tossing her napkin on the table and scooting her chair back. "Count me out."

"Wait a minute," Anne insisted. "I think it's a good idea for two reasons. One, to pay our respects. And, two—it might put a lot of things to rest."

"What do you mean? What things?" This from Barbara Jean.

"The fact that some of us have been seeing Kathi. Or someone who looks like Kathi. I know whoever he was, she gave me a fright. And Liz and Francine weren't exactly blasé about their encounters, either."

Francine stole a quick look at Margie. The redhead had a look of panic on her face.

"Going out to the grave," Anne continued, "would put it all into perspective. Once we see it again, we'll know she's really dead and didn't mysteriously live to try and scare the rest of us to death."

"I see what Annie means," Francine said, no longer repelled by the suggestion. "I think it's a good idea. In fact, since we're all together, we might as well go this afternoon. We might not get another chance."

"No!" Margie jumped up. She was shaking so hard she could scarcely stay on her feet. "I'm not going. I'm going home."

"Hey, wait a minute. There's nothing to get upset about." Liz was at Margie's side and had thrown a sympathetic arm about her shoulders. "You'll feel better if we go. Really you will."

"Liz, I can't. I'm sorry." She gulped at the air. "I guess I never got over what happened."

"Margie, none of us ever got over it," Francine told her in a firm, steady voice. "But there's nothing to be frightened of at this late date. Anyway, we'll all be together. Nothing will happen to any of us."

"I know. It's just that . . . I just can't." Margie was on the verge of tears.

"Yes you can. We all can." Anne also rose from

311

her seat and reached for her purse. "I'm going to the powder room to freshen up. Then we'll go, okay?"

Barbara Jean shrugged. "Fine with me." She looked at Margie. "If Margie doesn't want to go—"

"We're all going," Francine insisted. "Margie's an adult like the rest of us. She can handle it." She picked up the flower arrangement from the center of the table and carried it with her as she led the way through the house.

"Sure she can," Liz said, patting Margie's shoulder. "Right, Marge?"

Margie nodded dully. What choice did she have? She would simply have to hang on until she could get away from them.

When Anne came out of the powder room, they piled into Francine's baby blue Cadillac and headed for Memorial Park.

The man who introduced himself as Jake Godfrey looked more like a football player than caretaker of a cemetery. Not tall, but very stockily built and extremely broad-shouldered, he appeared to be in his mid-thirties. He greeted each of his callers with a firm handshake and a dazzlingly bright smile and apologized for not being able to tell them where Kathi Harcort's plot was without checking his files.

"I know the whereabouts of everyone who's come here within the last five years," he said, his light blue eyes traveling from Vali to Francine to Margie and then back to Vali again. "Matter of pride, you might say. But beyond that . . ." He drifted off and shrugged his massive shoulders. "If you'll excuse me while I check, it won't take a minute."

The women nodded and watched in silence as he left the reception area with quick, broad strides. As soon as he was gone, Francine burst out in giggles.

"What a hunk!" she hooted, widening her eyes with great exaggeration.

"And to think, we found him here at Memorial Park!" Barbara Jean added, following Francine's lead.

"I think he has eyes for Vali," Anne declared. "Did you see the way he was looking at her?"

Vali gave them a disgusted look. "Oh, come on. Give me a break."

"I think you're mistaken, anyway," Liz said, serious-faced. "It's obvious to me the man's a necrophile. He gets off on corpses."

"Of course! That's why he knows their whereabouts!" Vali exclaimed. The idea was greeted with fresh giggles. "I wonder if he's into men as well as women."

"Hey, we'd better keep it down," Barbara Jean warned, looking furtively toward the door from which Jake Godfrey had exited. "He'll be back any minute."

"It's a good thing Kathi died before he got here," Anne said in a stage whisper. "She certainly wouldn't be safe."

The cry that tore through the room was so shocking, they all momentarily froze. It was like something out of a ghost story, more of a wail than a cry, carrying an almost unearthly quality.

It was Liz who realized it had come from Margie. The slender redhead was crouched against the back wall, hunched over as if she was in mortal terror.

"Hey, Marge," Liz cried, rushing to her side and putting a protective arm around her. "What's wrong?"

Margie was gasping for breath, but after a moment she managed to speak. "I think you're terrible—all of you! Saying those things about that man. And Kathi—" She broke off and began to sob.

"Yeah, I agree. It was in rotten taste," Anne replied, looking almost as miserable as Margie. "It just popped out. I'm sorry."

"Forget it. We're all a little tense," Vali said, attempting to act as conciliator. "All the business about seeing Kathi's double, and then coming here . . . Margie?" She moved toward the sobbing woman tentatively.

"She's all right," Liz told her, stroking Margie's hair as she soothed her. "She's just a little on edge. Right, Marge?"

Margie nodded and made an attempt to pull herself together. She straightened up and blew her nose with the hanky Vali offered. "I'm sorry. I'll be fine in a minute."

"Is someone having a problem?" Jake Godfrey was looking worried. No one had been aware of his return to the reception room.

"No," Francine told him. "Everything's cool." She flashed a smile that could have competed with his own. "Did you find out what we wanted to know?"

"It's all right here." He waved a piece of paper and motioned for them to gather round while he explained. "This is a map of Memorial Park. We are

314

re." He pointed to a building drawn at the right
wer corner. "And your friend is resting here." He
ed a red pencil to mark the route. "If you drive out
the cul de sac and turn right, you shouldn't have
y trouble. The area you want is called Peaceful
oll. Kathi Harcort is in plot number seven."

"Thank you." Francine took the paper. Somehow
e had become in charge of this expedition.

Jake Godfrey nodded. "If I can be any more help,
st give me a holler." He smiled again. "It was nice
eeting you ladies."

They each murmured something in reply, and
ith Liz still supporting Margie, they trooped back
it to the car. No one spoke as Francine maneuvered
e black-topped road that wound between graves
arked with everything from elaborate statues to
mple cement headstones.

"This is giving me the creeps," Barbara Jean
nally whispered to Vali. But Vali merely grimaced
d inclined her head toward Margie as if to warn
arbara Jean that such a comment could cause
other burst of hysterics.

"Peaceful Knoll. This is it." Francine pulled the
r to a stop. They were at the top of a small hill. Two
ige chestnut trees shaded the graves which dotted
e area. One grave looked fresh and was covered
ith a blanket of drooping yellow roses.

"It's starting to look familiar," Anne observed as
ey climbed out of the car. "I can even remember the
eather that day. It was cold—raw, you might say.
lthough I think I was shivering as much out of
ight as of cold."

"There weren't nearly as many graves then," Vali

said softly, walking gingerly between the markers. "I remember feeling like Kathi was going to be up her all alone."

"Wait. There it is." Francine stopped and pointe to a simple tombstone which measured approxi mately two feet in height. The lettering, in plain block print, was still readable, although thirt winters had obviously done their work on the façade

In Loving Memory, the first line read. And the the name. *Katherine Amelia Harcort.* The last lin contained the dates, *July 20, 1940–October 31, 1957*

"I didn't know her middle name was Amelia," Li said as the six of them stared at the bold reminder o the tragedy of their teen years.

"I didn't even know her name was Katherine, Vali added. "Although, I guess it had to b something like that."

"God, we were all so stupid in those days," Barbar Jean mumbled. "We didn't know which end wa up."

"You know, I have half a mind to tell someon what really happened," Liz announced. "We didn commit a crime. Her family would feel better if the knew what really happened."

"Except we don't know where her family i anymore," Anne reminded her. "And what goo would telling do, anyway? It would just open up ol wounds."

"I think Anne's right," Francine said. She ben down and placed the flowers she'd brought from home in front of the tombstone. "Hello, Kathi," sh said softly. "The Loreleis have come to pay ou respects. We miss you. And we hope you are restin n peace."

The little speech caused the others to stand in awed silence. Francine's gesture had been oddly touching. Barbara Jean wiped a tear from her face with the back of her hand.

Then, as Francine rose and backed away, another figure flung itself on the grave. Margie was on her hands and knees, moaning aloud and talking as if Kathi could actually hear her.

"We're sorry!" she screamed, so loud her voice seemed to carry across the knoll and down to the valley below. "Kathi, forgive us! We didn't mean for anything to happen to you! We didn't want you to die! It was just an initiation! A hazing! It was all in fun! Oh, God, Kathi—please, please forgive us!" Her body was wracked with sobs, her face contorted with distress. For a moment, the others were too shocked to do more than stand by and watch as she groveled on the neatly manicured grave.

Then Liz stepped forward to comfort her once again.

"No!" Margie screamed as Liz's hand touched her shoulder. "Leave me alone. Can't you see I'm talking to Kathi?"

"But Kathi can't hear," Liz said gently. "Get up, Margie, and come with us. This isn't doing anyone any good." She reached out again; but Margie twisted out of her grasp, and Liz decided to give up. She and the others exchanged panicked glances as their friend continued to moan and speak in a voice so low they couldn't catch the words.

"Margie . . ." It was Vali who had stepped forward this time. "Margie, we have to go now." She stood a

317

short distance away and regarded her anxiously.

For a moment more, Margie continued to crouch on Kathi's grave. Then, suddenly, the moaning stopped. She sat up on her haunches and looked back at the others. Her face held a beatific smile.

"It's all right," she said, as if in wonder. Her gray-green eyes looked clear and untroubled. "Kathi says she forgives us." Slowly, she stood up and looked at them each in turn. When her eyes landed on Francine, she took a step toward her and reached out her hand. "Thank you for suggesting this, Francine. I don't know how I could have been afraid. Kathi's fine. She's at rest. She's happy."

"Yes, of course she is," Francine answered, taking Margie's hand and leading her back to the car. The others followed slowly, their hearts pounding, their legs weak. "She doesn't want us to worry about her anymore."

As manageable as a new-born kitten, Margie allowed herself to be ushered into the front seat between Francine and Liz. "Kathi's home," she murmured as Francine put the Cadillac in gear and moved slowly forward. "Home."

Chapter Seventeen

The girls' gym served as both dressing room and "Green Room" for the performers taking part in the Pow Wow. The Loreleis sat on benches in front of make-shift dressing tables and fussed with their hair and makeup.

"I feel like a whore," Barbara Jean said, peering at herself with a distasteful expression.

"Hey, all right!" Francine joked. "Maybe we could make a little money on the side."

"Listen, you two," Anne said in disgust. "I made you up that way on purpose. Don't you know you have to wear a lot of makeup in order to be seen properly on the stage?"

"I think it's terrific," Vali deadpanned. "From now on I'm going to wear this when I go to the supermarket."

Margie lit a cigarette. It had been years since she'd smoked, but she'd been carrying a pack in her bag for the past week. "What time is it, anyway?" she asked. "Shouldn't we be upstairs?"

Liz shook her head. "They said they'd call us in plenty of time. We don't come on till the end, anyway."

"Who knows that last turn we do before we bow?" Anne asked, getting up from the bench and making her way to a part of the gym which was free of furniture and performers' belongings. "I'm still having trouble with that."

"I know it," Vali told her. She rose and offered a demonstration. In their bright yellow leotards and matching tights, the women reminded themselves of escapees from a canary farm.

"Maybe we should all go over it," Liz suggested. "How about getting into our slickers? That way we'll be all ready."

The Loreleis obediently filed onto the floor in the center of the gym. Their tap shoes clicked smartly on the polished wood.

"Umbrellas? Where are the umbrellas?" Vali looked around worriedly.

"I have them right here." Anne retrieved them from an open locker and quickly passed them around. The umbrellas, like the slickers, were fashioned of transparent plastic. The handles and ribs were painted yellow.

"We don't have music down here so we'll have to hum," Francine directed. "Everybody ready?"

There was a moment of scuffling to get into position and then Vali gave the count.

"Five and six and seven and eight. We're sing-in in the rain. Just sing-in' in the rain . . ."

Five pairs of tap shoes resounded as they moved across the floor in rhythm, five open umbrellas twirled behind their shoulders, making delicate frames for their smiling faces. Barbara Jean, standing on the sidelines, watched and tapped her toes to the music.

"What a glor-i-ous feeling— Damn! What's this?" Francine broke off as she danced across a scrap of paper that had mysteriously appeared on the floor. "Who dropped this? It broke our tempo."

No one claimed the paper. "Give it to me. I'll throw it away." Liz reached for it, but Francine pulled her hand back.

"Wait. We'd better see what it is first. One of us may have dropped it without realizing it." She opened the folded sheet, her coppery eyes quickly taking in the content. When she looked up, her face was angry. "All right, you turkeys. Which one of you wrote this?"

"Wrote what? What does it say?" Anne snatched the note from Francine, read it, and blanched. "I don't believe it," she murmured as she handed it on to Vali.

Liz and Barbara Jean peered over Vali's shoulder as Vali read aloud.

"Dear Loreleis. Come to Our Lady at eight o'clock. This is important. You won't be sorry." Vali took a breath before reading the name at the bottom. "Kathi."

"This isn't even funny," Liz declared, snatching up the note and crumpling it into a ball. She threw it across the gym floor angrily. "This Kathi thing is going too far."

"Well, don't look at me," Anne answered indignantly. "I didn't write it."

"Neither did I," Barbara Jean announced.

The others disclaimed the note with equal fervor. Except for Margie, who was looking as if she'd seen a ghost.

"Margie?" Liz approached her gingerly. "Do you know anything about this?"

"It's K-Kathi," Margie said faintly. "She wants to talk to us."

"Then it *was* you." Barbara Jean heaved a sigh of disdain. "Margie—"

"But we have to go," Margie interrupted. "It's after eight o'clock now."

The other women exchanged glances.

"We have a dance number to do, remember?" Francine, too, was becoming impatient.

"But there's still time before we go on. Like Liz said, we're at the end." Margie had an urgent look about her. "Our Lady is just across the street. We can be over there and back in ten minutes."

"What if Kathi has a lot to say?" Barbara Jean muttered facetiously.

"I think we'd better humor her," Vali whispered, looking at Margie in alarm. "Otherwise, she won't go on, and we'll blow the number."

"Maybe we could just run over there and back," Francine suggested. "Once she sees the church is empty, she'll calm down."

"I hope so," Barbara Jean said. She was becoming angry. "I've had enough of this Kathi shit. And Margie's a candidate for the looney bin."

"It'll all be over soon," Anne said encouragingly. "The Kathi bit, the reunion, everything. In the meantime, I think Vali's right. Looney or no, we'd better humor her."

The others nodded in agreement. Liz returned to Margie's side.

"All right, Marge, let's go. But if Kathi's not there, we're coming right back."

"And if she *is* there, we're only staying a few minutes." Francine choked as the last of her words me out of her mouth. "I can't believe I said that," she mumbled as she followed the others out of the gym and up to the entrance on the building's first landing.

The night was warm, but a cloud cover blocked out the moon. "I hope to God no one sees us," Barbara Jean said through gritted teeth. "We look like idiots running around out here in these costumes."

"All I can say is, the priest had better not be in the church," Liz responded. "He'll think he died and went to the big aviary in the sky."

"There won't be anyone at Our Lady," Francine told them. "The church has been closed for at least a year. The whole block's being torn down to make way for the new center."

Francine's information was confirmed by a sign tacked to the church's double doors declaring the place closed and advising parishioners to try Sacred Heart or Monte Casino.

"Well, so much for this little adventure," Barbara Jean said flippantly. She was turning to go when Margie pulled open one of the doors and slipped inside. The others, looking dismayed, followed suit.

Inside, the church was pitch black. Not even a candle burned in the foyer. The air smelled of decay.

"What are we supposed to do now?" Vali whispered to Anne.

Margie heard the question. "Come in to the main part," she said, her voice sounding calm and certain.

"Kathi's waiting for us there."

Holding each other's hands for support, the women made their way to the inner church, willing their eyes to become accustomed to the darkness. They groped about and found that the heavy wooden pews still existed.

"Let's slide into these pews and sit down," Liz suggested. "There's no point in going down any farther." They settled themselves in two different rows, taking comfort in the closeness of each other's bodies in what was an eerie, if ridiculous situation.

"We'll give it five minutes," Francine announced, her voice echoing in the vastness of the empty auditorium. "Then we'll have to get back to the school."

"God forbid we miss the performance," Anne declared dryly. "After all the work we did on that routine."

"We'll make it," Liz assured them. "We had plenty of time when we left."

They sat in silence for a few more minutes. Then Francine rose and stepped out into the aisle. "That's it," she said flatly. Finding she was able to see faint shadows in the darkness, she walked straight toward the door. The others rose and filed along behind her.

The click of the lock was unmistakable. The sound caused Francine to stop short and the others to gasp audibily.

"That wasn't what it sounded like—was it?" Vali's voice sounded weak and frightened.

"I don't know. I'll check it out." Francine walked rapidly to the door and tried the handle. It wouldn't move. The door was locked tight.

"Well, I'm not going to stand for this." Barbara Jean turned around and started back to the auditorium. "There's a door in the back. I remember from last time. And windows." She walked briskly down the aisle in the direction of the altar.

"Hold it. Don't come any farther."

The voice was coming from somewhere in front of them. It sounded high pitched. Unnatural. Once again the women stopped and held their breath. Their hearts were pounding in their ears.

"Who's there?" Anne called out. "Who's speaking?"

Vali groped for the hand nearest hers, found it, and held tight.

"I should have known you'd forget me." The voice had an injured tone. "You never really liked me."

"It's Margie," Francine whispered. "She's trying to make us think she's Kathi."

"Let's go along with it," Liz said. "We've got to jolly her into opening the door."

Anne was the one who ventured to speak to the unseen voice. "Kathi?" she asked, forcing herself to sound pleasant and unafraid. "Is that you?"

"So you do remember me." In an odd way, the voice sounded like Kathi's. High and wispy.

"Of course we do," Anne answered. "How could we forget?"

While Anne was attempting conversation, Liz was toying with something on the floor. She had stepped on it first, and now she bent down to pick it up. The minute her hand touched it, she knew it was a packet of matches. "What is it you want?" she called out as her fingers fumbled to remove one from the pack.

"I want to be a Lorelei."

"But you *are* a Lorelei." Francine was speaking now. "We asked you to join us, remember?"

"But I was never a member. I was never initiated."

"Of course you were," Anne told her. "It was right here in this church. You must remember that."

"But it was never . . . finished."

Liz struck a match against the flint paper on the front of the pack. A tiny spark flew. Then . . . nothing.

"Kathi." It was Vali's voice now. She sounded calm and firm. "I think we should talk about this another time. We're due back at the school. We're doing our number for the Pow Wow. We have to get back before they announce us."

The voice in the dark was cold. "You can't go back. Not until the initiation's over."

Frantically, Liz fumbled for another match. She pulled it from the pack and struck it across the flint. It flared up, startling the others. Liz moved quickly up the aisle, holding the small flame before her. When she reached the person in front, she illuminated her face for the others to see. Margie was standing before them, dressed in a long black clerical robe.

Immediately, the others breathed easier. Now that they had proof, they could deal with her better. Liz reached out to touch her, attempting to guide her toward the door.

"Come on, Mar—I mean, Kath. Let's get out of here now. You must unlock the door."

"Take your hands off me!" Margie pulled away with a violent gesture. The match flickered and died.

326

n the suddenness of Margie's move, Liz dropped the acket containing the others. She stooped to pick it p.

"No! No more matches!"

Through the darkness, Liz saw the glint of omething in Margie's right hand. It was long and ooked like steel. Margie, she realized with shock, had knife.

"We're having an initiation. Not mine. One of ours."

"Margie, please. Stop this. We have to go." Barbara Jean was taking the direct approach. Playing along seemed useless. Her voice was sharp nd commanding.

Margie ignored her. "Come up to the altar with ne. All of you."

They heard the rustle of her robe and her soft ootsteps as she climbed the three steps leading to the ltar. Suddenly, another match flared. A candle was it. And then another. And another. "I'm sorry hey're not black," Margie said. "I couldn't find lack."

The women could see now. A series of candles—hirteen in all—had been placed around the altar. Margie was concentrating on lighting them. She ooked pale—and totally mad. She stopped what she vas doing and faced them as they still huddled below.

"I said come up here."

One by one, they joined her at the altar, Liz going irst, Barbara Jean bringing up the rear.

"I have robes." Margie pointed to a pile of clerical garments lying off to one side. "There's one for each

of you." When no one moved, she commande[d]
impatiently, "Get into them, goddammit!"

The women slipped the robes over their costume[s.]
They felt very hot. The church was so airless, Vali fe[lt]
as if she might faint.

"All right. Who's going to volunteer?"

"Volunteer?" Anne was speaking. "For what?"

"To go through the initiation. I want to be [a]
member this time. I want to call the shots."

Wearily, Liz tried again. "Margie, this is reall[y]
kind of silly. We're all grown up now. Kathi['s]
initiation was thirty years ago."

"You!" Margie shouted, whirling on Liz. "You'r[e]
IT! Lie down on the altar. Inside the circle o[f]
candles."

Liz stood motionless. She decided to try to cajol[e]
her once more. "Margie . . ." Her voice was soft an[d]
persuasive. "Honey, please . . ."

"I said lie down!" Margie snapped. She held up th[e]
knife she had brandished earlier. "And that's jus[t]
what I mean!"

In the auditorium of John Ross High Schoo[l]
Marilyn Morrison Cantrell was entering the stag[e]
from the wings. She was carrying a violin.

"We know you don't want to hear this," Roc[k]
Wyatt, the show's MC, was saying wryly. "Go[d]
knows, we all heard it enough when we were i[n]
school. But here she is, playing it till she gets i[t]
right—Marilyn Morrison Cantrell and 'The Ho[t]
Canary!'"

As good-natured raspberries resounded from th[e]

audience, Frank Bragg sat quietly. He looked at his watch. Eight fifty-five. It was almost over. Barbara Jean and her friends should be coming on soon.

Marilyn Morrison Cantrell played the number well. She ran her bow whimsically over the strings, producing the "cheep cheep" of the canary and, in one case, the meow of a cat. When she finished, the audience stood up and applauded, many of them laughing and calling out good-natured barbs.

"Atta girl, Marilyn! I think you've got it!"

"Hey, Marilyn, how come you never practice that tune?"

"One more time, Marilyn. Let's hear it again!"

This last cry was joined by others, and in a moment the entire audience was shouting for a reprise. Marilyn grinned, looked at Rick for a go-ahead, and launched into the whole thing over again.

Frank sighed and settled back into his seat. What else could one expect at a class reunion? When Marilyn's performance came to its end, the violinist walked off the stage beaming and holding her violin up in a gesture of triumph. Frank wondered if she would ever play "The Hot Canary" before such an enthusiastic audience again.

"And now," Rick Wyatt announced grandly. A drum roll sounded. "The act you've been waiting for for thirty years. The number that set a million teeth on edge." He grimaced and the audience laughed. "The Loreleis and 'Singin' In The Rain!'"

Wild applause swept through the auditorium. Eager anticipation was in the air. The drum roll sounded again. Then a piano kicked up the intro.

All eyes were front and center as the familiar

refrain burst forth. "La *la* la la la la . . ." Nothing
No dancers in plastic raincoats and memorabl
yellow tights tapped out from the wings. Rick rushe
back on stage and signalled for the pianist to stop

"I guess they didn't hear their cue," he explained
peering toward the wings on the opposite side
"Their hearing aids must be tuned out. Hey, girls
You out there? I know you want a big fanfare, bu
this is ridiculous!"

He turned back to the audience, shrugged, an
motioned to the pianist to begin again. "And a *on*
and a *two* and a *three* . . ." He shuffled off a la Jacki
Gleason.

Again, the intro. Then the melody. Again, the lac
of response. Frank didn't bother to see what woul
happen next. He was on his feet, rushing toward th
exit.

Liz was lying motionless in the circle of candles
Vali, Francine, Barbara Jean and Anne stood outsid
the circle, their bodies rigid with fear. Margie wa
standing over Liz. The knife she held was poise
above Liz's heart.

"There should be chanting," she said suddenly
"Chanting to the devil."

"Margie, no!" Anne cried frantically. "We wer
just kids then. The chanting didn't mean anything."

Margie looked up, her eyes glittering oddly. "Bu
the devil came, didn't he? Something evil happened
didn't it?"

"But we didn't *mean* it to!" Vali's voice wa
choked and quivery. "We didn't want anything t

happen to Kathi! It was a joke, a stupid kid's game."

"But something *did* happen," Margie replied. "And now Kathi's going to make it happen again." She turned back to Liz and lifted the knife.

Liz opened her eyes. She saw Margie's pale face, the wild look in her glazed eyes. She saw the point of the knife glittering ominously. *This is it,* she thought dully. *And I can't even pray.* She closed her eyes. The knife was inching downward.

"Stop it! That's enough!" The stranger's voice came from somewhere in the church auditorium. The four women outside the circle whirled around. Margie straightened up and stiffened. Liz remained where she was, her heart pounding furiously.

Someone was moving toward the altar, walking with determined, swift strides.

"Put down the knife. Let her get up."

As she came nearer, her features could be made out in the candlelight. A delicate, heart-shaped face. Vibrant green eyes. Pin-point-sized freckles. A cloud of red-gold hair.

Kathi.

For an instant, they all froze. Then an agonized scream rose from the center of the circle of candles. It came from the depth of Margie's soul. Limply, as if in slow motion, the woman holding the knife collapsed.

Liz scrambled to her feet as a flash of fire blazed upward. "Help!" she cried, shrugging off her robe and sprinting into action. "Margie fell into one of the candles. Her clothes are on fire!"

Instantly, the others rushed to help. They took off their own robes and threw them over Margie,

331

attempting to suffocate the flames. "It's okay!" Barbara Jean called out. "We've beat it out!"

Even as she spoke, they saw the line of fire travel across the old, dry carpeting and find fuel in the altar drapery. Flames blazed up, threatening to engulf the entire church.

"Quick! We'll have to carry her!" Liz shouted. "Someone see if you can find the key!"

Vali, Francine and Anne struggled to get Margie's unconscious body to the foyer. They laid her on the floor and felt for a pocket in her tattered robe.

"The pocket's burned off. It must have fallen out."

"We've got to get the door open." Barbara Jean tried the lock once again. "Maybe we can force it."

"Let's all push together," Liz commanded. "Everyone. Use all your strength."

Five shoulders heaved at the double door. They moaned. The lock held fast.

"Help! Fire!" Barbara Jean yelled at the top of her lungs. The others joined in the cry.

The flames were threatening the auditorium now. The dry, unused church was going up at a furious pace. The roar of the fire could be heard in their ears. Their noses and eyes were filled with smoke.

"Dear God! Somebody save us!" The high, thin voice gave them a start. It wasn't coming from one of them. They'd forgotten the girl who was Kathi.

Barbara Jean began to howl. She didn't know which was more terrifying—the girl or the fire.

The thundering crack of the door alerted them all. Their necks whipped around to watch the battering ram splinter the lock and break open the door. The sound of sirens filled the air.

"Get them out of there!" a man's voice yelled.

The women clamored for the safety of the outdoors. "Wait!" Liz yelled. "Somebody help me with Margie!" Francine turned back, but a fireman shot past her and scooped the unconscious woman into his arms.

"Anybody else hurt?" he asked gruffly.

"No. Everyone else is all right."

"Then get the hell out of here."

They collapsed on the sidewalk across the street, coughing and crying and gasping for air. Barbara Jean felt the familiar warmth of strong hands on her shoulders. She turned to find herself face to face with Frank Bragg.

"Frank! How did you know?"

"We'll talk about it later. Are you all right?"

"Yes." Barbara Jean coughed. "Oh, God, Frank. I thought it was the end."

"It almost was." He held her close, as if she were a precious child. Barbara Jean leaned into him, gaining strength from his body.

"It was Margie," she told him, too keyed up to remain quiet. "She thought she was—" She broke off as she felt Frank's grip on her relax. She had to regain her balance to keep from falling down. She looked at him, bewildered. His face was turned slightly in the direction of someone several yards away. His eyes were wide, staring. His features were frozen.

Slowly, his mouth began to work. At first, there was no sound. Then a word made its way up from the back of his almost paralyzed throat.

"Kathi."

Barbara Jean turned toward the direction of his

gaze. The girl with the red-gold hair was on her feet, staring at Frank. She blinked and moved slightly closer, as if she could not believe what she was seeing. Barbara Jean was mesmerized as green eyes and brown locked together, shutting the rest of the world out. Then the girl broke into a run.

Frank stepped away from Barbara Jean, held out his arms, and smiled as the girl ran directly into them.

"It's really you," she cried as she snuggled into the warmth of his embrace. She kissed him full on the lips and murmured blissfully, *"Daddy."*

Chapter Eighteen

"So you see, we didn't actually 'kill' Kathi. Our crime was running away and leaving her after she died."

Margie shifted slightly in the heavy hospital bed and frowned at Vali. A bandage covered her right ear, and her right shoulder was completely wrapped up. Her slight movement caused her to wince. "She had a bad heart?" she asked, struggling to comprehend what she had just been told.

"She was born a 'blue baby.' That means her heart had a congenital defect to begin with. And when she was a child she had Rheumatic Fever, which made her heart even weaker. She was never expected to have a very long life." Vali was seated on a chair next to the bed. Her golden hair was smooth and shiny, and she was wearing an expensive sundress. The terrifying events of last night were not evident, either in her appearance or her manner.

"But her heart stopped because she was frightened." Margie was still not convinced.

"Well, yes. You could say that. The Black Mass caused palpitations because she was nervous. But if it hadn't been the initiation, it would have been something else. She wasn't even taking the medication she was supposed to take."

Margie was silent. Thoughtful. "You said she had a baby."

Vali nodded. The expression on her face indicated this was a fact that even she found difficult to grasp. "She gave birth the summer before she started her senior year at John Ross. Her parents sent her to Baxter from Wichita to get her away from the boy."

"*That's* why? She said it was because they went to Africa." Margie seemed utterly bewildered.

Vali reached for her hand and held it. "She lied to us, Marge. About a lot of things."

"She was so pure. Virginal. She was going to become a nun."

Vali couldn't suppress a grin. "She wasn't even Catholic. Remember her funeral? It was at the *Baptist* church. I remember wondering about it at the time."

"I remember being surprised her parents were there. That they could get here from Africa so fast."

"They weren't in Africa, and her father wasn't a writer. It was all fantasy, an act she adopted. When her parents sent her away, she felt like an outcast, an untouchable. She made up a whole new history for herself. Including a religious fervor."

"But we hated her for it. Resented her."

Vali sighed. "I know. It's why we put her through the Black Mass." She shook her head. "God, kids are stupid!"

"What . . . what happened to the baby?" Margie gently slipped her hand from Vali's and reached for he glass of orange juice sitting on the bedside table.

"She was put up for adoption. A couple in Illinois ecame the parents."

Margie sipped her juice through the straw. "And hat was . . . ?" She stopped. She already knew the nswer, but it still seemed so incredible.

"That was Christina. The girl we kept seeing. .lthough, she's not a girl. She's a young woman. Born thirty-one years ago."

"But she was wearing Kathi's clothes. Driving her ar." Margie returned the glass on the table. She ooked wan and tired.

"That's because Margie's aunt and uncle still had hem. They didn't know where Christina was, but hey kept everything in case she should try to find her eal family. Which she did."

Margie heaved a deep sigh. "It's all so complicated. still don't understand."

"You will when you've had time to digest it all. I'm till reeling from the news myself."

"Vali . . ." Margie reached out and Vali took her hand again. "The others. Do they hate me? I don't emember much, but—"

Vali didn't allow her to finish. "Of course they lon't hate you. You were sick, Marge. You weren't esponsible for what you did."

Margie leaned back and closed her eyes. "All that ime in the sanitarium. I thought I was cured."

"Well, I don't know very much about that," Vali old her. "But your doctor did say something about our not opening up to anyone. They were treating ou for . . . uh . . . a split personality. Kathi was on our mind so much, there were times when you

337

actually thought you were her."

Margie swallowed hard. "I know. That time I wen
looking for the Crippled Children's Home . . . an
the dedication I phoned in to Big Burke . . . but i
hadn't happened in years. I was sure it was over."

"According to Dr. Feinstein, it couldn't be cure
completely because you never told anyone the whol
story about what happened in high school."

"That's not quite true. I told them about how I wa
back then. The school tramp. The goodtime girl
Vali, I hated doing all the things I did!"

Vali smiled at her. "I know. We all hated some o
the things we did. But you covered up the part abou
Kathi. That's why it festered in you all that time, wh
you 'separated' and became Kathi at times."

Margie looked at her urgently. "You talked to Dr
Feinstein. Does he think I'll ever be normal?"

"You *are* normal." Jerry's voice boomed from th
doorway. Margie looked up at him and smiled
"Now that your secret's out, the wound is clean. It'
all over, baby. I've got my wife back." He walked t
the bed and kissed her unbandaged cheek.

"Well." Vali stood up. "I guess that's my cue to
leave." She, too, leaned down and kissed Margie
"Don't try to put things together just now. What you
need is plenty of rest and tender loving care." She
smiled at Jerry. "The last of which you are definitel
going to get from this man here."

Margie looked at her gratefully. "Thanks fo
coming. Will I see you before you go home?"

"Sure thing." Vali's eyes clouded. "I'm not ever
sure when I'm leaving."

Jerry offered her his hand. "'Bye, Vali," he said

armly. "I can see why you were Homecoming Queen."

Vali flashed her silvery smile and walked briskly from the room.

Donald was waiting for her downstairs.

"How is she?" He was disturbed by her troubled face.

"Margie? She's going to be fine." The smile she offered him was not so bright.

Donald put an arm around her shoulders. "And you? Are you going to be fine?"

Vali looked up at him. Her aquamarine eyes were full of confusion. "Donald? Could we drive out to the lake?"

He shrugged. "Whatever you want."

"We have to talk. It might be easier out there."

Barbara Jean and Frank sat in a corner booth in the coffee shop at the Lancelot. Barbara Jean's breakfast of scrambled eggs and sausage patties remained untouched. Frank toyed with a cheese omelet.

"I'm surprised you even showed up this morning," Barbara Jean said admiringly. "To find a daughter you didn't even know you had . . . I'd've thought you'd have wanted to spend every minute with her."

"Christina and I have the rest of our lives," Frank replied. He looked at her unhappily. "You and I have less than an hour."

"Yeah." Barbara Jean played with the paper napkin in her lap. Woody and the kids were on their way in to pick her up. When they'd heard about the fire, they'd insisted. Kerry would drive her mother's

car back to the farm, and Barbara Jean could blam
her broken arm on last night's events and not have
confess to her moment of madness at Baxter Stadiun

"I want you to know this past week meant a lot
me," Frank said. "Not just because of what I foun
out about Kathi. Because of you."

Barbara Jean remained silent. Frank studied he

"I know you think I was using you."

"Well, weren't you?" She gave him a lopsided grir
"You've already told me you came to Baxter to fin
out what happened to Kathi. Your job was made a lo
easier when you ran into me that first day."

"Look, I'm not terribly proud of the way
behaved. I didn't lie to you, exactly, but I didn't te
you the truth, either."

Barbara Jean sighed and leaned back against th
tufted red naugahyde. "It still seems unreal to me
That you and Kathi were lovers. That you had
baby."

"The baby part seems unreal to me, too." His fac
tightened. "All those years! The Harcorts lived thre
blocks away, and they never said a word. Even afte
she died . . ."

Barbara Jean shook her head. "They told you sh
was dead months before it actually happened. I gues
they were too embarrassed to tell you a second time.

"At least Bill Harcort had the decency to tell me th
truth at the end. Or most of it, at least."

"He told you Kathi had been sent to Baxter? But h
didn't tell you why?"

"He told me he and Kathi's mother had decided sh
should be sent away so the two of us would b
separated. They decided to tell me she was dead so

340

ouldn't try to contact her."

"God. How painful that must have been for you.
o be a kid and be told the person you're in love with
dead." Barbara Jean thought fleetingly of Larry
olloway. They had been parted, too, only Larry
ad been the one sent away.

Frank inclined his head. "I knew her medical
istory. She wasn't very strong. I guess that's why I
ought the story so readily."

"And they told her *you* were dead?"

He nodded. "Original, isn't it? I was at ROTC
amp that summer. They said a practice mine went
ff or some such thing. Shit." He hammered the table
disgust.

Barbara Jean became thoughtful. "There's some-
ing else I don't understand. When Mr. Harcort—
ill—finally told you she'd been sent to Baxter,
idn't he tell you who the relatives were?"

"He just said her aunt and uncle. He died before I
ad brains enough to ask their names. I was in such
ock. I did check the Harcorts in the phone
irectory, but the aunt was the sister of Kathi's
other. And she was already dead."

Barbara Jean shot him in understanding look. "So
hen you saw Anne on TV . . ." She looked at him
or confirmation.

"When Bill died, he left me a box of memorabilia
e and Helen had kept. Old letters, photographs.
here was a picture of the Loreleis." He swallowed
ard. "It was taken at Kathi's funeral."

Barbara Jean nodded soberly. "And you recog-
ized Anne from that? Thirty years later?"

"No, of course not. It was her name that was the

341

clue. After Kathi got over being mad at them, s
wrote voluminous letters to her folks about all t
Loreleis. Anne Eastman was a name that cropped
often.'' He took a swallow of water. "Thank G
Anne didn't change it or take her married name.

"So when she mentioned the reunion on the ta
show, you wrote down the date and showed u
And,'' she added, "Christina did the same thing.'

"Not quite. Christina was already here. When t
adoption agency opened its records to her, she four
the names of her aunt and uncle. She'd been stayir
with them for several weeks before I got here.''

"Incredible.'' Barbara Jean looked at him wor
deringly.

Frank slid closer to her in the booth and reache
for her left hand. "The whole thing's incredible.'' H
paused. "Barbara Jean . . . I know your husband
coming for you.''

"And my six kids.'' Barbara Jean grinned.

"And your six kids. I'm sure you'll be glad to se
them.'' He looked at her wistfully. "Look . . .'' H
cleared his throat and started again. "I'm not a hom
wrecker. I'd never ask you to do anything rash. W
don't even know each other all that well. It's onl
been a week . . .''

"Frank.'' Barbara Jean looked into his eyes. "Wha
is it you're trying to say?''

His grip on her hand tightened. "Just that . . . i
you ever decide your life is going in the wron
direction . . . if you get tired of the farm . . . an
Woody . . . will you get in touch with me?''

Barbara Jean leaned over and kissed his cheek. Sh
smiled at him. "Thank you, Frank. Thank you fo

ying that."

"I meant it, honey." He seemed at a complete loss.

"Whether you did or not, it was wonderful to hear. And whether you 'used' me or not, this week with you has changed my life. Well, not my life," she corrected. "My attitude about my life. And about myself. You made me feel desirable again. Like a real woman."

"Believe me, you are every bit of that."

"Thank you. And I'm going to act like one again. My problems with Woody were as much my fault as his. I see that now. I let myself go, had no pride." She stopped and took a deep breath. "I'm going to make my marriage work, Frank. But thank you for this week."

Frank nodded and slipped his hand from hers. He smiled his old engaging smile. "Now that that's settled," he said brightly, "suppose we send these cold eggs back to the kitchen and start over again? I'm suddenly ravenously hungry."

Barbara Jean laughed. "The first time I ever lost my appetite, and you had to give it back to me!" She reached for the menu as he motioned for the waitress.

"What I want to know is, who called the fire department? How'd they get there so fast?" Anne and Liz were in Anne's room at the hotel. Liz was perched on the bed watching Anne pack. Anne was the one who asked the question.

"Apparently, it was Frank Bragg. He was at the school, watching the Pow Wow. When we didn't make our entrance, he went looking for us."

"But why would he look in the church? Barbara Jean didn't—"

"No, no one told him about our link to Our Lady. He went down to the gym to see if we'd missed our cue. When he found it empty, he got worried." Liz paused. "Remember that note we found on the floor? The one from Kathi?"

Anne nodded.

"I'd wadded it up and thrown it back on the floor. Frank found it. He smelled smoke as soon as he got to the church door. Fortunately, there's a pay phone on the corner."

Anne dropped a pair of shoes into her bag and shook her head. "They say truth can be stranger than fiction. I believe it now." She turned back to Liz. "Margie must have been planning that initiation for some time. She even had the candles and the robes."

"And the knife." Liz shuddered at the memory. "Apparently she took the stuff over there earlier in the day. She doesn't remember much about it, but Jerry says there were some black robes missing from their dry cleaning establishment."

Anne was thoughtful. "Liz? What now? Are you going back to Moscow?"

Liz nodded. "Tomorrow morning. What about you?"

"I'm off to New York. I'm up for a new play, and my agent called and said Robert Wagner asked—" She broke off and smiled. "Actually, there's a part on a soap opera I'm supposedly right for. I'm going to try for it."

Liz grinned. "Good for you. You can tell me all about it at our fortieth reunion."

The two women looked at each other. "The fortieth!" Anne hooted. "Won't that be a blast?"

Francine snapped her cosmetic case shut and reached for the phone to call the bell captain. She'd spent the previous night at Brookfield Manor; after the fire, Baron had refused to let her out of his sight, but she'd come back to the Lancelot today for her clothes.

Before she could dial the bell captain, a knock sounded on the door. Sure it was one of the Loreleis come to say goodbye, she dropped the receiver back onto its cradle and went to open the door.

Arthur Brookfield was there.

"No, wait. Please," he begged as Francine tried to close it in his face. "I'm not going to give you any trouble. I promise."

Francine looked at him. He seemed subdued, even contrite. She shrugged and motioned for him to enter. "Sorry I didn't make it to your house last night," she said sarcastically. "Something came up."

"I know. Believe me, I know. Francy, I'm sorry. It must have been terrible for you."

"It wasn't exactly a lot of laughs."

"Are you all right?" His worry seemed sincere.

She gave him a tight smile. "Yeah. I'm fine."

He took a step toward her. She shrank back. "I'm not going to touch you. Trust me. Although," he added softly, "when I heard, all I wanted to do was hold you."

Francine was unmoved. "How *did* you hear?"

"I was there. At the Pow Wow. I slipped in at the

345

last minute. Not even Dad knew I was there."
Francine looked at him questioningly. "Right after
your act failed to show up, someone ran into the
auditorium yelling that the church was on fire.
Everyone ran to help."

"You included?"

"Me included. But by the time we got there, the
firemen had shown up. I'd have gone on home, but I
heard someone say the Loreleis were inside."

Francine caught her breath. The memory of last
night was closing in on her. "So you stayed?"

His blue eyes were somber. "Francy, *of course* I
stayed. Despite everything, I—" He broke off,
frustrated. "I saw Dad there. And Barry. They were
beside themselves. Especially Dad. He . . . loves you,
Francy."

She looked straight into his eyes. "No shit."

His shoulders slumped dejectedly. "You, have a
right to be mad. I've acted like an ass. I'm sorry."

She looked surprised. "The great Arthur Brookfield—sorry?"

"Okay, I'm sure I deserve all this sarcasm. I just
want to say I was wrong about telling Barry. When I
saw the two of them last night—Dad and Barry,
ripped apart because you were in danger—I realized I
have no business interfering in my son's life. I lost the
right to do that twenty-six years ago."

Francine breathed a relieved sigh and smiled.
"You mean that, don't you?"

"Unfortunately, yes." They locked eyes for a
moment. Francine was first to look away. "Have you
seen your friends today? The other Loreleis?"

"I talked to Anne and Liz. The story behind what
happened is incredible."

346

Arthur nodded. "Barry filled me in on a little of it this morning. When I called to see how you were. I take it the girl he brought to the house was the daughter of your friend who died."

Francine shook her head wonderingly. "Isn't that bizarre? She's thirty-one years old, but she looks exactly the way her mother looked at seventeen. She even has a birthmark on her shoulder that resembles a cloven hoof. And she was wearing Kathi's clothes. Apparently she's the type that shops in antique clothing stores anyway. They were right up her alley."

"Obviously she fooled Barry, too."

"She lucked out, running into him. She'd been following the six of us around out of curiosity. She'd read about us in her mother's diary, and she wanted to see what we were like. She didn't even realize she was scaring us."

"She was in the church, too?"

"That was the weirdest part of all. She saw us leaving the high school and followed us over there. It was so dark we didn't see her, until later, when she saved Liz's life."

Arthur smiled affectionately. "Poor Francy. Think you can forget all this?"

Francine smiled back. "Sure. In about a hundred years." She gestured toward her luggage. "Feel like giving me a hand with these?"

Arthur moved to gather up the suitcases. "Gladly. Where to?"

Francine sighed. "Home. Thank God."

They drove to a secluded spot on the lake's south

shore. The morning was already hot, but the ai
seemed fresher out there. They got out of the car and
walked to the bank. The lake was quiet. A lon
outboard motor could be heard somewhere in th
distance.

Vali looked out at the water.

"Looks just the same."

Donald smiled. "Lakes don't change much."

She stood quietly for several minutes, gathering
her thoughts. Then she turned to him.

"I'm going to ask Chase for a divorce."

Donald tensed. It was more than he'd dared hope
for. He moved closer to her and reached out to touch
her. She stepped just out of his reach.

"It's not what you think. It doesn't have anything
to do with us."

He looked bewildered. "Then I don't understand
Why . . . ?"

"It's never been right with Chase and me. Oh, he's
a wonderful man. Bright and honorable and hard
working. But the two of us together, we don't—" she
struggled for the word—"fit." She took a deep
breath. "Continuing our marriage wouldn't be fair
to either of us. Chase needs a wife who's a *wife*
Someone whose whole world is her husband's world.
The perfect homemaker. The perfect hostess."

Donald looked at her. "I'm sure you were all those
things."

"I tried to be. But I wanted more. I'm too
independent. I feel confined in his world."

"You have your charter company."

"And I love it. But it's been a source of friction
between us since I started it." She turned to Donald

with an anxious look. "I'm going to be letting him down. I should probably stick it out and see our marriage through. It's not as if I can't bear it. But . . ." She sighed. "Last night, at the church, I thought I was going to die, and I realized I hadn't lived. Not really. Not for me."

He frowned slightly. "What about the kids?"

"They're cool. They'll handle it. Anyway, they aren't kids anymore. They're adults."

"Will you stay in Connecticut?"

She shrugged. "Probably not. Without Chase, there's nothing for me there. I can get an airplane charter anywhere."

Donald was thoughtful. His face was clouded. "Vali," he said at last. "You said this doesn't have anything to do with us—"

She stopped him before he could go on. "Donald, seeing so much of you this week has been incredible for me. For one thing, it's reaffirmed my belief that I was right in marrying you all those years ago. You're a terrific guy. I'm proud to have been loved by you. Ben and Kevin are lucky to have you for a father."

"Val—"

"No, wait." She put a gentle finger to his mouth. "I know what you're going to say. I've felt it coming all week. I know you think you still love me. Maybe you really do. But what happened at this reunion . . . it was all too fast. We don't know each other anymore."

"We were married for four years."

"That was a long time ago. We're different people now."

He swallowed back the lump that threatened to

349

form in his throat. "Couldn't we get to know eac[h] other again?"

"Yes. Maybe we could. Maybe we will. But it'[s] going to take time."

He looked at her carefully. "Are you saying there'[s] a chance for us?"

"Yes. But it's only a chance. Wherever I go, we'l[l] stay in touch. We'll see each other when we can. I[n] time . . . well, if it's right, we'll know it." She looke[d] up at him and smiled. "Okay?"

He nodded. "It'll have to be."

Vali reached out to him, and he stepped toward he[r] and gathered her into his arms. They kissed long an[d] lingeringly. Sweetly, with a hint of the passion the[y] both knew was waiting for release.

"I love you, Vali."

"I love you, too, Donald. I'm unsure about a lot o[f] things. But I love you."

He cupped her face in his hands and smiled dow[n] on her. "You'll be certain again. You wait and see."

They walked hand in hand back to the car.

Liz saw the police car pull up as she neared th[e] hotel parking lot. She tried to pretend she hadn'[t] noticed and walked briskly toward her car. Th[e] police vehicle cruised along behind her, setting he[r] nerves on edge.

"All right, Everly, stop right where you are."[
]Bobby Langencamp's voice boomed over the lou[d] speakers. Liz froze. *Oh, God*, she thought des[-]perately, *why didn't I get out of here sooner?*

When she heard the car door open and shut, sh[e]

350

rced a quivery smile and turned around.

"Bobby, I—"

She broke off as she saw the perplexed look on his
ce.

"I actually think I scared you. What's the matter,
zzie? Think I came to arrest you?"

"Well, I . . ." She was so flustered she didn't know
hat to say. "Bobby, about last night—"

He took a step toward her. "Yeah, listen, that's
hat I came to talk about. I hope you didn't wait up
o long."

"What?" Liz eyed him warily. She'd spent the
ght at her parents' condo. After the fire, she hadn't
en thought about Bobby.

"One of the guys got sick and I drew his duty.
elieve me, it wasn't my idea."

"I see." Liz relaxed. "I wondered."

"I suppose you're taking off?"

"I have to get back to the embassy, yes."

Bobby made a face. "Moscow. Doesn't sound too
ot."

She smiled. "It's a living."

He nodded and scratched his head thoughtfully.
Well, listen, it's been good seeing you again."

"Thanks. You, too."

"Don't suppose you'll be coming back any time
on?"

"I doubt it. Russia's a long way away."

"Think there'll be another reunion?"

"I don't know. Maybe."

He grinned. "Well, if you come back for it, save me
night, okay?"

She nodded. "Okay. Sure."

"And watch out who you take money from, hear?"

"I will. I definitely will."

As the police car drove off, Liz looked at her watch. Four thirty-eight. The bar at the Baxter ought to be filling up about now. She considered, and reconsidered. The heightened risk gave her goose bumps. Should she?

Definitely not, she decided. But, maybe . . . She got into her car and started the engine. *Maybe I'll just stop in for a drink.*